HE WOULD HAVE HER
IN ANY WAY
AND EVERY WAY HE CHOSE.

To teach her a lesson she would never forget. To ignore her pleas for gentleness and patience. So he ripped the tattered buckskin skirt from her just as a fierce gust of wind slammed into the enclosure, almost knocking Martay from her feet. With one steadying hand he held her up. While fierce lightning skittered within feet of them, and the winds and the rains grew more angry and intense, Night Sun, as tumultuous and as violent as the worsening storm, stripped Martay naked.

He sat back on his heels then, anticipating her fear, expecting the tears and the begging. But Martay defied him. Proudly she stood there, bare and wet and beautiful, her emerald eyes shining with unashamed desire, her hands outstretched to him, beckoning him to take what he'd uncovered.

"*Savage Heat* is dynamite . . . exploding sensuality. Nan Ryan is one of passion's leading ladies."
—*Romantic Times*

Other Dell books by Nan Ryan

CLOUDCASTLE

SAVAGE HEAT

NAN RYAN

A DELL BOOK

Published by
Dell Publishing
a division of
Bantam Doubleday Dell
Publishing Group, Inc.
666 Fifth Avenue
New York, New York 10103

ISBN: 0-440-20337-6

Printed in the United States of America

Published simultaneously in Canada

February 1989

10   9   8   7   6   5   4   3   2   1

KRI

For my little sister
Judy Jonas,
courageous, cheerful, and cherished

SAVAGE HEAT

1

NEW YORK CITY
JUNE 2, 1879

The lamplight reflecting in the depths of his cold black eyes, a dark man sat reading *The New York Times*. He smiled suddenly, laid the newspaper aside, and slowly lowered his long, lean legs to the floor. Rising from the overstuffed chair where he'd been lounging lazily for the past half hour, he moved, silently, across the deep custom-loomed English carpet to a highly polished mahogany drum table on the far side of the spacious room.

A lifetime of keen cautiousness made him look out the window of his eighth-floor Buckingham Hotel corner suite—first down Fifth Avenue, then up Fiftieth—before dropping the heavy velvet drapery back into place and lifting the stopper from a cut-glass decanter. The smile had disappeared and his harshly planed face was set with cold determination. Yet he felt a tingling excitement spread pleasantly through his tall frame as he poured himself a bourbon, downed it in one easy swallow, then poured another.

He returned to the chair, picked up the newspaper, and

read, one more time, the society page article beneath a roto-gravure picture of an extraordinarily pretty young woman.

Chicago's "Golden Girl," Martay Kidd, the beautiful, blond Miss, educated at Manhattan's exclusive ladies' academy, Miss Bryan's, on Park Avenue, whose shining presence has brightened many a New York social gathering, plans to "rough it" this summer in Denver, Colorado. The heiress to a vast gold-mining fortune, Miss Kidd is the only child of Brigadier General William J. Kidd. From his post at Colorado's Fort Collins, the general says he's eagerly awaiting his daughter's early June arrival. The emerald-eyed beauty is to be the houseguest of Colonel and Mrs. Dolph Emerson, one of Denver's first families and old friends to the general.

Again the dark man lowered the paper, a near-Satanic smile curving his full lips, and neatly tore the photograph from the paper, placing it inside the breast pocket of his fine white silk shirt. Then, summoning a hotel steward, he issued orders in a low, soft voice.

"Book a berth for me on this evening's midnight train to Denver. Have my things packed within the hour. Make certain a cab is here for me by no later than a half hour before departure time." He paused, then added, "and send a wire to Mr. Drew Kelley, 1201 Broadway, Denver, Colorado, informing him of my June 8th arrival."

The uniformed steward shook his graying head in puzzlement. "Suh, didn't you just arrive this afternoon from Boston? We thought you were going to stay here with us for a week."

The dark man drew some bills from his pocket and pressed them into the steward's palm. He said, "Wish I could, but something's come up. I have no choice. I must leave."

"I sure hate that. Yes, suh, I sure do," said the hotel steward, and reluctantly allowed himself to be ushered out of the room.

Pacing restlessly back and forth, hands shoved deep into the pockets of his tight black trousers, the dark man paused and drew out the small photograph he'd torn from the newspaper.

It was the girl's eyes he studied. They seemed all too familiar, though he'd never met her.

His own black eyes narrowed as his long dark fingers reflexively closed tightly around the photograph, crushing it cruelly in the palm of his hand.

CHICAGO, ILLINOIS
JUNE 3, 1879

Martay Kidd's brilliant emerald eyes were shining as she dressed for her last evening in Chicago. Though she'd charmingly told all her friends not to make a fuss over her leaving, she was not surprised, nor displeased, that several had chosen to ignore her requests and had thrown lavish parties in her honor.

Tonight was to be the last one. A wine supper at the Lake Shore mansion of wealthy steel baron Farrell T. Youngblood, Sr. Farrell T. Youngblood, Sr., and his wife, Laura, were presently out of the country, touring Europe, but their twenty-two-year-old son, Farrell T. Youngblood, Jr., was in residence, and very much enjoying having the run of the house.

A classically handsome man with light sandy hair, strikingly blue eyes, an aristocratic nose, and boyish dimples, Farrell Jr. had diligently tried to persuade Martay to give up her foolish notion of spending the summer in Denver. He was, he told her, falling hopelessly in love with her, and if he could, he would forbid her to go.

That's when Martay had decided for certain that she would go. She was fond of Farrell. After all, he was quite worldly and very handsome and great fun. Or had been until she'd allowed him to kiss her a few times and he had immediately started talking of marriage. That had chilled the relationship. He couldn't seem to understand that she meant it when she said she had no interest in marriage.

"Please believe me, Farrell," she had told him only the night before, "I enjoy your company and I consider you one of my best friends, but I have no intention of marrying." When his face fell and a hurt expression came into his blue eyes, she hurried on, "It isn't you, it's me. I value my freedom and I plan to keep it for a long, long time."

"What nonsense," said Farrell. "You can have all the freedom you want with me. I'm not the jealous kind." His brows lifted accusingly. "If I were, we'd have been at odds long before now."

Martay laughed, unbothered by the jibe. She knew very well that people gossiped, but she didn't care. She had no desire to be one of those hothouse flowers who got an attack of the vapors if a man so much as kissed their hands. She would tell anyone who asked that she had kissed not one but three handsome young men in the past two years and she planned to kiss a darned sight more before she was too old to pucker.

If gentlemen, even highly regarded gentlemen, could go about kissing their pick of the pretty girls, why couldn't it work the other way round? It could. She would kiss whom she pleased, when she pleased, so long as he was no one's husband or sweetheart.

"You're purposely misunderstanding me, Farrell. I know you're not jealous, and I appreciate that very much. I'm trying to make you understand that I've no desire to be the young married matron with a baby at my breast by the time I turn nineteen, and then another child coming every year thereafter." Farrell's pale face blushed at such frankness, though her boldness was one of the very reasons he was so enchanted by her. "I am certain many girls marry, not because they are madly in love but because they want a man to take care of them."

"Well, young ladies do need . . ."

"I don't. With my mother's inheritance, I'm quite rich in my own right. There's nothing I could ever desire that I can't have. I've no need of a man to provide me with the fine things in life. I can provide them for myself. And," she pointedly added, "have the freedom and time to enjoy them."

"You are truly exasperating, Martay," he had said, dejected. "Still, I believe in time you'll change your mind. That you'll grow up and realize how important a husband and family really are."

"You sound just like my father," Martay said. "His fondest hope is to see me safely married before I reach another birthday." She shook her golden head. "I suppose he's afraid I will create a scandal."

"Dearest, I'm sure your father only wants—"

"My father wants what's best for him. I want what's best for me." She laughed then, shrugged her slender shoulders, and said, "I suppose we're too much alike, Father and I."

"Is there nothing I can say or do to make you change your mind about Denver?" pleaded Farrell.

"No. It's Denver for the summer." She smiled at him then and said sweetly, "But autumn will come before you know it, and I'll be right back here in Chicago, ready for parties and the opera and rides along the lake shore." She toyed with his lapel.

Farrell captured her hand, drew it to his lips, kissed the soft palm, and said plaintively, "I hope you're right, my dear." He shook his sandy head. His high brow knit. "Denver is not all that civilized. It's full of sourdoughs and gamblers and fugitives and loose women. And they say renegade redskins still roam the Rockies. I'm afraid . . ."

"Well, I'm not. I'll be completely safe in Denver."

* * *

Martay smiled now, recalling their conversation. Instead of frightening her, Farrell's warnings had only added to the building excitement she felt regarding her upcoming visit to Denver. She'd been "completely safe" for eighteen years. Too safe. A dash of danger would be fun. Unafraid, she was anxious to be on her way to Colorado and the promise of new adventure.

All about her spacious cream-walled bedroom stood half-open steamer trunks and valises and hat boxes. Colorful summer dresses and elegant ball gowns and delicate underthings and soft kid leather slippers peeped from the many matched ivory leather suitcases.

Martay sighed with pleasure and her green eyes sparkled with delight. In less than eight hours she would board the train and be gone! And in less than a week she would see her father again. She'd not seen the general for more than six months and she'd missed him dreadfully. She knew he must have missed her as well or else he would never have agreed to her coming to Colorado. This would be the first time ever she had been allowed to visit him in the field.

Martay grabbed up a gold-handled brush, began stroking her long blond hair, and envisioned Denver, Colorado. She pictured it to be a wild, untamed town high in the magnificent Rockies, where decorum and convention took a backseat to adventure and gaiety. A place where gunfights still erupted on city streets and ladies of the evening strolled down the avenues right in broad daylight. A town filled with swaggering gold-rich entrepreneurs and handsome nimble-fingered card sharks and big rough-and-rowdy cowboys. Smooth-tongued hustlers and down-and-out beggars and fierce, savage Indians.

She could hardly wait to get there!

"I don't like it, Martay. Not at all," said a perplexed Farrell T. Youngblood, Jr.

It was midnight.

The festive party had ended with all the laughing guests piling into buggies and carriages and escorting Martay to Chicago's busy train depot. She stood now just outside her private railcar, California Gold, a cherished extravagance her father had encouraged when she turned eighteen, the previous August.

"Farrell, don't look so morose. It will only be for three months."

"Only?" he intoned, feeling as though it were a lifetime. "That's too long. Come back sooner. Return in time to celebrate your nineteenth birthday in Chicago."

"All aboard," called a chubby-faced black man as the train's whistle gave a loud, sharp blast and steam hissed from the mighty engines.

"It's time!" Martay said excitedly, lifted her gloved hand, and waved good-bye to all her friends. "See you in the fall," she shouted, to be heard above the noise. "Thank you all for my wonderful party."

She stepped onto the stairs and looked at Farrell. He was so forlorn, she leaned down and kissed his cheek. "I'll write."

"No, you won't," he said, knowing her all too well.

She smiled and started to object, but he suddenly pulled her from the steps, crushed her to him, and kissed her ardently, eagerly, mindless of the crowds witnessing his fervent display of passion. When finally he tore his lips from hers, he murmured, almost apologetically, "Just so you won't forget me."

The train had started to move, wheels turning on the track. Martay, grateful for the opportunity to escape, said, "I must hurry!" lifted her flowing skirts, and dashed up the steps. In seconds she was rolling away, pulling out of the station, while Farrell, his face flushed with emotion, ran alongside the moving train. Martay sighed with relief when the train picked up speed and he could no longer keep up. He stopped, out of breath but still calling to her, while she stood in the open doorway and waved a linen handkerchief.

"It's time to get inside," said Lettie from behind her.

Martay nodded, turned, and impulsively hugged the big Irishwoman who had tended her since the day she was born. "Oh, Lettie, can you believe it! We're finally on our way to Colorado!"

"The only place you're on your way to right now is bed," said Lettie, hands on ample hips, her plain, ruddy face screwed up in a frown of disapproval. "Up half the night, kissing gentlemen in public, going across the country. What next?"

Undaunted, Martay happily whirled around and around. "Indeed, what next? I don't know, and that's the fun of it, Lettie. I'm going to a new place, I'll meet new people, and I'll do things I've never done before."

"I don't know what's got into the General." Lettie took Martay's arm and jerked her to an abrupt stop. "A young girl's got no business going off to the wilderness." She started to unhook Martay's exquisite pale yellow ball gown.

Martay stopped her. "I can undress, you go on to bed. You must be tired."

"A little. My arthritis is acting up and I . . ."

"Poor Lettie. Get some sleep. Is Dexter . . ."

"That no-account Dexter's been asleep in his quarters since before nine o'clock. Fat lot of help he's going to be on this trip."

Martay could hardly hide her delight that Big Dexter was fast asleep and therefore couldn't be his usual nosy self. She knew she didn't need to worry about Amos, the family cook. If she knew Amos, he'd found a dice game somewhere on the train and wouldn't return to the California Gold until it was time for her breakfast.

Lettie, Big Dexter, and Amos were the only servants accompanying her to Colorado. The rest of the staff would remain in Chicago, taking care of the big house on Michigan Avenue. She'd miss them. Her mother had died when she was four years old, so Lettie and the others had raised her. They had their faults; Dexter was lazy, but he was also big and powerful and would lay down his life for her or the General. Amos was a hopeless gambler, but one of the best cooks in Chicago. And Lettie—well, Lettie was becoming increasingly hard to get along with. Martay put it down to the "mysterious change" she'd heard matrons whisper about. Lettie had turned fifty-one last winter and on the coldest of days she went about fanning herself, saying she was burning up.

"You're too hard on poor Dexter," said Martay, smiling up at Lettie. "And too hard on yourself. Go on to sleep." Martay put a fist to her mouth and yawned dramatically. "I can hardly hold my eyes open. I'll just fall right into bed."

"You sure you don't want me to help you get ready?"

"I can manage nicely, thanks."

"Well, all right. Don't be staying up reading any of those trashy dime novels, you hear me."

"I heard you. Now, good night."

Again Martay sighed with relief when Lettie left her alone. And then she smiled; raced to the vanity; looked into the gold-rimmed mirror. She snatched up a pot of lip rouge and quickly repaired the damage from Farrell's last lusty kiss. She impatiently smoothed the mass of tousled blond curls falling about her bare ivory shoulders, jerked the low-plunging bodice of her yellow gown up over the swell of her full breasts, turned out the lamp, and quietly tiptoed to the rear door.

The California Gold rode six cars ahead of the caboose. In front of it were the dusty chair coaches and shipping cars. Behind it were the sleeping and first-class coaches. Martay slid the big, heavy door of her stateroom open and stepped out onto the platform.

The fast-moving train had already left the lights of the city far behind and was now traveling over the rolling moonlit countryside. The wind blew so strongly into her face, Martay felt tears spring to her eyes and her long skirts whip about her legs.

She hurried to the next car, jerked the door open, and stepped inside. She made her way down the aisle where elegantly clad gentlemen were smoking cigars and talking of the stock market. Three well-dressed ladies were traveling together. A couple of brash young soldiers smiled and winked at Martay, and she smiled back. A child, breaking away from his weary, distracted mother, grabbed Martay around the knees and held on for dear life, saying, "Do you have candy?"

"No. No, I'm sorry," Martay said, smiling down at the adorable blond boy.

"Tyrone, turn loose of that pretty girl's dress," came the quick reprimand from Tyrone's mother.

He obeyed, and, smiling, Martay took a step forward and realized the hem of her dress was caught on something. She looked down. The delicate lace of her petticoat had somehow become snared on the toe of a man's gleaming black boot. Martay started to speak but saw that the man was obviously asleep. His head was resting on the seat back, his black hat pulled low, completely covering his face.

Half irritated that his foot had been in her way, Martay sat down on her heels to disengage her petticoat from his boot toe. While she was there she cast a curious glance at the man, who was traveling alone. His dark frock coat lay on the seat beside him. His cravat was untied and his white linen shirt was open at the throat. Long dark fingers were laced atop a flat abdomen, and a broad, powerful chest rose and fell evenly.

And long, lean legs, encased in fine black trousers, were sticking out into the aisle.

He shifted slightly and Martay held her breath. And for some reason the hair on the nape of her neck rose. Jerking the caught lace from the shiny boot, she heard it rip, but didn't care. She rose and hurried back down the aisle, feeling as if someone were after her. Her heart pounding, she stepped back inside her own gleaming stateroom and slammed the heavy door, whirling to lean back against it.

Then immediately laughed at her foolish attack of unease. Humming to herself, she undressed, turned out the gaslit lamp, and climbed into her big, soft bed. Her slender arms flung up over her head, she smiled in the darkness and thought about the glorious days ahead.

In moments the happy young woman, lulled by the monotonous clickity-clack of the wheels on the track, fell into a dreamless sleep.

In the middle of the night, while Martay slept peacefully in her stateroom, a tall, dark man stood alone on the observation deck at the back of the moving train. Cupping bronzed hands against the night wind, he lit a long brown cigar. The flare of the match briefly lit his chiseled face, the tiny flame making twin reflections in his black eyes.

He lowered the match and did not blow it out. The wind extinguished it. The cigar clamped firmly between his even white teeth, the man lifted a booted foot up to rest atop the wrought-iron railing. His eyes narrowed and, reaching down, he drew a tiny piece of torn lace from the toe of his gleaming black boot.

Rolling it slowly between thumb and forefinger, he smiled in the darkness.

2

After five days, Martay was growing restless and bored, despite the opulence and comfort of her "moving hotel" with its satinwood paneled walls, Queen Anne chairs with hand-embroidered rose upholstery, blue Frederickian sofa imported from Germany, and Louis XVI bed. It was almost noon and still she had not dressed. Her tumbled blond hair falling about her face and down her back, she still had on a lace-trimmed satin nightgown and matching robe. Her feet were bare.

Sighing loudly, she rose from the secretary, where she'd spent the past hour writing notes to her friends back in Chicago. After long, uneventful days of the train's snaking across the Great Plains, she'd grown tired of looking out the windows. There was nothing to see but mile upon mile of flat, high prairie, the sameness of the scene occasionally broken by a herd of cattle being driven to market by a handful of weathered drovers.

Wondering dismally if Denver was to be as tedious as this flat, lonely eastern part of the state, Martay made a face and flung herself down on the white velvet recamier, entertaining, for the first time, the idea that she might have made a big mistake by promising to spend her entire summer in Colorado.

She sighed again and closed her eyes, the idleness making her sleepy. She was just beginning to doze when Lettie came into the room and announced, arms folded, "Rocky Mountains straight ahead."

Martay's lassitude melted away and she was up off the daybed and at the window as quick as a cat. Pushing aside the curtains, she stuck her head out, squinted into the brilliant Colorado sunshine, and gave a great whoop of glee.

Before her, on the far, far western horizon, rose the majestic Rockies, their tallest peaks dusted with snow, their color, from her vantage point, a cool, deep, inviting blue.

Awestruck, she studied their grandeur unblinkingly for several minutes before she pulled her head back inside so swiftly, she bumped it. Ignoring the minor pain, she flew to Lettie. "Please run my bathwater, I must get dressed!" She slid the long sleeves of the satin robe from her arms and raced to the big armoire.

Shaking her gray head, the big Irishwoman smiled, her young charge's mercurial nature ever an amazement to behold. She said, "Honey, you got plenty of time. We won't arrive in Denver until tomorrow morning."

June 8 was a perfect day in the Rockies. Warm, but not summertime hot. Clear, the sky a robin's-egg blue with only a few high scattered puffy clouds floating aimlessly. Air thin and clean.

Martay, beside herself with excitement, looked every inch the "Golden girl" as the Chicago, Burlington and Quincy pulled into Denver's Union Station. Attired in a well-cut traveling suit of pale blue linen, her gleaming golden hair swept atop her head and covered with a saucy blue straw bonnet, white kid gloves on her pale, slender hands, and a smile as big as Colorado stretching her luscious Cupid's-bow mouth, she stepped down from her private railcar and felt every eye in busy Union Station turn her way.

Her own emerald eyes were anxiously surveying the crowd, looking for a noble head whose pale gold locks had turned to gleaming silver. She spotted him almost at once. Still a vitally handsome man at forty-seven, he was striding purposely forward, a young blond soldier at his side.

Martay hurried down the steps and started toward him, pushing through the throngs, murmuring "Excuse me" and "I'm sorry" until at last she reached him and found herself swept up into his arms and whirled around as though she were still a child.

"Daddy, Daddy!" she murmured, tears of happiness stinging her eyes, "it's been so long."

"Too long, angel," said her father, his strong arms threatening to squeeze the very life from her. At last he lowered her to her feet, cupped her flushed cheeks in his hands, and kissed her. Then drawing her under his right arm, he said, "Honey, I want you to meet a very fine young officer, Major Lawrence Berton."

"My pleasure, Miss Kidd," said the smiling blond man, his warm brown eyes crinkling at the corners as he held out a square freckled hand.

"I'm glad to meet you, Major Berton," said Martay, placing her small hand in his and feeling his blunt fingers firmly grip hers.

"Major Berton's agreed to have lunch with us, Martay. Isn't that grand?" said her father.

"Why, my goodness, yes," Martay answered, smiling up at the major but secretly wishing he had not come along. It would have been so lovely to have had a long, leisurely lunch all alone with her father. Her mild disappointment increased when she saw the four stocky military men standing beside the waiting carriage. She'd forgotten, almost, that her father never went anywhere without an armed military escort. She supposed it was necessary; she wanted him to be safe, of course, but it got awfully tiresome having strangers trail him every time she was with him.

Her father slid an arm around her narrow waist, leaned down, and said, "My God, I've missed you, sweetheart." And Martay's dashed spirits promptly lifted.

Touching the crown of her blue straw bonnet to his medal-bedecked chest, she said happily, "We've the whole summer together and it's going to be wonderful."

"That it is, my sweet girl," said the beaming general.

Martay was laughing sunnily by the time she stepped up into the carriage. Her father followed her up and sat down beside her, promptly putting a long arm protectively around her, while Major Berton took the seat across from them. The black carriage driver spoke in low, calming tones to a team of matched, nervous sorrels while waiting for the general's military escort to mount their horses. The four big men, their alert eyes moving constantly over the crowd, swung up into their saddles to ride alongside the carriage.

Being in a lively holiday mood, Martay took the pin from her straw hat, drew the hat from her head, and tossed it onto the seat by the spread-kneed major. Studying him from beneath full dark lashes, she noted that he was really quite handsome in a shy, cute way, like a great big overgrown boy, all scrubbed clean and on his best behavior. His eyes were a warm shade of brown, his nose patrician, his mouth just a shade too large, lips wide and full. He was stockily built, but there was no fat on his frame. His massive shoulders strained the fine blue blouse of his uniform and his summer whites pulled against hard, muscular thighs.

Impulsively Martay snatched her hat back up and moved across to sit beside the handsome major, never realizing just how much the simple act delighted the nervous young soldier. Or the general.

Depositing her hat upon the major's left knee, she told him a humorous anecdote about her father. Blushing, he laughed, casting nervous glances at his commanding officer. The general had thrown back his silver head and was laughing heartily, not minding that he was the butt of the joke.

But it was Martay's sweet bubbling laughter that carried on the high, thin air. And it was her gilt-blond hair that glistened so brightly in the warm Colorado sunshine.

Standing on the street outside the terminal, a man's attention was drawn by the sound of a girl's infectious laughter. Squinting, he looked toward the coach with its military escort. His black eyes lifted and went at once to a glorious mane of shimmering golden hair.

He raked long, dark fingers through his own raven locks, stepped into a waiting carriage, and said, "The Centennial Hotel."

Martay found Denver to be a charming city. Though not as large as Chicago, it was, in many ways, even more exciting. And best of all, her father spent a great deal of time with her, much more than she had hoped for. The first three days she was in the city, he, too, stayed at the Emersons' Larimer Street home.

It was wonderful.

The Emersons, such thoughtful, sensitive people, allowed the Kidds to spend their long summer afternoons alone together on the back terrace of the estate, just being lazy. Sipping cool drinks and enjoying the spectacular scenery, father and daughter made up for lost time.

On the evening before General Kidd was to return to his post, Major Berton came for dinner. The meal was superb, the dinner conversation pleasant, and the handsome Major Berton kept stealing covert glances at Martay. She was well aware of the warm brown eyes on her, though she pretended not to notice, acting as though she were paying very close attention to her father as he spoke.

"At last," said the general, setting his coffee cup back in

its fragile Ceralene china saucer, "this part of the country is a fine place to live, since we've about rid it of hostile savages."

Colonel Dolph Emerson smiled and said, "We've not completely solved the problem, Bill. There's always handfuls off the reservations, causing trouble. And there's still a few diehard Sioux and Crow renegade bands who refuse to give up and come on in."

"Ignorant heathens!" said William Kidd. "Mindless, less than human creatures! They should all be shot down like mad dogs!"

Martay was not shocked by her father's outburst. She'd heard it many times before. For as long as she could remember, he'd preached about the worthless, worrisome redskins and he'd bravely fought in many an Indian battle; he had the scars to prove it.

She shared his views on the redskins and thought it outrageous that for years they'd roamed wherever they pleased, terrifying the brave white settlers who peacefully traveled west. She'd reacted with horror to the countless stories of the massacres, the ungodly atrocities the wild savages had committed against the whites.

"Is that old bastard—ah, beg pardon, ladies," said General Kidd, "is Sitting Bull still hiding out up in Canada, the sneaky coward?"

"The last I heard he—"

"Goddamn him!" said General William Kidd. "When Grant was president he said that since we couldn't kill all of them, we'd starve them into submission. My thought then, as now, is, Why the hell couldn't we kill them? It's taking too damned long to starve the parasites."

Martay was growing bored with the subject. When her father got wound up, he could talk for hours about the "vile redmen." Letting her eyes drift casually over to Major Berton, she caught him staring at her. And she impudently winked at him. He blushed to the roots of his light hair. She continued to hold his flustered gaze while politely waiting for

Colonel Emerson to finish the long-winded reply he was making to her father's last statement.

When finally he did, Martay seized the opportunity to say, "If you will kindly excuse us, Major Berton and I will go out on the front veranda and catch the evening breeze." She paused, and smiled prettily at the officer. "There's a full moon rising, I think."

"Why, yes, yes. You young folks go on out and enjoy yourselves," said General Kidd, magnanimously.

"Thank you, sir." Lawrence Berton rose and hurried to pull out Martay's chair. Helping her to her feet, he looked at his hostess. "Mrs. Emerson, I don't know when I've enjoyed a meal more."

Betty Jane Emerson smiled warmly at the big blond man. "Major, you're welcome at our table anytime. You've a standing invitation."

When the handsome couple had stepped out onto the broad, flower-scented veranda, General Kidd said, "He's a fine boy, don't you think, Dolph?"

"By all means," answered his host, then grinned and added, "and the fact he's the only son of a man who has very close ties to President Hayes's White House doesn't hurt, now, does it?"

"Ties, hell," said General Kidd. "Strings. And Senator Berton pulls the strings." The two old friends laughed while Betty Jane, shaking her head good-naturedly, lifted a hand and signaled a servant for more fresh coffee.

Outside, a full white moon was indeed rising, its brilliance bathing the padded wicker settee where Martay and Lawrence sat. Looking up at the romantic moon, Martay said, "Isn't it beautiful, Major?"

Lawrence Berton looked only at her. The most breathtaking woman he'd ever seen. Masses of golden curls were glowing silver in the moonlight. The wide-set emerald eyes, shaded by thick, long lashes, flashed with appealing mischief. Her small turned-up nose was adorably cute, and her mouth with those dewy, Cupid's-bow lips made him ache to taste them.

"Yes," he said, "so beautiful."

Abruptly her eyes snared his and she said, "You must tell me about yourself, Major. I want to know everything!" And she stared right at him in a way that made the snug collar of his uniform blouse pinch his neck.

But, dutifully, he told her something of himself. He told her that he had been put in her father's command only three months previously and that he had never met a finer man than the general. Told her he was an only child, that his home was Richmond, Virginia, that he had graduated at the top of his class from West Point ten years ago, and that, no, there was no girl waiting back in Virginia.

After speaking steadily for a good five minutes, he stopped, laughed, and said, "Forgive me. I'm not usually so talkative." Shyly he reached for her hand. "Please, Miss Kidd, tell me of your life in Chicago."

"Oh, gosh, there's not much to know," she said, allowing his broad hand to draw hers atop his knee. Then she proceeded, with no more coaxing, to tell him how her beautiful mother, Julie Kidd, had died when she was only four years old. She volunteered that she herself was a very wealthy woman, that her mother had owned a number of rich-veined gold mines in California and had passed them on to her. When Lawrence had respectfully interrupted to remind her that married women could not have separate property, Martay promptly set him straight.

"Ah, but you're mistaken. In California all property owned before a woman's marriage or acquired afterward by gift or inheritance remains hers and is not under her husband's control. It's part of the state constitution. My mother was from California. She married my father at the Presidio in San Francisco. The property fell to her lawfully, and she willed it to me before I was born, held in trust until my eighteenth birthday. And now it's all mine."

She spoke with such authority, he had no doubt she was right. Before he could comment, she shocked him so he was entirely speechless when she said, with frank straightforwardness, "Tell me, Major, would you like to kiss me?"

Lawrence Berton swallowed, then swallowed yet again. He tried to speak, but the words would not come. So the mute major gently pulled the beautiful, brazen golden-haired girl into his frightened arms and tenderly kissed her.

When their lips separated, he embraced her, his mouth and nose pressed into her glowing golden curls. Martay, her face against his broad shoulder, caught a glimpse of someone lurking in the shadows. She tensed, then began to tremble.

Pushing away, she said, "Major, someone is spying on us!"

"Where?" he said, pulled rudely back to reality.

"Out there, at the edge of the yard! I saw someone. I know I did."

"Don't worry, no one could get by the general's guard," said Lawrence Berton, rising, "but I'll take a look around." He hurried across the vast yard, ready to slay any dragon for the fair lady. He found no one. But the Emerson's cat, a black panther-looking feline, flashed through the undergrowth when he approached the edge of the yard.

Laughing, he returned to tell Martay it was nothing more dangerous than a curious tabby. "See. Look to the left of that elm." He pointed.

Peering out, Martay saw, at last, the gleaming cat eyes shining out of the darkness. She laughed and said, "So it is. Only Ebony out for his evening prowl."

Still, that odd sense of being watched remained, and she said quickly, "We really should go back inside, Major."

3

On June 11, a hot, still Wednesday afternoon, two well-dressed gentlemen sat in the deserted oak-paneled bar of the gleaming new Centennial Hotel on Denver's downtown Tremont Street. The two were attorneys, as well as close, loyal friends, having spent years reading law together at Harvard. The pair, as different as summer and winter in both looks and temperament, nonetheless got along quite well. They were, on this lazy, warm afternoon, languorously passing the time talking cases.

Or had been. Until the subject turned to women.

Drew Kelley, a twenty-five-year-old strapping light-haired sunny-dispositioned Denver native, tipped his chair back on two legs and looked at the man across from him.

"My God, Jim, don't you have enough women? Why this interest in a girl you've yet to meet?" he said, studying the friend whom he had never fully understood, despite their having shared quarters at Harvard for more than four years.

Jim Savin, twenty-four, a tall, spare man with coal-black hair and blacker eyes, was staring moodily into his glass of wine, idly rocking the stemmed glass in his long, dark fingers, watching the slow swirl of the pale rosé as it moved in a spinning vortex.

It was Jim Savin's third day in Denver and he was bored. And impatient. Finally lifting his black eyes from the wine's hypnotic dance, he smiled and said, "I've my reasons, Drew."

Drew Kelley simply nodded. He knew it would do no good to question Jim further. He said, "How will you be introduced? She's the daughter of the regiment. Surrounded by handsome young officers."

"I'll find a way," answered Jim Savin calmly, picking up his glass and drinking the remainder of his wine. "Now . . . since you insist we visit Mattie Silks tonight, I think I'll go up to my room and have a bath and a nap."

Drew Kelley's face brightened. "You won't be disappointed, Jim. Mattie has only high-class, exotic women in her house."

"Sounds great," said Jim Savin, thinking it sounded just the opposite, agreeing to go only because his friend was so eager to show him Denver's wild side, the famous red-light district. "Pick me up at nine."

"Will do," said Drew, shoved back his chair and stood up, tossing several bills onto the table.

Jim rose and they walked out into the Centennial's impressive marble-floored lobby, shimmering now with varicolored light from a bright alpine sun coming through the stained-glass windows. A giant skylight six stories above the main lobby gave it a feeling of great height. A huge open fireplace of smooth, shiny white carrara marble stood cold on this hot June day.

As the two friends sauntered unhurriedly toward the gleaming glass front-doors, a sudden commotion caught their attention. A dozen chattering females swept out of the ladies' parlor, where they had lunched. At once the vast lobby seemed engulfed in a cloud of stylish silk frocks and French perfumes and veiled hats and tossing curls and high, feminine laughter.

"Oh, no," said Drew Kelley under his breath, and Jim turned to see a thin, raw-boned matron quickly bearing down on them. She had in tow a pretty, curvaceous young woman with flaming red curls peeking from under a ridiculous beige hat with feathers.

Jim smiled. "A hopeful mother trying to interest you in her charming daughter?"

"Hardly. The copper-haired beauty is the wife of a very jealous man, a Colonel Thomas Darlington. The stringy old gal is Bertie Gillespie, a widowed nosy friend of Mother's who says whatever pops into her head."

The ladies reached them, and before Drew could introduce Jim, Bertie Gillespie jutted out her rouged cheek for Drew to dutifully lean down and kiss. Then, as her snapping blue eyes landed on Jim Savin, she said, "Drew, who is this dark, good-looking stranger?" She poked a sharp elbow into the ribs of the redhead beside her and thrust a bony hand out to Jim. "I'm Bertie Gillespie, you handsome devil, and it's a cryin' shame I'm not twenty—even ten—years younger."

Gallantly, Jim lifted the thin hand clinging tenaciously to his, brushed his lips to it, and responded, "My dear, I'm Jim Savin, and I've a feeling you can hold your own with women half your age."

Bertie Gillespie hooted with laughter and, still gripping his dark hand, said, "Jim, you smooth-tongued rogue, this pretty thing with me is Regina Darlington. But don't go getting any ideas. Her husband is a powerful military man." At last she reluctantly released Jim's hand.

Jim's black eyes shifted to the redhead. She smiled, but did not extend her hand. "Mr. Savin," she acknowledged, tipping her head and setting the feathers atop her hat to fluttering.

"Mrs. Darlington," Jim returned, then fell silent while the talkative Bertie Gillespie, turning her attention to Drew, fired a host of questions at him, giving him no time to answer. As the elderly lady talked, Regina Darlington, though pretending interest, kept stealing glances at Jim's dark impassive face.

With Bertie Gillespie's one-sided conversation and Drew's nodded replies, it was established that Jim Savin was an attorney, was visiting Denver for an indefinite stay, and was a guest at the Centennial. When finally the long-winded woman found all that out and more, she turned to Regina Darlington and said, "If you're to drive me home, my dear, let's go. That horrible steamed trout we had for lunch has given me a bad case of indigestion." She patted Jim's cheek, turned, and marched off.

"Yes, be right there," said Regina Darlington, remaining where she stood. Then, eyes rising to his, she said softly, "Ah, Mr. Savin, it so happens I'm to give a talk at our next ladies' luncheon on the law as it applies to the vote for women." She paused, glanced around, and added, "It would be ever so helpful if I might interview you on the subject."

Jim smiled down at her and said, "Anytime at all, Mrs. Darlington." He lowered his voice so only she and Drew could hear. "Room number six eighteen."

A deep flush started in the V where the woman's expensive beige suit jacket met at the swell of her full breasts. It spread quickly over the pale apricot flesh of her throat and up to her lovely face. Without a word, she nodded good-day, turned, and walked away.

"I think," said Drew, after her shimmering beige skirts had disappeared through the heavy glass doors, "that the lovely Mrs. Darlington is interested in more than the vote."

"You say she's married to a colonel?" Jim's half-hooded black eye's were still on the door.

Drew nodded. "Still a bride. Married less than a year."

Jim Savin made no reply.

Not an hour later a gentle knock came on his hotel-room door. It was the hottest part of the afternoon; all the shades were lowered against the fierce sun. Just out of his tub, Jim stood pouring himself a bourbon, a white towel knotted atop a hipbone, wrapped around his bare, damp body. Unhurriedly, he took a drink of the whiskey, not bothering even to glance at the door. He knew who was standing on the other side.

Again it came. Soft yet anxious knocking.

Jim slowly drained his glass, then moved barefooted across the dim room. When he swung the door open he was not surprised to see the flame-haired Mrs. Regina Darlington nervously smiling up at him.

"Oh, my . . . I've come at a bad time, Mr. Savin," she said, her wide eyes quickly moving over his bare, glistening chest.

"Not really, Mrs. Darlington," said Jim. He took a step back and stood aside, neither inviting her in nor suggesting she return another day. Looking straight into her eyes, he raised long, bare arms and ran his fingers through his thick black hair, still wet from his bath.

Mrs. Darlington hurried inside.

When Jim closed the door after her, Regina Darlington whirled about, pressed her back against it, and said, breathlessly, a hand raised to her tight throat, "I . . . I came to . . . to interview you."

Jim smiled at her and braced a hand on the doorframe by her head. "Ask me anything, Regina."

Her senses were immediately assailed by his potent male presence. She was vitally aware of the fathomless black eyes, the sensual lips, the long, lightly muscled arm only inches from her shoulder. His bare gleaming chest with a long white scar beginning below his left collarbone and extending down to his ribs, made her feel as though she couldn't take a deep breath.

"Ah . . . yes, yes . . ." she stammered, "would . . . would you like to . . . to . . . get dressed?"

"Would you like me to?" His black piercing eyes held hers, neither accusing nor inviting, inscrutable.

He was not making it easy. Regina drew a shallow, labored breath. "I'm not sure," she admitted, blushing, feeling as though those hypnotic black eyes could read her guilty thoughts.

"Ah, well, then, suppose I help you decide." And his free hand moved to the buttons lining the center of Regina Darlington's stylish beige afternoon suit as he said, "I believe you mentioned a curiosity regarding the law and women's rights?" His black gaze holding hers, with one hand he deftly flipped all the buttons open while she swallowed convulsively and felt faint and weak, and the feathers on her bonnet quivered.

"Ye—yes, for . . . for my speech at the ladies' luncheon." The suit jacket was entirely unbuttoned. Jim casually pushed it apart, revealing full, high breasts covered only by the slick beige satin of her chemise.

"Perhaps," said Jim, "instead of my getting dressed, you should get undressed."

"No. Certainly not," she managed, trying to sound indignant, and made a halfhearted attempt at pulling the suit jacket back together. But her trembling hands fell to her sides when Jim, hand still braced against the doorjamb, the muscles of his inner arm pulling as he flexed his splayed fingers on the smooth wood, toyed with the lace trim of her filmy satin chemise. Then, curling his long, dark fingers inside the straining fabric, he casually lowered it until the wispy garment was nothing more than a tight lace-trimmed frame for the bare breasts he'd so boldly released.

The mere feel of his heated black eyes on her naked breasts made them quiver with sensation and the hot flames of desire rise within her. And when Jim licked his lean forefinger and languidly drew a wet, teasing circle around each rosy crest, Regina Darlington shuddered involuntarily and, breaking their locked gazes, lowered her eyes to the skilled fingers so expertly tormenting her aching nipples into hard, telltale points of passion.

The dark, dark hand against her pale flesh coupled with the sight of his obvious arousal—that rigid male flesh so provocatively outlined against his white towel—brought a rapid escalation of the torrid heat engulfing her.

Still, when he asked, "My dear, have you decided?" she felt compelled to say, "Yes. Yes, I have. I certainly have no wish to take off—ooooh," she softly moaned, lost in the pleasure of the moment. She caught herself and hurried on, "Mr. Savin, I didn't come up here to get undressed."

Abruptly the talented fingers stilled and the dark hand dropped from her breasts. Jim Savin nodded, turned, and walked away. "Then perhaps we'd better wait until another day to do the interview, Mrs. Darlington. I was just about to take my afternoon nap." He paused beside the turned-down bed, its spotlessly clean white sheets, cool and inviting in the too-warm room.

Stunned and hurt that he would give up so easily, Mrs. Regina Darlington, her lovely face almost as red as her hair, knew instinctively that if she let this opportunity pass, there would not be another with this strange, cool man.

"Jim!" she gasped, and hurried to him, her wet-nippled bare breasts bouncing with her steps. Not stopping until she stood facing him, all pretense gone, she reached anxiously out, undid the knot atop his hip, and pulled the white towel away, dropping it to the carpet. Her eyes hungrily sliding down the dark, sleek animal body, her lips fell open and she moved even closer—so close, her naked aching breasts brushed Jim's bare chest. "Jim," she said again, and brazenly she cupped her hands low around him, thrilling to the feel, the texture, of the crisp black hair of his groin.

"Yes?" said Jim, standing there naked, bare feet apart, arms at his side, his erection complete.

Regina's shaky fingers slipped inquiringly up the length of pulsing satin power to its tip. A ripple of pleasure raced through her and she said, "I do want to get undressed. I want to be as naked as you." Stroking eagerly, awed by the size and heat of him, she murmured, "I want you to make love to me."

"My pleasure, Mrs. Darlington," said Jim Savin, and smiling at her, he removed the feathered beige hat from her copper curls. Letting it fall to the carpet at their feet, he bent his dark head to kiss her.

For the next two hours Jim Savin gave the colonel's misbehaving wife exactly what she had come for.

4

She stood on the west sally port in the morning sunshine, her expectant eyes on the fort's main gates. The provost marshal, Colonel Thomas Darlington, a tall, lanky man with rich brown hair and a well-trimmed mustache, stood beside her, hands locked behind him.

Martay found it difficult to pay close attention to the colonel's polite conversation when she was straining eagerly to hear the first sounds of approaching horses. Giving only perfunctory replies to his questions, she waited on the porch of the main compound, her view of the outside world totally obscured by the fort's high, thick walls. Only glimpses of the towering mountains were visible through the deep embrasures for the heavy guns.

Impatient, she looked around at the only things she could see: the barracks, the casements, the north powder magazine, the deep, circular rifle pits with their huge black guns, the stone revetments, the flagstaff with its colors waving gently in the morning breeze.

Atop the parapets, straight-backed young soldiers, issue-rifles atop their uniformed shoulders, marched back and forth, and Martay found herself wishing she could join them. From up there she could look far out into the distance and catch the first sight of the returning troops.

". . . and would be honored to do it," Colonel Darlington was saying.

Knowing she'd been rude, Martay turned to the man and said, honestly, "Colonel, I'm terribly sorry. I'm afraid I was not really listening." She gave him a wide, full-lipped smile then and admitted, "I get such a thrill when I see the mounted cavalry come riding in that I . . ." she laughed then and added, "well, I suppose I'm truly my father's daughter. Being inside a fort, around proud military men, makes my heart beat faster."

Her statement caused the colonel's shoulders to go back a full inch. He smiled warmly at her, his own heart swelling with pride. "Miss Kidd, I find your candor—and your admiration of the men serving our country—absolutely charming." Posture erect, he added, "I share your enthusiasm. I get a great sense of security when I hear the bugle call tattoo or the gun fired for retreat."

Martay said, "Now you're sounding like my father."

The colonel laughed and replied, "And you, my dear, remind me a great deal of my lovely wife, though she's a few years older. Your lively spirit and appreciation of the military is much like my Regina's. In fact, I'm sure she would enjoy knowing you."

"I'd be pleased to meet your wife, Colonel Darlington," said Martay, fighting the urge to let her gaze drift back toward the gates.

"I'll ask Regina to call on you at the Emersons' one day soon." A fleeting darkness passed over his features, was gone as quickly as it had come, and he smiled once more. "I'm afraid she has too much idle time on her hands with me at the fort most all the time. We've been married less than seven months, and Colorado is not Regina's home. I encourage her to make lady friends to ease her loneliness."

Martay sympathized. "I think I understand something of how your wife must feel. My father has been in the military since before I was born; he's gone months at a time and it's hard. I miss him terribly."

He nodded. "You know, I'll bet Regina would like to have a party for you. We just completed our home up in the Denver foothills and she's been anxious to entertain and show it off."

"That would be very nice," said Martay, for want of a better reply.

"Good. Then it's settled," said Colonel Darlington, quietly surmising that a splendid party at his new west Denver mansion for the visiting daughter of his commanding general could be highly beneficial to his military career. And planning the fête would give his beautiful, cherished wife something to occupy her time—for at least a few days.

"You're too kind, Colonel," said Martay, "it's really not necessary to . . . to . . ." She fell silent and quickly turned her head, listening. Then her lovely face broke into a wide grin when the definite echo of horses' hooves striking hard-packed earth announced the return of the garrison. "It's them," she said excitedly, "they're back!"

At that moment, two trim young officers hurried to the tall front gates and threw the heavy bolt, opening the protective fort to its conquering heroes.

Into the dusty quadrangle rode the command, guidons fluttering in the breeze, horses whinnying and snorting, weary soldiers smiling broadly, glad to be back after four days in the saddle.

Martay, feeling her heart drum pleasantly, saw him at once, the most flamboyant cavalryman on the Great Plains. Her father.

He rode at the head of the command. He was dressed in his blues, a double row of brass buttons going down his tunic to its tight waist. The yellow piping of a commissioned officer decorated the trousers, and his shoulder boards bore the single silver star of Brigadier General, United States Cavalry.

His black felt campaign hat was jauntily tacked up on the left side, the drawstring pulled tightly beneath his firm chin. Suede-gloved hands held the bridle of his prancing iron-gray stallion and the toes of his tall black boots, spit-polished to a mirror brightness, were thrust deep into silver-trimmed stirrups. His saber glinted in the bright Colorado sunshine.

Like a great Shakespearean actor on opening night, Brigadier General William J. Kidd played his real-life role with intense concentration and dramatic flourish; this fort was his stage, the troop his audience.

They, and his lovely young daughter, who he knew, though he looked neither to the left nor the right, was watching his grand performance. It was moments like these that were best. The thought of one day giving all of it up was painful to him, and yet he knew he must.

In a few short years he would be too old to play the lead, to ride a magnificent steed into a remote army outpost at the head of his command. Too old to lead brave young warriors into battle against the barbaric redskins. Too old to sleep on the cold ground in some pitched camp in the wilderness. Too old to cut a dashing figure on the dance floor when he visited Washington City.

Suddenly the general felt a twinge of melancholy in the middle of triumph. If not this life he loved, then what?

A post in the President's cabinet, by God, that's what! Wield some power in the nation's capital, take his satisfaction —and his applause—from the decision making enjoyed by only a handful of men. Respected men. Lauded men. Powerful men.

At last the general looked toward the sally port, where his daughter was to be waiting.

And there she stood. A lovely willowy girl with gleaming golden hair. A true vision in a cobalt-blue dress, smiling prettily, a slender arm raised, waving to him. A beautiful girl any young man would be proud to call his wife.

And if General Kidd had his way, he'd choose the young man who one day would call her his wife. He hadn't excelled in tactics at the academy without learning a great deal about silent maneuvering and surprise attacks and gaining confidence of the unsuspecting.

His daughter was going to marry Major Lawrence Berton; he would see to it! That's why he'd invited her to Colorado for the summer, and why he'd allowed her to visit Fort Collins today. He would, over the next several weeks, implement the strategy called for and gain, he felt certain, the reward he was seeking.

Major Lawrence Berton for a son-in-law.

Soon there would be grandchildren to be shared and enjoyed with that other grandfather, Virginia senator Douglas Berton. And by the time the firstborn was out of short pants, grandfather Berton would no longer be a senator, he'd be the President of the United States of America. And Martay and the children, lonely without their hero husband and father who was often away, bravely protecting his country, might decide they'd be comfortable living on Pennsylvania Avenue. Just move right into the White House with President Douglas Berton!

General Kidd was pleased to see that Martay was at this moment smiling at Major Berton, who was riding just behind him. He didn't need to turn in the saddle to know the major was smiling back. Since young Berton had first laid eyes on Martay at the Denver train station, it was obvious the senator's son was smitten. Too obvious. He'd have to speak to the boy about hiding his innermost feelings for a time.

Martay, unfortunately, was not the kind of sweet, demure young lady who was anxious for the total devotion of a fine, upstanding young man. She claimed she had no desire to marry for a long time. She had some tomfool notion in her head that she was supposed to have a life of excitement and adventure, do as she pleased, as though she were a man! God, where had he gone wrong?

"Daddy, why were you frowning at me when you rode in?" Martay asked when the general bent to kiss her cheek. He'd dismissed the tired command, climbed down from the iron-gray, tossed the reins to a waiting private, and strode across the parade ground, returning Colonel Darlington's crisp military salute.

"Frowning? Why, Angel, I didn't know that I was." He smiled warmly then and shook hands with Darlington. "Thanks, Colonel, for looking after my little girl."

"The pleasure was mine, General," said Colonel Darlington. "Martay and I have become friends, and, as I was telling her, my wife wants to throw a party for her. I hope you'll be able to attend, sir."

"Wouldn't miss it," said the general. Then, to Martay, "Walk me to my quarters. I'll clean up and we'll have lunch in the officers' mess. Then I'll show you around."

"Lead the way, General," said Martay, taking his arm and nodding to Colonel Darlington.

Lunch was most enjoyable for Martay. Seated at a table with eight attentive officers, she was entirely in her element. Charmed by her wit and beauty, the gentlemen soldiers remained at the long table after the dessert plates had been cleared away and coffee had grown cold in their cups.

And they were disappointed when the general placed his napkin on the table and rose, announcing, "I'm sure you'll excuse us. I've promised to give Martay a tour of the fort."

The officers rose and not one, but three, rushed to pull out Martay's chair. And when, after bidding them good day, calling each by name, she swept out of the mess on her father's arm, the enchanted officers smiled and shook their heads and agreed that the general's beautiful daughter was all he'd said and more.

Martay and her father stepped back out into the glaring

sun and strolled across the parade ground toward the hospital. "I thought, child, we'd spend a few minutes cheering the lads in the infirmary. Get that behind us."

Before she could respond, and right on cue the way the general had planned it, a skinny young lieutenant rushed across the plain toward them. Apologizing for the interruption, he informed General Kidd that he was needed in his office.

Acting as though he were truly annoyed, the general shook his silver head and said, "Angel, I'm sorry."

Martay sighed. "I understand, Daddy. Promise you won't be long."

"Promise," he said. Then, looking over her head, he smiled and added, "Why, there's Major Berton. Perhaps he can keep you company while I'm tied up."

So it was Major Lawrence Berton who escorted Martay to the hospital, then showed her the bakery, the wood yard, the chapel, and the icehouse as the afternoon wore on and still her father did not return from his important meeting.

Martay didn't mind too much. She hadn't seen Major Berton since the evening at the Emersons' and had been mildly disappointed when he failed to appear for lunch in the officers' mess. Besides, he was much more patient about answering her many questions than her father would have been.

At midafternoon the pair strolled leisurely along the ramparts, and Martay, having seen everything there was to see, admitted, "Larry, I'm getting a little tired. I was up before the sun this morning. Perhaps I'd better go to my quarters and rest before dinner."

"Of course, Martay. I'll walk you there."

"No," she said, "I want to go to Daddy's office and see what time we'll be dining."

Inside the general's office at that moment, an Indian sat across from General Kidd, drinking his second glass of whiskey while the general questioned him.

"You're sure? I thought he was up in Canada," said General Kidd.

The Crow scout scratched at a jagged scar beside his left ear. "I'm telling you, General, Sitting Bull's got a big band of hostiles, half-breeds, and foreign Indians together. He and Gall are roaming again in the U.S., south of the boundary line." He swilled the liquor and held out his empty glass for more. "I've talked to a number of reliable people who've seen their main hostile camp. They tell me there's five thousand Indians. Two thousand of them are warriors."

"Goddamnit to hell!" thundered the general. "Where are the bastards getting food and ammunition?"

"They say the half-breeds have been trading with the hostiles and furnishing them with ammo. You know how sneaky half-breeds are."

General Kidd nodded and said, "I'll get a wire off this afternoon, see if we can't have a good man sent up to Fort Keogh with a strong force to break up their camp, separate the doubtful Indians from the hostiles, and force the foreign Indians back north of the boundary." He slammed his fist down atop his desk as his face grew a fiery red. "Damn Sitting Bull! Damn all those pigheaded, surly, foolhardy Sioux! Don't they know they cannot fight the United States Cavalry! I'll not rest until they're wiped from the face of this earth!"

"Nor will I," said the Crow, with no emotion.

"All right, Scar, if that's all you have, go. Get out of here. My daughter's visiting the fort and I don't want her to see you." He smiled then, and rising, came around the desk to put a hand on the Indian's shoulder. "I've taught her that all redskins are alike. She might be frightened if she saw you here."

The Crow scout gave no reply. He reached over, picked up the half-full bourbon bottle from atop the desk, turned it up to his lips, and took a healthy swallow. Wiping his mouth on the back of his hand, he rose and left the room.

* * *

When Martay and Lawrence Berton neared the long, low building that housed the general's office, the door suddenly opened and a stocky, fierce-looking Indian stepped out onto the porch. Instinctively Martay stopped, wrapped her hand around Lawrence Berton's elbow, and drew close to him.

"Who is he?" she whispered, her wide, shocked gaze on the ugly, badly scarred copper face with its glittery black eyes and huge nose and fleshy lips.

Patting her hand, Lawrence Berton said reassuringly, "That's Scar, Chief of our Crow scouts." He urged her on toward the building. "Scar's harmless."

The squat-bodied Crow looked up, noticed them, and stood, unmoving, watching their approach, an evil smile spreading over his uneven features. His eyes went to Martay and stayed. Martay tried not to look at the frightening, repulsive man, yet couldn't keep from it.

He stood with his moccasined feet wide apart. His dirty buckskins stretched tautly, vulgarly, over bulging muscular thighs and rode low beneath a thick, heavy belly. His shirt, a faded calico, had had the sleeves cut from it at the shoulders, and he was flexing and unflexing his beefy fists, causing the tendons and veins in his huge, powerful arms to stand out in grotesque relief. Those arms, like his ugly face, were badly scarred. Dirty black hair, parted in the middle, hung to his shoulders.

When Martay and Lawrence were but a few short feet from the staring Crow, the door directly behind the Indian again opened and General Kidd marched out.

"Still here, Scar?" he said, and the Crow scout, not bothering to answer, stepped from the shaded porch and walked away, disappearing around the corner of the building.

Only then did Martay's racing pulse return to normal.

5

"**H**ave you noticed," Martay said to Lettie, her maid, as the big Irishwoman helped her dress for a morning of shopping with their hostess, "that everyone wants to please Betty Jane?"

Lettie nodded. "It's not hard to see why. Mrs. Betty Jane Emerson is a lady in the truest sense of the word."

"She is, isn't she," Martay said musingly. "Still, it's hard to understand how a woman so quiet and modest commands so much admiration." She tilted her head thoughtfully. "She gets almost as much attention as I do."

"No!" exclaimed Lettie in fake horror, clasping her hands to her breasts. "Is there no justice?"

"Oh, I didn't mean it like it sounded," defended Martay. "It's just that . . . well, she isn't exactly pretty, and her conversation is not all that sparkling. And," she added, with an inflection of mild distaste, "she looks at Dolph Emerson as though he were a god, instead of a fifty-year-old man with thinning gray hair."

"Perhaps in her eyes Colonel Emerson is still the dashing young cadet she fell in love with thirty years ago."

Martay frowned. "Mmmmmm. I suppose. I asked her if she never tired of deferring to him, and you know what she said? She smiled and told me she always did just as she pleased, so long as it pleased the colonel. Isn't that tragic, Lettie? The poor woman has subjugated herself to a man for all those years!"

"Child, you don't know what you're talking about. Betty Jane Emerson is a very happy woman. While you may have noticed the way she regards the colonel, you've failed to see the adoration in his eyes when he looks at her. He thinks Betty is beautiful, and she is."

"She is?"

"Inside. Mrs. Emerson is so pretty inside, it makes her pretty outside."

"Hmmmm," murmured Martay, and mulled it over in her mind. "Maybe I'll try to be more like Betty Jane." Lettie exploded with laughter. Frowning, Martay demanded, "What's so funny about that?"

Shaking her head, Lettie said, "Honey, you're about as different from Betty Jane Emerson as it is possible to be."

Hands going to her hips, Martay said, "Well, perhaps I am a bit more self-centered than . . ."

"A bit?" interrupted Lettie, still smiling. "Child, if you ever had a thought that didn't focus on yourself, I'm not aware of it."

Emerald eyes snapping with anger, Martay shot back, "Why, how can you say a thing like that? I most certainly do not . . . I . . . never . . . I . . ." She faltered and stopped, and a small smile began to spread over her mobile features. And she said, whispering, suddenly afraid they might be overheard, "While Betty Jane Emerson seems to derive great satisfaction from always putting others first, I for one am not quite ready for sainthood."

Grinning, Lettie answered, "You can say that again."

"I will, then. I want a great deal more out of life than to be the respected mistress of some man's home."

"What more is there?" asked her maid.

"I don't know," admitted Martay, "but I intend to find out. Now, get me a pair of clean gloves. Betty Jane's promised to take me shopping."

"I'm giving a grand party. You must come."

"No."

"But I want you to . . . to . . . mmmmmm . . . darling. . . ."

"I said no."

"I wish you would . . . I . . . we . . . ahhhh . . ."

Dark, tapered fingers swept enticingly over pale trembling flesh, and the woman lying naked atop the cool white bed arched her back as the words died in her throat. Unconsciously straining upward, she sighed, breathed through her mouth, and languidly flung her slender arms up over her head. Savoring the delicious, tantalizing preliminaries to full-blown passion, she tried valiantly to continue the conversation, to pretend that she was not yet ready to surrender totally, that she was not completely aroused.

"But, darling," she murmured, purposely keeping her voice level, "you must come . . . come to my . . ." A foolish little smile touched her lips as that warm, skilled hand cupped a full white breast and a dark, handsome head bent to brush a kiss to its darkening crest.

"I despise parties," he said, his voice low and emotionless, his lips and tongue toying with a peaking nipple.

Gritting her teeth with pleasure, the woman's slender fingers went immediately into the thick raven hair of her lover's head. Almost frantically grasping the silky black locks, she pressed him to her, murmuring, "My . . . my . . . parties . . . are . . . are . . . different, darling."

"They're all the same," he said, his words muffled as his warm mouth slid up to her throat. The woman was momentarily stung by his statement. She felt this strange, compelling man who made such hot, devastating love to her was actually speaking, not of parties but of women. Although he'd never been anything but gracious and accommodating, and unfailingly passionate, she felt sure that their heated sessions of afternoon delight meant little or nothing to him. And there were times when he lay above her, his lean, sleek body bringing her to a height of pleasure she'd never before experienced, that the deep black eyes looking into hers were as cold as his lips were hot.

"No. No, that's not . . . it isn't . . . mmmmmm . . ." Giving herself up to the burning flames enveloping her, she forgot about the planned gala. Sighing, she writhed and arched and strained while her dark experienced lover drove all logical thought from her head with his burning lips and magical hands and lithe body.

She basked in the sweet torture for as long as she could, glorying in the things he did to her, the erotic methods he knew of arousing her, the shocking love words he elicited from her. And finally, drowning in a scalding ocean of desire, she begged, just as she did each time they were together, for him to give her all he had.

"Please, please, my love . . ." she breathed as the heat between her pale parted thighs blazed out of control.

Agilely he moved into position, and the woman gasped as the hard, pulsing length of him slid swiftly into her. For one brief instant she felt as though that throbbing power invading her with such brutal force would surely spell her end, but she didn't care. What a lovely way to die; impaled upon this beautiful naked prince of love.

Then he started the slow, deep thrusts she'd come to crave as her arms entwined around his neck and she looked once more up into those black, fathomless eyes that impaled and invaded her with a force equal to the deeply buried pulsing male flesh.

For the next hour the man made love to the woman,

bringing her to climax again and again, before seeking his own release. His dark body glistening with a sheen of perspiration, he finally eased off the limp and sated woman and stretched out on his back.

She lay quietly beside him for a time, sighing and smiling, her long auburn hair a tumbled mass of curls about her bare apricot shoulders, her eyes misty with satisfaction. Easing herself up onto an elbow, she watched the even rise and fall of the dark, gleaming chest with the fascinating white scar he refused to speak of. She knew he was on the verge of dozing. His eyes closed, girlishly long black lashes rested on the high, slanting cheekbones, and his mouth had lost some of its hardness.

Knowing it was past time to leave, her thoughts were pulled back to reality. And to her upcoming party. Placing a small white hand on his flat belly, she said softly, "Jim, darling, please say you'll come to my party. I do so want it to be a success and I've promised an interesting mix will attend."

Not bothering to open his eyes, Jim Savin said, "No, Regina."

Pouting, letting her fingertips lightly tickle his stomach, she said, "Jim, is it because you feel guilty about us?" She smiled then and added, "You said yourself you're always more than willing to 'entertain a military man's wife.' Isn't that what you said?"

"It is."

"Then come, darling. I'll not give us away. My husband will be there, so I'll hardly get the chance for more than a couple of dances with you; but the girl I'm giving the party for is said to be quite hard to impress, so I'm determined to have a number of handsome, charming people there. At first I had planned to invite all ages, but I'm just not going to do it. I told my husband I'll not allow anyone over thirty-five years of age to attend. That way there won't be a bunch of stodgy old folks there watching every move so they can gossip about it. Besides, that will leave out Betty Jane and Dolph Emerson, as

well as the girl's father, and I'm sure she'll enjoy herself more
if they're not there breathing down her neck. I do so want
Miss Kidd to . . ."

Hooded eyes slowly came open and the lithe bronzed body
tensed. He heard only snatches after that as Regina Darlington chattered on, explaining she was intent on having the
most extravagant party that Miss Martay Kidd of Chicago,
Illinois, had ever attended. At last she concluded, saying,
"My goodness, where has the time gone? I shall be late getting home and the colonel is coming in from the fort this
evening." She shook her auburn curls, swung her bare legs to
the floor, reached for her silk stockings and, giggling naugh-
tily, added, "I must wash your scent from my body before he
arrives. I hope Thomas isn't in an amorous mood, because
I'm so . . ."

Interrupting her monologue, Jim Savin said casually, "I'll
be there." One shapely leg raised, the sheer silk stocking
pulled up to her knee, Regina Darlington's hands stilled and
she turned quickly to look at him, her eyes questioning. He
smiled lazily at her. "I've changed my mind. I'll come to your
party."

Martay lingered in her bath.

Almost asleep in the long marble tub, she lay totally relaxed, her neck resting against its rim. Golden tresses pinned
haphazardly up, her head lay back on the pillowed headrest
and her slender arms were draped along the tub's sides. Her
long legs were stretched out the full length of the enormous
bath, toes pressing the smooth marble. Gallons of hot, steaming water filled with scented, foamy bubbles covered her re-
clining form, the thick suds reaching just to the tops of her
full, high breasts.

It was two hours until time to leave for the Darlington
party. Enjoying the sweet lassitude claiming her, Martay was
in no particular hurry to get dressed, nor for that matter was
she eagerly looking forward to the occasion. It wasn't that she

didn't like the Darlingtons; she found Colonel Thomas Darlington to be a most pleasant gentleman, and the one time she had met Regina Darlington, the pretty red-haired woman was both gracious and friendly.

Martay yawned and sighed.

Languidly she picked up the perfumed soap and dampened sponge from the small gold-and-white tubside table and began rubbing the two together, elbows still resting on the tub's rim, head still pressed against the pillowed headrest.

She felt sure it would be a carefully planned, elegant party with mountains of tempting foods and bouquets of cut flowers and an orchestra and dozens of interesting guests. And she would, she knew, behave as was expected of her. She would laugh and flirt and dance and convince everyone that she was having a wonderful time and she'd do everything within her power to make the others enjoy themselves as well.

Martay lazily placed the lathered sponge atop her bare left shoulder and slowly spread a soapy trail down her arm. Changing hands, she repeated the action on her other arm. Then dipped the soapy sponge into the hot water and brought it up to her throat.

No, she was not looking forward to the Darlingtons' party, and the reason she wasn't was that she was to be escorted by Major Lawrence Berton and she didn't want to go with him and she felt downright mean about it.

But there it was.

She faced the truth now as she sat in her hot tub in the privacy of her bathroom. She did not want to spend her entire evening with Larry. She didn't really want to spend any more of her evenings with Larry, because she could tell that he had fallen in love with her, though she'd known him for only six weeks. He was beginning to behave just like Farrell T. Youngblood, Jr., back in Chicago.

Again Martay sighed wearily and wondered if there would ever be a man in her life who did not turn into a spineless, moonstruck boy after she'd shared a few moonlight kisses with him.

The abrasive sponge moved around her slippery left breast in a slow, tickling circle.

What would it be like, she wondered dreamily, to meet a man so fierce and strong, he could overpower her with the sheer strength of his will. A man dark and handsome whose cocksure manner and natural arrogance could not be altered by her. A compelling, godlike creature whose very presence would render her totally speechless and awed. A virile, untamed male who could silence her with a look, frighten her with a word, tame her with a touch.

The warm sponge, guided now with both her hands, was moving over Martay's wet belly, and she realized, guiltily, that the nipples of her breasts, now fully above the water, were standing out in twin erect peaks. Face hot, she continued to conjure up an image of the man she was yet to meet. And as her daydreams grew more vivid, more real, the untapped passion deep within her rose ever closer to the surface.

An underlying fire that was totally foreign caught her by surprise, spreading through her bare wet body with unsettling speed. A tickling, thrilling feeling that made her long legs tense, her back arch, her breath grow short. An intense heat, far hotter than the steamy bathwater, was centered between her pale thighs, and the telltale nipples of her breasts were now tingling points of sensation.

Frightened yet intrigued by this new experience, and never one to back away from pleasure of any kind, Martay remained as she was, allowing the abrasive sponge to roam at will over every inch of her trembling, ignited body. And she closed her eyes once more, the better to imagine the tall dark man she could almost see beneath closed lids.

With her eyes tightly shut, she surrendered completely to her enchanting charade.

It was his dark hands that guided the soapy sponge so tantalizingly over her bare, burning body. His gentle coaxing that caused her knees to fall apart in expectation. His commanding touch that moved unerringly toward . . .

"Martay. You better get out of that tub," came Lettie's intrusive voice from just beyond the door, "you're going to burn completely up." Martay jumped as if she had been shot.

Face flaming red, she leapt up, sending water splashing over the tub's rim, and reached anxiously for a towel.

"Be right out," she called, her heart pounding as the heat that had claimed her body was replaced by a definite chill.

6

An hour later Martay descended the stairs, looking very much like a shining angel come down to earth. The ball gown she was wearing was of shimmering white silk and was of the latest fashion. Small capped sleeves that left her slender arms bare were attached to a closely fitted bodice that continued to a deep point on her flat stomach. The dress was cut quite low, displaying lovely ivory shoulders and the swell of her pushed-up breasts. Its waist was very tight and the skirt was molded snugly from her rounded hips down to her knees, where it flared dramatically, making it possible for her to walk and to dance.

Her golden hair was parted in the middle, pulled to the back of her head, and caught there with a pearl-and-gold barrette. Glowing, perfumed curls fell halfway down her bare back and danced prettily with every step she took. Pearl earscrews clung to her small shell-like ears, and a long strand of cultured pearls caressed her bare throat. Her gloves were white satin, as were the dainty dancing slippers peeking from beneath her rustling white silk skirt. She carried in her hand a fragrant white gardenia.

Martay reached the bottom of the stairs and, not bothering to take one last look in the tall hall mirror, swept into the drawing room, where her father and the Emersons were gathered. Pausing in the arched doorway, she waited until all three pairs of eyes were on her. Then she smiled, held out her arms, and spun about so that they might get the full effect.

They did.

Though all were used to her spectacular beauty, she took their breath away. Never had she looked lovelier, more fragile, more innocent. Betty Jane Emerson clasped her thin hands to her breasts and sighed. Colonel Dolph Emerson, bolting up out of his chair, rushed to take her hand, saying, "Child, you are truly a vision in gold and white!"

Her father, rising also, remained where he stood, his green eyes locked on his lovely daughter, his chest filled with pride and with fear. God, she was so breathtakingly pretty and so damned naive for all her coquettishness. Was such a dazzling creature ever safe? Could he trust even Major Berton not to take advantage of this fair child? Would Almighty God watch over such appealing innocence?

"Daddy, you are staring at me," said Martay as she entered the big room on Dolph Emerson's offered arm.

"Yes," he said, and smiled at her. "I am staring. I'm staring just as every other man will stare at you this evening. You're exceptionally lovely tonight, angel. Prettier than I've ever seen you."

Dropping Colonel Emerson's arm, she came to her father, stood on tiptoe, kissed his cheek, and teasingly accused, "You've said that before, Daddy." Before he could reply she had hurried to the long brocade sofa where Betty Jane Emerson was seated. Dropping down beside the older woman, Martay took one of Betty Jane's hands and lamented, "I do so wish you and the colonel and Daddy were coming to the party."

Betty Jane smiled. "So do I, dear, but Regina Darlington explained that she is having only the young set this evening because she thought you'd enjoy it more." She squeezed Martay's slim fingers. "I think that's very thoughtful of Regina, and perhaps it will be fun for you young folks to be free of the elders for one night."

"Well, I disagree and I think it's . . ." Martay was interrupted by the loud hammering of the front-door knocker.

"That's your young man," said Colonel Emerson, and went to let him in.

In his dress military blues with his face scrubbed shiny clean and his blond hair carefully brushed, Major Lawrence Berton, smiling broadly, entered the room looking boyishly handsome and appealingly bashful. When he caught sight of Martay, the big smile left his face and he swallowed hard. Courteously shaking hands with General Kidd and bowing politely to Betty Jane Emerson, he stared, speechless, at Martay as she rose gracefully from the couch and said, "Hello, Larry. How nice to see you this evening."

Not trusting his voice, Major Lawrence Berton just nodded and grinned and was grateful when Colonel Emerson clapped him on the back and said, "Son, what you need is a drink."

The small glass of good Kentucky bourbon was indeed just what the nervous major needed. Soon he was engaged in polite conversation, relaxing a bit, and eager to get the beautiful silk-gowned Martay alone for the ride up into the foothills of the Rockies.

Half an hour later the handsome pair had said their goodnights and were headed for the front door. While they stood in the foyer with Lawrence carefully draping Martay's delicate lace shawl about her bare shoulders, General Kidd startled them both.

He came charging toward them, his face strangely set, his green eyes almost wild. "Child," he said, his voice rough, and he grabbed Martay and hugged her, crushing her to his broad chest.

"Daddy," she said, feeling the trembling of his big solid body, "what is it?"

Patting her slender back and giving her one last squeeze, he said, "Nothing, sweetheart. I just wanted to hold my baby girl one last time." He released her, setting her back.

Her hands still clutching his ribs, she smiled up at him. "Don't be silly. You may hug me whenever you please."

"I know," he said, "I am being silly."

But after he had bid them good-night and the carriage had rolled away down the avenue, and he had ordered the two mounted horseman, "Don't let her out of your sight tonight," and had returned reluctantly to the veranda, he stood there alone in the gathering dusk, again wondering how long his lovely daughter would remain as safe and as innocent as she was on this warm July night in 1879.

Feeling a squeezing pain in his heart, General Kidd shook his head wearily and started back inside. But an arriving messenger stopped him.

Brigadier General William J. Kidd had been ordered to Washington on the next train leaving Denver.

The Darlington ballroom was undoubtedly one of the grandest in the state. Regina Darlington took great pride in the huge white ballroom with its hand-carved pine Corinthian columns, crystal chandeliers, and white marble fireplace. The room, covering the entire back of the mansion, was one hundred feet long and sixty feet wide. The ceilings were twenty feet high, and a half-dozen sets of tall French doors opened onto a long, wide stone gallery that overlooked back gardens and well-tended lawns sweeping toward the edge of the property where tall firs and aspens and cedars became the forested mountain.

The Darlington home was located on the highest inhabited point in the west Denver foothills. From its lofty heights far above the sprawling city, those inside enjoyed total privacy and seclusion. From the mansion's large drawing room and banquet-sized dining room, it was possible to see every twinkling light of Denver, to feel the city's life and energy.

The rear ballroom offered quite a different experience. Guests dancing there felt as though they were truly high up in the remote mountains, and more than one elegantly gowned lady, taking the air on the stone veranda, had squealed delightedly as a white-tailed fawn skittered across the lush yards.

Coyotes howled plaintively from out of the dense woods, and bobcats, their sleek coats flashing in the sunlight, chased frightened antelope within sight of the house. And more than once Colonel Thomas Darlington, enjoying a late-night smoke alone on the stone porch, had seen the unmistakable gleam of a panther's eyes, though he never shared that information with his wife or their guests. He did caution against couples strolling too far from the well-lighted house at night.

At a quarter before nine, Regina Darlington, gowned in vivid lavender faille, swept down the winding marble staircase, diamonds glittering at her throat and wrist and falling in long, swaying showers of light from her delicate earlobes. Her new Paris gown was scandalously low and daring, its décolletage barely concealing the large nipples of her full breasts, which were purposely pushed high by a tight, torturing corset she endured for beauty's sake. The long lavender skirt fitted like a second skin down to her knees, where the faille met heavily gathered lavender chiffon, the fluffy fabric swirling prettily about her feet.

Reaching the ground floor, Regina Darlington went at once to the first mirror, a ceiling-high gold-framed glass wiped spotless each day by industrious servants. She stood looking at herself, well pleased by what she saw. With a pink-nailed hand she smoothed the straining fabric covering her rounded bosom, then let her fingers glide down her rib cage to her hip.

She drew a deep breath, smiled at herself, and licked her wet red lips. A shiver of excitement ran up her spine. In less than an hour Jim Savin would be here, inside her home. He would see her at her loveliest in her opulent hillside mansion. Regina felt that her impressive home was but an expensive, tasteful frame for her fair beauty, and if there was ever a man she longed to have see her at her best, it was the mysterious, compelling Jim Savin.

She knew nothing of the man, nothing, other than the fact that he was an attorney who had read law at Harvard with the Kelley boy. He never talked of himself, and when she asked questions, his only response was a smile or a casual shake of his handsome head. More than once she had tried to find out exactly what business he had in Denver. Would he be remaining in the city indefinitely or was he just here for a short time? Did he plan to practice law in Denver? Was he looking to buy a home?

Satisfactory answers to her questions were never forthcoming, and Regina was afraid that on one of those occasions when she cautiously slipped up to the Centennial Hotel for an afternoon of ecstasy she would find him gone. For good.

The idea was devastating.

She'd had many lovers, before her marriage to Thomas Darlington, and after. But none could compare to Jim Savin. There was a barely submerged savage side to his nature that frightened and excited her beyond belief. At the same time there was a coldness, an uncaring attitude, that hurt her feelings yet intrigued her greatly as he must surely intrigue every woman he met.

The thought suddenly caused Regina to frown at her mirrored image. Young Martay Kidd was undeniably pretty, if somewhat too tall and slender. And Denver was buzzing about the Chicago girl's unquenchable thirst for adventure. Would Martay behave like a rude, spoiled child and throw herself at the fascinating Jim Savin while her poor bewildered escort looked on helplessly?

"The brazen little bitch," Regina said aloud. "How dare she come to my home and behave like a trollop. If she thinks she can lure a man as worldly as Jim Savin away from me, she's another think coming!"

"What did you say, dear?" came Thomas Darlington's voice from inside the vast ballroom.

Regina hurriedly put a sweet smile back on her face, turned toward the ballroom, and floated straight to her husband. Fussing with his black cravat, she told him, "I said some of our guests are now coming."

"Oh, really?" Thomas Darlington drew the gold-cased watch from his pocket. "Perhaps you're right. I have three minutes of nine."

Regina had already stepped away from her husband. She gave the big room a sweeping inspection, needlessly rearranged a leafy palm resting in a tall Ming vase, checked to see that the gilt opera chairs were neatly lining all the walls, gave her upswept red hair a pat, and went forth to meet her guests.

It was twenty minutes past nine when the carriage transporting Martay and Lawrence Berton rolled to a stop on the circular driveway before the magnificent Darlington house. The melancholy Martay had experienced earlier was gone and she was her old self again. Ready to talk and laugh and dance and have a fabulous time.

To her surprised delight, Larry had been charming company on the short trip, neither pressuring her for kisses nor exclaiming over and over again how lovely she looked. He had, instead, held her hand warmly in his square freckled one and entertained her with amusing stories of his soldier's life at Fort Collins. Wondering at the change in him, she listened attentively and thought that if he continued to behave in this new, more sophisticated fashion, she might grow to care for him.

Martay had no idea that her uncharacteristically composed escort had been counseled by her father. Stubbornly resolved to have his way, General William Kidd had carefully coached the major on how he should behave if he had any hopes of winning Martay's heart.

"Son, you can't go mooning about if you want her. Be a man. Be decisive. Be reserved. Hell, be distant, make her wonder. It'll work. Women like that sort of thing, perverse creatures that they are."

The major would have been amazed to know how well the advice had served. After the first awkward back-sliding moments when he'd walked into the Emersons' house and seen the radiant Martay, Lawrence Berton had managed to behave as the general had instructed; and Martay, surprised, pleased, and puzzled, found him to be far more charming than he'd ever been before.

So by the time the couple arrived at the party, a composed Major Berton was sweeping a laughing Martay up the stone steps and into the glittering entryway. There they were met by beaming Regina Darlington and her husband, the colonel.

"So happy you could come," trilled Regina. "We're all going to have a lovely time tonight."

7

Jim Savin reclined atop his bed at the Centennial Hotel. One lone lamp was burning, casting a circle of honeyed light over the polished mahogany table on which it rested and a portion of the deep, expensive carpet beneath. The light did not reach to the bed where Jim was lying. Stretched out on his back, one long arm folded beneath his head, he was smoking a thin black cigar in the darkness.

A nighttime quietness had descended over the big hotel. Many of the early-retiring guests had gone to their rooms as ten o'clock approached. An occasional carriage rolled by on the street below, the sounds of horses' hooves striking pavement, wheels turning, and fleeting snatches of the occupants' conversation drifting up on the thin, dry air and in through the open sixth-floor window.

Jim lay totally still except for the movement of his hand bringing the hot-tipped cigar back and forth to his lips. But he was far from relaxed. His long, lean body was as tightly coiled as a stalking panther's, while his thoughts, as he stared at the ceiling, were as disciplined as a school marm's as he clicked off in his mind all the arrangements that had been completed, and the steps of his master plan that remained to be carried out.

This morning he'd gone down to the Curtis Street stables and taken his horse; the one he had purchased his first day in Denver and had been training ever since. A big shiny black with heavy mane and tail. A powerful animal with prominent eyes, a sharp nose, small feet, and delicate legs. The beast, he had been told when he bought him, was tricky and dangerous, but could run like the wind and had unmeasured stamina.

Now the mount waited, high up on the mountainside, saddled and hidden in the darkness of the pine forest. Just six miles from where the stallion was tethered, inside a long-abandoned line shack, were the Navy Colt .45, the well-oiled Winchester rifle, blankets, food, candles; all he would need for the twenty-four-hour wait.

From the mantel across the hotel room, an E. Howard clock began its hourly chiming. Jim Savin waited. Waited until the ten rhythmic strikes had ended. When all was quiet once more, he reached over and carefully snubbed out the fire from his burned-down cigar, making sure each orange spark had cooled and completely died in the crystal ashtray. Only then did he rise from the bed.

Naked, he crossed the dim room.

A neatly pressed black tuxedo with satin lapels was draped over the mahogany valet. A snowy white shirt lay across a chair. Onyx studs were tossed carelessly atop a tall chest beside a pair of black patent-leather shoes. In the top drawer of that chest was one pair of gentlemen's long black stockings and one set of white linen underwear.

The naked man suddenly stretched like a big, lazy cat. Going up on bare toes, he raised his long brown arms high up over his head and clasped his hands together. He stood there poised on his toes for a moment, then allowing his heels to sink back down to the soft carpet, he leaned back from the waist; way, way back, until he felt the tight muscles of his shoulders and belly and groin pulling tautly. Then in one quick fluid movement he brought his raised arms forward, bent from the waist, and touched his flattened palms to the floor directly in front of his bare brown toes.

Ten minutes later, impeccably dressed in fine evening clothes, Jim Savin stood downstairs at the cashier's desk. A drowsy hotel clerk jumped down from his stool and hurried forward. While Jim drew a roll of bills from his trousers pocket, the thin-faced man said, "Mr. Savin, all your luggage has been shipped, just as instructed." He cleared his throat needlessly and added, "We sure hate it that you're checking out of the Centennial, we've enjoyed having you, sir. Catching the midnight train back east?"

Jim made no reply.

Smiling easily at the curious man, he counted out enough money to pay for his six weeks stay, added a generous gratuity for the staff, put the rest back into his pocket, and walked out into the night. Right on schedule a rented carriage rolled to a stop before the Tremont Street entrance of the Centennial, and Jim stepped into it. When the landau reached the western edge of town, Jim opened the tuxedo jacket, lounged back on his spine, plucked at the creases of his trousers, and stretched his long legs out before him.

It was just ten minutes past eleven o'clock.

"I sure hate this, Bill," said Dolph Emerson, as the general placed the last of his personal belongings in the valise that lay open on the bed. "Martay will be so disappointed."

"I know," said William Kidd, "but I've no choice. I must leave for Washington tonight. President Hayes has called for a counsel of his top military advisers."

"I see," mused Dolph Emerson. "I had hoped that sharp fight Colonel Miles's troops had up by Frenchman's Creek last week would have scattered the hostiles."

General Kidd gave a disgusted shake of his silver head. "Colonel Miles had a troop of the Seventh Cavalry, a company of the Fifth Infantry, and about fifty Indian scouts, and still only managed to kill a bare handful of the savages." Again he shook his head. "Chased three or four hundred of them for twelve miles and then let the hostiles get away, north of the Milk River. They say old Sitting Bull and Gall were with them." William Kidd ground his teeth viciously. "Instead of catching that midnight train east to Washington, I wish to hell I was mounting a horse to ride into the Dakotas."

"Bill, don't you think you're getting a bit too old for Indian fighting?" said his friend.

For an instant William Kidd's green eyes blazed with anger. "Too old? By God, I've never been in better shape in my life! I can still out-soldier any of these young pups and I . . . I . . ." His words trailed away, then he began to smile sheepishly. And he admitted, "You've heard this before."

His old friend smiled warmly and laid a hand on General Kidd's shoulder. "I have, my friend, and it's the God's truth. No finer soldier ever lived than you. But, Bill, you serve your country better by going to the White House to confer with President Hayes than by riding up into the Badlands."

William Kidd sighed wearily. "I suppose." He closed the valise and lifted it from the bed. "Now I must get to the station. You'll look after Martay for me?"

"You know I will."

Downstairs, Colonel Dolph Emerson walked his old West Point comrade outside into the hot, still night, where the family carriage was waiting to transport General Kidd to Union Station.

The two men shook hands in the moonlight, and General Kidd said suddenly, "I should never have allowed Martay to come out here." Before Dolph Emerson could respond, the general had bounded up into the carriage and departed.

Beneath one of five magnificent chandeliers lighting the long white ballroom, Martay Kidd turned about on the polished floor in the arms of Major Lawrence Berton. The sweet strains of a waltz came from an alcove where the ten-piece orchestra was concealed behind garlands of cut flowers.

At half past ten the party was in full swing and dozens of couples were on the floor, the ladies' colorful gowns contrasting beautifully with the solid white ballroom. Other guests had already hurried into the dining room to sample Regina Darlington's splendid buffet.

One of the first shimmering ice sculptures ever to be seen in Denver reigned supreme atop a long, impressive banquet table draped in white damask. An imposing six-foot-long beautiful frozen panther seemed to prowl gracefully down a mountain of white damask amid strategically arranged huge silver platters bearing ribs of beef and sliced spring duck and broiled fresh trout and roast quail with wine sauce and grilled salmon and rosemary-scented lamb. Beyond the many kinds of meats was an array of vegetables, both plain and exotic, and two dozen different desserts.

White-gloved waiters served the feast to hungry young people holding out fine Limoges china plates. Others who had already visited the buffet sat about on the silk opera chairs in the ballroom, or upon the grand staircase, or outdoors on the stone veranda, balancing the china plates on their laps, dabbing at their mouths with fine Irish linen-and-lace napkins, and washing the delicious food down with vintage French champagne from sparkling crystal flutes.

The waltz ended, and Lawrence Berton's hands dropped away from Martay's narrow waist as he said, "Would you like supper now, Martay?"

She thought for only a moment. "No, Larry. I'm not hungry, but you go ahead."

"Sure you don't mind?"

She did, but she didn't say as much. "Of course not. You go on. I'll freshen up." She was surprised he could be interested in food when she was willing to dance every dance with him. Larry was not behaving like himself. Not at all.

His hand at the small of her back, he guided her to the

base of the stairs, smiled down at her, and said, "I'll see you back in the ballroom in a half hour."

She nodded, lifted her white silk skirts up to her slim ankles, and gracefully climbed the stairs, knowing very well that Larry was standing below, watching. Pausing when she reached the second floor landing, she turned to look down, intending to favor him with a smile.

But he wasn't there.

Mystified and half miffed, Martay whirled about and hurried to the beige-and-white salon appointed as the room where young ladies were to retire if they wanted to freshen up and rest for a few minutes. Teeth grinding, Martay was growing more than a little annoyed with Larry Berton. Immediately she realized she was being foolish. After all, it was eleven and they'd not yet eaten a bite. Larry always had a hearty appetite, as did she. Except tonight. For some reason, she had no appetite. None at all.

Martay was not the only one with no appetite for food.

Pacing restlessly in the spacious beige-and-white salon, Regina Darlington felt she might never be hungry again. Where was he? Each time an arriving guest had stepped into the white ballroom, she had looked toward the entrance, her heart speeding, expecting to see him, elegant in his evening clothes with his raven hair gleaming under the chandeliers, his cool black eyes seeking her out.

It hadn't happened.

It was almost eleven and he had not shown up. Damn him! Where was he? Why had he promised he would come if he never meant to?

"Oh, excuse me, dear," Regina said as she almost bumped into Martay.

"Mrs. Darlington," said Martay, "a lovely party. I can't thank you enough. I'm having a wonderful time."

Forcing herself to smile, Regina said, "I'm glad. Have you been to the buffet yet?"

"No, I'm far too excited to eat anything. And you?"

Again Regina smiled. "I'm too excited as well. Perhaps we'll both be hungry later. I'm serving an early breakfast spread around two A.M. Nothing fancy, mind you. Strawberries and cream. French pastries. Omelettes and smoked ham. The usual."

"I shall wait and . . ."

"Dear," Regina interrupted, "you haven't seen . . . that is . . . ah, have you met all the guests here this evening?"

"Every one of them," Martay proudly announced.

"Hmmmm," Regina responded. "If you'll excuse me, I should get back downstairs. Relax here for a while, you must be winded after all that dancing." And she was gone.

Regina hurried down the stairs and into the white ballroom. Eyes eagerly scanning the dancers, she looked for him without success. Waving away her husband's invitation to dance, she proceeded into the dining room. A queue of hungry guests were still passing along before the food-laden table, filling their plates, but his tall form and dark noble head was not among them.

A feeling of despair came over Regina. It was foolish, she knew, to be so disappointed, but she couldn't help it. This party was as much for his benefit as for Martay Kidd's. She had so wanted to show Jim Savin that she was not simply the frustrated, lonely wife of a rich army colonel who sneaked up to his hotel room for afternoons of stolen ecstasy. She was a respected lady of great poise and beauty, looked up to and admired by the city's gentry, capable of ruling over a vast estate with confidence and ease.

Sighing, she went back toward the ballroom, telling herself he would come, he had to come, and when he did, she'd find a way to get him alone. That thought chased away her gloom and a mild flutter of excitement took its place. How thrilling it would be to make love to Jim Savin in her own home while a party was going on around them. Her mood elevated, Regina smiled and circled the large dance floor.

Tapping the shoulder of Major Lawrence Berton, she said,

"I told my husband, the colonel, I'm just so disappointed I could weep."

"Ma'am?"

"That's right. I told the colonel that the handsomest man at my party hadn't so much as asked for one single dance." She stepped closer, head thrown back, lashes fluttering. "Are you going to make me suffer, Major?"

"No. No. I . . . would you care to dance, Mrs. Darlington, ma'am?"

"Regina," she corrected, and put her arms around his neck. Locking her hands behind his blond head, she purposely moved so close to him her breasts lay against his blue uniform blouse and her hips pressed against his. "Yes, Major, I'd love to dance with you."

After a couple of dances, Regina thanked Lawrence Berton, then insisted he meet a lovely brunette at the edge of the crowd. No sooner had she introduced the pair than Regina pushed them both toward the floor.

While Lawrence Berton was taking the smiling girl in his arms, Martay was starting back downstairs. And a late-arriving guest was stepping into the empty foyer. Not even a servant was there to greet the gentleman. He was alone. His back was to Martay; she saw only that he was tall and lean and had hair a deep midnight-black. She paused midway down the steps, suddenly nervous, strangely reluctant to go further. Her fingers tightly clutching the polished banister, she realized her heart was behaving erratically, skipping beats, and the palms of her hands were moist.

She waited anxiously for the man to turn around so she could see his face. But he never did. He walked straight toward the dining room. As soon as his tuxedoed back disappeared through the double doors, Martay lifted her skirts and rushed the rest of the way down the stairs. Following him directly into the dining room, she looked eagerly about, longing to get a glimpse of his face, but couldn't find him. Intently she studied every group, seated and standing, and still failed to locate him. Puzzled, she even asked two or three people if they had seen a tall black-haired man come into the room, a guest who had just arrived. None had.

Sighing, wondering why she cared about some dark-haired stranger, Martay pushed him from her mind and looked about for Larry Berton. Not finding him there either, she wandered back into the ballroom. She stopped short, not believing her eyes. Larry was on the dance floor. And a pretty brunette girl was in his arms. The girl was listening intently to what he was saying and looking up at him as though he were the most exciting man she had ever met.

Martay was not jealous, but the girl's undisguised interest in Larry heightened her own. He was quite handsome tonight with his pale blond hair and arresting smile. And the fact he had hardly waited until she was out of sight to dance with another clearly showed he was not as totally snared by her charms as she'd presumed.

When the music stopped, Lawrence escorted the young lady back to her group of friends and came to join Martay. She waited for him to stammer and turn red and apologize for dancing with another woman, but again he surprised her. He neither stammered nor blushed nor so much as mentioned the other girl.

Instead Lawrence smiled at Martay, commandingly took her in his arms, and drew her out onto the floor. And when after several silent cheek-to-cheek dances he said, "Let's go out-of-doors," Martay was quick to agree.

It was well past midnight as they stood on the deserted veranda. A full moon had risen and was now sailing high over the mountains. The scent of honeysuckle sweetened the cooling air, and soft music from inside floated out through French doors thrown open to the night.

"It seems we're all alone," said Major Berton, turning to lean back against the smooth stone railing. He looked down at Martay and smiled.

"Yes," she answered, glancing about, "all alone." And

putting her arms around his neck, Martay, with the white gardenia in her hand, boldly pulled his head down and kissed him so soundly, the major's knees buckled.

When their lips separated, a man's voice, very near and sounding apologetic, said, "Excuse me, Major," and the pair turned to see a uniformed servant. In his white-gloved hand he was carrying a small silver tray, atop which lay a small envelope. Raising the tray, he said, "a message for you, Major Berton."

"Thank you," said Lawrence, picking up the envelope and hastily ripping it open.

"What is it?" asked Martay, seeing the look of annoyance in his eyes.

"I'm wanted upstairs by my superiors." He lowered the note. "You'd think whatever it is could wait until morning. I must go, you understand." He took her arm. "Shall we?"

"I'll wait here, Larry. It's too warm inside." And she gave him a meaningful smile that promised more kisses upon his return.

"Sure you'll be all right alone out here?"

"Just fine."

"I'll go, then, but I promise to be back in ten minutes."

"I'll be waiting. And, Larry, bring me a glass of punch when you come. I'm thirsty."

He touched her cheek and smiled. "Meet you right here in ten minutes with the punch." He hurried away, but when he reached the French doors, he turned back to look at her.

She blew him a kiss and laughed, the sound of her laughter floating out over the gardens. When he'd gone, she turned to look out at the magnificent scenery. Sighing with contentment, she tilted her head back and looked up at the towering majestic Rockies. Their tallest peaks were still dusted with snow, the moonlight turning them a glistening silver. After studying their splendor for several long moments, she let her eyes return to the nearer surroundings. To the flower-laden gardens and the sprawling well-tended lawns and finally to the thick forest beyond.

She caught sight of movement at the edge of the dense forest. Something flashed rapidly across her line of vision, an animal or creature with such startling swiftness, she lost sight of it. Then it stopped and Martay saw, shining from out of the blackness, a pair of gleaming animal eyes.

Transfixed, she stared unblinking at those light-reflecting eyes, her hands gripping the stone railing, her breath caught in her throat. It seemed as though those frighteningly awesome eyes, the only two points of light in a sea of blackness, had mysteriously locked her in place so that she could neither move nor look away.

For what seemed an eternity to Martay, she stood there alone, scarily hypnotized by those eyes. Then suddenly there was nothing there, only a thick, unrelieved blackness.

A chill raced up Martay's spine and her hands felt icy. Her throat was tight and very dry. She was frightened, though she didn't know why, and she hoped that Larry Berton would return very soon.

And as though he had read her thoughts, a hand came out of the shadows and passed her the promised punch. Relieved, Martay smiled and, looking only at the refreshing drink, eagerly reached for the glass. But before she could take it, an unsettling fact registered in her brain. The dark, tapered fingers holding the glass did not belong to the square freckled hand of Lawrence Berton.

Like a fawn sensing danger, Martay's alarmed green eyes flew up to a handsome hawklike face with eyes as black as midnight. She opened her mouth to scream, but before any sound came, the glass of punch had been tossed away and the long, dark fingers and a snowy white handkerchief were clamped tightly over her open lips.

A feeling of acute dizziness immediately claimed Martay, but fleetingly she struggled as she was pulled against the rock-hard body of her assailant. Effortlessly she was lifted up into his arms and he agilely leapt over the stone railing and was running as soon as his feet touched the ground. In seconds they'd crossed the moon-splashed lawns and were into the forest, and Martay, feeling a strange lassitude coming over her, foggily realized that the hand was no longer covering her mouth. She was free to scream. But the effort was too great.

Vaguely aware of a muscled chest beneath her cheek, she drew in a much needed breath. His scent, clean and unique and masculine, mixed with that of the dying gardenia she still foolishly clutched in her hand. Desperately she fought to make out his features, to find out who was holding her so tightly in his arms, but she could see nothing but a pair of ebony eyes gleaming like an animal's in the thick, cloying darkness.

Those strange, mesmerizing eyes shining brightly in the blackness were the last thing she remembered. Then even they disappeared as total darkness engulfed her.

8

"**M**artay?"

Puzzled, Lawrence Berton stood looking about the empty veranda, holding two cups of icy punch. His irritation was rising. If this were someone's idea of a joke, even Martay's, he failed to see the humor. Foolishly he had dashed inside and upstairs as soon as the servant had delivered the message saying he was wanted by his superiors, only to be met by Colonel Darlington and told that no one had summoned him; there was to be no meeting.

"This is a party, Major," Thomas Darlington had reminded him.

"But, sir," Lawrence Berton had protested, holding up the folded note, "this message was signed by you, and I . . ."

"What message? I signed no message. Someone's having sport with you, Major." And Colonel Darlington had grinned and added, "It appears to me one of the many young men anxious to beat your time with Miss Kidd has cleverly maneuvered to get her alone for a few moments."

"No. No, sir, I don't believe . . ."

"Well, I do, Major. You've apparently failed to notice the looks of envy you've been drawing from a majority of the men here."

"I can certainly believe that, sir," Lawrence said proudly.

Major Darlington clamped a hand down atop Lawrence Berton's muscular shoulder. "You're a lucky man, Major. Now get on back out there to your sweetheart before some fellow steals her away."

And so Lawrence Berton, mildly annoyed, had hurriedly stopped by the table where a gigantic carved-crystal bowl held gallons of icy pink punch, nodded yes to a servant's offer to pour, and carefully balancing the two brimming cups, had gone back out to claim what was his.

But where was she?

"Martay?" he called again. "Martay, where are you? I've brought our punch." He turned his head, listening, looking. The huge stone porch was silent. "Martay, answer me."

Lawrence Berton's irritation turned to downright anger. Major Darlington was right. Obviously one of the unattached males present had called him away on false pretext, then hurried outdoors to charm Martay. Lawrence Berton immediately began considering who the guilty party might be. Captain Haynes? He was always trying to move in on somebody's date. Lieutenant Brooks? He was a known ladies' man. Samuel Baker? Sam had made no bones about the fact that he wanted Martay.

Gulping down one cold punch, then the other, Lawrence Berton set the empty glasses atop the smooth porch railing and hurried down the back stone steps into the manicured gardens. Jaw set, he went in search of the woman he loved, ready to fight any unscrupulous cad who might, at this moment, have Martay alone out in the moonlight.

Major Berton's anger had given way to mild apprehension after twenty minutes of scouring the vast grounds, both in back and in front of the mansion. His careful search had turned up a half-dozen courting couples enjoying the warm mountain moonlight, but not a trace of Martay.

Dashing back inside, Lawrence Berton wandered through all the downstairs rooms, his eyes anxiously seeking a head of gold-gilt hair, a shimmering gown of white silk.

"Excuse me, Miss Brady, Miss Hanson." He hurriedly mounted the stairs to meet a pair of descending young ladies. "Did either of you happen to see Miss Kidd upstairs in the ladies' salon?"

"No," they said in unison. Then Miss Brady, the one with chestnut curls, teased, "Major, everyone knows she went out into the moonlight with you." She tapped his broad shoulder with her folded fan. "Don't tell me you left her out there alone and lost her." She laughed then, as did Shirley Hanson.

Realizing suddenly how very irresponsibly he had behaved, Lawrence Berton muttered, "Jesus Christ! Dear God in Heaven!" And the heart inside his broad chest beginning to pound with alarm, he bounded down the stairs and sought out his host.

Within minutes the orchestra no longer played, guests no longer danced, sweethearts no longer strolled in the moonlight. While the ladies, twittering nervously and holding hands, gathered in the vast white ballroom, every man present began a thorough search for the missing guest of honor.

Nothing.

Not a sign of Martay Kidd.

A decisive Colonel Thomas Darlington ordered a mounted search of the wooded acreage surrounding his big estate. In a remarkably short period of time, dozens of young gentlemen, dressed in their evening duds, thundered out of the stables astride fast horses, Colonel Darlington and Major Berton leading the way.

It was after three in the morning when the frustrated horsemen came riding back to the mansion in defeat. They had not found her. Miss Martay Kidd was very definitely missing.

At almost four A.M., in an upstairs study of the lighted Darlington mansion, a heartsick Major Lawrence Berton, his blue jacket cast off, circles of perspiration staining his shirt, related again and again to a circle of looming military superiors exactly what had led up to Martay's disappearance.

It was past four in the morning when the bearer of the bad news galloped up to the Emersons' Larimer Street home. Inside, a wide-awake, worried Colonel Dolph Emerson, upon hearing the approaching hoofbeats, drew an easy breath at last, turned and smiled at his robed wife, Betty Jane, and said, "They're home."

Betty Jane Emerson's eyelids slid closed in relief and she sighed. Then, opening her eyes, she immediately clutched at her husband's forearm, saying softly, "Now, Dolph, please don't be too hard on the boy."

"Hard on Major Berton? Why, Betty, I ought to horse-whip him! Keeping that child out all night when he promised he'd have her home at a . . ."

"Now, Dolph, you're forgetting what it's like to be young and in love." His reply was a snort and a shake of his balding head. "You are," his wife went on, gently. "Remember the Fourth of July Ball back in forty-nine when we . . ."

"Hush now, darling, they're on the porch." And not waiting a moment longer, Dolph Emerson strode into the foyer and jerked open the heavy front door. He saw not the tall, muscular major and Martay but a skinny young lieutenant standing before him.

"What's the meaning of this, Lieutenant?" said Dolph Emerson.

"Colonel, sir, with apologies from my superior, who is in the field," replied the nervous officer, "I'm afraid I have some very bad news."

It was straight up four A.M.
A lone rider, on a deep-chested dun gelding, pulled up on

the reins, bringing his mount to an abrupt halt atop a rocky overhang above the sleeping city of Denver. Only a few lights were still twinkling below in the valley. The full moon had set and the summer sun had not yet tinged the eastern horizon with color.

The rider sat for only a moment, then nudged the gelding back into movement. If he were to be in and out of Denver under the cover of darkness, as planned, he could wait no longer.

Down the rocky, timbered slopes the rider guided his horse beneath the towering trees and across boulder-strewn crevices in the early morning blackness, reciting silently to himself the instructions he had been given, the orders he had sworn to carry out.

"You're to ride into Denver and go straight to the Larimer Street home of a Colonel Dolph Emerson. Place this envelope under the door, lift the door knocker several times, making sure you've roused the household, then flee back to your horse, remount, and ride away before the door opens. Don't come back here; don't return home. Go south, spend the winter with Running Elk's people, and I'll see you in the spring."

The rider was so preoccupied with his thoughts of successfully carrying out the all-important mission for his friend, he failed to notice, as he rode into a wide upland clearing, a trio of mounted men lying in wait. They'd heard him lunging down the mountainside, his horse whinnying and loosening boulders as he came.

As soon as he spotted the ill-kempt men, he pulled roughly on the reins, the bit jerking his gelding's head up. But it was too late.

"Get him," shouted a big, bearded man, grabbing for the startled gelding's bridle. The rider managed to wheel his gelding away, but he didn't get far. The men gave chase in the darkness, overtaking the rider not a half mile from where he'd first seen them.

His hand flattening protectively over the breast pocket

where the all-important message lay against his rapidly beating heart, the rider was jerked down from his horse and unceremoniously killed by the three drunken vagrant gold prospectors.

It was a robbery, of sorts.

They took from the knife-butchered body the few coins he carried in a tiny worn leather purse. They also took, after prying away the still-clutching fingers, a message from inside the rider's breast pocket. An impressive white parchment envelope with a shiny gold seal securing its flap.

Striking a match so that he could see, the largest of the three, the big-bellied, bearded Benjamin Gilbert, held the envelope between soiled thumb and forefinger as though it were precious, studying it carefully.

His match went out.

"Light a goddamned match, Eli," Gilbert snapped at the young, skinny boy who was still frantically searching the warm body, hunting for hidden treasures.

A match flared, then a second, as Johnny Batemen, the third member of the drunken trio, moved closer, and the big man painstakingly separated shiny gold seal from fine parchment and unfolded the letter. Squinting, he peered thoughtfully at the bold, neat handwriting as though he were carefully reading it.

A snort of derision from Johnny Batemen caused big Benjamin Gilbert's head to swing around. "What's so all-fired funny?"

"You," said Batemen. "You could have the secret to the mother lode there in your hand but it wouldn't do you no good. You can't read." And he hooted with laughter, as did young Eli Wills.

Big Benjamin Gilbert looked fierce for only a moment, then he, too, laughed. They all three laughed because not a one of them could read or write. Not a word.

When they'd calmed a bit, Benjamin Gilbert said, "Reckon this here gold seal might be worth something?"

"I'd save it, you never can tell. Might be something valuable," replied Johnny Batemen, rising. Looking down at the man they'd killed, he nudged the body with the toe of a scarred boot, scratched his itchy chin, and said, "Wonder what this ignorant redskin was doing with a fancy envelope sealed with gold?"

His black eyes had not left her for the past hour.

She lay exactly as he had placed her when they'd reached the abandoned line shack. On her back atop the cot, one small hand resting on her waist, the other beside her hip. Her head was turned to the side, facing him, her golden hair fanned out on the pillow, one thick lustrous lock falling over her left shoulder and across the swell of her pale bosom.

She looked as innocent and helpless as a baby lying there with her soft lips partially open, her green eyes peacefully closed. Long, dark lashes cast feathery shadows on her ivory cheeks. Her nose, small and proud, was that of an adorable child. But when, still slumbering soundly, she sighed and drew a deep, shuddering breath, her soft, full breasts swelled atop the low-cut bodice and the shimmering white silk of her gown pulled provocatively across a flat belly and flaring feminine hips.

This was no child.

As he studied her sleeping form, he thought she was a spoiled, beautiful woman who looked upon her too-easily snared lovers as mere playthings, toys to be chosen and discarded with equal carelessness. Much like Regina Darlington and so many others he'd known in the past four years, this lovely golden-haired temptress lying before him now, her pale, fragile beauty making her appear angelic, sweet, untouched, was in fact as brazen and promiscuous as the rest. Of that there was little doubt. He had observed her behavior for the past six weeks.

His jaw hardened.

He was glad he would have her only for twenty-four

hours. With her deceptively innocent brand of beauty, she was as dangerous as her heartless, murdering father.

He turned his head and looked out the window. A faint hint of gray was seeping over the eastern horizon. She would waken soon. He'd used only a minute amount of the chloroform, just enough to ensure her silence until they were safely away from the Darlington estate and inside this distant shack so that her screams, when they came, could not be heard. It had been almost four hours.

His eyes returned to her face.

She gave a little short sigh and again turned her face in his direction. A tiny muscle twitched beside her soft mouth. Her lashes began to flutter.

Martay began slowly to shake off the chains of unconsciousness, struggling to wake up. She drew in a breath and tried, unsuccessfully, to open her eyes. She swallowed and licked her lips. And tried once more to open her heavy, heavy eyelids.

Managing to open them barely a slit, she found her vision blurred, fuzzy. She blinked, and blinked once more, then allowed her lids to slide closed. And she rested. Shortly, eyes still closed, she tried to lift her arms, to move her hands, but couldn't. She moaned softly. And trying again, finally got her eyes to open fully.

For a long moment she saw only shapes and muted color and the glow of a lamp from somewhere. Then movement caught her attention and she stared, unblinking, as a man slowly came to his feet to loom tall and menacing before her.

He stood there silent and made not a move. In the heavy lassitude still weighing her down, Martay languidly studied him, unsure where she was and with whom, but as yet unafraid.

Looking down, she stared at his feet. And, her head still foggy, she didn't think it the least bit strange that he wore soft, intricately beaded moccasins or that elkskin leggings covered his long, lean legs. A buckskin shirt, fringed at shoulder and hip, stretched across broad shoulders and lay unlaced and open down his smooth, dark chest.

Her curious gaze lingering on a white scar slashing across his muscular chest, Martay frowned imperceptibly and languidly allowed her eyes to drift up over his gleaming throat to his face.

As motionless as a statue, the harshly chiseled features were half in shadow, half in bold relief. A proud, fierce face with a cruel, sensual mouth, an arrogant nose, and high, slanted cheekbones that gleamed copper in the lamplight.

The horror of realization finally dawning, Martay felt her entire body become paralyzed with fear as her eyes flew up and locked with his. He stared down at her.

And those eyes—those cold, mean, killer-black eyes—were unmistakably those of a fierce, untamed savage!

9

The force of his black, unblinking eyes was so strong, Martay was unable to move or even to scream. That powerful, hypnotic gaze held hers as though she were a helpless bird charmed by a deadly snake. And for several tension-filled minutes the pair remained transfixed: he standing above, tall and dominant and frightening; she lying below, small and powerless and afraid, all the while those black, fathomless eyes snaring the green, pleading ones.

It was he who finally broke the spell, lowering his eyes briefly, setting her free. And releasing himself as well.

With those compelling eyes no longer locked with hers, Martay felt the invisible bonds fall away. She flew into action immediately. Rising to her knees, she began to scream at the top of her lungs. She screamed and screamed, her heart pounding with fear, tears pouring down her cheeks.

Her captor, continuing to stand just as he had since the first moment she'd opened her eyes, calmly watched her. Moccasined feet apart, he remained in that casually arrogant stance, crossing his long arms over his chest, waiting. Waiting for her to calm down.

Cowering there on the bed, her face bloodred, her golden hair a wild, tousled mane spilling about her shaking shoulders, Martay continued to scream until, tired of hearing the unpleasant sound, the dark man said, in a voice soft, yet deadly cold, "That's enough."

She screamed all the louder and shook her head violently, like a thwarted child throwing a temper tantrum. A muscle flexed in his lean jaw and he took a step forward. Her eyes grew wilder and, fearing for her life, Martay instinctively sprang forward to meet him.

With a swiftness that surprised him, she scrambled from the bed and came at him with claws bared, lashing out to scratch his face, her eyes those of a cornered animal. But she was no match for him. Before sharp nails touched smooth brown skin, his long fingers had captured her fragile wrists.

Standing so close she could feel his warm breath on her face, he said, "If you won't behave, I'll have to tie your hands."

Outrage now mixing with her fear, Martay glared up at him and wrenched free of his grasp. She whirled about and raced for the door. He got there before her, turned, and blocked her path. Trapped, terrified, Martay doubled up her fists and began pounding on his hard chest, sobbing loudly.

He stood flat-footed and absorbed the blows, knowing it was useless to try to reason with her. It was too soon. She was far too upset and frightened. It was best he allow her to tire herself.

When she continued to pound on him and to kick his shins, the toes of her satin slippers banging the sharp bones again and again, his respect for her spirit grew. He wondered if she would ever give out. She looked as fragile as a leaf in the wind, but she fought like a fearless warrior woman.

Crying and tossing her head, her breasts rising and falling

with exertion, she continued her attempt to beat him senseless.

Afraid that she was too stubborn for her own good, that
she would continue to fight until she passed out from exhaustion, he decided to end it. Effortlessly he caught her flailing
left hand and spun her about so that he was standing behind
her. Holding her wrist in a viselike grip, he brought a long
arm around her shoulders and jerked her back against his tall
frame.

Martay's right hand was still free. She wasted no time
raising it to hit at his head. A glancing blow connected with
his right ear and brought a buzzing he knew would be with
him for several minutes. Hearing his sharp intake of air and
knowing she'd stunned him, Martay tried again.

This time it didn't work.

She'd never know how he managed, but instantly she
found both her arms quickly pinned to her body and his
wrapped tightly around her. She squirmed and screamed and
threatened, and finally, so weary she could no longer struggle,
sagged limply back against him. Weak, her face hot and shiny
with tears and with perspiration, she stood there panting for
breath, a feeling of deep despair invading her very soul.

Frightened as she was, she could no longer fight. She
couldn't even remain standing without his support. She had
no choice but to lean on him. Coughing with sobs, she let her
head tiredly fall back on his shoulder. Screams no longer tore
from her raw throat; she was too weary even to scream. Salty
tears beginning to dry on her hot face, Martay stood there
trembling in the enveloping arms of a wild, dangerous redskin.

She could feel, beneath her back, the powerful pounding
of his heart. His scent, that smell of clean masculine sweat
and hot skin, was strong in the air. The tall, lean body was
touching her all too familiarly from chest to toes, his flat
abdomen and long, hard thighs pressing her bottom and the
backs of her legs so closely, she could feel the leashed power

emanating from him, the muscle and bone straining against his taut flesh. Worse, a dark muscular forearm was pressing her breasts as his arm crossed her chest and he gripped her shoulder to hold her immobile.

There was no longer any sound in the too-warm room save her rapid, nervous breathing and his slow rhythmic breaths. Strangely calm at last, Martay was willing to rest for a time; he was too. As they rested, dawn broke over the mountains, spreading fingers of gray pervading light over the rugged terrain and stealing in through the broken windows of their shelter.

It was during that quiet interlude that Martay grasped the curious fact that the powerful Indian holding her had spoken to her in English. At least that was in her favor. She could communicate with him. She could offer him money; he would know its value. Probably he was one of the reservation Indians out looking for . . . what? A white woman?

A violent shudder went through her. He was going to rape her! He would rape her and kill her! Dear God, no. No!

Martay jumped when her captor, in a low, casual voice, said just above her ear, "I'm going to take my hands away. Don't try anything foolish. I'm not a patient man." And all of a sudden those binding, sinewy arms dropped from her and she was free to step away from the constant heat and close intimacy of his tall frame. She did immediately, and felt the floor coming up to meet her.

She was hauled up into his arms before she completely crumpled. The sudden movement had left her dizzy, and she felt as though she might faint. Reluctantly allowing her forehead to fall onto his chest, she tried desperately to gather her wits, to renew her spent energy.

Feeling that even to lift her head was more than she could manage, Martay proudly did just that. She looked again into those cold black eyes and foolishly spoke exactly what was on her mind. "You're going to rape me and then kill me, I know you are, you filthy beast!"

His black eyes narrowed. "A Sioux warrior does not make war on women and children."

"Then put me down this instant and let me go!" she demanded weakly.

"You'll be gone in twenty-four hours," he said noncommittally as he looked directly into her eyes.

More terrified of his intense gaze than of the strong arms that bound her, Martay lowered her eyes to the level of his dark throat, noting the strong pulse throbbing there beneath the sweat-slick bronzed skin. "Why have you captured me? What do you intend to do with me? How did you get me? I don't . . . I . . ."

He gave no answers to her barrage of questions. Instead, he carried her to the cot and sat her down, then took a seat beside her. Martay shook her head in confusion, trying to recall what had happened.

The last thing she remembered was standing alone on the back veranda at the Darlington party. Waiting for Larry Berton to bring her punch. How did she get from there to here? And just where was here? How could a wild Indian have snatched her right from that moonlit veranda? Hugging her arms to her ribs, she tried to stop the trembling of her cold, tired body. And she tried to recall exactly what had happened.

And through her mind flashed the memory of all those premonitions she'd had for the past several weeks. That feeling that someone was watching her, that something bad was about to happen to her.

"What do you want with me?" she asked, her voice faltering.

He said nothing.

Martay turned and looked again at the chisel-faced man sitting beside her. Silently he drew a cigar from inside his saddlebags and lit it, slowly puffing it to life.

In a voice gone high and shrill, she said, "Why me? Why have you brought me here?" No reply. Total silence. He didn't bother to look at her. Angrily, she said, "Answer me, damn you!"

The dark head did not turn. Staring straight ahead, he pulled smoke deep down into his lungs, then leisurely released it. Finally, he spoke. "It doesn't matter. This time tomorrow you won't be here."

Martay swallowed hard.

All day and all night alone in the wilds with a forceful, hostile Indian! What might happen in that length of time? True, he spoke perfect English and he had bragged that Sioux warriors didn't make war on women, but could she believe him? No. Her father said the Sioux were the meanest of all the Plains Indians, that they raided and robbed and killed for the sport of it. You couldn't trust them as far as you could throw them. They were sneaky and dangerous.

"Please"—she heard her weak voice take on a begging tone— "please let me go and I'll never tell anyone about this." He made no reply, just leaned back against the wall, stretched his long legs out before him, and smoked quietly, his hooded eyes fixed on some point across the room.

"I have money." She tried another tack. "I'm quite rich; very rich in fact. I own gold mines all over northern California and Nevada. You'll have more money than you've ever seen in your life if you'll release me."

His black eyes came back to her. "I don't want money."

"But you must. Everyone wants money." She shoved her tangled hair from her eyes and pointed out, "With money you could buy all kinds of pretty things at the trading post." She thought she detected a look of interest. His lips seemed to soften and stretch into a near smile. Triumphant, she hurried on, explaining excitedly, "Yes, you could buy lots of colorful fabric and jewelry and beads. Take presents back to all your brothers on the reservation." She smiled at him. "Why, with enough gifts, you could probably buy any squaw you chose."

The smile left his lips and Martay's heart stopped when his mouth thinned into a tight line and his black eyes turned icy. He said, his anger barely controlled, "In the language of the Sioux there is no such word as squaw. That's a white man's word." He put the cigar back between his even white teeth. Looking again at the stationary spot, he added, "Nor do Sioux maidens spread their legs for a few trinkets." He ground down viciously on the cigar. "That custom, it seems to me, also belongs to the white race."

Incensed, Martay quickly replied, "How dare you suggest that a white girl would . . . they most certainly do not . . . I would never . . ." Her voice trailed away. Her face had gone deathly white and her slender body jerked with anger and anxiety.

He sensed she was near hysterics again. Hoping to avoid any further physical outbursts, he rose to his feet and tossed the smoked-down cigar out the door. Standing before her, he said, "Lie down and rest. You look pale and tired."

Knowing suddenly that if this strange, cold savage didn't let her go right now, this very minute, she would never again be free, Martay impulsively reached out and grabbed his shirt-front. Wadding it in her hand, she drew him down to her until their faces were mere inches apart. "Please," she pleaded, her eyes filling again with tears, "please."

She felt a small measure of hope flood through her as those fierce black eyes softened for one fleeting instant, but that instant passed and she was looking once again into fathomless depths of harsh, cold obsidian.

"Rest now," he said, pulling her clutching fingers free of his soft elkskin shirt and gently easing her down on the cot. He took the satin slippers from her feet and set them on the floor beneath the cot. Pulling a blanket up over her, he tucked it in around her shoulders and said, "You'll be free in twenty-four hours."

Telegrams flew.

Within eight hours of her abduction from the Darlington

party, Martay Kidd was the focus of a massive manhunt that covered the whole state of Colorado.

When General William Kidd's eastbound train pulled into the Bethune station shortly after eight o'clock in the morning, he was given the shocking news. He immediately detrained, climbed into the saddle, and headed back to Denver, stopping only for fresh mounts along the route.

By mid-morning, the hills and canyons around Denver were swarming with blue-coated cavalrymen. The commanding officer at Fort Collins had sent half the garrison in search of the missing woman. When General Kidd arrived in the city and was apprised of the situation, he angrily fired off a message ordering all the remaining cavalry, save a skeleton crew of twenty, out of the fort and into the mountains to look for his daughter.

Told that Major Berton had led a detail into the high country within hours of Martay's abduction, the worried general slammed a fist down on the table and swore, "I'll have Berton's hide for this! Goddamnit all, he'll be court-martialed and hanged for his negligence if my daughter is harmed!" He turned and grabbed at the nearest blue blouse he saw. "Find her, soldier! We've got to find my sweet child!" His green eyes swam with tears.

"We will, sir."

"We've got to find her. We've got to," murmured a weary, heartsick Major Lawrence Berton as he rode up a steep evergreen forested shoulder of the towering Rockies at mid-afternoon.

"We will, Major," comforted a middle-aged leathery-faced captain riding knee to knee with the younger man. "We'll find her."

Major Lawrence Berton wanted desperately to believe the captain. But a chill ran through him despite the heat of the day and the circles of sweat soaking his blue blouse. He had a terrifying premonition that he would never again see the beautiful golden-haired Martay Kidd.

Fighting back a sob of panic, Major Lawrence Berton kicked his bay into a gallop, shouting over his shoulder, "We must find her before night. We must!" And he led the saddle-weary detail farther into the canyons and crevices where the terrain was so rough and forbidding, it would be possible to hide there forever.

He heard the distant neighing of a horse.

In a flash the Sioux was on his feet, the Winchester rifle in his hand. He cast a quick look at the woman. She was sleeping again, but he couldn't count on her remaining asleep. If she wakened and cried out, they'd be discovered.

Peering warily out into the sloping green forest, he laid the weapon aside and went to the cot. Throwing a long leg over her, he straddled her, his knee resting on the bed beside her hip. Keeping one foot on the floor to support his weight, he leaned down and swiftly placed a brown hand over her mouth. His touch brought her instantly awake and a pair of terrified green eyes looked up at him.

"Don't scream," he said softly. "I'm not going to hurt you, but I want to make sure you're quiet. I'll have to put a handkerchief in your mouth for a while." She shook her head violently and made soft mewing sounds, her eyes wild. He paid no attention. He drew a snowy white handkerchief from an inside pocket and quickly gagged her while she lay trapped beneath him.

"Now," he said conversationally, looking down at her, "do exactly as I tell you and you won't get hurt. Understand?" She glared at him. He slid his long, lean fingers into her hair at the side of her head. "I said, 'do you understand?'" The fingers tightened, holding her head immobile. She nodded. "Good." He released the hair and, reaching down, scooped her shoes from under the bed, slid down the length of her body, and deftly put the slippers back on her feet.

Then in one fluid movement he was off the bed and pulling her up and guiding her toward the open front door. When they reached it, he picked up the Winchester and walked out onto the shaded stoop, bringing her with him. He looked down at her, took her hand, and reading the puzzlement in her eyes, said, "We're going to take a little walk."

Was this it? she asked herself. Was he going to take her into the woods to kill her so he could bury her body away from his cabin. Her eyes darted to the gleaming rifle he carried under his right arm. Would he take her deep into the trees, lift the steel barrel to her temple and fire? Would her death be mercifully quick or would he rape and torture her first? Would he throw her down and tear the white silk dress from her? Would he rip her fine French underthings to shreds, then cruelly force himself on her again and again? Would he scalp her and tie the long, bloody locks to his belt?

Would she live to see another sunrise?

Her heart pounding so furiously it was painful, she died a thousand deaths on the way to what she felt sure were her final minutes on the earth.

They were climbing now, he leading her up a rocky, treacherous path that was so narrow, she had to follow behind. Hobbled by her tight skirts, she stumbled after him, her hand in his, her legs weak. She was jerked along and at times lifted when she couldn't manage because of her dress. Out of breath, gagging on the handkerchief, she bumped into him when her captor stopped abruptly.

His arm coming back to hold her close, he turned his head and listened. Martay listened too, and heard the clanking of bits, the creaking of leather, and the whinnying of horses. She froze. More savages coming to join him? A celebration of some sort with her a part of their uncivilized entertainment? Dear God, no. Not that! Not the horror of being passed around among a dirty murdering band of Indians bent on doing unspeakable things to her before they finally tired of the game and burned her at the stake!

In seconds she heard men's voices. The voices carried on the thin alpine air and Martay's panic rapidly turned to relief as she heard a man's deep, clear voice addressing a companion. "Captain," he said, and she knew. It was the Army! They'd come for her. Her father had come for her. Thank God, oh, thank God! By suppertime she'd be safely back inside the Larimer Street mansion and this animal holding her would be dead.

She was pulled back from her pleasant reverie when her captor edged out farther onto the huge, flat boulder they had climbed. He halted then, moved her around in front of him, and crouched down on his heels, bringing her down with him. Her feet curled to the side, she was forced to sit between his spread knees and she ground her teeth when his fingers wrapped around her throat and he urged her head back against his chest.

Brushing her hair back, he put his lips against her ear and whispered, "Make one sound and it will be your last."

His hand left her throat. He reached a long arm out and pulled back a leafy tree-branch. Slowly he leaned forward, the motion of his chest pushing her forward with him. She turned her head to look at him. His face was beside hers, his smooth dark jaw lightly touching her temple. The black, black eyes were scanning the mountain slope below. She knew by his fierce expression he had caught sight of the approaching soldiers.

She turned, held her breath, and looked out over the lowered tree branch. There, a hundred feet below and some fifty yards away, rode a half dozen blue-uniformed troopers led by a big, powerfully-built man on a bay stallion. His blond hair gleamed in the bright sunlight, and recognizing Major Lawrence Berton, she made a gurgling sound deep in her throat.

Instinctively she lunged forward, trying to call to him, praying she'd attract his attention, that he'd look up and see her there above. But a strong bronzed arm quickly came around her waist and jerked her back so quickly, her head rocked on her shoulders and she felt the hard muscles of the Indian's chest bump against her shoulder blades.

And with both his long arms trapping her inside, the Sioux calmly lifted his Winchester, poked the barrel through the thick foliage, took dead aim, and waited.

10

Martay's heart stopped beating.

She couldn't call to the unsuspecting Larry Berton and his troopers. She couldn't jump up and wave her hands about. Trapped inside a pair of strong copper arms, she could only wait for the inevitable shot to ring out, ending Larry's life, then the others'.

The mounted troopers had ridden closer; so close, they could have whispered and she would have heard them. They had halted below; their tired horses snorted and blew. Men coughed and spat. And a voice she'd last heard promising warmly to "be back in ten minutes with the punch" now sounded tired and distraught as Major Lawrence Berton said, "She can't be up there. A horse could never climb those steep rocks." He added, almost as an afterthought, "And neither could a man."

"I agree, Major," a soldier answered. "Let's rest the horses here for an hour, then turn back southeast to rendezvous with the rest of the search party."

Martay looked at the Indian's face as the soldiers dismounted. In moments the weary men would be lying about on the ground, smoking, relaxed, rifles laid aside, forage caps pulled low, eyes closed. The silent Sioux could pick off the half-dozen men before they knew what had happened.

The Indian's expression had changed not at all. Save the occasional flickering of his black lashes, his dark face might have been carved of the stone they sat atop. The raised rifle rested against his right cheek, its sight an inch from his eye. Martay's gaze went from his face to his dark right hand. A long, lean finger was curled around the trigger, gently caressing.

Tensed, she waited. Waited for that deadly finger to gently squeeze. Waited for the firing to begin. Waited, mute and helpless, for the senseless slaughter of the tired troopers, and for her own end as well.

Long minutes passed.

The Indian neither fired nor lowered the rifle. Completely puzzled, Martay kept stealing glances at the impassive face as a terrible tension built. What on earth was he waiting for? She almost wished he would go ahead and fire, get it over with. Nothing was worse than this waiting. But he did not fire.

Staring at him, she noted a trickle of perspiration slipping out of his hairline and down over his left temple. She followed its slow, steady progress over the dark skin until it came to rest in the corner of his left eye. He neither reached up to brush it aside nor did he blink it away. It clung there, poised for an instant on a long, dark lash, glittering like a diamond in the sunshine, before falling directly into his eye. If it burned or bothered him, he gave no indication.

While Martay squirmed and twisted as much as possible within the encircling arms, the Sioux was completely motionless. Crouched there on his heels in what she was certain was a terribly uncomfortable position, he remained just as he was. And did not fire a single bullet at the dozing troopers.

Those were the longest, worst moments of Martay's life. Imprisoned inside the parted thighs and powerful arms of a

man who seemed less than human, she felt she'd been there
for as long as she could remember; would be there forever.
The blistering afternoon sun beat down on her uncovered
head, turned her fair skin a flushed pink, and covered her
bared arms and shoulders with a sheen of perspiration. Trick-
les of the tickling, salty moisture ran down her hot face, pooling behind her knees and between her breasts.

Her head ached dully and her neck, caught against the
Sioux's rock-hard shoulder, was growing stiff. Her lips were
dry and bruised from the damnable gag, and her throat was
parched and scratchy. She was in agony, both physically and
mentally. She feared and despised the calm, nerveless Sioux
beside her. Martay now knew what her father meant when he
said Indians loved toying with their prey.

After what seemed more like an eternity than only one
hour, the soldiers began to stir. The Indian waited until he
knew they had mounted and were departing. Only then did he
move, and Martay instinctively shut her eyes against the horror that was about to happen.

But no shots rang out, and finally, opening her eyes just a
little, she was shocked to see that the Indian had lowered his
Winchester. He had pulled back a heavily-leafed tree limb and
was looking after the departing troopers, his black eyes calm.
And he allowed the mounted troopers to ride away unharmed.

Swallowing with difficulty, Martay looked after the
soldiers too. Watching Larry Berton trotting away, his blond
hair gleaming in the Colorado sunshine, she was at once relieved that his life had been spared and angry that he'd left
her behind with a dangerous savage. He might have tried a
little harder. He had given up too easily. He'd assumed no
horse nor man could scale the steep cliffs, but the Indian,
carrying her, had made it up by the light of the moon.

Her heart sinking, she watched until the soldiers were out
of sight; then, sighing wearily, she turned to look at her captor. His glance touched, then dismissed her. At last he laid

aside the Winchester, sat down on the flat rock, stretched out his legs, and untied her gagging handkerchief.

Coughing and spitting, Martay turned around to face him. "Why did you do that?"

"Untie the gag? You want it back on, I'll be . . ."

"That's not what I'm talking about and you know it!" Suddenly realizing she was still sitting between his legs, she scrambled up on hands and knees and crawled over him, anxious to be as far from him as possible. "Why didn't you shoot the soldiers?"

Shrugging, he said, "Should I have?"

Martay ground her teeth. "They'll be back, you know. You won't get away with this! My father is a powerful general and he loves me very much."

"I'm counting on that," said the Sioux, and agilely rose to his feet. Reaching up behind his head with one hand, he jerked the hot elkskin shirt up and off.

Frowning, Martay shaded her eyes and looked up at him. He stood there in the unfiltered sunlight, his smooth, hairless chest gleaming with sweat, and the thought skipped through her mind that what they said was true. Indians really didn't have any hair on their chests. And she innocently wondered, Was the rest of their bodies hairless as well?

Her gaze was drawn to a scar that began at his right collarbone and slashed a path across his brown flesh to below his left rib cage. The scar was starkly white against his dark skin, and smooth and wide, as though it was very old and had grown as his body had grown. Obviously he'd been viciously cut when he was a child.

Her eyes climbed to his face.

"Get up," he said, and reached out to help her stand.

Ignoring the offer, she rose to face him. "Never doubt that my father will save me, Indian. You've picked the wrong captive this time!"

The Sioux slipped a hand into the waistband of his low-riding buckskins. Sliding long brown fingers inside the tight pants, he rested his palm against his flat, bare stomach and said, "You're the right captive, Captive."

His flip reply was lost on Martay because he'd unconsciously drawn her attention down to his naked abdomen. Eyes helplessly pulled there, Martay couldn't keep from noticing how the buckskin trousers fell away from his firm, flat belly, exposing his naval and two inches of a line of heavy black hair leading downward from it.

As her eyes flew back up to his face in embarrassment, the guilty thought raced through Martay's head that her earlier question had just been answered. Indians certainly did have hair on their . . .

"Yes! You've picked the wrong one," she said, her voice shrill.

"You're repeating yourself," he said, and in his gleaming black eyes she detected a brief flash of amusement that she found highly irritating and insulting.

"Are you making fun of me, Indian?" she snapped, hands going to her hips.

His answer was a blink of his hooded eyes and a hand on her shoulder. "Let's go, Captive."

She tried to shrug from his grasp but was unsuccessful. His long fingers wrapped tightly around her arm and in minutes he had firmly guided her back to the cabin. Pausing on the stoop, he said, "I know you're hot and uncomfortable. There's a small snow-fed stream just up the slope. Would you like to bathe?"

Skeptically she eyed him. The thought of a refreshing bath sounded wonderful. She could almost feel the cold, clear water on her heated, itchy flesh. "Where would you be?"

"On the bank," he said matter-of-factly.

She glared at him. "I'd go forever without a bath before I'd allow you to . . ."

"Makes no difference to me, Captive. I thought refined white ladies bathed daily."

"They do," she quickly retorted. "What about you, Indian?" She'd heard the stories of their disgusting filth.

"Ah, well, you know us heathens," he said, "we rarely bathe." Then: "What about some food. You hungry?" He urged her inside the cabin.

It was the first she'd thought about food, though she'd not eaten for more than twenty-four hours. Despite the circumstances, she was starving, but was not about to share a meal with a dirty, ruthless savage.

"I'm not hungry," she said haughtily, watching as he lifted his saddlebags from a shadowed corner.

She expected him to pull out some rancid buffalo meat or an ear of too-hard corn or something equally unappealing. She stared, unbelieving, when he placed two clean china plates on the table, laid napkin and silverware beside each, then drew from the bags a perfectly delicious-looking prime roast beef.

Shaking her head in confusion, Martay stood there watching as the Sioux sliced the beef, then a loaf of French bread, and some cheese. From a canteen he splashed red wine into a couple of long-stemmed crystal glasses and motioned for her to sit. She loftily refused. He shrugged disinterestedly, slid down onto the bench, picked up a white linen napkin, shook it, placed it on his left knee, and said, "Sure you're not hungry? I had assumed your appetite for food was as healthy as your other appetites."

She paid no attention to what he was saying. Her busy mind had quickly deducted that the food, china, and silverware she saw before her had undoubtedly been stolen. She envisioned her cool captor sneaking into some wealthy rancher's remote mountain home in the dead of night and taking what he wanted. And she wondered, Had he calmly slit the throats of the sleeping family while he was at it?

Instinctively taking a step backward, Martay's hand went to her aching throat as the Sioux, ignoring her, began his meal. Expecting to see him tear large chunks from the meat and gluttonously wolf it down, she grudgingly admitted, after silently watching him, that his table manners were impeccable; far, far better than those of many white people she had dined with in the past.

Save for the fact that he was naked to the waist and his skin was darker than that of any man she'd ever known, he might have been a handsome, aristocratic gentleman seated across from her at an elegant banquet. She could almost picture him in a delighted hostess's tall-ceilinged dining room with perfectly tailored evening clothes draping his tall, lean frame, his raven-black hair gleaming in the candlelight.

Martay shook her head as though to clear it.

Such thoughts were foolish. This strange man was a ruthless Sioux, wild and dangerous, no matter how polished he appeared as he calmly cut the beef with a stolen sterling knife and sipped his wine from a stolen crystal flute. Chances are he'd be just as mannerly when he coldly slit her throat with that same gleaming silver knife.

The hand at her throat automatically tightened and Martay felt as though she might be sick. Eyes never leaving the Sioux, she moved backward toward the cot, not stopping until she felt its edge against the backs of her legs. Fighting the uncontrollable fear that was rising to choke her, she sank down on the cot, determined she'd get hold of herself, figure a way out of this nightmare.

Almost at once she realized the careless Indian had allowed her to get behind him. He sat with his back to her, leisurely enjoying his meal, irresponsibly giving her an opportunity to attack. Her heart began to pound with elation.

His Winchester stood against the doorframe. The Navy colt lay on the table, out of his reach. Absorbed with his food, he was vulnerable, perhaps more vulnerable than he would be again. Now was the time to strike.

Biting her lip, Martay looked about for something she could use to hurt him. If only she had that other sharp knife lying, unused, beside her empty plate. What a dunce she was;

she could have had that knife in her hands if only she had agreed to eat and had sat down at the table. No matter. She'd have to find something else. Something to strike him on the head with.

Her eyes swept hopefully around the room. Everything that could inflict a deadly blow was out of reach. Soon he'd be finished with his meal and up from the table and her opportunity would be forever lost. Her shoe! That's all she had; it would have to do. She'd bash him over the head and hope it would at least stun him until she could grab one of the guns. Once she had the Colt, she'd blow his brains out and climb on the big black stallion tethered outside and ride away.

Martay cautiously lifted her feet and took off her white satin slippers. Laying one aside, she lifted its mate in her right hand. Then, heart drumming against her ribs, she rose. She remained standing where she was for a moment, watching, getting up her courage.

The Sioux continued with his meal, arrogantly, stupidly, neglecting her. Shoulder blades slid and lifted beneath sweat-slick dark skin as he cut small bites of the rare roast beef and raised the wineglass to his lips.

Martay gripped the white slipper tightly, holding it so that she could bring the sharp heel down on his head with all the strength she possessed. As silently as if she herself were the Indian, she crept forward, almost light-headed with the anticipation of freedom. In seconds she stood directly behind him and, not daring to draw a breath, she raised the shoe above his bent head. Instantly she brought it down, putting the full force of her body behind it, striking a blow sure to render her captor senseless.

It happened so fast, it was a blur.

A dark arm shot up and long fingers stayed her hand an inch from his skull. Silverware clattered to the china plate and wine spilled from the overturned glass and Martay was jerked down across the Indian's lap. Too startled even to scream, she found herself looking straight into those cold black eyes as he held her cradled there in the crook of one powerful arm. His fingers cutting into the flesh of her wrist, he said in a low, slow voice, "Turn loose."

A tiny little whimper escaped her open lips as she surrendered her useless weapon to him. He took the satin slipper from her and brought it up close to her face. He said, "I see you've a lot to learn." She trembled against him, dreading the sure punishment, wondering what he would do. "Shoes," he said, looking at the raised slipper, "are something you wear on your feet." He dropped the slipper noisily to the floor. "That's all shoes are for. You were coming to the table, so I can only assume you meant to dine." He reached over and picked up the sterling knife from beside her plate.

Holding it directly before her frightened face, he said, "I believe this is the instrument you'll need to enjoy your meal. Take it." Martay looked at him, her green eyes wary, fearful. "Take the knife, Captive, and use it instead of the shoe," he said, a dangerous edge to his voice.

Afraid to take it, afraid not to, Martay finally held out her hand. He placed the sharp, gleaming knife atop her open palm and let his hand fall to her knees.

Slowly Martay's cold fingers closed around the knife's carved hilt. Hope springing up inside her again, she swiftly assessed the tricky situation. She was draped across his lap with one of his arms wrapped securely around her. His other hand was resting on her knees.

As though he could read her mind, the Sioux said, "What are you waiting for? Try it." And they both knew what he meant.

Her spirit as untamed as his, Martay quickly rose to the goading challenge. Wild-eyed, she screamed and plunged the knife straight into his bare belly. And did nothing more than scratch him.

His hand was swifter than a striking reptile. He stayed the blade just as it touched his bare skin. His eyes, and hers, went to where the sharp point had pricked the flesh. As they watched, a tiny circle of bright red blood appeared.

"Look at me," he commanded, taking the knife from her, tossing it back to the table. Martay, terrified, slowly raised her eyes from the surface wound where a tiny trickle of crimson blood oozed onto his dark, smooth skin. Their gazes locked, his hand covered hers, and he guided her forefinger directly to the superficial wound.

She felt the wetness of his blood on her fingertip and recoiled in distaste, trying to pull free. But he would not let her. He forced her to leave her finger pressed to him until it was smeared with his warm, wet blood. Only then did he lift it up before her face.

And he said, "Let me offer congratulations. You're the first person who's tried to kill me"—he paused, his black eyes on her bloodstained finger— "that I've allowed to live." Cruelly he urged her finger toward her parted lips. His eyes narrowed into slits of black fire, he said, in a voice coldly commanding, "Taste it, Captive. I assure you it's the last taste of my blood you'll ever get."

On the verge of hysteria, Martay, sure he was insane, dutifully licked his blood from her finger, the taste salty to her tongue, the act repugnant. When her finger was free of blood, the Sioux urged her off his lap and rose. Casually he examined the small cut on his belly, picked up the table napkin, and blotted away the remaining blood.

"The sun will set soon," he said evenly, as though the past few electrifying moments had never taken place. "Sure you don't want a cool bath before bedtime?"

She could only shake her head no as, dejectedly, she stood holding to the table for support, her legs weak. Through the open door the last precious rays of a lowering sun streamed in, bathing them with gold-red light. Fighting back fresh tears of despair, Martay sadly watched the fading light and felt that her hopes were fading with it. Soon darkness would settle over the mountains and her father and Larry and the rest of the troopers searching for her would make camp for the night. And she would be defenseless and alone with this strange, paradoxical savage whom she'd just tried to kill.

And had failed.

11

"**S**ir, with all due respect, it would be foolhardy to press on in this darkness."

General William Kidd turned in the saddle to look at Colonel Thomas Darlington. Squinting in the moonlight, he thundered, "Goddamnit, Colonel, my little girl is out there somewhere in the night!"

"I know, General," replied the heartsick Colonel, feeling he was directly responsible for Martay's disappearance. The girl had been enjoying his hospitality, was in his care, and he had failed to ensure her safety. For that, he would never forgive himself. "We'll find her, General, come sunrise." Even as he spoke the words, they sounded hollow.

General Kidd, his sun-creased face haggard, his green eyes clouded with agony, wearily nodded. "Give the command, Colonel. We'll camp here for the night."

The two officers, along with a force of armed troopers, had reached Eldorado Springs, fifteen miles northwest of Denver. It was well past midnight. It had been almost forty-eight hours since the general had last slept.

Within moments of making camp, the majority of tired troops were fast asleep, but the middle-aged general remained awake. Staring into the fire, his shoulders slumped, his big hands wrapped around a mug of hot coffee, General Kidd worried. Worried as only a parent can about a beloved child. Worried that his precious daughter was lost and cold and frightened. Worried that some unscrupulous cad attending the Darlington party had found Martay so luscious and innocent, he'd taken her against her will.

General Kidd ground his teeth, and hot, stinging tears again filled his tired eyes. His chest constricted with pain and he felt impotent and helpless for the first time in his life. He who had led valiant warriors into many a rousing battle, had struck fear into the heart of his enemy, had killed more men than he could count, was powerless against this faceless foe who had stolen from him the only thing worth fighting for, the only person left on earth he truly loved.

The general was not the only worried soldier out in the field on that August evening. No less than three hundred mounted cavalrymen were camping in the distant hills and plains surrounding Denver; their mission the same as the general's. Find Martay Kidd.

Major Lawrence Berton had been in the saddle most of the day. His detachment was camped fifty miles east of the general, on the banks of Horse Creek. He, too, was wide awake, though the hour was late. Lying on his back, his head resting on his saddle, the big blond man stared up at the rising moon and wondered if Martay was somewhere nearby watching the moon come up. Or was she already dead? He shuddered and clenched his teeth.

And in her mansion in the foothills of West Denver, Regina Darlington was also wide awake. In her lace-and-silk-hung bed, she sat propped up against the tall headboard, sipping hot milk from a delicate cut glass. She hoped it might help her to sleep. She'd slept only fitfully since the terrible tragedy had happened more than twenty-four hours ago.

She sighed and looked out on the moonlit balcony. Setting the milk aside, Regina climbed down from her big soft bed and padded across the specially woven Turkish rug to the open French doors. She stepped out onto the broad balcony, mindless of the fact she was barefoot and wearing only a thin, gauzy bed gown.

Cool night breezes pressed the frothy gown to Regina's ample curves and lifted tendrils of her unbound auburn hair. She stood at the railing and worried. She worried, of course, about the missing girl, whose body might even now be lying hidden somewhere out there on the estate grounds in the brilliant moonlight. She worried also that it was from her home, her party, that the flirty little brat had been taken. Through no fault of theirs, she and Colonel Darlington might be considered responsible in some way. Why, it could even hurt the colonel's career, and she did so long to be a general's wife.

Something else worried her as well.

Only moments before the Kidd girl was reported missing, Regina had bumped into the handsome Jim Savin in a deserted back corridor. Overjoyed that he had finally shown up, she'd rushed up to him, glanced hurriedly about, and said, "Darling, you did come! I'm so glad; why don't you make it a point to introduce yourself to Martay Kidd, then meet me in the summerhouse in half an hour."

His reply had been a wink, a nod of his dark, handsome head, and then he had immediately left her and gone in search of Martay. When a half hour had passed, Regina had been in the gazebo at the east edge of the verdant garden, waiting breathlessly for Jim Savin's kisses, hoping she could persuade him to make love to her there in the shadows while laughing couples promenaded within a few feet of the summerhouse. As she'd waited, she had grown beside herself with excitement. The danger of being caught would add such a delicious dash of spice to their heated lovemaking, she was sure it would be an incredible experience.

But Jim hadn't come.

And when, twenty minutes after she'd ducked into the gazebo, she sensed a great flurry of activity, she hurried back to the mansion to learn that Martay Kidd was missing. Someone else was missing also, though she didn't mention it to anyone. Jim Savin had curiously disappeared about the same time Martay was taken from the veranda.

Regina Darlington shook her auburn head. She was being ridiculous. It was coincidence, nothing more. Her savage lover was, at this very hour, stretched out on his bed at the Centennial. Unfortunately, owing to Miss Kidd's disappearance—damn the trouble-causing little bitch—she could not go into Denver tomorrow afternoon and slip up to Jim's room. Until the girl was found, Colonel Darlington would be in and out of the mansion at all hours. Regina couldn't count on her husband's sure and prolonged absence as she could when he was at Fort Collins.

As a member of a search party, he might ride in home at any minute, and if he found her gone, there would be questions. He was such a jealous fool she could hardly breathe when he was around.

Pouting, Regina turned to go back indoors, hoping to high heaven they would find Martay Kidd soon. The thought of going for a week or more without seeing Jim Savin made her feel quite tense and restless. Inside, she climbed back into her bed, stretched out on her back, and stared at the frilly canopy above, worrying.

She just could not sleep.

Martay could not sleep.

It was almost midnight. A full white moon had risen. It's silvery light streamed in through the open door and broken windows of the small shack where she was held captive by an enigmatic Indian who had grown more mysterious as night approached.

Through the hot, still day he had behaved as though he were tolerating her presence because she wouldn't be with him for long. He'd said as much, more than once. Said she would be free within twenty-four hours, said it as if he meant it.

When sundown had neared, he was listening, looking, with an even greater intensity than he'd shown throughout the long tiring day. As though he expected someone to arrive at any second. Long before the sun completely dropped from sight behind the western mountain peaks, he had taken up his post outdoors on the stoop, the Winchester in his hands, his black eyes scanning the dense forest below their rocky redoubt in unblinking expectation.

Watching from inside the cabin, Martay had witnessed the slow, sure hardening of his chiseled features, the angered narrowing of his black eyes, the pulling and flexing of the powerful muscles beneath the smooth dark skin of his arms.

Now, at midnight, he slowly rose to his feet; the first time he'd moved in the past two hours. Martay, seated on the cot, tensed as he filled the doorway. He stood facing her, blocking out the moonlight, casting the cot into darkness.

She strained to see his face; couldn't. He hadn't spoken a word since sundown and she jumped when, from out of the darkness, his voice, deep and soft, said, "Why aren't you asleep?"

She swallowed, then swallowed again. "Wh-why aren't you?"

He moved in out of the doorway. Moonlight again lighted her face, though his remained in shadow. He said, "Lie down, Captive."

She stayed as she was, terrified he had notions of lying down with her. "I'm not sleepy," she said, her breath coming in rapid, nervous little gulps.

He moved toward her. She shivered.

He stood just above, looking down at her, his black eyes gleaming like an animal's. He laid a hand on her bare shoulder and Martay sat there, paralyzed with fear, unable to move. His face was icy cold, but his long, dark fingers were warm upon her chilled flesh as he slid them over the curve of her shoulder and down her arm to the tiny, white silk cap sleeve that had fallen.

With a touch as delicate as a surgeon's, those fingers took hold of the slippery fabric and the stone-faced Sioux slowly pulled the dainty sleeve back up over her trembling shoulder.

"You'll catch cold," he said, his eyes going to the shadowy valley between her full, quivering breasts. "There's a blanket at the foot of the cot. Cover yourself." And he turned and walked away.

Martay anxiously snatched up the blanket, hurriedly pressed it to her bosom, and swore to herself she'd stay awake forever. She'd not dare close her eyes again in the presence of this mystifying Sioux with his warm, gentle hands and cold, brazen eyes.

The Sioux pulled his fringed shirt back on against the evening chill. He then sat down in the doorway, leaning his back against the wooden frame. He held the rifle between his bent knees, its barrel pointed up, and pulled a cigar from his pocket. A match flared, then went out, and he sat there smoking, the glow of the cigar lighting his face.

Martay watched him, baffled. He hadn't harmed her, but he hadn't released her. As long as she was with him, she was in great danger. He was a terrifying, forceful savage. A creature of the wilds. As cold as the mountain snows.

Determined she'd not take her eyes off him, she wet her lips and made an attempt to engage him in late-night conversation.

"My goodness," she said, trying to sound calm, "it's hard to believe the nights are already so chilly. At home in Chicago it's still quite warm. Is it warm where you live?"

No answer.

"I like Colorado though. I suppose you've spent a lot of time in these mountains, or did you come down from the North? I'll be honest I don't know a great deal about where the Indians live and . . ." she talked on and on, pausing for his answers, answers that never came. After a fruitless half hour she was still chattering nervously when all at once his cold, calm voice interrupted.

"Captive," he said, "be quiet."

No one had ever told Martay to shut up before, but she wasted no time obeying his command. Feeling as though he had slapped her face, she fell silent. Sagging tiredly back against the wall, she tried to swallow the lump forming in her throat, but couldn't manage. Afraid she'd annoy him if she cried, she let the hot tears slide down her cheeks and wept as noiselessly as possible. Still, it must not have been quietly enough because all at once he rose.

Blinking furiously, her heart thundering, Martay watched him cross to her. And when he loomed tall and terrifying before her, she defended herself like a child to a disgruntled parent.

"I . . . I . . . can't help it," she sobbed, "I didn't mean to . . . to . . ."

"I know," he answered, the deep timbre of his voice sending a chill up her spine. He took the clutched blanket from her cold hands and Martay felt herself being gently eased down onto the cot. Every nerve in her body cried out against what she knew was about to happen.

She was flat on her back now, her tear-filled eyes on his dark face. The blood was pounding in her ears. Any second she would hear the ripping of her clothes as those dark hands callously stripped her. She tried to lift her arms, to hit at him, but she couldn't do it.

The force of his presence was too strong, too powerful. She was conquered by it as surely as if he had beaten her into submission. She could do nothing but lie here, his subdued captive, praying silently that the cruel, hard mouth would not be too punishing on her trembling lips, that the dark, deft hands would be gentle on her sensitive flesh, that the lean, lithe body would be mercifully quick in its intimate invasion of her own tense body.

12

A look of cold determination on his starkly chiseled face, he bent to her. Martay, staring up at him from frightened tear-filled eyes, couldn't stifle the grateful sob that tore from her lips when finally she realized his true intention. Instead of tearing the clothes from her, the Indian swiftly unfolded the blanket and spread it neatly over her chilled, jerking body. Meticulously tucking it in around her bare shoulders, he straightened, looked down at her, and said, "Night, Captive."

"Th-thank y-you," she sputtered, confused, relieved.

He went back to his post in the doorway and Martay, slowly turning her head to watch him, wondered for the thousandth time what this strange abduction was all about. Puzzling over it, she lay there in the moonlight, determined she'd stay awake all night. She didn't trust the Sioux, not for a minute. Likely he found this cat-and-mouse game amusing in a dark, sinister way. She was not fooled. While he appeared to have a human side, she could not forget his true nature was that of a wild, untamed savage.

Martay was soon yawning sleepily.

She blinked, trying desperately to keep her eyes open, to remain wide-awake. But she was so tired and the soft blanket was so warm and the raven-haired man was so quiet. She drifted off to sleep. At some point during the night, she awakened. The moon was still high. She looked immediately toward the door. It was empty. Her dark jailor was not there.

Before she'd had time to consider escape, she heard a step, and caught sight of him outside. He was walking directly toward the shack and he was shirtless again. Moonlight shimmered on his bare wet shoulders and the thick black hair of his head. The idle thought skipped through Martay's sleepy brain that he had lied. Indians did bathe. That's where he'd been. He'd waited until she slept, then slipped up to the stream for a bath. Her eyes sliding back closed, she inhaled deeply, her half-slumbering senses foggily recalling the clean masculine scent of his sun-heated flesh when they'd crouched atop the rocks earlier that day.

When next Martay awakened, bright sunlight was filling the cabin and her captor was nowhere to be seen. She bolted upright. Wary of a trap, she carefully pulled back the blanket, swung her legs to the floor, and stood up, looking all about. Hastily pushing her long, tangled hair behind her ears, she started for the door.

On the stoop she paused, looking around, unable to believe her good fortune. He was gone. The mean-faced Indian was gone! Perhaps he had fallen asleep somewhere out in the woods. Thinking of nothing but flight, Martay rushed down the steps and to the path leading from the hut. Scolding herself for forgetting her slippers, she picked her way along, carefully scaling a network of huge, smooth rocks. Topping the last skyward-pointing boulder, she stopped, looked down, and shook her head.

Tons and tons of fallen rock, pushed from higher up in the mountains, had fallen to construct a natural fortress, completely concealing the small shack and making it impossible to get down or up. The tumbled boulders, the work of a gigantic rock slide, had left room-sized stones stair-stepped down the mountain; the distance from one to the other as much as eight feet.

A hot summer wind was blowing through the mountains, scattering tiny pebbles about, pushing them down the enormous monoliths. The sound of the skittering stones striking the solid rock in their descent before soundlessly coming to rest far down the mountain made it disappointingly clear that an attempt to get down would be suicidal.

The force of the winds blew Martay's loose hair about her face and pressed the silk of her dress against her willowy frame. A dark cloud passed over the brilliant sun and a few huge, wet drops of rain hissed on the rocks. Then the sun reappeared, brighter than ever.

Martay stood there atop the precipice, frustrated, wondering how she could possibly get to the valley below, unaware of the black eyes calmly watching her.

He stood, rigid, on a ledge just above, his moccasined feet wide apart, his arms crossed over his chest. A muscle jerked beside his full mouth. His eyes had been on her from the moment she came from the shack.

What a beauty she was, standing there barefoot, her classic profile etched against the clear blue sky, her golden hair afire in the summer sunlight. The wind was whipping the shimmering tresses about her head and molding the white dress to her slender, tempting curves. Her bare shoulders were proudly erect, her chin raised defiantly high.

The title Golden Girl fitted her. She was exactly that, with her white perfumed skin and red petulant lips and heavily lashed emerald eyes and spun-gold hair. Standing there in the sun and wind, the exquisite golden girl looked as proud and untamed, as untouched and unspoiled, as the glorious scenery framing her fair golden beauty. There was about her an appealing blend of helplessness and haughtiness that made him want to take her in his arms and protect her, yet at the same time forcefully bend her to his will. And she exuded an innocent sensuality that was far too alluring for her own good. Or for his.

His lids slid low. Suddenly he was unreasonably angry with her.

She didn't belong here. And he didn't want her here.

He wanted only her father.

Silently he scaled the rocks down to her. Aware that if he called out it would startle her and she might tumble over the cliffs, he made no sound as he came up behind her.

Softly he spoke at the exact instant his arms enclosed her. She screamed and briefly struggled, calling him names, before going limp against him. If Martay's heart was beating fast, his was beating faster. Suddenly there was a different kind of tension between them as they stood there in the wind and the rain atop the rocky promontory on that hot August morning. Both felt it. Both fought it.

He recognized it for exactly what it was. Martay did not. She knew only that every time she was near this man, held in his arms this way, she felt a strange excitement that was separate and apart from her fear of him. Never had she experienced anything like it before. The hot-cold, dizzying sensation puzzled her.

It made her captor angry. Made him want to hurt her, to cast her roughly away from him. Or to roughly draw her closer. Standing there behind her, his arms wrapped tightly around her, her warm, slender body leaning against his, he shut his eyes, inhaled her sweet scent, and silently cursed her for her desirability. And himself for his damnable weakness.

She never knew.

Abruptly, he turned her to face him and said, his tone flat, his face devoid of expression, "Back to the cabin."

"You told me I'd be free by now," she said, her brilliant green eyes accusing. Stinging raindrops peppered her upturned face, her bare throat and shoulders, the tight, low bodice of her dress.

His jaw hardened.

He didn't answer. He picked her up and carried her back across the rocks, down the path, and into the shack as lightning cracked above their heads and echoing thunder quickly followed. He ducked in out of the rain and set her on her feet.

She tried again. "It's been twenty-four hours. You promised you'd let me go." She raised her voice so he could hear above the sudden summer storm.

"I lied," he said coldly, failing to explain that he was as baffled and disappointed as she. He could not imagine why General William Kidd had not come for his only daughter. He had waited for the General all day yesterday, couldn't believe it when night fell and still he had not come.

"You red bastard!" Martay shouted, and came at him. He held her off with one muscular forearm, neither swayed nor upset by her tirade. Actually, he much preferred this screeching, clawing little hellion to the calm, quiet woman that had stood in his arms moments ago. He'd never been moved by loud, ill-mannered females; found them anything but attractive. So he was glad she chose to behave like a brassy bitch.

Quickly bored with her screaming and scratching, he unceremoniously grabbed both her wrists in one of his hands, dragged her to the cot, and flung her down on it. When she started to rise, he placed a spread hand directly atop her heaving chest and said, "Stay down, Captive. I don't want to hurt you."

She stayed down.

He was cold and uncommunicative for the remainder of the day, as though he were angry with her. It seemed to Martay, cautiously watching him, that his physical appearance changed before her very eyes. The harshly planed, handsome face grew harder still, the stark features more severely defined. The high, slanting cheekbones struck her as more prominent, the shadows beneath them deeper, darker. The full, sensual mouth had thinned noticeably and the black eyes had grown more scarily mean. He looked, and acted, more Indian than ever.

Fierce. Cruel. Hostile.

The long day passed and his mood did not soften. They shared a meal in strained silence, and when it was finished Martay was glad when he went outdoors to sit on the stoop. Night came and with it uneasy sleep and unanswered questions. Why was he so angry with her? Why hadn't he released her?

The third day of her captivity was no better. The Sioux was sullen and silent. And Martay didn't dare bother him. His dark countenance was so forbidding, she stayed as far from him as allowed and nervously lowered her eyes when he loomed near. But it rained again in the afternoon and he came inside to sit and stare glassy-eyed at her.

On the fourth day her nerves were so raw, she jumped every time he moved. Her menacing captor neither looked nor acted like the same man she'd awakened to see on the first morning in the cabin. That first day he'd at least been civil, talking to her, and at odd moments he had seemed, and acted, almost like a white man. No more. He was all Indian, silent and mean and terrifying.

Martay was miserable. Her white silk dress was soiled and tight and uncomfortable. Her hair was a dirty, tangled mess, and she felt as though it had been four weeks since she'd had a bath instead of four days. Since her captivity began, she had done nothing more than sponge off her face and hands and throat from a pan of cold water. She hated him; he had bathed every night and, she suspected, again in the afternoon while she napped, and she hated him for it. He went about clean and comfortable while she suffered.

By noon of the fifth day Martay knew he was planning something, though she didn't know what. She cringed when he came toward her, a rope looped over his shoulder. Her spirit not yet broken, she rose to meet him.

"You will not tie me up and torture me, you bloodthirsty bastard!" she shouted, her emerald eyes blazing fire, though her heart hammered with fear.

Paying no more attention to her than if she were a cranky three-year-old, he pushed her back down, knelt before her, put the satin slippers on her feet, and led her out of the shack. Outside, the big black was tethered close to the shack. It stood shaking its head and whickering. Ignoring the whinnying stallion, the Indian guided her past and into the rocks.

"Where are we going?" she demanded, stopping.

"Down," was his one-word reply as his fingers tightened on her upper arm and he forcefully impelled her across the treacherous terrain. Martay labored down a narrow, steep slope, dislodging small rocks that kicked up more rocks, causing a dusty avalanche below that rose to choke her. Coughing and gasping, she stopped stubbornly, only to feel a firm hand on her shoulder and the order to "keep going." She did, though her legs were already weak and the sun was harsh and the thin air hot.

The rising spires of the sandstone cliffs were narrowing, the path becoming increasingly harder to traverse. In her dainty dancing slippers and form-fitting skirt, it was next to impossible for Martay to go farther. She glanced back at the Indian, her eyes looking for understanding. His answer was to pluck her from the rocky ridge and toss her over his left shoulder as if she were a sack of grain.

She bellowed in outrage, the sound of her shrieks echoing through the rocky crevices. He paid no attention. He continued agilely down the stair-stepped ledges, pausing when he came to the first dangerous drop.

"Hold on," he commanded, and when she objected, he turned sideways so she could see the precarious path he meant to carry her down. It was a six- or eight-foot drop down to the next ledge. Knowing he meant to jump to it, Martay obediently wrapped her arms around his trim waist and shut her eyes.

With one arm around her legs and a splayed hand clamped firmly on her bottom, the Indian leapt to the rocky shelf below and Martay made not one sound, though his hard, muscled shoulder was digging into her stomach and her breasts were bouncing against his deeply-cleft back.

Gritting her teeth against the discomfort and the fear, she intermittently opened and closed her eyes, dizzied by glimpses of rushing rock and clear blue sky seemingly sailing past her in an upside-down world as the surefooted Indian leapt from rock to distant rock as agilely as if he were a sleek mountain cat.

A few scary moments after their frightening descent had begun, he was lowering her to her feet in a wide, level valley. And while she was shaken and drained and perspiring and laboring for breath, the exasperating Indian stood there looking as cool and composed as if they had been out for a Sunday stroll in the park.

Martay was far too spent to put up a fuss when he let the rope slide from his right shoulder and stepped closer.

"Here," she said loudly, and thrust out her wrists to him. "Tie me up, gag me, beat me, I don't care anymore." She defiantly threw back her head, "You hear me, Indian? Do you?" As usual, he did not answer, so she shouted all the louder. "I just don't care!"

The Sioux gently pushed her toward a tall pine, drew her arms around its trunk, and tied her hands with the rope. He stepped away.

She glared at him. "What?" she said, hatefully. "You're not going to gag me? Surely you don't mean to . . . to . . . where are you going?"

He was walking away from her, his back to her, toward the rocky ramparts they'd come down. Over his shoulder, casually, "To get the horse."

"To get the . . . are you crazy? That horse couldn't possibly make it down those rocks! No horse could. . . . Are you listening to me?" He wasn't. He was already beginning the climb back up. "Come back here," she shouted, "don't you dare leave me alone!"

The only answer she got was the showering of pebbles slipping down the mountain, loosened by his moccasined feet as he nimbly climbed. Martay squinted in the sunlight, watching, until finally she lost sight of him. Letting her head fall to her chest, she sighed, thinking that the mute, ill-tempered Indian was not only mean, he was stupid.

True, he had obviously gotten her and the horse up the rocky mountain, but he surely had taken a less forbidding path back on the other side. There was absolutely no way he could get that horse down . . . down . . .

Martay lifted her head, looked up, and her heart rose to her throat. There at the very pinnacle of the tallest upthrust of rock, the big black stallion with the Indian astride stood perfectly still, outlined against the cloudless blue sky. The pair appeared to be a magnificent statue, poised there, unmoving, the stallion's black coat and the Indian's black hair shimmering in the brilliant sunshine.

What happened next was impossible to believe, though she saw it with her own eyes. The Indian leaned low over the horse's neck and spoke into its ear. Immediately the big brute started down the series of jutting precipices, leaping from one ledge to the next, fearlessly jumping six- and eight-foot bluffs, his hooves heavily striking stone the only sound in the afternoon stillness.

That and the thunder of Martay's heart.

Awed, transfixed, she watched the amazing pair drop steadily lower, expertly taking plateau after plateau, wondering as she watched if the next leap would be the one to shatter the horse's spindly legs. She expected, at any second, to see horse and rider plunge to their deaths at her feet.

Half disappointed that it didn't happen, half relieved as well, she tried to appear unimpressed when the Sioux rode the mighty stallion right up to her, threw a long leg over its back, and dropped to the ground. The horse lowered its proud head and gently nudged her with his velvet muzzle. He made soft, neighing sounds, and Martay couldn't help herself; she smiled and murmured softly, "Yes, boy, you were grand. Wonderful. You must surely have wings on your feet."

"And me?" said the Sioux, revealing for the first time a human side. Typically male, he was almost boyish in wanting her approval, his face softening minutely as he slipped the rope from her wrists, freeing her.

Martay didn't care what he wanted, or needed. Bringing her hands up to pat the stallion's smooth face, she said hatefully, "You're a fool. You might have killed this magnificent animal."

"I never kill beautiful creatures," he said pointedly, his black eyes impaling her.

She peered up at him. "What do you do with them?"

"Take them home," he responded, drawing the reins over the mount's head, and swinging back up into the saddle. The horse, anxious to be off, danced in place, nickering, and Martay thought for a moment the Indian intended to ride away and leave her. But he nudged the stallion closer, reached out a long arm and hauled her up, placing her across the saddle in front of him.

"You . . . you're going to take me home?" she ventured hopefully, grasping at the thin thread of hope, wondering if she dared.

He nodded. "I'm taking you home." She smiled at him, a great rush of happiness sending color to her pale cheeks. Then he added, coldly, "My home."

"Your home?" she echoed dumbly, her smile slipping as the truth dawned. "You most certainly are not taking me to your home, Indian!" She raised a hand to strike at him.

He caught it easily and, pressing it flat against his chest, said, "Stop calling me Indian. I'm no Indian. Indians are from Calcutta. We are The People."

The blaze in his black eyes made her immediately contrite.

Martay nervously replied, "Well, I don't know what else to call you. You've never told me your name."

"Hanhepi Wi," he said. "My Lakota name. Night Sun in your language."

"Night Sun." She repeated the name, pulling her hand free of his imprisoning fingers. "Now that I know yours, I'll tell you my . . ."

"Miss Martay Kidd," he interrupted, "or do you prefer 'Golden Girl'?"

Her lips fell open. For a long moment she stared at him. "But how could an Indian . . . I mean . . . you've known all along? How could you possibly? I've never seen . . . what do you . . . where are you taking me?" A terrible tightness was gripping her chest.

"I told you, we're going home. Home to the Powder River and Paha Sapa country." He could tell by her expression that she had no idea where the Powder River or Black Hills were. He said, "North to the Dakota Territory, Golden Girl."

And he kicked the black into a canter.

13

The President of the United States of America, Rutherford B. Hayes, from his Oval Office in the White House in Washington City, authorized the following: A punitive military mission against parties, known or unknown, involved in any way in the abduction of Miss Martay Kidd of Chicago, Illinois, from the Denver, Colorado, home of Colonel and Mrs. Thomas Darlington.

The President, appalled that such a foul deed had befallen the child of the country's bravest, most respected general, dispatched additional United States cavalrymen to the state of Colorado. Five days after Martay's disappearance from the Darlington estate, thousands of troopers, from as far away as California and Texas, were scouring the mountains and canyons and plains of Colorado with orders to "find her alive."

Virginia Senator Douglas Berton, close confidant of President Rutherford Hayes and father of the distraught Major Lawrence Berton, had himself boarded a train for the mountain city within an hour of hearing the news. The senator, his right leg lame from a riding accident suffered years before on his rolling Virginia horse farm, could not head up into the wilds with the others, but his presence in Denver helped defuse an otherwise volatile situation.

It was only natural for the fiery General William Kidd, beside himself with worry, to blame the major who had foolishly left his daughter alone and vulnerable. General Kidd was furious with young Berton, as well as with the two big, burly bodyguards who had been charged with the responsibility of "keeping that child safe."

The general had refused to listen to the flimsy excuses of the two military guards. Their passionate pleas for understanding— "Sir, we could not go inside; we weren't guests at the party. There was no choice but to remain outdoors. We followed the pair right up to the front door of the Darlington mansion. What more could we do? Be reasonable, General"— fell on deaf ears.

The general was in no mood to be reasonable and his face was red and his green eyes blazed fire when he raised a big fist in the air and thundered, "By God, you'll both be court-martialed and hanged, do you hear me? Couple of cry babies who don't have enough sense to get in out of the rain, God-damnit! Why the hell didn't you police those estate grounds? Answer me that! What were you doing all that time? Holding hands out on the front porch like a couple of old maid sisters, by God!"

The general was no easier on Major Berton when first they came face-to-face after the tragedy. Losing his head completely, he reached out, grabbed the younger, bigger man by his tunic collar, and shouted into his face, "You dumb Tidewater, Virginia, bastard, I'll have your hide for this, you hear me? Any man that has no more gumption than to leave a helpless girl alone in the night should face a firing squad immediately! No!" he shouted, his fury mounting, when Major Berton asked for a chance to explain. "I will not listen to your sniveling excuses. There is no excuse, soldier! You lost my little girl and if you don't find her, I'll kill you myself, so help me God!"

The general was speaking those very words, and meaning them, when the senior senator, Virginian Douglas Berton, walked into the high-ceilinged room where the two officers stood facing each other. Without so much as a glance at his tall blond son, the wise, unflappable senator stepped up to the red-faced general, clasped him on the back, and said reassuringly, "General Kidd, we'll find your daughter. Come, I'll pour you a drink." He smiled kindly at the wild-eyed general and, gently urging him toward the drink trolley, continued to speak in low, calm tones. "Your good friend and mine, President Rutherford Hayes, has dispatched additional troops and pledged punitive measures against all responsible parties and has sent me here to convey to you his deep, heartfelt concern and personal affection."

The aristocratic, smooth-tongued senator managed to calm the anxious general. Minutes after the senator's arrival, he and the general sat, knee to knee, facing each other, in big, overstuffed easy chairs, talking quietly, sipping their Kentucky bourbon, unwinding.

And when, after an hour spent together thus, they rose from their chairs and shook hands, the exhausted general, his eyelids heavy, his shoulders slumping, had agreed to climb the stairs to one of the many guest rooms in the Darlington mansion to get some much needed sleep before going back out into the field to rendezvous with Colonel Thomas Darlington.

No sooner had the general's tall frame disappeared into the marble-floored corridor than Senator Douglas Berton at last turned to his silent, miserable son. Shaking his silvery head, the senator held his arms out wide. As if he were still a little boy, Major Lawrence Berton stepped into his father's comforting embrace and unashamedly sobbed.

Patting his tall son's shaking back, the senator said softly, "Son, haven't I always handled it? And I will this time too. Don't you worry. There, now, there. Shhh, hush before someone comes in and sees you like this. It's all right, Larry, all right."

While the two men stood embracing in the drawing room and the weary general stretched out on his back in a guest room, Regina Darlington, restless, bored, and tired of all the military coming in and out of her home, fretted in the privacy of her white boudoir. Her nerves were every bit as taut as those of her unwanted houseguests. She had been cooped up here at the mansion for five long days and it was beginning to tell on her.

Regina heaved a sigh of disgust and temperamentally jerked back a gauzy curtain to look out at those responsible for the constant commotion. Tight-trousered troopers milled about on the pebbled circular drive below, laughing and talking, their voices carrying on the thin, dry air.

The very idea of her husband making her home a temporary command post for the Kidd girl's searchers! How thoughtless he was to subject her to such discomfort and total lack of privacy. She could hardly leave her suite of rooms lest she trip over a cavalryman.

Not that she didn't appreciate the sight of handsome uniformed soldiers sprawling about on the lawn, but there were too many! With dozens about all the time, she had no chance to get acquainted with any of them. It might have been fun had there been only a couple.

She smiled wickedly as she considered how different, how pleasant, the long, hot August days could have been if the pair of tall, dark-haired young men lounging now on the steps directly below her were the only ones about while her husband was miles away. She'd seen the way the healthy young animals had cast covert glances at her when they thought she wasn't looking. Oh, yes, the three of them could have had some good times indeed.

Her smile fled and again Regina sighed.

It was impossible with so many around. She might as well

have been all alone. No, this was worse. If she were alone, she could ride into Denver and see Jim Savin.

The thought of the darkly handsome Savin caused her to lose all interest in the two young troopers on the front steps. Allowing the curtain to fall back into place, she left her post at the front windows. Oh, how she wanted to see Jim. Now. This very minute.

Her chin lifting determinedly, Regina Darlington decided she would do just that. She couldn't bear it another day. She couldn't. She'd been patient long enough. Besides, how long might this circus continue? No one knew. It could be days more, or weeks. They might never find the girl. Was she, Regina, to suffer forever? No. And she wouldn't. She would make some excuse to the general and to the arriving Virginia senator.

Half an hour later, an elegantly turned-out Regina Darlington entered the drawing room, extended her gloved hand, and smiled prettily at the distinguished silver-haired senator, who gallantly bent to kiss her hand as he said, "My dear, I'm Senator Douglas Berton. How beautiful you are and how kind to allow me to be a visitor in your home."

Preening as she always did when a handsome or powerful man paid her a compliment, Regina let her lashes flutter seductively and replied, "Senator Berton, you're the one who is kind. I'm not really a beauty." But her expression told him she thought differently. She reluctantly took her hand from his, adding graciously, "And we're honored you'll be staying with us, Senator Berton. You're welcome here for as long as you wish to stay."

"Hopefully this ordeal will soon be over," said the senator.

"Yes," she replied, making her face appear appropriately grave. "We're all praying for Miss Kidd's safe return." She brightened at once, smiled, and said, "Lunch will be served in the dining room in precisely half an hour, Senator."

He smiled too. "It will be a pleasure to be seated at the table with you, Mrs. Darlington."

"Oh, dear, me. I . . . I'm sorry, Senator, I won't be dining with you."

"No?" His silver brows rose slightly.

"No, you see I was just on my way into Denver. I do so hate to appear rude, but I've an old friend who is in ill health and I've not checked on her since all this began." She laughed, nervously. "The poor thing must feel I've deserted her."

"By all means run along, Mrs. Darlington, and do not concern yourself with me. I'm quite tired after the long train ride. I'll have lunch, then lie down for a needed rest, if I may."

"Yes," she said, "you do that, sir." She moved in the direction of the hallway. He followed. "I shan't be too long in town." She walked to the marble-topped table in the foyer, picked up a picnic hamper covered with a snowy damask cloth, held it up, and said, "Soon as I deliver this food to my sick friend and stay for a short visit, I'll come home. May I count on you to be my dinner companion this evening, Senator?"

"By all means, my dear."

"Good. Then I'll be on my way." She turned at the door and gave him one of her most devastating smiles, fully aware that this well-bred senator was said to be a favorite in that chosen inner circle surrounding the President of the United States. She intended, while Senator Douglas was her houseguest, to make certain he never forgot the hospitality and friendship extended by the Darlingtons. "Dinner's at eight-thirty, Senator. Shall we make it a formal affair, despite the depressing circumstances?"

"Mrs. Darlington, I shall count the hours."

Well pleased with herself, a smiling Regina Darlington, the picnic basket over her arm, descended the stone steps, enjoying to the fullest the attention she effortlessly attracted. Young soldiers turned to look at the curvaceous copper-haired woman sweeping out to the waiting carriage. Pretending she had no idea that a dozen pairs of eager eyes were on her, she paused beside the carriage and turned to wave to her illustrious silver-haired houseguest, who was standing on the veranda watching with as much interest as the troopers. Senator Berton bowed slightly from the waist and smiled warmly at her.

"Hmmmm," she murmured happily to herself as she settled back against the deep claret cushions for the long ride into Denver. It was going to be quite a lovely day after all. A sultry afternoon in Jim Savin's arms, then a leisurely candlelit dinner alone with the powerful, charming senator. Afterward she'd suggest perhaps a game of whisk or a stroll in the moonlit gardens before a nightcap shared in the colonel's study before a cozy fire.

Regina was still smiling when she knocked briskly on the door of Jim Savin's Centennial Hotel suite. When the heavy door opened, she said excitedly, "Oh, Jim, I could wait no longer, I . . ." Her words trailed away and she stared, unbelieving, at a short, large-bellied man standing before her in his long cotton underwear. Foolishly looking past him, into the room, she demanded, "What are you doing here? What have you done with Jim?"

"Ma'am?" said the balding man.

"Jim Savin. What are you doing in Jim's room?"

"This is my room, ma'am. Been here for the past five days."

"Dear God, no," said Regina, starting to tremble, the covered basket containing the French champagne and Russian caviar and English biscuits and Belgian bonbons sliding, forgotten, down her arm. The half-dressed man caught it before it could fall.

"Here, ma'am, you almost lost your . . ."

"Give that to me," said Regina as she snatched up the basket and flounced away. Uncaring what he might think, she went directly downstairs and to the hotel employee behind the front desk. "Jim Savin," she said at once, "where is he? Has he moved to another suite?"

"Mrs. Darlington," replied the hotel employee, "Mr. Savin is no longer in the house."

"No longer . . . what do you mean, 'no longer in the house'?" Her eyes were snapping with frustrated anger.

"The gentleman checked out five days ago."

"Checked out?" she repeated shrilly. "But why? Where did he go? When will he be back?"

"I'm sorry, Mrs. Darlington. Mr. Savin didn't say what his destination was. He left quite unexpectedly one evening."

Regina's heart began to pound. "One evening? What evening?"

"Why I believe it was the evening of your gala for Miss Kidd." The man's face went grave at once. "Such a pity about Miss Kidd, isn't it?"

"Yes," she murmured, stunned, and suddenly feeling very uneasy. "A pity." And she turned and walked away, anxious to be out of the Centennial, back inside her carriage, away from questioning eyes. Her head had begun to pound as violently as her heart. Her stomach was jerking involuntarily by the time she sank back against the coach seat.

In her heart she knew that Jim Savin was responsible for Martay Kidd's disappearance. Her first impulse was to rush immediately back home to her mansion and tell Senator Berton and General Kidd. She could envision their joyous response to the unexpected breakthrough; the good news she'd thrown into their laps. It would be easy enough to track down a handsome Harvard-educated attorney and his bubbly, blond companion. Such a celebrated pair couldn't avoid detection forever. Both Savin and the girl were used to the pampered, privileged life led by the very wealthy. While Jim and Martay —she didn't doubt for a minute that the girl had gone willingly with him—might find it delicious fun to spend a couple of days in some remote lovers' hideaway in the wilds, they'd soon miss silk sheets and chilled wine and all the other things that made life worth living.

Suddenly furious that her prized lover would prefer the vapid Martay Kidd to her, Regina Darlington was very anxious to get back home. She would expose the presumptuous, unprincipled bastard, Jim Savin. She'd tell Senator Douglas Berton and General William Kidd that Savin had taken the girl. What a celebration there would be when they learned the truth. Both relieved, influential men would be forever grateful to her, Regina Darlington, wife of Colonel Thomas Darlington.

Already planning for a bright future, Regina saw happy days stretching ahead. Days spent in the very middle of all that bustle and excitement and power and glamour of the nation's capital. Nights turning about on the White House ballroom floor in the arms of ambitious congressmen and important senators and visiting titled royalty. Polished counts and noble kings and the President himself!

All at once Regina sat straight up, a stricken expression spreading over her face. Whatever was she thinking of? What had she almost done!

Her hand went to the buttons at her throat. Quickly she flipped them open, feeling flushed and ill.

She couldn't tell on Jim Savin. She could never tell because if she did, how could she possibly explain her visit to his hotel room to find him gone. To find that he had been gone since the night of Martay's disappearance. She couldn't dare tell of her suspicions without raising dangerous suspicions about herself.

"Damn you, you bastard," she snarled to the absent Jim Savin. "I hate you!"

14

"**D**amn you, you bastard," Martay snarled at the impassive Night Sun, "I hate you!"

"So you mentioned earlier," replied the tireless Lakota chieftain, his back still ramrod-straight, black eyes still alert, after the long hours in the saddle.

Squirming and miserable within his encircling arms, Martay wondered if this impervious savage would ever tire. They had left the line shack in the late afternoon, heading north along the foothills of the towering Rockies. She had assumed that they would make camp at sunset, but the sun went down and still they rode on, despite her demands that they stop.

Reminding him that civilized people got hungry at mealtime, she was handed the last of the roast beef and bread from his saddlebags, but he never slowed the big black's steady pace. Famished, she choked down the food, spitefully devouring every last bite, hoping he would starve! If he minded, he didn't let on. He continued to guide the big steed over a treacherous path, seemingly uncaring that there was no food left for him.

That had been hours ago. How many, she didn't know, but by the weariness in her bones she would have judged that at least six hours had passed. Still they rode on. And with each passing hour, she hated the cool savage more. If Martay had ever doubted that Indians were totally different from the white man, she no longer did. Not only did Night Sun possess superhuman strength and could endure endless discomfort without complaint, he was completely immune to her insults.

And to her charms as well?

Martay was far too exhausted to flirt with the stone-faced Indian tonight, but perhaps soon, maybe tomorrow, she'd give it a try. If she could turn him into a fawning admirer, he would let down his guard and make it easy for her to slip away from him. Just steal the big black and ride alone back to Denver! Why hadn't she tried it earlier? She was yet to meet the man who could resist her when she played the coquette. Surely even Indian males shared certain susceptibilities with their white counterparts.

"Will we ever stop?" she asked angrily, shifting as much as she could within the restraints of binding silk skirts and hard, ungiving arms.

"In a while," he said, not looking at her.

"Hmmmp! 'In a while' with you means sunrise. I can't go any farther without sleep."

"I know." He glanced at her at last, then away. "Go to sleep."

"Here? Like this?" She glared at him. "I'm not one of your damned—" She caught herself before she said "squaws." "Indians may be able to sleep atop a moving horse, I am not."

"Then you'll have to wait," he said, unmoved.

"Damn you, damn you. I hate you, hate you, hate you!" she shouted, crossed her arms and reluctantly laid her head against his chest, knowing she would not get one wink of sleep until this heartless man stopped for the night. Looking up at his hard-planed handsome face, silvered by the moonlight, her anger evaporated and she involuntarily trembled. He must have noticed, because his arm tightened around her. She felt the hard muscles pressing against her shoulders, a silent reminder of all that dormant power and of her vulnerability.

The suggestion of latent force silenced her as words could not. It was dangerous for her to bait him; she would do it no more. She would stop complaining no matter how long they rode on. She would lie here quietly in his arms and rest as best she could. Certainly sleep was out of the question.

That was the last thought to run through Martay's mind. Giving a tiny little shudder of exhaustion, her eyes closed and her head dropped forward. Sound asleep.

Night Sun knew the moment slumber overtook her. Her tensed body went limp and her breathing changed. Only then did his black eyes lower, and gently he shifted, so that her head fell back to be more comfortably cushioned against his arm and shoulder.

He stared at her.

Asleep, she looked the complete innocent with those snapping green eyes closed and the silky dark lashes shadowing pale cheeks. The contemptuous mouth, relaxed now, was soft and dewy, lips slightly parted over small white teeth. A gleaming lock of golden hair—silvered by the moonlight—had fallen across her right cheek, the feathery ends resting atop the swell of her bosom.

Night Sun slipped his little finger beneath the silky strand and gently pushed it back from her beautiful, sleeping face. But the curling ends still lay upon the luminous flesh exposed by her low-cut bodice. A vein pulsed on his forehead. With thumb and forefinger, he plucked the silky hair, held it for a moment, rubbing it tenderly, then placed it over her bare shoulder.

He felt a tightness in his chest, an unwanted emotion stirring in him. She was so sweet-looking, so helpless. Like a trusting child, safe in a loving parent's care.

He forced his eyes from her and purposely hardened his heart. Teeth clenching, he made himself remember the reason she was here. Made himself recall another trusting child, safe in a loving parent's care.

Black eyes glazing, Night Sun felt it all come flooding back. The sounds, the sights, the smells, of that fateful morning so long ago.

He was sleeping soundly in his warm tipi beside his grandfather, Walking Bear, on that frosty November morning in 1864. The rest of Black Kettle's camp slept as well. The Cheyenne chieftain, believing the white chief, Scott Anthony, when he'd promised that the Cheyenne would be under the protection of Fort Lyon as long as they remained in their Sand Creek, Colorado, camp, was so confident of his people's safety that there was no night watch.

Ten-year-old Night Sun was startled by the first crack of rifles and the neighing of horses. Still, he was not frightened. Not at first. In the heaviness of sleep, he thought it was only the beginning of the day-long wedding celebration he'd been looking forward to for weeks.

Night Sun, riding his favorite paint pony, had traveled far from his Paha Sapa home to Black Kettle's Sand Creek winter camp in the Colorado Territory. There was to be a great celebration: the marriage of his Lakota aunt, Red Shawl, to the noble Cheyenne warrior, Kills His Enemies. They had all come down with Red Shawl—his beautiful mother, Pure Heart; his grandfather, Walking Bear; and his grandmother, Gentle Deer.

The Cheyennes were loyal friends of the Lakota, and Black Kettle was pleased that his fiercest warrior was to marry the daughter of the respected Lakota chief, Walking Bear. Black Kettle, welcoming them with much fanfare and hospitality, had every reason to be content that winter.

For the first time in years his people felt safe; the white man was treating them humanely. Black Kettle was pleased.

The soldiers at Fort Lyon had invited him there, had listened to his concerns, had promised him his people would be under their protection; he need fear no soldiers.

Not an hour after the arrival of his welcomed Lakota guests, Black Kettle proudly brought out his treasures to show his old friend Walking Bear. A big smile slashing across his sun-wrinkled face, the Cheyenne chief thrust out his chest, pointing to medals the Great Father, Abraham Lincoln, had given him when he had visited Washington City. Impressed, Night Sun, eagerly reaching up to touch the gleaming silver medals, felt his grandfather's firm hand on his shoulder. He turned, looked up at his grandfather's stern face, and saw the slightest touch of envy in the old man's eyes.

Night Sun backed away but couldn't keep from whistling appreciatively when Black Kettle lovingly unfolded the United States flag that Colonel A. B. Greenwood, Commissioner of Indian Affairs, had presented to him. And Night Sun was awed when the Cheyenne chief solemnly declared that Colonel Greenwood had told him that "as long as that flag flies above you, no soldiers will ever fire upon you."

Walking Bear shook his graying head. And in the Lakota tongue, which his friend, Black Kettle, understood, he said, "It is good. May your people, and mine, enjoy lasting peace and no longer fear the white soldiers."

Black Kettle beamed.

Placing a square hand atop Walking Bear's broad shoulder, he replied, "I take pride in assuring my Lakota friend that his beloved grandson"—he glanced down at Night Sun—"and all his people enjoy complete safety here in my winter camp."

The two proud chiefs shook hands, and it was Walking Bear, smiling now, jealousy forgotten, who said, "Let the celebrating begin."

And it had.

For ten days and nights there had been much laughter and gaiety. Night Sun had been catered to and spoiled by old friends, none caring, any more than the Lakota cared, that he had been fathered by a white man. They cherished him as they did all their children, and he was never called half-breed.

Here at the Cheyenne camp he was just the sturdy-bodied, rapidly-growing grandson of the fierce old Lakota warrior Walking Bear. And because he was the chieftain's only grandson, adored by the old man, he was allowed to stay up late nights. And on more than one night there had been much merriment; some drinking and passing of the pipe and occasional gunfire as spirited braves rode their ponies among the tipis and fired at the twinkling stars in the black winter sky.

Night Sun snuggled more deeply down into the warmth of his buffalo robes. He had nothing to fear here in Black Kettle's peaceful camp. The gunfire he heard was that of a handful of Cheyenne braves. Most of Black Kettle's warriors were away hunting buffalo as they'd been told to do by the trusted white soldier, Anthony. Black Kettle would never have left the women and children unprotected if there was any danger.

"Grandson, wake up," shouted Walking Bear, and Night Sun felt his arm would be jerked from its socket, so forcefully did his grandfather grab him.

"What is it, Grandfather?" The child blinked at the old man.

"An attack!" hollered Walking Bear as the blue-coated murderers swept through the village, the snow muffling their hoofbeats. "Go to the women. Hurry!" He shoved Night Sun from the back of the tipi, then snatched up his rifle and went out to meet the enemy.

Obeying his grandfather, Night Sun dashed around the bend in Sand Creek, stopping for nothing, while from down the creek mounted troopers were advancing at a rapid trot, guns raised. The camp was mass confusion. Sleepy, bewildered people were rushing out of their lodges, partially dressed. Warriors shouted and ran back inside for their weapons while women and children screamed and dogs barked and frightened horses neighed loudly.

His heart pounding in his bare chest, Night Sun waded across the bend of the icy creek, trying desperately to reach his mother. He saw, fluttering in the cold winds, Black Kettle's American flag rising high above his lodge in the winter dawn and heard the chief calling to his people not to be afraid, that the soldiers would not hurt them.

Night Sun nodded, bobbing his head as he ran. It was all right. Everything was okay. All he had to do was get his mother and aunt and grandmother back to where the other women were gathering beneath Black Kettle's flag. There was no danger. Black Kettle had been promised that as long as the United States flag flew above him, no soldier would fire on him.

Splashing up out of the frigid water near his mother's tipi on the snow-covered banks, Night Sun saw White Antelope, an old Cheyenne chief who had seen seventy-five winters, walk confidently toward the approaching command. Speaking in perfect English, he said, "Stop! Stop!" and held up his hands. Then he stopped and folded his arms to show that he was not afraid.

The soldiers shot him down.

Arapahoe Chief Left Hand came rushing from his camp, hurrying his people toward Black Kettle's flag. But he, like White Antelope, was unafraid, and seeing the troops, folded his arms, saying he would not fight the white man because he knew they were his friends.

They shot him where he stood.

Night Sun bit back a scream of horror and hurried on to find his mother. Calling her name loudly, he dashed into the tipi where she'd slept. But he was too late. His beautiful loving mother, a woman who had never spoken an unkind word against the white man who had fathered her son and left her, lay dead with a bullet through the heart that had been broken so many years before.

Falling to his knees beside her, Night Sun threw his arms around her and begged her to speak, though he knew she would not. Tears streaming down his cold cheeks, he murmured against her still-warm throat, "They'll pay for this, Mother. I promise."

He lifted his head, brought a trembling hand up to close her staring, sightless eyes, then leapt to his feet, shouting, "Grandmother, Grandmother."

The camp was total mayhem.

Tipis were burning and terrified people were running and gunfire filled the air. Warriors were herding the women and children together to protect them, and Night Sun ran barefooted across the snowy ground toward them, hoping to find his grandmother and aunt.

The horrors he saw before he reached the gathering would stay with him forever.

A pretty girl, no older than fifteen years, came running out of a burning tipi, begging for mercy, her arms upraised toward the mounted troopers. A blue-coated devil pulled her up onto his horse and thundered away. Shouting for the soldier to halt, Night Sun ran after them, trying to save the frightened girl, but another mounted cavalryman overtook him, drew up even, and kicked him in the back with a spurred boot.

When Night Sun rose from the snow, the soldier and the terrified girl had disappeared.

Oblivious of the blood streaming down his naked back, Night Sun continued the search for his loved ones, dodging thundering horses and whizzing bullets and slashing sabers. In his flight, he saw a four-year-old boy, sent by the women, walk out into the melee carrying a white flag of surrender. Immediately the child was riddled with bullets. He saw women chased down and brutally raped. He saw bodies lying in the snow, all of them scalped. Others decapitated by striking sabers. There was the body of old White Antelope with his genitals cut off. And fleeing women and children painfully slashed with sabers, then left alive to suffer.

Night Sun stumbled over the body of a fallen warrior.

Struggling to rise, he saw that it was his grandfather, Walking Bear. The old chief would walk no more. He was dead; his flowing gray hair gone, his broad, proud chest still, his life-blood flowing down to stain the white snow crimson.

Night Sun wasted no time grieving for his dead grandfather. Walking Bear wouldn't have wanted that. He was the man now. He would take the fallen chief's place. He would be responsible for Gentle Deer and Red Shawl, if they were still alive. He shot to his feet and went to find them.

He found his aunt, Red Shawl, first. He heard her terrified screams; picked them out above all the other women's screams, and flew toward the horrible sound. A soldier had dragged her behind one of the smoldering tipis and had cruelly raped her.

"No!" screamed Night Sun, and ran toward them, but the soldier was already rising, buttoning his pants. Grinning, the trooper swung back up into his saddle and wheeled the big horse away, leaving the battered, bruised woman to suffer.

Red Shawl lay naked in the snow. Blood was oozing from her open mouth, from her right ear, and from between her bruised thighs. She screamed anew when Night Sun fell to her side; then, as she recognized him, tears of relief slipped down her cheeks, and as he drew her discarded dress up over her abused body, she whispered to him, "Night Sun, kill me. Please kill me."

"No," he said, violently shaking his head. "You'll be okay, Red Shawl. I'll take care of you." He patted her battered, freezing cheek.

"I don't want to live," she said tiredly, and as if on command, a soldier, riding past, shot her in the temple. "Thank you, Night Sun," she said, smiled sadly at him, and died.

Knowing what a modest maiden Red Shawl had always been, Night Sun took time to redress his dead aunt, then he was again up and gone, searching for his grandmother.

The smell of gunpowder and blood and death strong in his nostrils, Night Sun raced frantically through the destroyed camp, desperate to find Gentle Deer. Soon, through the thick, drifting smoke, he caught a glimpse of her, not fifty yards away. Brave and resourceful to the end, she was herding a handful of terrified children to the safety of the trees at the camp's edge. In her arms she was carrying a crying infant, which she handed to one of the older children when they reached the sheltering pines. Shooing the children from her, she turned and hurried back to gather others.

"Grandmother!" shouted a thankful Night Sun.

Hearing his voice, she turned, and it was then that a mounted trooper, his blond hair gleaming in the rapidly rising sun, rode close and fired, the bullet entering Gentle Deer's right temple and exiting the left.

"Grandmother!" Night Sun shouted again, and raced to her side. She was on her knees in the snow, blinded but alive. Night Sun knelt beside her, wrapped his short arms around her, and told her not to worry.

"Night Sun!" she warned, hearing the hoofbeats of the returning trooper. He looked up to see the blond-haired soldier riding down on them. Pushing his blinded grandmother from him, he rose to his feet to shield her from further harm, shouting, "Stay away from her!"

The young captain reached the pair, pulled up on his mount, smiled, drew his saber, and placed its sharp point atop Night Sun's right collarbone. Then, laughing heartily, his vivid green eyes shining, the soldier playfully slashed a bias line across Night Sun's thin chest to below his left ribs.

While blood streamed and the officer laughed, Night Sun narrowed his black eyes and warned, "You better kill me, soldier. If you don't, I'll kill you."

The green-eyed, blond-haired captain, laughing still, nodded, drew his revolver, and took dead aim. Night Sun, bare feet apart, eyes deadly cold, never flinched.

But before the trooper could squeeze the trigger, a senior officer, shouting to be heard, commanded, "Enough, Captain! Let's go."

At once the soldier holstered his weapon, said to Night Sun, "I'm going to let you live, Injun," and rode away, leaving behind a blinded old woman and a bleeding young warrior who would never forget the face of a green-eyed, blond officer. From that moment, it was forever etched in Night Sun's memory.

"But I won't let you live, green eyes," vowed Night Sun, calmly. "One day I'll hunt you down and kill you. That I promise."

15

"I hope they let her live," said an anxious General William Kidd, his face haggard, eyes red-rimmed from lack of sleep. He rose from his chair to pace once more. "Who in God's name would have taken her? And why haven't we heard anything? It makes no sense. None."

Senator Douglas Berton took another sip of brandy. It was past midnight. He had enjoyed a sumptuous meal alone with the mistress of the house, Regina Darlington. Afterward, she had shown him around the large estate, insisting they stroll in the moonlight, then share a drink in the study. At half past eleven, he had begged tiredness and climbed the stairs to his room. Seeing the light beneath the general's door, he had knocked and entered to find General Kidd pacing restlessly, too worried to sleep, his dinner tray untouched.

"General," he said, purposely keeping his voice level, soothing, "if someone has taken Martay, it would indeed make no sense for them to harm her. I'm sure the child's quite safe."

The general stopped his pacing. "Then why haven't I been contacted? Tell me that."

"I can't," admitted the senator. "Surely any day now . . ." His shoulders lifted; lowered. "Try to think, General. Who are your enemies? Who would have reason to . . . to . . . cause you grief? Whom have you so infuriated . . ."

"Nobody!" interrupted the general. Then, "Hell, lots of people. Show me a man who makes no enemies and I'll show you an incompetent fool."

The senator nodded. "That's true. But I'm speaking of a person or persons who have such violent hatred of you, for deeds done or imagined, that they would kidnap your daughter."

General Kidd dropped tiredly down into a chair, leaned forward, and raked his fingers through the thick, silvered hair at his temples. "I've never done anything bad enough to another human being to warrant this. I'm a bit abrasive and ambitious, God knows, but I've never . . . hell, I've never even killed a man except for Rebs in the War and the goddamned Indians, and that doesn't count."

"No. No, of course not."

As the general and the senator talked together in the Darlington mansion on that warm August midnight, a bearded, big-bellied, half-drunken gold seeker was chasing a laughing black-haired woman around the red-walled boudoir of a Cheyenne, Wyoming, brothel. Big Benjamin Gilbert finally caught her, grabbing the hem of her revealing red satin gown, and together the laughing pair tumbled into bed.

Afterward, while the sated, loudly-snoring gold prospector lay spread-eagled atop that rumpled bed, the woman routinely went through the pockets of his discarded trousers. She found little of interest. No folding bills. No gold coins. Only an envelope with a shiny gold seal.

She lifted it close to the low-burning lamp. On the envelope was written: General William J. Kidd. The woman turned over the envelope, drew out the letter, and began to read.

General Kidd:
I have your daughter. I'm in a line shack exactly six miles northwest of Denver. It's your life for hers. Come alone, within twenty-four hours or . . .

A stirring from the bed across the room caused the woman to look up. The big man was rousing. Hurriedly she stuffed the letter back into its envelope and shoved it back inside the trousers pocket, wondering why Benjamin Gilbert would have such a message and if it had any value. Answering herself, she shook her head and crossed to the bed. She'd never had a General Kidd as a customer; she would have remembered a name like that.

Raising a foot, she kicked the sprawling man. "Get up," she shouted, "and get out of here. Other customers are waiting."

Sputtering and snorting, the naked man got up and dressed. Grinning broadly, Big Benjamin Gilbert left the woman's room ten minutes later, promising to see her again when he got back from Montana.

"I'll bring you pockets full of gold nuggets," he promised, giving her cheek a smacking kiss.

"Sure, sure," she said, skeptical. Benjamin Gilbert had been bragging about his next big strike ever since she'd known him, and that had been for five years. "Don't come back here without it."

He laughed, slapped her on the bottom, and lumbered down the stairs and out into the night. Mounting a buckskin gelding, he rode out of town alone and was intercepted an hour later by a pair of roving, whiskey-drunk Crow braves. The Crows, furious that he was carrying no money to purchase more liquor, killed the big prospector and took from him a letter with a shiny gold seal.

But neither of them could read it.

Sometime after midnight, Night Sun pulled up on the reins, bringing the tired, lathered black to a stop beneath a sheltering conifer. The abrupt halt roused Martay, but she didn't open her eyes. She snuggled more closely to Night Sun, burying her face against the warmth of his chest, inhaling deeply, on the verge of drifting back into deep slumber.

But a voice, far colder than it had ever been before, ordered, "Wake up, Miss Kidd. Now."

Martay's eyes flew open. She looked up at the dark-visaged Indian and felt her blood turn to ice. Night Sun's expression was fierce; he looked at her as though he hated her, as though he might scalp her at any minute.

Roughly he took her arm and pushed her off the horse, then dismounted. Having no idea why he was so unreasonably angry, Martay stood there in the moonlight, trembling, wondering what he meant to do next.

Ignoring her, Night Sun unsaddled the exhausted stallion and drew off the bridle so the horse could crop the tall, sweet grass and drink from the cold brook that trickled down the mountain. Martay jumped when he took the pack and saddlebags and flung them at the base of the conifer.

Then Night Sun turned to her.

She waited for him to speak, but he said nothing. He took a step toward her and she cringed. He stood there towering over her. Fearfully she searched his face for some explanation, some indication of his intent. His black eyes held a fierce, murderous look that rendered her speechless and terrified.

A surge of rage swept through Night Sun as he looked into Martay's flashing green eyes. Eyes so like the ones of the laughing blond officer on that cold November morning back in sixty-four. Eyes he had never forgotten. Eyes that had haunted his dreams.

Eyes so like her father's.

The hurt and the hatred still potent as ever, Night Sun felt himself losing the rigid control he had always prided himself on. He wanted to hurt her; had to hurt her.

Stepping forward, he wrapped his hands around Martay's pale neck, fingers lacing together behind her head, thumbs meeting at the base of her throat. Martay's own hands flew up to grip his strong wrists, her nails biting into the bronzed flesh.

She was certain he was going to kill her. The blood roared in her ears and she waited for the powerful brown fingers to tighten and choke the life from her. Too frightened to scream, she clung to his wrists and stared into his murderous black eyes, praying he would make it mercifully quick.

Seconds dragged by.

Blind hatred for this cruel animal mingled with her fear. Certain he was savoring this last bit of heartlessness, Martay had no idea of the war that was raging within him.

A part of Night Sun longed to do just as she feared, to slowly, cruelly, choke the very life from her beautiful body. Kill her and cast her aside as though she were a piece of refuse, just as the soldiers had killed and cast aside his mother. Or draw his pistol, put it against her temple, let her feel the cold steel barrel, then squeeze the trigger, just as her father had done to his defenseless grandmother.

He ground his teeth.

He couldn't kill her. Murdering a woman was too abhorrent. He would rape her. Rape her as brutally as the soldier had raped his aunt, though this girl would not suffer as Red Shawl had suffered. Red Shawl had been an untouched virgin; this frivolous, fun-seeking "golden girl" had undoubtedly had lovers.

Night Sun's hands left Martay's throat and she swallowed convulsively, grateful for the reprieve. It was short-lived. His face still deadly mean, he grabbed her arm and jerked her up against his tall, hard body. His fingers went up into her hair, tangling there, tightening. Roughly he jerked her head back. Her face, eyes frightened, lips parted, was tilted up to his. Her hand lifted to push in vain on his ungiving chest.

Quickly Night Sun bent to her, his hard, brutal mouth covering hers in a kiss of such savagery, Martay whimpered her outrage at the harsh, intimate invasion. Mindless of her reaction, he deepened the kiss, his tongue thrusting forcefully, his hand holding her head rigid.

It was no heated kiss of passion; it was a cold assault of hatred. An act of aggression so blatantly hostile, Martay felt as though the long, intrusive kiss itself would kill her. He was drawing the very life from her; taking her breath away, violating her.

Martay screamed loudly when his hot, demanding lips finally freed hers. And louder still when that punishing mouth went to the side of her throat. She felt his sharp teeth graze her sensitive flesh and was afraid he would viciously bite her. That concern paled in comparison, when she realized his true intent.

"No!" she screamed as his dark head moved lower and his powerful lips and thrusting tongue covered bare quivering flesh. He was fiercely kissing the swell of her breasts, atop the low-cut dress. Pulling his hair wildly, Martay gave a strangled cry of relief when his head lifted just as his open, questing lips reached the straining silk of her bodice.

He stared at her, his black eyes burning with a near-demonic light, his lean body shaking with rage and desire. Again his hot mouth covered hers and Martay was powerless against such superior strength and fierce determination. Lustily he kissed her, grinding his passion-hardened lips against hers, plundering the deepest recesses of her mouth with his tongue, robbing her of breath and of sanity.

When, finally, after what seemed an eternity, his heated lips lifted, Martay gasped frantically for air and swallowed convulsively. But before she could speak or cry out, those merciless male lips were again on hers and he was expertly, effortlessly sucking her tongue into his mouth. And she was shocked and horrified to realize that his deep, intrusive kiss was stirring her own blood.

Dear God, what was happening to her?

Martay felt herself half responding to fierce kisses born of pure hatred. He hated her, this savage Lakota whose mouth held hers prisoner, and she hated him. Hated him! But his lips . . . those blazing hot lips . . . they were burning right through her, searing away logical thought and prudent reserve and valid fear.

Her eyes sliding closed, Martay swayed limply to him. And heard Night Sun moan as his lean, hard body pressed closer, his knee seeking entrance between her legs. The strong muscular arm that was wrapped tightly around her, holding her intimately close, loosened its grip, and before she knew what was happening, Night Sun had pulled her tight silk dress up so high, his knee could go between her own.

It was Martay's turn to moan.

An incredible wave of heat surged through her chilled, trembling body as his hands, strong and sure, caressed her thighs; thighs now bared to the cool night air. And to his warm, stroking fingers. Dizzy, heart pounding, Martay winced, then shuddered, when Night Sun pushed his knee, no longer encumbered by the confines of her dress, between her legs and, gripping her hips, guided her pelvis to meet his rock-hard thigh.

That muscular buckskin-covered thigh at once began an intimate rhythmic rubbing, pressing the satin of her underwear against sensitive female flesh that rapidly heated to such bold, breathtaking intimacy. Martay's arms hung limply at her sides, but it was all she could do to keep from wrapping them around his neck.

Night Sun's lips abruptly left hers. He lifted his head and stared down at her, and she had no choice but to grip his fringed shirtfront lest she fall. For what seemed a lifetime to the bewildered Martay, Night Sun kept her as she was, his hands clutching her naked thighs, lifting her, lowering her, moving her back, moving her forward, forcing her to ride his ungiving leg.

Their gazes were locked. Martay's breath was soft, shallow. Night Sun's was loud, heavy. And his mouth, that cruel, beautiful mouth, was slowly descending to hers again. Martay, helplessly surrendering to his searing, savage kiss, was jolted back to harsh reality when Night Sun abruptly ended the blistering kiss and pushed her so callously from him, her head rocked on her shoulders.

In confusion she stared at him. That confusion turned to terror and dread as he smiled coldly and roughly flung her down on the grass. Landing on her stomach, Martay frantically rolled over and saw, to her horror, that the unfeeling Lakota had removed his shirt; the long, slashing scar gleamed deathly white against his bare, dark chest.

His hands were at the leather-laced fly of his tight buckskin trousers.

"No," Martay begged, full comprehension of his intent finally washing over her. Rising to her knees, tears springing to her frightened eyes, she pleaded, "Please . . . please don't do this."

He stood just above, tall and dangerous and determined. Desperate, Martay crawled closer, threw her shaking arms around a long, muscled leg and bowed her head. "Please," she sobbed heartbrokenly, "please."

The muscles tightened tensely in his leg. His fingers paused on the leather laces. He looked down at her. Golden head bent, her cheek was pressing against his upper thigh, her arms were wrapped tightly around his leg, fingers tenaciously clinging. She was sobbing loudly, her slender shoulders shaking uncontrollably.

His fury, his rage, his passion, fled.

Teeth clenching so tightly, his jaws ached, Night Sun laced up his buckskins. Then, drawing a deep, slow breath, he laid a cradling hand atop her bowed head. His touch made her jump and cry all the louder. He sighed wearily, bent, and put his hands on her shoulders.

"I'm not going to hurt you, Martay," he said softly.

"No!" she wailed, and clung tightly to his leg, on the verge of hysterics, past reasoning.

He stood there in the moonlight while she wept and screamed and trembled. When her wracking sobs had turned to tired little hiccoughs, he eased her arms from his leg and crouched down before her.

Her eyes were swollen and puffy, her nose was running, her lips were trembling, her teeth chattering. The sight of her, so pitiful, so distraught, made his heart hurt.

"Oh, God," he ground out. Immediately he sat flat down on the grass and pulled her onto his lap, murmuring, "Shhh, shhh," when she tried weakly to resist. Finally realizing he was not going to hurt her, Martay, more tired than she could ever remember being, relaxed against him, sighing gratefully. Night Sun quickly pulled a clean handkerchief from his pants pocket and wiped the tears from her sad, beautiful eyes and hot, fevered cheeks. Then he brought the handkerchief to her nose and gently commanded, "Blow." She did.

And she didn't fight it when he wrapped his arms around her, cradling her close to his chest, warming her chilled, slender frame with the heat of his body. Curling against him, Martay instinctively put a flattened palm on his stomach and laid her cheek against his bare warm chest. Lulled by the sure, steady heartbeat under her ear, she soon fell asleep.

Night Sun felt the muscles in his neck tighten.

Martay's long golden hair spilled over his supporting arm, tickling him, enchanting him. Her pale, slender fingers, gripping him, were flexing and unflexing on his naked stomach. Her parted lips were against his throat, her breath sweet and moist. Her full, soft breasts, barely covered by the soiled white silk, pressed intimately against his bare, heaving chest, and her firm, rounded bottom was too close, much too close, to his stirring groin.

Night Sun drew a shallow breath and let his long fingers sweep fleetingly over the shimmering white silk draping the youthful curve of her left breast. He closed his eyes.

This beautiful girl—the most temptingly exquisite creature he had ever seen—had fallen asleep in the arms of a man who had, only moments ago, meant to rape her.

He forced himself to move his hand from her soft breast.

He opened his eyes and smiled at the bitter irony. If this sleeping girl knew he wanted her far more now than when he'd forcefully kissed her, she'd know it wasn't safe to be sleeping in his arms. Before, his passion had been pure rage; now it was growing desire. No longer did he want to hurt her; he wanted to make love to her.

"I'm sorry," he said to the girl, who could not hear him as his attention was drawn to faint red marks on Martay's graceful ivory throat. Teeth marks. His teeth marks. His black eyes clouded with pain and frustration and a pulse throbbed in his tight throat. "I'm sorry," he repeated, "sorry I ever took you from that party."

16

Gently, Night Sun laid Martay on a soft bed of grass, taking care not to wake her. He pulled a blanket from his gear and covered her against the chill night air, then drew his fringed shirt back on and stretched out beside her. Close, but not touching.

He lay there on his back, head cradled in his folded arms, staring broodingly up at the summer moon, his thoughts troubled.

Taking her had been a mistake. Already he regretted he'd done it. Regretted she was lying here beside him. Regretted he could turn his head and see her beautiful angelic-looking face.

Forcing himself not to turn his head, not to look at her, he rolled to a sitting position, clasped his hands around his knees, and rested his chin on a muscular forearm.

Why hadn't her father come? The general must surely have gotten the message; no one was more reliable than Little Coyote. He had chosen Little Coyote to deliver the all-important letter because the small, quick brave could be depended on to carry out orders without question. Little Coyote had vowed he'd see to it the message got to General Kidd at the Emersons' Larimer street residence.

So then why?

Several detachments of soldiers had ridden very near to the rock-concealed shack in the five days he'd kept her there, but the general had not led them. Was he too big a coward to come, even to save the life of his daughter? Or could something have happened to Little Coyote? That question couldn't be answered for months. The messenger was to ride directly from Denver south to Running Elk's camp and not return home until the spring.

Night sun pondered for a long time before finally lying back down.

There was nothing to do but carry out the second part of his plan. He had warned the general in the letter that if he did not come for his daughter within twenty-four hours, she would be taken from Colorado north to the Dakota Territory.

Night Sun ran a hand over his face.

He had not planned to take her anywhere, so sure had he been that her father would come for her. Now there was no choice. He couldn't back down. He'd have to take her with him, and that could only bring more trouble for his beleaguered people. An American general's daughter held hostage in a Lakota Sioux camp could bring down the entire U.S. Army on their heads.

Night Sun thoughtfully closed his eyes. And, exhausted from the long hours in the saddle, soon fell asleep.

It was midmorning when Martay awakened feeling uncomfortably warm. Her lips were dry and she licked them, opening her eyes to bright, pervading sunlight. She turned her head and saw the sleeping Night Sun lying beside her, face turned in her direction. Immediately the recollection of last night's brutal embrace came back and Martay shuddered and stifled a scream. Her first impulse was to flee.

Silently she stared at the sleeping Lakota through narrowed green eyes, not fooled by the peaceful, handsome face.

In sleep he appeared placid, harmless; Martay knew differently. He was a dangerous primitive savage and she had to get away from him.

Very carefully, Martay lifted her head. Night Sun didn't move. Relieved, she rolled her shoulders up and immediately felt the pulling of her hair. Frowning, she looked down to see long, bronzed fingers grasping the tangled golden ends. Taking great pains not to disturb him, Martay gingerly turned over onto her side. Then, very carefully, very slowly, she went about bending back those restraining fingers, one by one, holding her breath as she did so. With a patience that was totally foreign to her, Martay worked at freeing the blond hair from his clasping hand, silently praying he would continue sleeping, her concentration so intense, she looked nowhere but directly at the task before her. After long pulse-pounding minutes, the last lock of hair was freed; she was elated.

Ready to spring to her feet, she cast a hurried glance at the Lakota's face.

And saw a pair of lazy-lidded black eyes calmly watching her. A shiver raced through her, though the sun was hot on her face and perspiration beaded her throat. Her hopes of escape dashed, she waited tensely for him to speak. Or to reach for her and finish what he'd started last night.

His eyes grew hard for a moment, then softened. He said, "Good morning, Martay."

She didn't answer. She forced her eyes from his, her fear escalating, her face growing rosy from the vivid recollection of his heated lips on her throat. From beneath lowered lashes, she nervously observed him.

"We're not going to ride today," said Night Sun, casually, as though last night's heart-stopping drama had never happened. Pushing his fringed shirt up to rub his hard, flat abdomen unselfconsciously, he added, "If you like, you may sleep longer."

Martay licked her dry lips, despising the cool, detached Lakota with a vengeance. His blatant sexuality offended her almost as much as his heartless cruelty. He exuded an aura of sexual menace so powerful, she was repelled, yet, perversely, at the same time drawn by it. He made the simple gesture of rubbing his stomach somehow sexual, and try as she might, she couldn't keep her eyes off those long dark fingers gliding lewdly over his bared brown belly.

"No. No, I'm not . . ." She cleared her throat and jerked her gaze up to his face. "Why aren't we riding?"

He yawned and stretched like a lazy cat. "It's not safe. These foothills are full of troopers. We'll wait until the sun sets, then ride tonight."

Knowing it was useless to argue, Martay nodded. "And what will we do all day? Hide?"

Abruptly he sat up and leaned uncomfortably close, propping a stiff arm behind her back. Instinctively she leaned away, but couldn't keep from staring at his mouth as he said, "No need to hide, unless I hear someone coming." His black, lazy gaze dropped to her soiled silk dress. "It'll be a good chance for you to clean up."

"I told you I have no intention of . . ." Her words trailed off as she looked into eyes of glittering flint.

"You'll bathe today, Martay," he said commandingly, "and while you're in the water, I'll wash your dress."

Forgetting herself for a moment, Martay sniffed haughtily, "That's all you Indians know about fine things. This dress is pure Chinese silk and must be very carefully laundered with mild . . . with . . ." Those black eyes were impaling her, daring her to continue. "Oh, very well."

Night Sun agilely sprang to his feet. "I'll take your underthings too," he said matter-of-factly.

Martay rose beside him, hands going to her hips. "You'll do no such thing! I am not about to . . ."

"Then you'll kindly wash them yourself before, or after, your bath. And wash your hair. It's a sight, and I'm tired of looking at it."

"Who do you think you are that you can order me

about?" she snapped. Martay was the one used to ordering others about.

"For you, Martay, I'm everything."

"I beg your pardon?"

"Everything," he repeated. "Your protector, your guide, your provider."

"My warden," she responded scornfully.

"That too," he said, with no trace of apology. "Now, take that bath, before I'm forced to give you one."

Knowing the strong, lean Lakota meant exactly what he said, Martay turned away and looked out at the noisily running brook, hunting a part of it that offered some privacy. She saw the spot not twenty yards from where they stood. Directly in the middle of the gurgling stream, the waters were swirling and splashing around a large, jutting spire of brown sandstone rock.

Pointing, she said, "You see that big upthrust of rock. I shall go behind it to bathe."

"Do that."

She frowned. "How do I get there?"

He shrugged wide shoulders. "Walk."

"I'll get wet."

"I would hope so," he said, then bent from the waist, drew a bar of Pears soap from his saddlebags, and laid it atop her palm. "Toss out the dress when you get there."

Her fingers curled around the soap. "If you spy on me while I don't have my clothes . . ."

"Martay, that's the last thing I'd want to do," he said, and meant it. If ever there was something he wished to avoid, it was the sight of this beautiful, spoiled temptress, naked in the summer sunlight with water shimmering on her bare, appealing curves.

Not believing him, but having little choice, Martay lifted her skirts to her knees and waded out into the water. It was cold, so cold, but she didn't complain. She waded directly to the rising spire of rock, cautiously circled it, and began, somewhat awkwardly, trying to unhook her dress. She had not, for as long as she could remember, dressed or undressed herself. Lettie, her faithful maid, had always been there to help her.

A wave of homesickness swept over Martay as she stood there in the thigh-high water, trying valiantly to disrobe unaided. She missed Lettie and Big Dexter and Amos. And all the other servants. She missed all her old friends back in Chicago. She missed the new friends in Denver. She missed the kind Emersons and she missed big Larry Berton and she missed her dear father. She missed . . .

"Martay, what are you waiting for?" A deep voice cut into her reverie. "Toss out the dress."

"I'll toss out the dress if I can ever get the blasted thing off!" she shouted, irritably.

"Shall I help?"

"Stay right where you are!"

Finally she was able to get the soiled silk gown undone and off, and after throwing it over the rock in the direction of Night Sun, she nervously looked all about, drew a deep breath, shrugged, and shimmied out of her naughty French satin underwear.

A high cloud passed over the sun, casting the chilled waters in dark shadow.

For several miserable moments, Martay stood there shivering. She felt so vulnerable without her clothes. Here she was, the envied "Golden Girl" of Chicago, Illinois, stark naked in a cold mountain stream somewhere in the wilderness, alone with a hard-hearted, hostile Indian who was taking her God knew where. Her heart drumming a rapid cadence, Martay crossed her arms over her bare breasts and trembled violently, hopelessness invading her very soul.

The sun reappeared.

Its fierce rays beat down on Martay's upturned face and bare shoulders, warming her, reassuring her. Forcing her fears aside, she smiled suddenly, feeling better, thinking that surely nothing too bad could happen on such a glorious summer day.

Soon Martay was enjoying immensely her long, refreshing bath there in the clean, rushing mountain stream. Sighing, she sat down on the smooth stone bottom and let the cold waters close around her shoulders. Dipping her head back so that her long, tangled hair was fully saturated, she took up the soap and gave herself a good scrubbing, savoring every delicious minute, forgetting so completely, at least for the pleasurable moment, her dire circumstances. She hummed softly to herself.

On the other side of Martay's concealing rock, Night Sun, crouching on his heels at water's edge, painstakingly washing her delicate silk dress, caught the sound of her humming and shook his dark head. He wondered at the questionable intelligence, the supreme arrogance of the foolish young woman who, naked and defenseless, could be humming a lilting tune as though she had not a care in the world, when only hours before he had come very close to raping her.

Night Sun ground his teeth.

The golden-tressed beauty was so used to being coddled and protected, she could not conceive of anything bad ever happening to her. It was evident that from the cradle this deceptively sweet-faced creature had effortlessly ruled those around her, never giving a thought to anything save her own comfort and enjoyment. In the weeks he had observed her in Denver, she had easily collected men's hearts as if they were mere trinkets to be added to a little-worn charm bracelet. Obviously she considered him no different from the others. So sure was she of her charms, she most likely supposed he would soon fall under her spell, like all the rest.

God, what a foolish, vain little bitch he had kidnapped.

Blissfully unaware of her captor's harsh mood, Martay splashed about in the water, laughing and shouting like the unthinking child he considered her. It was wonderful to bathe after all those uncomfortable days and nights in her hot, sticky clothes. Splendid to be naked in a cold, clear stream under a hot alpine sun. Soaping her long, tangled hair, she gave her scalp a good, vigorous rubbing, then ducked her head to rinse. She came up sputtering and laughing, lost in a world of her own.

When her hair was squeaky-clean and her satin underthings had been washed out and her bare body was as fresh and slippery as if she'd reclined in her big marble tub back in the Chicago mansion, Martay, almost reluctantly, pulled the wet, lacy underwear back on and climbed out of the water. Taking a seat on the slanting face of the huge rock, she ran her fingers through her long, sopping hair, drew it all together over her left shoulder, and wound it like a rope, squeezing the water from it.

Then she stretched out on her back to allow the hot sun to dry her wet underwear. Shading her eyes with a bent arm, she lay there totally relaxed, satisfied for the moment, unwilling to think past this hour. The heat of the sun felt good on her chilled body. She stretched, sighed, and swept her arms up behind her head. A pleasant languor claiming her, Martay was lulled by the peaceful repetitive sound of the rushing water, of birds singing sweetly from the trees on the bank.

She smiled to herself.

If the circumstances were only different, she would actually be enjoying this outing immensely. Never in her life had she trekked into the wilderness, bathed in a cold mountain stream, lain in the hot sun in her undies.

The distant report of a rifle made Martay's eyes fly open.

"Martay!" shouted Night Sun, and she heard him splashing into the water. By the time she sat up, he was rounding the granite boulder, his dark face forbidding. Before she could speak, he plucked her from the rock, lifted her up into his arms, and dashed back through the stream, carrying her, the water slapping at his buckskin-clad thighs.

"What is it, Night Sun?" she asked when he stepped onto the bank.

"Gather up the gear," he commanded, his voice authoritative. Automatically she reached for her wet dress, anxious to be covered. His hand atop her shoulder stopped her. "Do as I tell you," he said.

She nodded and went about grabbing up their things. Minutes after they'd heard the shot, they had deserted their streamside camp and were crouched inside a deep fissure of earth so narrow, the big black bumped his sides entering it. Hidden by thick, tangled undergrowth, the narrow-sided crevice was the ideal hiding place, save for its lack of space.

Martay obediently took a seat on the blanket Night Sun tossed on the rock floor. He crouched on his heels before her and placed a vertical finger across his closed lips, indicating she was not to make a sound. She nodded. And almost laughed at his foolishness when he turned about, pulled the black stallion's head low, and said something into its ear. She had no doubt he was telling it to remain quiet also, as though a dumb animal could understand him.

Men's voices were getting steadily closer. Martay tensed, waiting. She looked at Night Sun, then at the stallion. The black had caught the scent of the approaching horses and Martay knew any second he would be whinnying madly. She watched as Night Sun calmly stroked the black's shiny coat, long, dark fingers gently patting, calming the beast.

The black's eyes were wild; his powerful neck was arched. His ears were cocked, nostrils flaring. But he didn't make a sound. Not a single whinny.

The fact that the mighty stallion remained obediently quiet for his bronzed master frightened Martay almost as much as last night's attack. Night Sun effortlessly exercised some strange, undefinable power over the big brute. She herself had felt the effects of that awesome power; and looking at him now, crouched there on his heels, gently stroking the big stallion, she had the sinking sensation that he could, if she didn't fight it, make her his obedient possession, just like the stallion.

Martay blinked in disbelief when the cocksure Lakota dropped his hand away from the horse, confident the trusted beast would remain totally silent. Night Sun turned about to face her, and in his expressive black eyes she read the message: "You, Martay, belong to me, just as the horse belongs to me. You will be just as dutiful, just as quiet."

Martay refused to let that happen. Damn him to hell! She would scream bloody murder! There were mounted soldiers within yards of them now. All she had to do was scream and they would hear her. There was nothing to keep her from it. No gun was leveled at her. Night Sun wasn't touching her. No gag was covering her mouth this time. There was no way possible he could keep her from crying out, and that's just what she'd do!

As if he had read her thoughts, Night Sun slowly reached out and cupped her bare shoulders with his hands. Martay swallowed nervously, preparing to scream. His warm fingers began to glide up and down her trembling arms, stroking, rubbing, calming. She opened her mouth, but, to her horror, no scream came. No sound of any kind. Nothing. She could not make herself scream or shout or call for help. She couldn't, for reasons she did not understand, disobey Night Sun. Mortified, furious, she looked angrily into his eyes. They were hot and dark. Her anger fled and she trembled.

And remembered, suddenly, that she was wearing only a wet satin chemise and daringly brief matching satin drawers that reached only to mid-thigh.

Night Sun's masterful hands continued to slide sensuously up and down her bare arms, his thumbs grazing her ribs. Shaking her head no, she forced herself to break contact with his heated, commanding gaze. Lowering her head, she was further mortified. The wet chemise clearly outlined her nipples, peaking from the cold of the clinging satin. Or from the warmth of those hot, dark eyes?

No! Her brain screamed, even if her voice would not work. No, no, no. This arrogant savage could not do this to her. He could not bend her will to his. He could not make her weak and breathless with his touch. She was not a damned dumb animal!

Night Sun unceremoniously took his hands from her. Then he leaned lazily back against the wall of rock and boldly observed her, his black eyes touching her more intimately than his hands had ever dared. Martay felt her breath grow short.

He was staring directly at her breasts, his eyes so intense, so hot, she felt the invading heat burn right through the damp chemise to the bare flesh underneath. Her breasts swelled painfully and her nipples hardened and ached and pressed against the restraining satin.

That dangerous black gaze slowly dropped to her quivering belly and Martay pressed her trembling knees more tightly together and wished there were more room in this close, hot redoubt. She was seated on the blanket with her legs curled to one side, her weight supported on a stiff arm. Had she planned it, she couldn't have chosen a more provocative pose, and yet there was no space for her to change positions.

So while mounted troopers cantered within yards of her, shouting and laughing and pondering just where the general's pretty blond daughter might be, Martay sat there, obediently silent, half naked, so snared by a pair of hot black eyes, she was totally oblivious of the world around her.

Martay was not entirely certain what was happening to her. She was not herself; was not in control; was guided by some intangible force so strong, she couldn't fight it. And didn't want to fight. Incredible warmth was spreading through her body, and she squirmed and postured and writhed, all the while looking straight at the lounging Lakota. Her swollen breasts and the insides of her thighs tingled and quivered and responded just as though his long, lean fingers were intimately touching her.

Frighteningly aroused, Martay licked her lips and threw back her head, arching her long, white throat. She extended her slender bare legs out as far as space allowed, rolling more fully onto her bottom to sit flat. And she raised her arms to push her long, clean hair atop her head, sighing, drawing a deep, slow breath, causing the rapidly drying chemise to pull and bind over her ample curves. And she never really realized she was posturing seductively for the black-eyed man across from her.

She was, as usual, thinking only of herself. Martay was enjoying this strange excitement and, as sophisticated as she prided herself on being, she was not quite worldly enough to fully realize what was happening. That this handsome, dangerous savage was making love to her just as surely as if his dark hands were on her. That she was giving herself to him, reveling in the erotic pleasure he was so effortlessly providing.

With his dark, sultry eyes he invaded, caressed, claimed for his own every luscious, sensitive inch of her undulating body. And she willingly, eagerly, surrendered herself to the powerful mastery of those incredible black eyes.

The strangely enjoyable interlude might have lasted longer, save for a tiny chipmunk. Frightened by a cavalryman's horse, the furry little creature skittered from its hole inches from Martay's left arm. The sudden, unexpected movement made Martay jump, and the man looking at her knew she was on the verge of screaming.

There was only one way to prevent it.

With a swiftness that gave Martay no chance, either to scream or to move, he was to her. He held her viselike in one strong, muscular arm, as though he would never let her go, and his lips, hard and determined, covered her soft, dewy mouth in a kiss meant only to silence her.

But she, like him, was still in a state of sweet sexual arousal, so her lips opened to him, letting him taste. His tongue penetrated and Martay sighed with exquisite pleasure. The kiss was hot and deep and long. So very long.

They kissed hungrily, anxiously, there in that small, dim place. Night Sun was crouched on his heels before her, his spread knees enclosing Martay's scantily clad torso as he pulled her up to him. Her head was thrown back to accept his kiss, her breasts pressing his chest. Her hands went up to grasp at the thick raven hair of his head as she sucked at his tongue and sighed and felt she could never get enough of this extraordinary man.

Night Sun prolonged the searing, voluptuous kiss long after its necessity had passed. When finally he dragged his burning lips from hers, the troopers had left the area. His heart thundering, he clasped Martay's head and pressed her hot face to his chest while he fought for breath.

Weak and trembling, Martay gasped anxiously for air, her sharpened senses assailed with the hot, thrilling scent of him. He smelled of clean sweat and sun-heated flesh and an unfamiliar male scent she did not recognize. She inhaled and wondered momentarily if his heart would pound right out of his chest, so heavy and rapidly was it beating.

Above her head, Night Sun's black eyes were closed in agony. His senses, too, were being assaulted with her essence. She smelled of soap-perfumed tresses and freshly scrubbed flesh and the unique, pleasing scent of sexual arousal.

More than that, he knew he could take her here, now, and she would give herself to him in sweet surrender. He forced himself to use his head, to remember who the girl in his arms was and why she was here with him. Made himself call to mind the green-eyed, blond-haired man who had fathered her. Made himself review all the times he had seen the shallow charmer on the arm of some worshiping male whose heart she carelessly crushed.

Better an aching groin than an aching heart.

Night Sun opened his eyes and stirred. Martay suddenly pushed on his chest. He pulled back to look at her.

"Don't," she said, somewhat shakily, "ever do that to me again, Night Sun."

"I won't, Martay. Believe me."

17

An extremely ugly, squat-bodied Indian sat in a comfortable white rocking chair on the sun-drenched veranda of the Darlington mansion. He was drinking straight Kentucky bourbon from a tall tumbler and smoking an expensive Cuban cigar.

He was Scar, chief of the Crow scouts. He'd ridden to this foothills estate to speak with General William Kidd, and the general, respecting the wishes of Regina Darlington, the genteel mistress of the house, had made no bones about the fact that Scar would not be welcome inside. It was, he told the badly-scarred scout, presumptuous enough that he had come here uninvited; that he was sitting here on the porch of such fine white people, drinking their bourbon and smoking their cigars as though he were company.

Scar's feelings were not hurt by the less than enthusiastic reception. He was not a sensitive man.

"What the hell do you mean, showing up on this estate?" said General William Kidd, his green eyes snapping. "Unless you've got news of my daughter, don't come around."

Scar crossed his muscular legs and took another drink of whiskey. "No news, General. But your daughter's the reason I came."

"Martay? You've heard something . . . you think you . . ."

"I've heard nothing. That's just the problem. I'll hear nothing unless I get around a bit. It's a waste of time for me to keep leading troops up into these mountains west of Denver."

"You've a better idea?"

"Give me a couple of months to travel. I'll ride up through the country, keep my ear to the ground, see what I can hear."

"I don't see how . . ."

"General, I've got plenty of contacts across the Plains. People who see and hear more than you'll ever know. I'll pay some visits, take a few presents—which you'll pay for—call in some favors."

"You think there's a chance of learning who took Martay?"

The beefy Crow licked obscenely at the chewed-up tip of his expensive cigar. "You never can tell. I have ways of wringing information out of the most secretive folks." He grinned then, his fleshy lips wrapped around the cigar, his flat brown eyes glittering evilly.

General Kidd scratched his jaw. "Hell, maybe you could find out something. Drink up, Scar, and be on your way. Time's wasting."

The obstinate Crow drained his glass, but rose, went to the drink trolley, and poured himself another. Without turning to look at the silver-haired general, he said, "I need a thousand dollars for the trip."

The general shot up from his chair. "A thousand dollars, my behind! There's a ten-thousand-dollar reward! You'll get your usual . . ."

"No, General. You'll give me a thousand dollars. I told you it is necessary to grease a few palms for information."

"I thought you were going to strong-arm your informers."

"That method will not work on everyone." He turned about and grinned. "Ladies like gifts."

General Kidd glared at the Crow. "You don't know any ladies, and the whores you visit sure as hell . . ."

"The trouble with you white men is you really think there's a difference." He laughed, a low, guttural laugh, and added, "Take the fine lady of this house, the one who's too refined to allow me inside her parlor."

"What foul thing are you suggesting, Indian?"

"That flame-haired woman is a bigger whore than any of those milky-skinned beauties down at Mattie Silks'."

"By God, get off this porch and out of my sight," said the general, nervously looking toward the open front door, his face growing red with fury. "Never a finer, purer lady lived than Mrs. Regina Darlington."

The scarred Crow chuckled nastily again. "Whatever you say. Now about that money."

"Draw cash from the paymaster and don't come back to these parts until you've word of my daughter."

"If I've heard nothing in a couple of months, I'll return to the fort." He set his empty glass down and walked to the edge of the veranda. "If I find her, I'll . . ."

Interrupting, General Kidd said, "You'll send me a wire, nothing more. I don't want you within speaking distance of my daughter. Now get out of here."

The muscular Indian grinned, nodded, and descended the stone steps. The general watched as he lumbered down the front walk and out to the circular driveway, where he mounted his sorrel gelding.

He disliked the Crow scout intensely. The man was obnoxious, sneaky, and dirty. He would have gotten rid of the ugly, repulsive Indian long ago, save for the fact no man, white or red, knew the country like Scar. The scout had a map of the entire plains in his head and he was a never-dry well of information about every tribe of Indian under the sun. He needed Scar. It was as elemental as that.

Still, the idea of that loathsome piece of humanity speaking ill of someone as high-minded and modest as Regina Darlington made his blood boil. It was common knowledge around the fort that Scar had an insatiable sexual appetite. There wasn't a whorehouse from New Mexico to Canada he hadn't visited. And there wasn't a woman he looked at he didn't lust after. Likely he found Colonel Darlington's pretty wife so desirable he wanted to believe she was of his kind. Preposterous! Utter hogwash. Why, never had he known a . . ."

"General." A soft, feminine voice startled him. "Why are you shaking your head so? Has something happened?"

He turned to see a sweetly smiling Regina Darlington coming onto the veranda. "Why, no. No, ma'am. I didn't realize I was . . ."

"Doesn't matter," she said. "Has that horrible heathen gone?"

"Yes, he has. I'm awfully sorry about his coming here. I know it must have frightened you half out of your wits when you answered the door."

Regina swept gracefully forward. Stopping directly before him, she said, "I'm just so very grateful you were here, General." She hunched her shoulders defensively, causing the delicate cap sleeves of her lilac summer dress to slip down her slender arms. "Whatever should I have done if I'd been here alone? Thomas down in Denver for the day . . . why, I'd have just been terrified."

General Kidd forced his eyes up from the enticing cleavage exposed by Regina's low-plunging neckline. He smiled warmly and said, "My dear, you're hardly alone. The senator's in the study. And had I not been here, the armed guard would never have let the Crow scout past."

"I suppose," she said, and again hunched her shoulders as

though the recollection of seeing the ugly Indian was just too much for her. Again the lilac sleeves slipped lower. Reaching out, she took the general's arm and asked casually, "When do you expect the senator's son to return?"

He patted her small white hand and told her, "Major Berton is due back at week's end. Saturday. Saturday afternoon I expect him."

"Mmmm," she mused thoughtfully. "You and Thomas plan to leave that day, I believe."

"Yes. Guess we'll miss the boy. Your husband and I are riding out early Saturday morning. Going northwest up to Greeley this time. May stay out for a couple of weeks." His green eyes clouded. "I've got to find my child."

"You will, General," said Regina Darlington, struggling to conceal a smile of pure pleasure. Her husband and the general out of her hair for a full two weeks.

And the distinguished Virginia senator to keep her company. And, for a couple of days at least, the senator's handsome son in residence.

Martay and Night Sun had hardly spoken for the past two days. Not since that kiss there in the narrow canyon, a heart-stopping kiss both wanted to forget. Silently, by the light of the moon, they made their way steadily northward, riding tandem atop the big black, stopping at sunrise to make camp and sleep through the day.

Martay had no idea where they were. Still in Colorado? Maybe. Wyoming or Nebraska? The Dakota Territory? She wasn't about to ask the sullen Sioux. She only knew that the overpowering vastness of the land they were traveling filled her with deep, pervading loneliness. It seemed they were a million miles from civilization, and with each mile they rode, her sense of isolation grew.

Deep in her heart she was certain a part of her life had ended forever. She had no idea what lay ahead, but any hopes of being returned safely to her father had passed. By now, after all these days and nights, she had more than likely been given up for dead.

Unshed tears stung Martay's eyes, and she closed them for a moment and swallowed the lump in her throat. She automatically laid her head back against Night Sun's hard chest.

They were riding the black down a rock-strewn hillside without benefit of the moon. It was early morning; the moon had set and the sun had not yet risen, so they made the crawling, punishing descent in total blackness.

As short a time as a week ago Martay would have been terrified to be traveling such a dangerous path in darkness. Now it didn't make that much difference. What future did she have? What if the big black stumbled and they all three plunged to their deaths in the valleys below. Would it matter? Why should it when the future ahead held only captivity in some remote Lakota Sioux camp surrounded by a band of barbarians.

Martay licked her lips.

She wasn't usually so despondent, but the past two days had been such long, trying ones. At a time when she most needed understanding, her savage captor had become distant and unreachable, and she didn't know what she had done to deserve such cold, uncaring treatment.

After all, he was the one who had kissed her. She sure hadn't wanted it; had hated it! Well, not hated it exactly, but hadn't . . . hadn't . . . responded . . . hadn't . . . Martay's cheeks suddenly felt hot. Try as she might, she couldn't fully force from her thoughts that kiss. That devastating kiss.

Never had she been kissed the way Night Sun had kissed her. It was as if she had never been kissed before in all her life. As if she'd never known what kissing was about. When she'd kissed Farrell Youngblood, Jr., in Chicago or Larry Berton in Denver, it was nothing like the way she'd felt when Night Sun kissed her.

Waves of heat crept through her at the vivid recollection

of that long, ardent kiss. She blushed in the darkness and was glad the man responsible could not see her face. A violent shudder surged through her; one of the many that had shaken her throughout the night.

"Are you all right?" came a deep baritone voice from just above her right ear.

"No, I am not!" she said, as hatefully as possible. And in truth, she wasn't. She was very uncomfortable. Her arms and legs ached and she was hot, far too hot, though the night air was cool.

By the time Night Sun had chosen a campsite near a shallow, trickling stream, Martay's teeth were chattering uncontrollably. Night Sun thoughtfully studied her face under the pinkening morning sky, and frowned. He reached out to take her arm only to have her jerk angrily away from him.

A muscle twitched in his lean jaw. In three long strides he caught up to Martay and pulled her back to him. He draped a hand across her forehead and felt his heart kick against his ribs. She was hot to the touch. He cupped her cheeks in his hands, ignoring her angry tirade. She definitely had a fever.

"I'll make your bed and you get right in," he said, dropping his hands away.

She shook her head. "I'm going to take a bath, it's hot."

"No, you're not."

She glared at him. "You're a real joy, you know that, Night Sun? You haven't spoken in two days and when you finally do speak, all you can say are three brief words: 'No, you're not.' Well, listen to my three words, 'Yes, I am.' "

His jaw hardened. "Can't let you."

"Three more words for you and my turn again. Okay? 'Cannot stop me!' "

"Want to bet?"

"Go to hell."

"Get into bed."

"Damn you, Indian."

"White woman stubborn," he said, the hint of a twinkle in his black eyes, full lips stretching wide.

"I'm in no mood for games," she shouted. "I'm hot and tired and dirty, and I'm going to take a bath in that stream!" Before her sentence was finished, violent chills wracked her and she looked up at him in puzzlement, as a child questioning what was happening to her.

His expression changed immediately. His voice soft, he said, "You're sick, Martay. You have a touch of fever. Why not wait until later in the day for your bath?"

Unable to keep her teeth from chattering, she reluctantly nodded, and the next thing she knew, she was lying on the soft earth, covered from toe to ears with blankets. And still she was freezing.

Martay's fever rapidly escalated and she was so cold and miserable, she didn't bother to object when Night Sun crawled under the blankets and held her shaking body tightly in his arms. Gratefully, she snuggled to him and slept fitfully as the sun climbed higher.

Through the day her condition worsened. She refused food. She took small sips of water, nothing more. Her eyes would open each time Night Sun's hand touched her forehead, her cheek, her throat, then the heavy lids would slide back closed.

It was twenty-four hours later, though she was unaware of the time passing, when Martay awoke to see a stranger standing with his back to her. Struggling to focus, she stared at the impeccably dressed gentleman so out of place here in this remote wilderness. Frowning, she puzzled over his presence, and wondered, fleetingly, if somehow she was back in civilization, rescued by the tall stranger.

Blinking, she studied him across the short distance separating them. The man stood before a small mirror propped up in the limb of a Juniper tree. He was combing his hair; hair as black as midnight. He wore a snowy white shirt that stretched across wide shoulders and disappeared at his narrow waist into perfectly tailored trousers of some fine black fabric. His shoes appeared to be of shiny black patent leather.

Martay smiled at her fevered foolishness and closed her eyes. There was no well-dressed stranger here with her. It was only her imagination again. Another of those strange dreams she'd had throughout the day and night.

Again she opened her eyes.

He was still there. His long arms lifting, shoulder blades moving beneath the white dress shirt, he continued to brush his black, silky hair. She stared, transfixed. And was still staring when he laid the brush aside and reached for an article of clothing draped over the tree limb. He picked it up and was shoving long arms down into the sleeves of the black tuxedo jacket when he turned to face her.

Night Sun!

She sat straight up, rasping his name in confusion. He was with her in a flash, kneeling beside her, his hands on her shoulders, his deep voice saying her name, calming her.

It was as though she were in a dream. He was Night Sun, but he wasn't Night Sun. He was no Indian; he was a white man. Or was he? He was so dark, so handsome, his beautiful white teeth flashing in the sunlight. His black eyes were . . . were . . .

It all came rushing back.

Standing in the moonlight on the Darlington's veranda, her fragrant gardenia sweetening the night air. Reaching out to take the glass of punch from Larry Berton's hand. Seeing instead the long, dark fingers wrapped around the glass and quickly looking up into a pair of gleaming black eyes. The gentleman in the evening clothes who had taken her from that veranda was . . . was . . .

"Who are you?" she murmured as the man she'd known only as Night Sun lifted her up into his strong arms.

He said, "You're sick, Martay, and I'm taking you to a doctor."

The next thing Martay was aware of was the unpleasant

smell of antiseptics and the sound of men's low, near voices. One was familiar. The other was not.

The deep, familiar one was saying, "Doctor, you must help her. Surely there's something, some medicine that . . ."

"Mr. Savin," the other interrupted, "your wife has Rocky Mountain fever and there is no known cure. I'm sorry." Quick, sure footsteps neared her. "What do you think you're doing?"

"I'm taking her out of here," said the firm, familiar voice.

"Don't be foolish, son. The girl's too sick to be moved. We'll make her as comfortable as possible; let the end come easy."

Too tired to open her eyes, too weak to speak, Martay felt herself being lifted up into a pair of strong arms and that deep, sure voice said, "The end for this woman is not coming for another sixty or seventy years." And he started across the floor, carrying her.

"Jim Savin, come back here! That poor girl is . . ."

"She's not going to die, Doc."

"Son, son, there's nothing you can do. It's the spotted fever. You can't save her!"

"I know the healer who will."

Martay was in and out of consciousness as Night Sun, protectively cradling her to his chest, rode the big black at breakneck speed over rolling grasslands straight toward his Powder River home. His dark face grim, he urged the stallion to run ever faster. The faithful foam-flecked beast obeyed, eating up the miles as though there were wings on his hooves.

At sunset Martay opened her eyes and, completely lucid and totally calm, though burning with fever, touched Night Sun's face and said, "I know I'm dying. It's all right, but please, won't you now tell me who you really are. White or Indian?"

He looked down at her, and as sick as she was, Martay

knew she'd never forget the expression in those beautiful black eyes. He said, "I won't let you die, Martay."

She said, "Please. Which are you?" and her pale hand lifted to finger the slick satin lapel of his expensive tuxedo jacket.

He said, "Neither. Both. I'm a mixed-blood. My father was a white man; my mother a Lakota Sioux. I'm Jim Savin in your world. In mine, I'm Night Sun."

Her hand fell weakly from his lapel and she murmured, "My lips are so dry, they hurt." Immediately Night Sun licked his forefinger, lowered it to her mouth, and circled her dry, hot lips. She smiled gratefully and said, "A half-breed?" He nodded. "Why the name Night Sun?"

"Night Sun means moon in our language. I was conceived under a full Dakota moon, born when the moon was full, and will one day die at full moon."

"Night Sun," she said, then: "Jim Savin." She repeated both names several times, weighing each, deciding which most suited the handsome half-breed. She was silent for a time, studying his harshly planed face, the high, slanted cheekbones, the arrogant nose, the sensual lips.

At last she said, "Night Sun, please don't let me die."

"I won't, *Wicincala*. Never."

18

The old white-haired Indian woman sat alone in her comfortable tipi on the northern edge of Chief Windwalker's Lakota Sioux summer camp on the grassy banks of the Powder River. Her sightless eyes closed in the wrinkled, coppery face, she was enjoying one of her favorite pastimes.

Gentle Deer had seen seventy-four summers, and like every human being on earth, she had favorite moments in her life; golden hours, happy times she would always remember. When she was lonely for the old days and for the people now gone on to be with the *Wakan Tanka*—the Great Spirit—she took those moments out of the reaches of her mind, where they were carefully tucked, and relived them.

The most precious of all was that spring in 1825 when alone she'd gone down to the Bad River for a swim as the sun rose. She was beautiful then and she knew it. Her hair was thick and raven-black and it reached to her hips when unbound. She was lithe of limb, supple and quick and strong, and all the braves looked on her with longing.

Reaching the cold, clear river as the rising sun bathed the waters a soft, shimmering pink, she stopped abruptly, and stared.

Atop a huge, slanting boulder that jutted out over the water stood a tall, magnificent warrior. A stranger to her; he was stark naked. His thick raven hair hung long and loose and his tall, gleaming body was nothing short of beautiful. His shoulders immense, hips slim, glistening thighs powerful, he was all any maiden could dream of.

Sensing her presence, the handsome warrior turned his noble head and looked directly at her. And without speaking a word, he invited her to be as bare and as free as he. Her heart pounding, she slowly, shyly, lifted her soft doeskin dress up over her head and released it. And she stood there naked in the rising sun while his warm black eyes admired her.

In the middle of the cold, clear river they met and knew when they came together that they'd spend the rest of their mornings together. And all their nights as well. They did not make love. They swam and laughed and touched, and later that same day the tall, magnificent Walking Bear brought a whole herd of horses to Gentle Deer's father and asked if he could marry her.

Within a week she was the adored wife of the fierce, indomitable twenty-five-year-old warrior, envied by every maiden in the huge Lakota tribe. And if those women had known what a gentle, loving husband the powerful brave was in the privacy of their tipi, they'd have been even more jealous.

A wide, pleased grin spread over the old woman's wrinkled coppery face and she sighed softly, recalling long love-filled winter nights and golden carefree summer days. Then the birth of their first daughter, and the second. And finally another warrior in the family, with the birth of the beloved *Hanhepi wi,* that mixed-blood grandson who, from the moment he'd opened his alert black eyes, had been a joy to them all.

Gentle Deer carefully, lovingly put the sweet memories back in their place and fell to dreaming. Her cherished grandson, now a grown man, handsome and strong and intelligent, had returned to his Lakota home to bring the bright sunshine back into her waning days. Night Sun threw back the flap of Gentle Deer's tipi, ducked his head, and entered. Then he stood just inside, smiling fondly on the blind white-haired woman he had missed more than he had realized. She appeared to be dozing; her sightless eyes closed. But as he stood there silently observing her, the white head lifted and the eyes crinkled merrily at the corners. She lifted her thin arms wide and said, *"Mitakoza."*

Night Sun threw back his dark head and laughed. Then hurriedly crossed to the seated woman, dropped to his knees, and embraced her warmly, saying, "Yes, it's your grandson." He kissed her temple affectionately.

"But how do I know you're actually here? This might only be one of my dreams." The brittle-boned old woman giggled happily and cupped her grandson's strong jaws in her thin hands.

"Does it matter?" he said. "I am here."

"You have been here all along; you'll be here forever." She pressed her withered cheek to his, then asked, "Is she with you?"

Night Sun pulled back to look at her. "Is who with me, Grandmother?"

"The fair-haired child-woman the *Wakan Tanka* showed me in a dream."

His high forehead knitted, and for a moment he was speechless. Then he gripped her thin hands and said, "There is a child-woman with me, and she's very sick with the spotted fever. I'm worried she might die."

The old woman asked, "Did you take her straight to Windwalker?"

"Yes, she's at his lodge now."

"Then do not trouble yourself, there is no more you can

do." She freed her hands from his and let her fingers roam inquiringly over her grandson's broad chest and shoulders. "You are dressed like a white man. You smell like a white man. Have you forgotten the ways of the people now that you've been to the white man's school and learned his customs?"

"You know better than that," he said, and captured her hands. "Don't forget you're the one who insisted I go to Harvard and read law."

"So I am," said Gentle Deer thoughtfully, having almost forgotten her urging pleas that her mixed-blood grandson take advantage of the education offered by his rich white father. Long before the boy had grown into manhood, she had clearly seen the approaching end to the Sioux's proud, free way of life. For her, it mattered little, she was old and her days on earth were short. But her cherished half-breed grandson had to be prepared for an uncertain future. He had fought going east, and agreed only because he hoped, by studying law, he could better help his people right the broken treaties of the past.

"Have you been well, Grandmother?" asked Night Sun, breaking into her thoughts.

"Do I not look well?" replied the feisty old woman, unwilling to burden the returning warrior with complaints of her failing health. She had what she wanted. Night Sun's return to his home before she died. Already she felt better.

"You look beautiful," he said, and touched her white hair, smiling. The smile fled, and he asked, "Grandmother, will you go to see the woman-child?"

"Ah, the impatience of youth," she scolded. "I cannot interrupt Windwalker at his medicine. I will go when the time is right, Grandson. When I am called on. Not before."

He did not argue. Nodding, he said, "I leave you now. I will go to my tipi and clean up. Then I'll wait at Windwalker's lodge."

"Do not disturb him, Grandson!"

"I won't. But I want to be close by in case the girl . . ." Night Sun didn't finish the sentence. He rose to his feet and left.

Martay slipped in and out of deep, dark unconsciousness. She fought against fever-induced dreams she could not distinguish from reality. She vacillated between resting peacefully in blissful, floating euphoria and struggling wildly against crushing, terrifying torment.

Smiling in her slumber, Martay sighed softly.

It was sunrise. In a weightless, wispy gown of sheer white batiste, she skipped through a vast field of wild roses. Roses of pure white with diamond drops of dew clinging to their ivory velvet petals. Their scent sweetening the clean morning air and making her dizzy with delight, she ran, barefooted, across the wet field, her long hair streaming out behind her, the wind kissing her face. She ran and ran until her legs were weak and her heart was pounding and she could go no farther.

She looked up and saw him waiting for her. A tall, dark God, dressed all in white, standing there in the sea of white roses, the golden sunshine shimmering in his jet-black hair. He reached out and drew her into his close embrace and she tipped back her head to look up into his beautiful black eyes.

Martay screamed in terror.

She was not looking into the beautiful black eyes. A broad, angular face was above hers, a face she did not recognize. And a voice she had never before heard said, "I will not harm you. Do not fear me." Martay, not knowing if she was awake or asleep, looked fearfully into his eyes, not believing she could trust him. But far too weak to fight him, her head dropped back to the pallet and her burning body went limp. Bending close, he said, "I am Windwalker, tribal chieftain of the Lakota Sioux and shaman to my tribe." Martay nodded weakly. "You are in my lodge on the banks of the Powder. Do you recall coming here?" he asked, his voice deep but gentle.

Martay did not answer. She turned her head and let her

tired eyes slide around the dim tipi. "Night Sun?" she murmured, suddenly terrified he had deserted her. "Night Sun,"
she said more strongly, her sick eyes questioning and fearful,
tears forming in their corners.

Pacing restlessly back and forth just outside in the darkness, Night Sun heard her speak his name. Dropping a just-lit
cigar, he hurried inside, disregarding Windwalker's command
to wait outside until summoned. His heart drumming against
his ribs, he went straight to Martay, took her fragile hand in
his, and said, "I'm here, Martay. Can you hear me? It's Night
Sun." He cast a quick, nervous glance at Windwalker.

The chieftain nodded, then silently retreated, stepping out
to breathe in the fresh night air. It was the first time in forty-
eight hours he had left Martay's side.

Focusing with difficulty, Martay blinked up at Night Sun.
He read the quick relief that came into her emerald eyes, and
her tears overflowed, spilling down her hot, flushed cheeks.
Squeezing his hand anxiously, she said, "I thought you'd left
me."

"I've been here all along," he said, and gently brushed the
tears away. "Right outdoors." He smiled at her.

She smiled back then and said dreamily, "Weren't the
white roses lovely?"

Knowing she was semiconscious, Night Sun said calmly,
"They were beautiful, Martay. And you were too."

She frowned and said, "You've never said that before."
Her eyes closed and she slipped back into unconsciousness.

A vein throbbed on his dark forehead. And he whispered,
"No. But I've thought it since the first moment I saw you."

Martay remained in the lodge of the Lakota medicine man
for three days. The shaman called on the Wakan Tanka, and
with the Great Spirit guiding him, he performed the secret
healing rituals of his ancestors. Passing an eagle's wing over
her face, he ordered the evil spirits of death to fly from her
body. He shook a great gourd rattle close to her ear to waken

her sleeping good health. He built the fire high and stripped her bare to her waist. Then, from a small leather pouch, he poured onto her chest and stomach a dozen sharp, gleaming panther's teeth to eat away the poison from inside her. He made a fist, pricked his vein with a sharp needle fashioned of buffalo bone, dipped a finger into the bright-red blood, and drew a crimson cross directly over her heart. Commanding the diseased, slowly beating organ to pump healthy blood like that he painted atop it, he repeated the process each time the blood dried on her breasts, using the fresh blood from his vein.

When he had done all that, and a dozen other things as well, he finally summoned Night Sun. It was late at night. The village was sleeping.

Night Sun hurried to the shaman's lodge on the east edge of the camp. Out of breath, he ducked in, his dark eyes questioning, fear making his chest constrict.

He looked immediately toward the sick girl. Her eyes were closed. She was either sleeping or she was . . .

He said, "Is she . . ."

Windwalker, his face solemn, said, "I can do no more."

"Will she die?"

"Only the Great Spirit knows," said the Mystic Warrior.

19

Dark thunderheads boiled up in the blue summer sky as the body was lowered into the newly dug grave. The small, solemn gathering bowed their heads respectfully when a tall, grim-faced man stepped forward and sprinkled the first handful of fresh dirt over the corpse. The man paused then, looked one last lingering time down at the departed, turned, and left.

While raindrops mingled with the tears on his cheeks, the tall man strode purposefully away, heartsick, shocked that someone so young, so strong, so vitally alive, could be dead.

Major Lawrence Berton quickened his step, anxious to be far from the post cemetery. While the regimental bugler blew Taps, the sad refrain carrying on the quiet, heavy air, and four able-bodied troopers came forward to complete the shoveling task, the gloomy major headed for his quarters and the bottle of Kentucky bourbon in his locker.

The quarters were deserted. The major was relieved. He didn't feel like seeing anyone. Didn't want to talk. Wanted only to drink alone, to numb his pain for a while.

Stripping off his rain-sprinkled blouse, the major drew out the bottle and a glass. Tossing down two full ounces of the whiskey, he made a face and poured another. The fiery liquid felt good burning its way down his throat and into his aching chest. He held up the near-full bottle and nodded his blond head. He would drink the whole damned thing, see if he could blot everything out. Martay's disappearance. And now this unexpected passing of a good friend.

He had tipped the glass up for the third time when a near voice said, "Major, I'm sorry."

Lawrence Berton's head swung around. The post surgeon stood in the doorway. Berton frowned as the short, balding physician, uninvited, advanced on him.

"We did all we could," said the doctor.

"It wasn't enough, Doc," replied Berton, tiredly. "Dane Johnson was twenty-five and strong as a bull. Surely there was . . ."

"Son, there is no known cure for Rocky Mountain spotted fever. Captain Johnson was an unlucky young man. He contracted a disease that's a sure death sentence."

Lawrence Berton was about to object further when another officer entered. The commanding officer, Colonel Thomas Darlington. With his eyes the colonel silently dismissed the bald-headed doctor and, sighing wearily, took a seat on the empty cot.

The dead man's cot.

Running a hand over the taut army blanket, Colonel Darlington said, "I know Captain Johnson's death hit you hard, Major. Especially coming right on top of . . ." He shook his head. Then, rising, continued, "Major, I'm ordering you off the post. Leave the fort immediately. Ride to my home in Denver. Stay there for a few days." He stepped closer to the taller, younger man. Putting a firm hand on Berton's shoulder, he said, "What works best for me when I'm combating grief, is to . . . ah . . . I understand Mattie Silks has some very beautiful women at her Holliday Street house."

Lawrence Berton blinked at Darlington. "Jesus, sir, don't tell me with a wife like yours you could . . ."

"My God, no! No. I didn't mean that. My wife's all any man could . . . Regina's so desirable I . . ." Darlington cleared his throat. "We're getting off the subject and I really don't think we should be mentioning my dear wife's name in the same breath with prostitutes."

"No offense, sir."

"And none taken, Major. Now, as I was saying, you're to go on immediate leave. Take a little pleasure from life. Get drunk. See the ladies." He grinned slightly, his face reddening.

Looking at his commanding officer, Lawrence Berton nodded. "Will you be riding in with me, Colonel?"

"No. In the general's absence I'll remain here, Major. Perhaps when you report back to duty at the end of your five-day furlough, I'll then ride in and take my place at the head of the Darlington dinner table. Until then, you may fill my empty chair."

"As you wish, Colonel."

It was nearing noon the next day when, tired and dirty and morose, Major Lawrence Berton rode up the circular driveway of the Darlington estate. Welcomed into the vast foyer by a polite servant, the despondent Berton quickly learned that General Kidd remained out in the field. That his father, Senator Douglas, was down in Denver, lunching with the city's politicos at Haw Tabor's Sherman Street mansion. That only the mistress, Regina Darlington, was at home and would be coming down shortly for lunch.

"Shall I have a plate set for you, Major?" asked the white-gloved butler.

"By all means," came a soft, feminine voice before Lawrence Berton could respond. He looked up to see Regina Darlington, stunning in a stylish dress of apricot faille, her red curls gleaming, standing at the top of the stairs. "You may go, Johnathan," she dismissed the servant.

"Yes, ma'am," said the butler, and disappeared into the back of the house. Lifting her skirts, Regina Darlington slowly, gracefully, descended to the waiting officer, her ruby-red lips turned up into an appealing smile of unmistakable welcome, her eyes boldly holding his.

Pausing two steps from the bottom, she stopped. Her full, barely concealed bosom was at his eye level. She purposely drew a deep, slow breath and said, "Major, you look so glum. What is it?"

"I just conducted the funeral of a fellow officer."

"My goodness, how upsetting for you. Whatever happened? Did the Indians kill him?"

"No, ma'am. He died of Rocky Mountain fever." His blond chin sagged on his chest.

She shook her head and the red curls danced. "Major, there's no cure for the fever. We all know that." She cupped his jaws in her hands and lifted his face. "Now, you are just going to forget all about deaths and funerals and . . . and . . . everything else that's been bothering you."

Recalling the colonel's advice, he was sorry he'd come to the estate. He should have ridden straight to Mattie Silks. Now he was stuck. At least through lunch. He said, "If only I could."

"But you can, Major. I'll help you. Besides, I'm ever so happy you're here. I thought I would have to spend the long, hot day all alone."

His eyes hopelessly drawn to the pale, perfect breasts, he said, "Allow me to go upstairs and clean up, then I'll . . ."

"No such thing," she scolded, moving one hand out to rest atop his broad shoulder. Toying with the golden oakleaf on his blue uniform blouse, she leaned closer and whispered, "Let's have our meal first. Then, who knows? Perhaps the handsome major could persuade the lonely lady to wash his back."

Major Berton was shocked. He was sure she must be teasing. True, she'd smiled flirtatiously at him many times and her sparkling eyes had looked at him in a manner no married woman ever had, but . . .

Regina stepped around him and swept directly into the sun-splashed dining room. His depression lifting, the major eagerly followed, charmed by her brash teasing. Certain that that was all that it was, still it wouldn't hurt to delay his trip to Denver until he'd shared lunch with the red-haired beauty.

At Regina's insistence Larry Berton took Colonel Darlington's place at the head of the table.

Regina Darlington, seated near him, said, "Already you're smiling, Larry. That's good. I like that. You have a cute, boyish smile I find most appealing." She picked up a ripe red strawberry from the silver fruit platter. "Tell me, Major, are you still a boy?" She dipped the berry into a bowl of thick, rich cream. "Or are you a man?" She popped the dripping fruit into her open lips, sucking it, nibbling, while her eyes held his. Then she swallowed it, leaving a circle of the ivory cream on her red lips.

Lawrence Berton automatically licked his own lips. "I . . . I'm a man, Mrs. Darlington."

She leaned up to the table. "Major, if you are, then why not do what you're dying to do."

"Ma'am?"

"Kiss the cream from my lips."

He swallowed, looked anxiously about, and remained undecided for only a second. Wondering if she'd stop him, he pushed back his chair, rose, and leaning over her, captured her chin with his hand. His lips covered hers and hers told his she most assuredly had not been joking. Larry Berton kissed the cream from her lips and dropped back into his chair, his heart drumming a rapid cadence.

It was a most enjoyable meal.

A bottle of the finest champagne had been brought up from the wine cellar and chilled. The pair drank as though the bubbly wine was lemonade, and Regina promptly sent a servant scurrying back down for another bottle. When it was carried in, chilling deep down in the icy depths of its silver bucket, Regina ordered yet another, planning ahead, envisioning an afternoon of tipsy lovemaking.

Major Berton was still not sure of her plans. He couldn't believe that Colonel Darlington's lovely wife would actually consider anything too improper with one of his regiment. Not right in her own mansion. No harm done if the lady flirted and teased and made him feel as Martay had once made him feel.

"Chill the third bottle and leave it in the summerhouse, Walter," Regina said, smiling. Then added quickly, ever mindful that she must not raise the servant's suspicion, "The senator likes the summerhouse. Perhaps he might enjoy a glass of champagne when he returns from town this afternoon."

"Yes, ma'am," said Walter, and went to do her bidding.

After that Regina made a great game of flirting outrageously with the delighted major while the servants, serving lunch, came in and out of the dining room. She was adept at the exercise. She'd done it many times before.

Major Berton's champagne glass was refilled every time it was emptied. The despair that had burdened him since Martay's disappearance lifted, and his good manners and gentlemanly behavior also went the way of his gloom. He was growing quite drunk and his keen sense of reasoning was more than a little impaired.

He looked at the beautiful woman finishing the last of her dessert. He grinned foolishly. He was taking the colonel's place at his table and he could take his place in bed as well if he liked. And he liked.

Draining the champagne glass, he slammed it down on the table, and said, "Come here, Regina."

Regina carefully blotted her mouth with a fine damask napkin, rose, pushed back her chair, and stood up. She swept over to the connecting door to the butler's pantry and called, "The major and I wish to drink our coffee without being disturbed." Then she closed the door and, smiling wickedly, went to stand beside Larry Berton's chair.

"What is it, Larry?" she asked ever so innocently, her eyes twinkling.

His answer was to take her arm and pull her down across his lap. "Are you a woman?" he slurred. "Are you going to finish what you've started?"

Before she could answer, his mouth was on hers, hot and hungry, and Regina Darlington couldn't have been more delighted. For a few dangerous, delicious moments, she allowed the aroused major to kiss and fondle her there in the dining room. She didn't stop him when he lifted her apricot faille skirts up past her dimpled knees. She sighed with pleasure when his big square hand caressed her creamy thighs and his mouth roamed hotly, hungrily, over her bare shoulders and down across the swell of her breasts.

But when the excited major raised his golden head and said huskily, "I want to take you right here, right now," Regina giggled nervously and shook her red head.

"Darling, darling, we can't. The servants. Go upstairs to your room. Then hurry onto the balcony and down the back stairs to the summerhouse. I'll be waiting there to prove I'm a woman who means to finish what she's started."

With that she got up and, her eyes going immediately down to the hard, heavy flesh straining the major's tight trousers, she put a hand to her throat and said, "Oh, Larry, let's hurry."

Breathlessly, Regina swept from the room, and as he left he heard her telling the servants that she and the major were finished with their meal; that the major was going upstairs to rest. That she had overindulged and was going to take a stroll around the gardens.

Eagerly Larry Berton climbed the stairs, hurried into the guest room, crossed it, and stepped out into the brilliant sunshine. He was across the balcony and down the back stairs in seconds and crossing the vast green lawn to the white summerhouse.

Regina, taking a moment to go to her room and freshen up, was shaking as she unstoppered her most expensive French perfume. The handsome blond major promised to be ardent and she had been without a lover since Jim Savin had disappeared. Dear God, she sacrilegiously prayed, please let Larry Berton be just half as good as Jim.

Giving her auburn hair one last pat, the trembling, excited Regina descended the stairs, hurried across the foyer and out the front door.

And stopped in her tracks.

"Good afternoon, my dear," said Senator Douglas Berton, coming up onto the veranda, his cane thumping on the marble steps. "Were you going out?"

"No. No, I was just . . . I had a heavy lunch and thought I'd take a short walk."

"Mind if I join you?" he said pleasantly. "I also overindulged. Tabor laid out a buffet fit for a king. A bit of exercise is just what we need."

20

She was so still. Deathly still. Her fair, beautiful face was chalky white against the dark buffalo robes. The once gleaming golden hair lay lank and lifeless around her slender shoulders. The lush cupid's-bow lips were cracked and burned from the fever that had raged for days. And the eyes, those expressive emerald eyes that telegraphed her every turbulent emotion, remained closed most of the time. When they did intermittently flutter open, they held no fire; neither hatred nor fear nor puzzlement.

"What have I done," murmured the dark tortured man seated cross-legged beside Martay's bed of soft buffalo furs.

It had been three days since Night Sun had moved Martay from Windwalker's lodge to his own tipi. In those three days he had not left her side, shaking his head no to offers of help from the women of the camp, even ignoring his beloved grandmother's suggestion that it didn't appear proper for a maiden to dwell in the tipi of an unmarried warrior.

Night Sun didn't give a damn how it appeared. He alone was responsible for Martay's being here, and for her fevered sickness as well; he would tend her. He did so tirelessly, catnapping for only minutes at a time, keeping a protective hand on her when he did doze, attuned to her every gentle breath, the slightest movement, each soft sigh.

He knew that had Martay been fully herself, she would never have allowed him to do all the things he did for her. The fact that she put up no struggle was a sure, frightening sign that she was gravely ill, still in danger of dying.

"Jesus God," he swore, "does Windwalker really have the medicine?"

"Never question the power of the Mystic Warrior," came a firm feminine voice, and Night Sun looked up to see Gentle Deer coming in out of the bright sunlight.

"Grandmother," said the tired man, "where are your manners? You are never to enter another's tipi when the flap is down."

She gave her grandson an impish grin. "How am I to know if the flap is up or down? I am a blind woman."

Night Sun rose. "You see everything."

"I hear everything as well," she reminded him. "You should not doubt the Great Spirit." She took his arm. "Help me get down."

Easing her to the mat beside Martay, he said, "I'm half white and that half is worried about this girl." The old woman laid a wrinkled hand on Martay's pale, dusky cheek. "Is she any better, Grandmother?" he asked, dropping down on one knee beside the old woman.

Gentle Deer's hand went to the slowly beating pulse in Martay's throat. The skin was cool and mottled. A bluish gray. She counted the beats. She pulled back the covers and placed a hand directly over Martay's heart. Then she moved down to Martay's bare, slender ankles, locating their pulses. And all the while Night Sun was leaning anxiously close, looking for any reassuring sign on the old woman's face. There was none.

Gentle Deer spread the covers back up to Martay's shoulders and sat back. She put out her hand for him to take. Swiftly he gripped it in his own and sat down beside her.

He said, "The truth, Grandmother. Is she better?"

Gentle Deer looked at her worried grandson. "She is no better," she answered honestly. "Night Sun, go out into the sunshine for a time. Ride with the braves. Hunt elk for our meal. Get out of this dark tipi; I will stay with the child-woman."

He shook his dark head. "She might wake and need me. I stay."

The old woman smiled. "How like your grandfather, Walking Bear, you are. Head as hard as stone." Her smile fled and she said, "When will you tell me?"

"Tell you what?"

Gentle Deer inclined her head toward the sleeping girl. "Who is she? Why is she here?"

"Not yet, Grandmother. Do not ask me now."

The old woman nodded, and did not press him. She knew Night Sun. He would tell her when the time was right. Now he was troubled by the white girl's sickness. She touched his taut brown cheek, wishing he were a boy again; that she might take him in her comforting arms and sing to him of the rivers and mountains and buffalo; that she could drive away his fears.

But her adored grandson was no longer a child. He was a man; a tall, proud Lakota chieftain, admired by the tribe for his intelligence, loyalty, and courage. He would have to suffer alone, and in silence.

"Help me up, Night Sun," said Gentle Deer. "I go now, but I will return before the sun goes behind the earth."

"I'll be here," said he, and turned his full attention back to the sleeping woman. He placed a gentle hand to the crown of Martay's head. "I only hope she will still be here."

Fur trappers and cowboys and gold prospectors looked up from their drinks when the powerfully built Indian walked into the saloon-brothel. Disgust shone clearly in their disapproving eyes, but the Indian, striding purposefully toward the back staircase, paid no attention. The stocky, badly-scarred redskin knew none would step forward to challenge his right to be there.

And he was correct.

A smattering of whispered insults followed him, but drinkers and gamblers stepped aside, allowing him plenty of room. Many of the patrons had seen the big Indian in saloons and brothels across the Plains. None wanted any trouble with the scarred, muscular man.

Scar's fleshy lips stretched wide into a smile. His brown glittery eyes, lifting to the second-floor landing, gleamed with anticipation. He knew what awaited in one of the red-walled rooms. Laughing now, a deep, guttural sound that came from way down in his powerful chest, the Crow scout climbed the stairs.

He was three days and a hundred miles out of Denver. He'd ridden relentlessly toward this white man's Cheyenne pleasure palace because the recollection of a pretty blackhaired woman with pale, pale skin who did anything he wanted her to do—as long as he had enough money—was still quite vivid in his mind, though it had been more than a year since he had seen her.

Stalking down the wide hallway, Scar called her name and opened doors, startling couples, causing prostitutes to squeal and the men with them to curse. He found her in the last room at the end of the hall. He flung open the door, marched in, and looking directly at the voluptuous black-haired woman, issued a one-word order to the lanky, bewhiskered man standing there in his long underwear.

"Out!"

Scar was undressing before the nervous man could grab up his clothes and get out the door. Bare-chested, the Crow stood there in the middle of the red room, flexing his scarred, heavily-muscled arms. Tendons in his huge, bull-like neck stood out beneath the copper skin as he grinned at the black-haired woman and said, "Remember me?"

The woman remembered the scarred Indian well. She smiled at him and promptly began disrobing, her busy brain toting up the extra money she would make this night. She was glad he was back. It bothered her only a little that he was ugly and badly scarred. And that he had a belly as large as a barrel that shook and rolled and undulated each time he moved. And that he was dirty and smelled to high heaven. And that his desires in sex were just this side of the bizarre.

He would, she knew, pay her five times what she usually made in an evening, and that happy fact made the dirty, fat savage a prince charming in her avaricious eyes. So when, his filthy buckskins discarded on the red carpet, the naked Crow sat spread-legged on a chair and invited her to get down on her hands and knees and crawl over to him, the black-haired woman didn't hesitate.

Much later, after the scarred Crow was sated, he lay atop the big bed while the tired, dutiful woman rubbed his bare, smelly feet. Scratching an itchy underarm, he said, "I hunt a woman."

The jaded prostitute replied, "I could go next door, see if Kitty will join . . ."

"No, no," he said, chuckling, setting his fat belly to shaking. "You all I want. You very good. I hunt missing woman for American general."

"Mmmm," she murmured.

"I must find her. I promise General Kidd."

"Who?" she said, looking up, eyes suddenly wide with interest.

"General William J. Kidd of the U.S. Cavalry has lost his gold-haired daughter."

The woman moved quickly up beside him. "I know that name! I know . . ."

"Know what?" said the Crow, grabbing her bare shoulders.

"The General's name. I've heard it . . . I . . . no, I've seen it on a letter! That's it. A letter addressed to General Kidd was in the pocket of one of my patrons."

Scar quickly sat up. His strong, short fingers cutting into her soft flesh, he drew her face close to his and demanded, "What did it say? Tell me."

"I . . . I . . . don't remember . . . I didn't read it all."

He shook her violently. "Think! What did you read? Who was it from? Tell me, damn you!"

"I . . . it said that he . . . he had the general's daughter. That's all I know."

"Who had her? Who?"

"I don't know. I don't remember."

The Indian's scarred face grew fierce. "You stupid white bitch. You cost me ten thousand dollars!"

"Sorry, Scar. I wish I could be of more help but . . ."

"The customer with the letter. Who was he?. Where is he now?"

"Benjamin Gilbert. He's a prospector, and when he left here he was heading for the Montana goldfields."

"Benjamin Gilbert," the Crow repeated. "Give me his description and anything else you remember of that night." His thick fingers went to her throat. "Do not lie to Scar; I will kill you if you do." He smiled then, a sinister smile, and his big hands slipped down her bare back, caressing, stroking. "And what a waste that would be. Who then would love me like my black-haired Wyoming whore?" He laughed heartily and drew her to him, crushing her to his chest.

In the high country of northern Colorado, on the grassy banks of the Poudre River, General William J. Kidd, weary after another long, fruitless day of searching, sat alone before a burned-down campfire while all around him tired troopers were sleeping.

His green eyes glassy, he stared into the flickering flames and saw, not the dying campfire but the huge marble fireplace of his Chicago mansion. Remembered the very first fire that was built there. The memory brought a smile to his wide lips.

He had moved the family—his beautiful wife, Julie, and their four-year-old daughter, Martay—from the East Grand Avenue house to the big white mansion on Columbus. It was summertime in Chicago and hot as the equator. But the golden-curled Martay had wanted a fire in the vast walk-in fireplace that graced the formal drawing room.

The General's smile grew broader.

"You want a fire, sweetheart; you just give that bellpull a jerk and order Big Dexter to get in here and build you one."

"Now, Bill," chided the lovely Julie, "you shouldn't be so indulgent. Besides, a fire in July? We shall die of heat."

Martay didn't waste a minute. She marched over, yanked on the bellpull, and when Big Dexter appeared in the arched doorway, she put her tiny hands on her hips and ordered, "Build a great fire in our new fireplace and be quick about it."

While the big black man blinked and nodded, General Kidd threw back his blond head and laughed loudly. Then he whisked the tiny girl up into his arms and said, "Sweetheart, you'd make one hell of a fine military officer."

"Bill!" scolded Julie. "I've asked you not to use coarse language in front of the baby."

"Why the hell not?" said Martay, squeezing her father's neck and giggling. The general laughed all the louder. And soon even the refined, serene Julie was laughing as they all sat on the deep, soft rug before the first fire built in their new home, drinking iced tea, fanning themselves, and finally, following their precocious four-year-old's wise lead, discarding unnecessary articles of clothing. Laughing as they did so and saying "Why the hell not?"

"Why the hell not?" General Kidd repeated aloud, and chuckled.

"Sir?" asked the approaching Colonel Thomas Darlington, snapping the general out of his reverie. He sat down before the low burning fire.

"Nothing. Nothing, Colonel. I was just thinking out loud."

Darlington nodded and drew a cigar from his blouse pocket. "Can't sleep, General?"

General Kidd said tiredly, "No, I can't." He smiled, wistfully, and said, "Did I ever tell you about the time when my daughter was six years old and her maid put her down for an afternoon nap?"

"No, sir, you didn't."

The general laughed and shook his silver head. "The little scamp climbed out the window, shinnied down the rose trellis, and was halfway to town before a neighbor, returning home, spotted her. God, she's been a handful from the beginning. I remember the time . . ." And he talked and talked, regaling Colonel Darlington with his daughter's childhood escapades, punctuating his sentences with bursts of deep laughter.

When finally he fell silent, the colonel, respectfully waiting a few minutes, finally gently suggested, "General, you really should get some rest."

"I know," admitted General Kidd. "But it's mighty hard to sleep knowing Martay's wondering why her daddy's not there to take care of her just like always."

21

It was the middle of the night. Windwalker's Lakota camp was sleeping; had been sleeping for hours.

But Night Sun remained awake, keeping his vigil over the sick woman. His black eyes on her, he lay stretched out on his side, head resting in the crook of his bent arm. Studying her perfect profile in the firelight, he picked up one of her small, cool hands and put it softly to his cheek. And for a foolish, daydreaming moment he allowed himself to imagine that things were very different.

The beautiful young woman was not sick, she was only sleeping peacefully. And she was not his captive, kidnapped and brought here against her will. She was his life's mate, content to sleep here beside him in this Dakota tipi for all the rest of her days.

"Martay." He spoke her name softly with tenderness and yearning. She never knew.

Night Sun drew the small hand around to his lips, turned it over, and kissed the soft, cool palm. Then he drew it down to his chest, turned fully onto his back, and totally exhausted, fell asleep.

Not half an hour later Martay roused. Slowly emerging from the mists of fevered unconsciousness, half awake, half asleep, she looked curiously around. The first thing her eyes fell on was a long, many-feathered war bonnet suspended from the far wall of the tipi, but its presence didn't frighten her. Neither did the large, round shield beside it, nor the lance, nor the banked fire in the center of the strange circular room.

In a calm, dreamlike state, Martay turned her head and saw him. Night Sun lay on his back holding her hand atop his chest. Smiling, she studied his handsome profile. And for a sweet, wishful interlude, she allowed herself to imagine that things were very different.

The darkly handsome man beside her was not a heartless savage who'd captured her. He was deeply in love with her, and they were not in a Lakota tipi in the hills, they were in a huge, soft bed in their fine city mansion where he would sleep beside her for a lifetime.

"Jim," she said quietly, trying out the name. But it did not sound right. "Night Sun," she murmured softly, her weak, thin voice filled with emotion. But he never knew.

Sighing, she slipped back into slumber. When Martay next awakened, she turned her head and found herself looking into the gleaming midnight eyes of Night Sun. Instantly she was outraged.

"What do you think you're doing? You get out of my bed," she demanded, a hint of fire in her dulled green eyes, and lifting a weak arm, gave his chest a push. "Get away from me!"

Night Sun was delighted. Her combative nature had returned; it could only mean she was a little better. He caught her flailing hand, wrapped his fingers around her fragile wrist, and said, smiling, "Ah, the sweetest words you've ever spoken."

"Let go of my hand!"

Nodding, he released her wrist, and agilely rising to his feet, inquired kindly, "How are you feeling, Martay?"

She frowned up at him. "Horrible. My legs and arms ache, and my head does too. My stomach hurts and my chest feels like someone kicked me. My throat is dry and my lips are . . . are . . ." He was smiling. She glared at him. "You think it's funny that I hurt all over?"

"Yes," he coolly replied, seeing a welcome touch of color rising to her pale cheeks, knowing instinctively she was past danger.

He turned and walked away, running his lean brown fingers through his disheveled black hair, ignoring the string of complaints she loudly voiced. "Where are you going?" she interrupted herself.

Pausing at the tipi's opening, he pivoted and said, "You want me to leave. I'm leaving." He grinned.

Struggling up onto an elbow, she demanded, "You come back here!"

"Lie down, Martay," said Night Sun. "I'm going for my grandmother. She'll give you something to make you feel better."

That morning, long before Night Sun and Martay had awakened, Gentle Deer had summoned Night Sun's boyhood friend, Lone Tree. When the strong, polite brave entered her tipi on the far edge of the camp, she served him some of the coffee Night Sun had brought her, and teased him about his upcoming marriage to the small, pretty Peaceful Dove.

His smiling eyes grew wistful and the quiet warrior said, "It is so long to wait. I never get to be alone with Peaceful Dove. I ask her father why the marriage cannot be now, in the Moon When the Wild Cherries Are Ripe, but he would not agree."

The old woman smiled at the impatience and eagerness of youthful lovers. She said, "Lone Tree, her father is wise. You will have many summers with Peaceful Dove. She will not be seventeen until the Moon of Drying Grass. Is best to wait."

He nodded, unconvinced.

The old woman smiled and said, "But I fix so you two can be alone." He looked at her with interest. "I need herbs gathered from the woods for the sick child-woman in my grandson's tipi. I have told Peaceful Dove's father she must go with you into the forest and show you which ones to choose." She saw the excitement leap into the warrior's eyes and laughed. "Go now. Peaceful Dove is waiting. But be back before the sun climbs too high. I must be prepared when Night Sun calls on me."

Grateful to the wise old woman, Lone Tree sprang to his feet, thanking her and promising to return in two hours, no later. He sprinted all the way to Peaceful Dove's tipi, and in moments the happy sweethearts were alone in the cool green woods.

They returned, flushed and happy, two hours later, carrying a basket of varied herbs. By the time Night Sun came rushing into his grandmother's tipi, she was seated there, waiting calmly for him, the basket of herbs gripped firmly in her hand.

"Grandmother," said Night Sun, ducking in, "you must come at once. The . . ."

"The child-woman is awake," she interrupted, smiling, and it was a statement, not a question.

Martay cringed when the short, wrinkle-faced Gentle Deer leaned over her. Pulling the soft fur robes protectively closer, Martay edged away from the touching, probing old gray-haired Indian woman, her aristocratic nose wrinkling with distaste.

Night Sun, standing above, felt his anger rising. In a voice that was calm yet commanding, he said, "Do as Grandmother tells you, Martay."

Martay reluctantly accepted the *wina wizi cikola* that Gentle Deer held out to her. And looking grumpily from Gentle Deer to Night Sun, she chewed the bitter licorice, making terrible faces and paying no attention to Gentle Deer's insistence that the herb would fight her miserable flu-like feelings.

Warned by his deadly black eyes not to make a scene in front of Gentle Deer, Martay also dutifully took the offered gourd filled with hot verbena tea and sipped it as the old woman smiled and said, "Is very good for your stomach. Drink it often."

But Martay balked when Gentle Deer ground up the bitter roots of *sinkpe tawote*, mixed them with gunpowder, and handed the concoction to her. "She is trying to kill me!" Martay said heatedly.

An expression of hurt passed behind the old woman's sightless eyes and she said, "Child, I would not harm you. I mean only to ease the painful aching in your arms and legs."

"I don't believe it," said Martay. Lifting snapping green eyes to Night Sun, she said more loudly, "I don't believe her. Get her out of here this minute!"

Holding his tongue, Night Sun took the mixture from his grandmother's outstretched hand and set it aside. Then he gently helped the aged woman to her feet, saying, "Grandmother, Martay is tired and irritable, not herself."

He escorted his grandmother back to her tipi, taking his time, engaging her in casual conversation, assuring her that he would call on her when she was again needed. He thanked her for coming, for helping.

No sooner had he ushered Gentle Deer into her lodge than he turned on his heel and headed straight back to his own tipi, his black eyes ablaze.

When Night Sun ducked through the opening, Martay knew he was angry. But she didn't know how angry. Lowering the tipi flap to ensure total privacy, he advanced on her, his handsome face a dark mask of fury.

For a moment he stood just above her, his eyes black slits of rage. He waited, coiled like a tightly wound spring, fighting to gain control of himself. At last he crouched down on his heels before her.

"In the white world, among the wealthy," he said, his voice deep, soft, "it may be accepted practice for pampered misses to be rude and disrespectful to their elders." His lean face was taut, the slanting cheekbones highly prominent. "You are in a Lakota Sioux camp. Here the old are honored and revered and treated with respect."

"I don't care, I'm not . . ."

"Never," he said, and a vein throbbed on his forehead, "never again speak to my grandmother in the manner you just did."

Martay swallowed. "I refuse to drink down some primitive god-awful concoction with gunpowder in it!" She turned away.

His bronzed hand shot out, captured her chin, and forcefully he turned her back toward him. Then, leaning close, he placed his hands on either side of her face and would not let her look away.

His killer-black eyes impaling her, he said, "There's one person left on this earth that I love. Gentle Deer. Be kind to her or answer to me." He released her face, his eyes still holding hers. "You will not be required to take Gentle Deer's medicine." He slowly rose to his full, imposing height, towering there above her. "If you wish to suffer, who am I to stop you?" He turned and walked away.

Her bottom lip trembling, Martay hissed under her breath, "You bullying bastard!"

Night Sun left her, and as much as she wanted him out of her sight, Martay felt uneasy the minute his tall, lean frame disappeared through the tipi's opening. Suppose the horrid old woman came back and forced the strange compounds on her? Or the camp's curious came to peer at her? Or, worse, came to harm her?

Martay felt a great measure of relief when she heard Night Sun's deep, distinctive voice just outside. He was engaged in conversation with another male, one he addressed as Lone Tree. But they were speaking in the Lakota tongue and she understood nothing. Curious, she listened, wondering what they were saying, supposing they were talking about her, discussing what they would do with her.

The voices rose and fell and Martay began to relax. Cruel and coldhearted though he might be, Night Sun was now her only link to the outside world. If he were not close by, there was no telling what the savages might do to her. Like it or not, she needed him, depended on him. And instinctively she knew that as long as she was considered his property, no other Lakota would harm her.

So she was glad that he remained close to the tipi. She felt protected as long as she could hear the deep timbre of his voice; knew that he was lounging lazily there in the sunshine, was so close she could call to him and he could be beside her instantly.

Martay rested through the afternoon and tried to be pleasant when Night Sun served to her hot, steaming broth at sunset and more verbena tea. She obligingly drank as much of both liquids as she could get down, hoping to mollify him.

She said, purposely making her voice soft, sweet, "I heard you outside the tipi this afternoon. It sounded as though you were visiting with a friend?"

"Yes, I was."

Martay sighed. What an exasperating man! He never volunteered information of any kind. "Who is the friend?"

"He's Lone Tree."

She smiled, determined to draw him out. "Have you known Lone Tree long?"

"Twenty-four years."

"For heaven's sake, you're at it again! Can't you say more than three words at a time?"

"Yes, I can."

"Oh, I give up."

"That's four words." He grinned. Angrily, she turned

away, showing him her back. He laid a gentle hand on her arm and said, "Lone Tree and I were born within a week of each other on the banks of the Powder River. We learned to walk and ride and hunt and fight together. We've spent many a happy day riding over these vast plains atop fast horses."

Martay slowly turned to look at him. His hand remained on her arm, but his black eyes were not on her. They were looking into the past.

"From the beginning we've had a friendly rivalry that made every feat we attempted twice as enjoyable. I couldn't stand to have Lone Tree beat me at anything. He felt the same." Night Sun smiled suddenly. "Lone Tree told me this afternoon he's finally beating me at something. In a couple of months he is marrying the prettiest girl in camp." His eyes dropped to Martay's face.

"Could you have beaten Lone Tree? Could you have had the girl?"

"The girl was twelve years old when I went away. A skinny little child."

"And now?"

"She's very beautiful. Large dark eyes and long raven hair and she is no longer skinny. Lone Tree is a lucky man."

Martay felt a sudden twinge of jealousy. "Are you envious?" she asked.

"Certainly not. He's in love with her, I'm not."

"Have you ever been in love?"

"I never have," he answered, and it was right back to the three-word replies from the dark, taciturn man.

22

The next hour passed in silence.

Night Sun, moving across the tipi from her, sat cross-legged and smoked a cigar, calmly watching Martay, wondering just how long it would take before she asked that he bring back his grandmother and her healing potions.

Martay, thrashing restlessly about on her soft fur bed, gritted her teeth and scrunched up her face against the discomfort of her intensely aching arms and legs. The pain had steadily worsened throughout the day. What had been only twinges at midafternoon was now, as dusk approached, nearly unbearable. Wondering how she could possibly make it through the long night, Martay, for a fleeting moment, lamented the fact that she had sent the old Indian woman away.

Mentally, Martay shook her head. No. She wasn't. She was not going to swallow some aboriginal mixture that might well kill her. She closed her eyes and wished for some of the blessed white powders Lettie favored for her migraine headaches.

Martay's eyes opened and she bit her bottom lip. She

looked across the dim tipi. Night Sun, his dark face awash in the last pink traces of a dying August sun streaming in the tipi's opening, was turned toward her. Quietly he was watching her, his forearms resting atop his bent knees, a cigar clamped between his teeth.

Smugly waiting for her to ask for help. Well, she'd be damned if she'd do it!

Sighing, she flexed her toes back and forth and stretched her tense legs out straight, wishing Lettie were here to massage the aching limbs. She rubbed her arms briskly and hunched her stiff shoulders and prided herself on not crying, even as the tears sprang to her eyes.

She was in agony.

Why couldn't Night Sun see it? He seemed to see everything else. She almost wished . . . she did . . . she wished he would bring back his grandmother. Maybe the old Indian woman could do something for her. Why hadn't Gentle Deer returned? Was it because Night Sun wouldn't allow it?

So miserable, she could no longer suffer in silence, Martay, hating herself for having to call on him for anything, softly said his name.

The cigar sailed out the door and Night Sun was beside her in a flash. "What is it?"

"About your grandmother . . . I . . . it's just that there's something almost eerie about her. She looks at me strangely, as though she is looking right through me."

Night Sun pushed a lock of damp golden hair from Martay's moist forehead. "Gentle Deer is blind, Martay. She sees nothing."

"Blind?" she peered up at him. "I had no idea. But she is so . . . How did it happen?"

She noted the minute tightening of Night Sun's hawklike dark face. And he hesitated a second before saying, "A United States Cavalry officer shot her in the head."

Martay gasped and stared at him. "I don't believe you! No

cavalry officer would shoot a woman. Not even a . . . a . . . "

"Not even a squaw?" he said, a hard edge on his voice.

"I wasn't going to say . . . I'm sorry about your grandmother and I . . . Do you think her potions might help the pain in my legs? I feel so terrible."

"Shall I ask her?"

"Would you?"

Gentle Deer cheerfully returned, bringing with her the magic potion of bitter roots, *sinkpe tawote,* and gunpowder. Martay trustingly swallowed it down, trying very hard not to make a face. She didn't quite manage, but reasoned it made no difference, since Gentle Deer could not see.

"I know it does not taste good," said Gentle Deer, "but it will make you feel better. You will rest tonight."

When Gentle Deer had gone, Night Sun reached immediately for the small gourd his grandmother had brought. The gourd contained a thick white salve to be used externally.

Martay, pale and suffering, opened her eyes when Night Sun knelt beside her and said in a low, soft voice, "Grandmother left something to be rubbed on your arms and legs."

And she blinked in surprise, but did not protest when he peeled away her covering robes of fur. In too much discomfort to care about modesty, Martay wondered immediately why she hadn't kicked off the hot fur covers long before now. This was much better. The fact that she was lying before Night Sun in her skimpy satin underthings was the furthest thing from her pain-clouded mind.

"What's in the mixture?" she asked as she watched Night Sun dab his index finger into the small gourd, remove it, and spread some of the white cream in the palm of his hand.

"Aloe leaves and a half-dozen secret ingredients," he said, rubbing his lean brown hands together, warming and thinning the salve in his palms. "I'm not sure."

Eagerly Martay lifted an aching arm. Night Sun took her small hand in both of his and began circular, rubbing motions, moving slowly, methodically, over the fragile bones of her wrist and upward to her forearm. He couldn't keep from smiling when Martay sighed loudly, a sigh of relief and obvious pleasure. His strong fingers slowly, gently, spread the soothing balm up to her elbow and beyond. "Feel good?"

Eyes again closed, she murmured, "Mmmmm. I've dreamed of this. Feels wonderful." She opened her eyes to look at him when he again dabbed long fingers into the thick cream and warmed it in his palms. Carefully hooking his little finger under the lacy strap of her chemise and urging it off her shoulder, he rubbed the lotion into the curve of her neck and shoulder.

Feeling the knotted muscles and tendons beneath her smooth white skin, he shook his dark head and pushed the other chemise strap down. Then placing both lotion-slick hands atop her bare shoulders, he kneaded and rubbed and worked to ease the punishing tautness from Martay's neck, shoulders, and upper arms, trying very, very hard not to be distracted by the swell of the lush, full breasts rising dangerously close to the sliding satin chemise's lacy top-edge.

Swallowing hard, he only nodded when Martay, moaning and sighing, and further showing her gratitude and enjoyment by stretching and inhaling deeply, murmured, "Magic hands, Night Sun." She closed her eyes and smiled.

Beads of perspiration rapidly dotting his dark hairline, Night Sun closed his eyes as well. But couldn't resist opening them immediately. Could not keep his gaze from admiring the twin crests of Martay's soft breasts, so alluringly outlined against the slick satin; and through his mind flashed that day he and she had hidden from the soldiers in a narrow canyon and she had sat opposite him in the soaking-wet chemise. The sleeping nipples he looked upon now had been pebble-hard that afternoon. And doubly tempting.

With his hands atop her shoulders, thumbs pressing just below her collarbone, Night Sun experienced an almost overwhelming urge to move his thumbs just a little lower; to brush them back and forth across those soft nipples until they peaked from his touch.

Martay's eyes came open. She caught the intense expression in Night Sun's black eyes and felt a strange rush of excitement herself. Wordlessly he moved his hands and the tension was gone. Abruptly, he moved down to her feet. He sat flat and, lifting her left foot onto his lap, began spreading the warmed thick lotion over arch and sole, pressing this thumb in the same pleasing circular patterns atop her high instep.

Martay softly giggled when his long fingers spread the aloe lotion between her toes.

Night Sun grinned, relieved that the tension of a moment ago had been broken. His grin broadened when she continued to laugh as he worked on both small feet. She was still smiling when he flexed and rubbed a slender ankle and began working his way up to the calf of her leg. But her smile became a nervous one when those long, bronzed fingers reached her dimpled knee and continued to climb.

She glanced at Night Sun. His copper face gleamed with perspiration and his chest, where the buckskin shirt was parted, was slick.

"It's warm tonight," he said suddenly and, draping Martay's lotion-slickened leg atop his bent thigh, reached behind his head and pulled his heavy shirt up and off, tossing it aside.

"Better?" she asked softly.

"Better," he said, and his hands were back on her.

But it wasn't better. Not for him it wasn't. Night Sun continued to spread the soothing lotion on pale, bare flesh so warm and silky to the touch, he couldn't help feeling his blood stir. He couldn't keep from wanting her, no matter how out of place and futile his sudden hunger was. And he reasoned that no healthy male—white or red—could let his hands caress the luscious insides of this lovely woman's pale thighs and not want to sweep away the covering satin and explore the concealed feminine sweetness beneath.

Though he didn't know it, Night Sun was not the only one affected. Martay, half drowsy now from the potion she had drunk, and further relaxed by Night Sun's massaging hands, felt a sweet yet disturbing lassitude envelop her. Senses at once dulled, yet heightened, she was suddenly aware yet unashamed that she was lying practically naked, with a bare-chested Indian, allowing his strong bronzed hands to massage areas of her body that no man had ever seen or touched. And she was liking it.

Stealing glances at Night Sun from beneath lowered lashes, Martay noted that the sculpted copper shoulders were glistening with sweat, and realized she, too, was perspiring. She was warm, far too warm, and it seemed to her that his firm fingers were spreading added heat with every bold stroke, with each manipulation of her muscles. Muscles that no longer ached.

That realization swept over her. She was not hurting any-more. Her arms and legs no longer ached. Night Sun had rubbed away the pain. She should tell him so; should let him know he could stop now.

"Night Sun," she said softly.

"Yes?" His black eyes lifted and met hers even as his hands continued to spread lotion and heat upward between her parted legs.

"N-nothing," said Martay, reluctant, however selfish and unfair, to have those magical hands leave her tingling flesh.

His gaze held hers for a second longer, and the dark, lean fingers that were skimming just under the lacy hem of her underpants, abruptly paused. It was, for each of them, the first moment they had become alarmingly aware of their inti-mate position. Night Sun honestly had no idea when he had moved, but he was no longer holding Martay's legs atop his lap. He was, instead, sitting on his heels between Martay's parted legs, his hands moving up her bared thighs as though he were her lover, poised to ready her for lovemaking.

Quickly he moved and at the same time commanded harshly, "Turn over."

Martay turned onto her stomach, and for her, the intimacy, the urgency, was gone. No longer looking at him, she relaxed completely as his hands were again spreading the lotion with its wonderful soothing balm.

"Hmmmm," she murmured, "cool. The aloe leaves make the lotion feel cool to the skin. So cool."

"Yes, cool," he said, feeling anything but, as he spread the slick liquid over the backs of her legs, his heated eyes devouring the rounded swell of her tight little bottom.

The massage continued until Martay's suffering had been completely stroked away and she fell blissfully asleep there on her stomach while Night Sun's hands worked on her bare, silky back.

Night Sun knew, by her deep, slow breathing, that she had fallen asleep. It was ironic. He had ended her suffering, and caused his own. Dark fingers skimming down her fragile spine, he drew a labored breath and allowed his hand to move down and fleetingly cup the curve of her soft bottom for one heartbeat.

Then shot to his feet, went for a cigar and match, and rushed outside, where he stayed for a long, troubled time, smoking in the darkness.

Under Gentle Deer's watchful, unseeing eyes and patient care, Martay quickly began to recover, and no one could have been more relieved than Night Sun. With the return of her health, Martay was once again herself, in every annoying way, and any tenderness and regard she had evoked in him went the way of her illness.

Back to being her spoiled, demanding self, Martay wasted no time insisting on privacy; she wanted a tipi of her own. She was, she haughtily reminded him, a lady. If he thought, for one minute, she was going to live in such close quarters with him, sleep in the same lodge, well he had another think coming!

"I gather," said Night Sun, pointedly, "your definition of a lady differs from mine."

Hands on hips, she asked, "What is that supposed to mean?"

"Exactly what I said. You don't know the meaning of the word."

"Look, half-breed"—she stepped closer, her chin lifted defiantly— "I really don't care what your opinion of me is. I'm telling you, I want my own place to live before another night falls!"

She got it.

And Martay, lying wide-awake that night on a soft fur bed in the tipi Night Sun had obligingly moved her to, wondered if she might have acted too hastily. The tipi, she was told, belonged to Little Coyote, a man who, like her, valued his privacy. The lodge was quite spacious and remarkably clean, but like Night Sun's, it was set apart from the rest of the camp. Now, lying there alone on that hot moonless night in the silence, she felt uneasy and found she couldn't sleep. She started at the least little sound, eyes wide, heart thumping. And wished, though she would cut out her tongue before she would have told him so, that Night Sun was sleeping just across the tipi from her. That she could glance over now and see the dark head, the bare, wide shoulders, gleaming in the firelight.

The man with the dark head and bare shoulders was also having trouble resting. He had told himself he couldn't wait to get Martay out of his tipi, out of his hair, out of his sight. She got on his nerves as no woman ever had. She sassed him constantly and complained and never, it seemed to him, shut her mouth. She asked endless probing questions, as no Lakota woman would have dared, and then griped loudly because he refused to supply the answers she sought.

Now he could relax. Now he could sleep without clothes again, as he had always done. Now he could have his old warrior friends in to visit and talk and laugh far into the night, just as in the old days. Now his large, comfortable tipi was his private domain again, all traces of the sharp-tongued, exasperating woman gone.

Naked, Night Sun lay atop his fur bed, arms folded beneath his head. He stretched his long, bare body out full-length and yawned. And slowly turned his head to look across the tipi to that other bed, the empty one, where, until tonight, tousled blond hair had spilled about slender ivory shoulders.

Night Sun felt the muscles in his bare belly tighten and he ground his even, white teeth. Arms came from behind his head and a long-fingered dark hand swept down over his hairless chest and across his stomach as his black eyes closed in self-disgust.

Jerking there on his naked belly, swollen and rigid and aching, was a part of him he could not control. Lying alone in the hot stillness of the dark night, he fought the desire that blazed at the mere recollection of her face and hair and pale, pale skin. It was not the first time his body had responded to the worrisome temptress.

Suddenly it was stifling hot inside his dark, close tipi. Night Sun rose from his bed, slipped into his tight buckskin pants, stepped into his moccasins, and ducked outside, drawing in a long, deep breath of fresh air, relieved to feel the cooling breezes on his face, his bare chest, his swollen groin.

His physical problem soon, if temporarily, solved, Night Sun went for a walk in the darkness, leisurely circling the perimeter of the sleeping camp, winding up very near to the isolated lodge where Martay slept. He stood, unmoving, for a long time and watched the cone-shaped dwelling.

He smiled ruefully in the darkness.

How out of place she was here. A rich, pampered white woman who had lived all her life in a fully staffed mansion, now sleeping alone in a tipi made of buffalo hides decorated with horses and coyotes and scenes of battles painted on its sides. Shaking his dark head, he turned and walked back to his tipi.

A little more relaxed after his walk, Night Sun stepped out of his moccasins and was unlacing his buckskins when he heard it. A loud, shrill scream. Coming from the direction of Martay's lodge.

Forgetting his half-unlaced pants, he grabbed up his Winchester and, barefooted, raced to her, his heart thundering in his naked chest. He reached her in minutes and found her cowering against the far wall, screaming hysterically.

Totally baffled, he went immediately to her, and pulling her up, enfolded her close to his chest with one long arm. He looked all about, gun poised at the ready.

"What is it?" he said anxiously into her hair. "Are you sick? Are you in pain?"

Martay's slender arms wound tightly around his waist and she buried her face on his chest. "N-no . . . I . . . I . . ."

"What, Martay?"

"A . . . a . . . big . . . ani-animal . . . was . . . was . . ." she stammered, pressing her face more securely into the curve of his neck and shoulder.

"An animal was here?"

"Y-yes . . . it . . . it . . . tried to . . ."

"I really doubt . . ."

Her blond head shot up. "It was here, I'm telling you!"

While she clung tenaciously to him, Night Sun slowly turned all around, his alert black eyes cautiously looking over the circular room. He stopped and squinted. There, directly beside the fur bed where Martay had been sleeping, were four long, wide slashes in the thick buffalo hide.

A shudder surged through him and Night Sun's protective arm tightened around Martay's slender shoulders. He need move no closer to know that a hungry panther had come down from the hills to prowl. The ripping sound had fortunately awakened Martay, she had screamed and frightened the beast away.

"Is help needed?" came Lone Tree's voice from just outside the tipi, and Night Sun suddenly realized others in the camp had been awakened by Martay's screams. There was the excited chatter of several braves.

"A panther," Night Sun called out in their native tongue. He made a move to go out and speak to the concerned men, but Martay refused to loosen her death grip on his waist. "The girl is safe," he called. "The cat got away. Go back to bed."

"Good night," called Lone Tree, and the men retreated, talking low about the panther problem that had grown with the thinning of the elk and buffalo herds.

Still Martay clung to Night Sun. "I was so frightened," she murmured, her lips moving against his collarbone. "Something was trying to get me and I saw these gleaming eyes and I . . ."

"I've got you," said Night Sun, gently stroking her trembling back through the wispy satin of her chemise. For a time they stood there embracing, her slender, quivering body pressed to the hard, comforting strength of his.

Her fingernails digging so deeply into the smooth, brown flesh of his back, he would have half-circle scratches come morning, Martay told him how scared she had been and how glad she was he had come so quickly and how she wished she had never left his tipi and asked would it be possible, did he think, for her to go back with him? At least for one night?

And all the while, as she spoke excitedly, relating what had happened, she was innocently pressing her slender, barely covered curves against a man who had, half an hour earlier, become aroused just thinking about her.

Above her golden head a pair of tortured black eyes slid half closed. Night Sun drew a labored breath, took her arm, and roughly set her back from him. She stared at him in puzzlement. Then it dawned on her that she was practically naked, and so was he.

His narrowed black eyes touched her breasts as her arms flew up to cross protectively over herself. Her wide green eyes were drawn to his exposed belly as his hand grabbed at the loosely hanging leather thongs of his half-unlaced buckskins. His eyes lowered to her long, slender legs, bare to mid-thigh. Her eyes climbed to the broad, smooth chest gleaming with a sheen of perspiration. Her breath grew short. His breath grew labored. She took a step toward him. He stood his ground. She didn't fight her rising emotions. He refused to give in to his.

Staring down the dangerous, stalking female swaying seductively closer, Night Sun snatched up a blanket and swirled it around Martay's bare shoulders. With one hand he held the ends together beneath her chin and said, in a voice gone as cold as his eyes, "Let's go. I'd like to get a little rest tonight."

Martay was not sure why he had so suddenly grown angry. But that was Night Sun. Kind and thoughtful one minute, cold and unreachable the next.

They trekked to his tipi in strained silence, and once inside, he remained mute, pointing a long finger toward her bed. She nodded and went there at once. Night Sun stretched out on his own bed and lay there in the darkness, still unable to sleep.

Damn her to hell! He couldn't sleep if she was with him, he couldn't sleep if she was not. Unreasonably angry, muttering oaths beneath his breath, he turned his back to her and closed his eyes. But he did not go to sleep.

Martay didn't suffer the same frustrations as her more worldly companion. Not yet awakened to full-blown sexuality, she never thought past kisses and caresses. So, feeling safe once more inside Night Sun's tipi, it was easy for her to drift toward slumber, even as she pondered Night Sun's warmth, then sudden coldness, back in Little Coyote's lodge. Sighing softly, thinking about his sullen, sensual lips, she turned her back to him and went to sleep.

Knowing the second her breathing changed, Night Sun turned onto his back and stared angrily at her. And he wondered, bitterly, who was actually the captive? Who the captor?

23

The next day a calm, cool Night Sun was again the one in control. While it aggravated him that a shallow, coddled creature like Martay Kidd could arouse him to the point of disturbing his rest, it was just that, an aggravation, nothing more. She was, as any man with eyes in his head could see, breathtakingly beautiful. And her seductive blend of insolence and vulnerability added to her erotic appeal. Still, it was only a physical thing. His body reacting to hers, nothing more.

Unworried and at ease, Night Sun stepped inside his tipi at midmorning, tossed a buckskin dress at Martay, and said, "Put this on. I'll show you around the village."

She didn't argue. Restless, eager to get outdoors, she smiled at him and said, "Turn your back."

"I'll do better than that." His voice was level, conversational. "I'll wait for you outside. But don't take all day."

Nodding at his retreating back, Martay jumped up and held the buckskin dress to her shoulders. The garment was entirely plain and shapeless. She frowned, sighed, and said aloud, "I wouldn't be caught dead in this thing!" And tossing it aside, she began the search for her own clothes. After several frustrating minutes, she found the neat bundle on the far side of Night Sun's bed.

White silk dress, high-heeled slippers, and torn stockings. The exquisite pearl necklace and earscrews were inside a pouch of soft leather.

"Martay, I'm waiting," came Night Sun's deep voice.

"In a minute," she called, and pulled the tight white silk dress over her head, smoothing the shimmering fabric over her curves. The stockings were past wearing, so she slipped her bare feet into the high-heeled slippers, and deciding the pearls were a bit too much for morning, left them inside their leather envelope. Hands behind her back, struggling with the gown's hooks, she hurried to a pine chest where she knew Night Sun kept his personal items. From atop it, she took a silver-backed brush and, pulling it through the tangles in her long, unruly hair, smirked, thinking that the handsome half-breed had most certainly transported some of the white man's handy tools to his wilderness camp.

"Martay," he called again, a trace of impatience in his voice.

"Coming," she said, and looking into his mirror, she bit her lips and pinched her cheeks to give them color, jerked at the low-cut bodice of her dress, fluffed at the cap sleeves, and went out to him.

"I'm ready," she proudly announced. His back was to her; he slowly pivoted. Never had she seen a pair of eyes change as swiftly as did his at that moment. Instantly they went from calm to fierce, and he took hold of her arm with such force, she almost lost her balance.

"What in the hell do you think you're doing?" he said, roughly shoving her back inside the tipi. Too stunned to speak, Martay shook her head in confusion. "Did you suppose I'd allow you to walk around this camp half-naked?" With each word his eyes became harder, colder, blacker.

"This is a stylish, expensive gown! You can't expect me to . . ."

"I expect you to keep yourself decently covered. Lakota women are very modest and they . . ."

"Well, I'm no damned Lakota woman and I refuse to go about in some hot, shapeless garment that does nothing for my coloring."

"You'll go about any way I tell you or stay inside this tipi for eternity. You're so vain . . ."

"I am not!" she hotly defended, "but the dress is . . ."

"The dress is coming off," he said, and taking her arm and jerking her about, he deftly unfastened the hooks she'd labored so painstakingly to close.

Insensed and insulted, Martay snapped acidly, "I'm a grown woman! You can't tell me what I'll wear." She slapped and clawed at the strong brown hands that were stripping the white gown from her body.

He didn't bother to reply, just kept on undressing her, no more bothered by her scratching than if a mosquito had attacked him. In seconds the white silk dress lay on the floor, and while Martay struggled Night Sun commandingly shoved her arms through the sleeves of the buckskin dress and lowered it over her head.

For a time she was caught inside; the smothering leather dress wrapped around her head and arms, hung there. Blinded and furious, she threatened him wildly until he took pity and jerked the buckskin garment down over her blond head. Her red, angry face appeared. He pulled the dress over her breasts and hips and was tying a belt around her waist while she continued to berate him hotly.

Breaking in, he said, "This will do nicely."

"It is shapeless and ugly, and I hate it!" She glared at him. "And I hate you as well."

"I can live with that."

"Well, I can't live with you," she shouted loudly, stepping

in to him, tipping her head back. "You are a stupid, arrogant savage!"

His jet-black eyes sharpened and he softly replied, "And you are a selfish, predatory bitch."

Refusing to allow the impossible, ill-tempered woman to embarrass him before his people, Night Sun waited until Martay's mood had softened, just as he had waited until she was properly, decently, dressed before he would take her outdoors.

Warning her that if she didn't wish to be imprisoned inside his lodge, she would keep a civil tongue in her head and behave as if she were a true lady, at last Night Sun ushered a docile Martay out into the brilliant Dakota sunshine.

It was almost noontime.

Martay looked around and inhaled deeply. Already the summer was dying; the deep azure sky had that autumn look about it. No hint of summer heat-haze. Just clean, crisp air and the slightest touch of morning coolness lingering even at this late hour.

Her anger forgotten, Martay marveled at the beauty surrounding her. It was her first venture outdoors since being brought, near death and unconscious, into the remote village. Windwalker's Powder River Lakota camp was pitched in a lush, high meadow along a protective, high ridge where colorful flowers spilled down the slopes and wild berries grew in abundance and birds sang sweetly from the branches of tall pines.

Walking along beside the tall, silent Night Sun, her eager eyes taking it all in, Martay commented, honestly, "I am pleasantly surprised. Your quaint home is really quite beautiful."

He cut his eyes to her, but he said nothing.

They were near the other tipis now, and dozens of Indians, men, women, and children, were outside, lined up in neat rows, as though they were expecting an important visitor to arrive. Suspicious dark eyes fastened on Martay. Instinctively moving closer to Night Sun, she whispered, nervously, "What are they doing?"

"Waiting to meet you," he said, and put a hand lightly at her back.

A sudden hush fell over the crowd. And there stood Windwalker, a powerful figure, invested with absolute authority over every man, woman, and child in camp. The chieftain was a man of great size, with a full head of black hair touched with gray, alert dark eyes, and large, amazingly gentle hands.

Martay, shaking the shaman's hand, recalled those kind, gentle hands touching her, caring for her through those foggy days and nights of raging fever.

"Thank you, Windwalker," she said, smiling at the Mystic Warrior, "for saving my life."

The chieftain's glittery eyes never wavered from hers as Night Sun interpreted. A hint of a smile spread over Windwalker's broad face, and his hand, still holding hers, tightened its grip for an instant.

Every eye in the village was on the two tall Lakota chieftains and the pretty blond woman. And when Night Sun guided Martay on through the camp, presenting her to his band, the morning promptly took on a festive air. Handsome half-naked brown-skinned children darted close to peer at her and to call to Night Sun. He flashed them the most incredibly disarming smiles, smiles Martay would have imagined him incapable of. Women twittered and giggled and looked from Martay to Night Sun, their gazes lingering on the dark chieftain, while the men nodded to them and smiled broadly and began to chant.

Leaning close to Night Sun, Martay, looking at the warriors and smiling appreciatively, whispered, "What are they saying?"

"Nothing, really. Foolish things."

"Tell me, please." She looked up at him.

"They are saying that you are lucky because . . . because

the returning mixed-blood chieftain is the bravest of all warriors. That no saber-toothed cat from the mountains nor sneaky Crow dog from the valleys can harm you so long as I have you."

"Mmmmm." The chants continued and Martay, smiling and nodding to the men, said, "What are they saying now?"

A muscle twitched beside Night Sun's full mouth and Martay could have sworn he flushed beneath his dark skin. "They say I am lucky too."

Martay felt exhilarated by the time Night Sun walked her back to his lodge. She had always enjoyed being the center of attention and she had certainly had that honor for the past couple of hours. She had been presented to every member of the tribe, and from the tiniest toddler, a boy called Slow One, to the oldest warrior, a deaf-mute named Speaks-Not-At-All, the Lakota Sioux of Windwalker's small band were clearly fascinated with Martay.

The Sioux were a handsome people. The village had more than its share of tall, strong-bodied braves and straight-backed pretty women. Cute, healthy children clung to their mothers' dresses and grinned at Martay. The warriors, married and single, looked on her with admiration, but with no hint of flirtatiousness. She supposed that was because they considered her the property of Night Sun. Some of the prettiest of the women stared at her with barely veiled expressions of jealousy, and it was not difficult to figure out why.

Of all the tall, strong warriors, none was quite as tall, quite as strong, quite as handsome, as Night Sun.

Typically female, Martay, relishing the envy she evoked, pointedly moved closer to Night Sun and, smiling charmingly up at him, slipped her hand around his arm, allowing her fingers to clutch possessively at his impressive rock-hard biceps.

She saw his black eyes flicker and read his thoughts. What is she up to now? But he didn't move her hand away, and Martay felt she had won a small victory of sorts.

Now, stepping inside the dim lodge, feeling wonderfully alive from the morning's excitement, she said happily, not wanting the pleasure to end, "What shall we do now?" She whimsically put her hands beneath her heavy blond hair and pushed it atop her head.

Night Sun drew off his shirt, tossed it aside, and picked up his rifle. "I'm going hunting."

The blond hair came cascading down around her shoulders. "I'll go with you."

"No you won't. I'm going with Lone Tree and some of the other braves. Women don't go hunting."

"When will you be back?" she asked, frowning.

He shrugged wide, bare shoulders. "Sunset."

"Sunset!" Her green eyes took on an angry glow. "What am I supposed to do all day?"

Laying the loaded rifle aside, he picked up the small, square mirror from atop the pine chest, handed it to her, and walked away, saying, "I'm sure looking at yourself all afternoon will be sufficient entertainment." He turned to face her.

"Oooh," she screeched, and hurled the mirror at his dark head.

His reflexes lightning-quick, his dark hand flew up and plucked the hurtling mirror from the air. Calmly placing it back atop the pine chest, he suggested, "Then why not join my grandmother in the . . ."

"I'm not about to spend my days with an old . . . with . . ." Her words trailed off and she looked fearfully at him.

His eyes held that wintry look. Coldly he said, "Then see if you can amuse yourself for once in your life." He picked up the rifle and was gone before she could reply.

Fuming, Martay stalked about after he'd left, growing angrier with each step, and hotter. Suddenly it was much too warm inside the close tipi. She rebelliously stripped off the hated buckskin dress, flung it on the floor, then flung herself down on her bed, thinking August in South Dakota was every bit as hot as August in Chicago.

Martay sat straight up.

August! She'd almost forgotten. It was August. What was today? The eighth or . . . no, the ninth. Only two weeks until her nineteenth birthday. She felt the familiar lump rise to her throat. She would spend her nineteenth birthday far from friends and family, with no presents or parties. No one here would even know it was her birthday. And back home they all thought she was . . . was . . .

Her hatred of Night Sun flamed anew. He was mean and cruel and insulted her at every turn. Handing her a mirror as though she were a foolish, vain, self-centered woman! Well, no one else thought she was. Well, except for Lettie, but . . .

Martay sighed wearily. Maybe she was a bit selfish, but who wasn't? Mr. Jim Savin Night Sun certainly was! He'd left her here to go off and enjoy himself, uncaring that she was alone and frightened and bored.

She ground her teeth. She was glad he had gone hunting, glad he was out of her sight, glad he wouldn't be back before sundown. She wished the selfish half-breed would stay gone forever.

Nothing would make her happier.

Astride the big black stallion, Night Sun rode away from the village, laughing, feeling more lighthearted than he had in weeks. It was good to be back with old friends. Good to roam these plains again atop a fast, responsive horse. Good to feel the hot Dakota sun beating down on his bare head and back.

With Lone Tree riding knee to knee with him, it was easy to forget the last four years had ever happened. That he had ever left his beloved Powder River home. Had ever gone East to Harvard.

That the beautiful Martay Kidd was waiting in his tipi,

because he had never met her, did not know that she existed. His bare, bronzed chest constricted and he dug his heels into the stallion's sleek flanks, determined he would forget, if only for a while, that she did.

24

When, the very next morning, Martay awoke to find that Night Sun had already departed, or else had never returned the night before, she felt her chest tighten with concern. A jolt of alarm slammed through her. If something had happened to him, what would become of her?

She shoved her hair behind her ears and hurried to get dressed. Not daring even to consider the white silk, she pulled the hated buckskin dress over her head, tied the belt at her waist with trembling fingers, crossed the tipi, and threw back the flap.

Barefooted, she headed anxiously up the path toward the center of the village, where only yesterday all the Lakotas had assembled to greet her and she had felt, for a brief time, almost happy. When she reached the edge of the clearing, Martay hesitated.

There was much activity in the village; people milling about, laughing, talking, horses neighing, dogs barking, campfires blazing. Unnoticed, she stood searching for that one dark face amid the others, her heart beating in her ears.

The minute he ducked out of a tipi on the east edge of the camp, she knew it was he. He crossed the clearing with those long, supple strides, and conversations lulled and every head turned. Smooth and powerful, he had that don't-fool-with-me presence she'd come to know so well, and to grudgingly admire. With his finely sculpted cheekbones and quick catlike movements, he radiated sheer magnetism that was impossible to ignore.

It was the first time Martay had ever been able to observe him without herself being observed by those piercing black eyes. Her finely arched brows knitted, she carefully studied the tall, lean copper-skinned specimen of manhood and felt her stomach flutter.

Night Sun reached a trio of men and stood, moccasined feet apart, hands shoved into his pants pockets, the soft buckskin shirt pulling across the hard, flat muscles of his chest. His raven hair, in need of a cut, touched his collar. His hard handsome face soon wore an expression of deep concentration as he stood and spoke quietly to the handful of nodding warriors.

All at once the fierce intensity was gone; his black eyes softened and he smiled that same brilliant smile she'd seen for the first time yesterday. It was so infectious, she smiled herself, and looked about for the child or children that had caused those wide, sensual lips to stretch into that appealing grin.

Abruptly, a couple of the warriors moved apart, opening up the small circle to her view, and Martay's smile fled.

A quartet of pretty dark-haired maidens had joined the braves; their presence was responsible for the swift change in Night Sun. If the women had lifted Night Sun's mood, they had the opposite effect on Martay. She felt suddenly betrayed and resentful. Foolish as it was, under such bizarre circumstances, she considered Night Sun to be hers.

Leaning against a heavily-leaved conifer for support, Martay shook her head at her own naiveté. How did she know that one of the women was not Night Sun's sweetheart? Anxiously she scanned the faces of the laughing, chattering women and felt her heart fall to her feet. Every one of them was pretty. And every one of them was looking up at Night Sun as though he were a god.

Martay's emerald eyes darkened with jealousy.

Her knees felt weak as realization swept over her. Night Sun had not returned to their tipi at sunset last evening as he had promised. When, finally, at well past midnight, she had fallen asleep, he still had not come home. And when she'd awakened this morning, he was not there.

Martay's eyes flew from him, across the camp to the tipi she'd seen him leaving. Was it the tipi of one of the pretty women standing with him now? The lodge of his sweetheart? His lover?

Green eyes rapidly turning greener, her narrowed gaze went back to the black-haired man who stood a head taller than the laughing, admiring girls surrounding him. Squinting, Martay observed each feminine face, sure she could pick the one who was Night Sun's sweetheart. It was easy, of course. She was the prettiest of the four. Small and delicate, her midnight hair, skillfully braided, reached well past her tiny waist. She looked very sweet, very quiet, very trusting, and Martay immediately surmised the small, pretty girl was exactly to Night Sun's liking. Someone he could order about as though she were a servant and she would obey him without complaint, as a well-trained puppy would. Then, after being bossed about all day, she was, at night, more than willing to allow him to . . . she would accept the burning kisses and . . . lie in the darkness and . . .

Martay spun around, half ill, and raced all the way back to their tipi. Inside she crumpled to the floor, clutching her churning stomach, while before her watering eyes swam visions of the small, beautiful Lakota girl, long braids unbound, lying naked in Night Sun's strong bronzed arms while he kissed and caressed and loved her through the long hot August night.

Two days later, boredom and bitterness mounting, Martay again strolled down into the camp. She'd not seen Night Sun for two days; she'd seen no one, and she was about to go mad. Cautiously peering at the sea of bronzed faces, she hunted his and, not finding it, asked a woman who was seated before a tipi and bent to some menial task if she knew where to find Gentle Deer.

The woman, unable to understand English, nonetheless smiled and nodded enthusiastically at the mention of the Gentle Deer's name. And she helpfully pointed. Martay looked in the direction of the pointing finger, then, shaking her head, turned back to the woman. "No. Not that one. I'm hunting Gentle Deer's tipi," she said. "Night Sun's grandmother. Gentle Deer."

The woman rose, bobbing her head, still smiling. "Gentle Deer," she said, and continued to point. She was pointing directly to the tipi Martay had seen Night Sun exiting two mornings before.

"Thank you," Martay said, and feeling a measure of relief, headed straight for the lodge. The flap was raised to the sun. Standing just outside, she hesitated, then called softly, "Gentle Deer, are you there?"

"Come in," came a deep, unmistakable male voice, and Martay felt the blood zing through her veins.

Blinking, she stepped inside the dim tipi and saw, lolling lazily on his stomach, elbows bent, chin supported in his hands, Night Sun. She felt a quick surge of affection slam through her. He looked for all the world like an innocent, precious little boy, his hair disheveled and falling over his high forehead, an appealing half-sleepy look to his hooded black eyes.

Near him sat his grandmother, mending a garment, smiling.

"I . . . I was . . ." Martay, feeling shy for the first time in her life, realized she was stammering and hated herself for it. "I wanted to visit Gentle Deer."

"I have been waiting for you to come," said the beaming, gray-haired woman. To her grandson: "Get up and make my guest welcome."

Night Sun stayed as he was. Almost imperceptibly he inclined his head, indicating Martay was to have a seat facing his grandmother.

When she started to sit, the blind woman said, "No, child, not way over there. Come closer."

Wondering how Gentle Deer knew how far away she was, Martay reluctantly came nearer and, dropping dutifully to her knees, frowned when Gentle Deer said, "A bit closer. Here, beside my grandson."

Martay obeyed, and found herself sitting not two feet from the sprawling sleepy-eyed man. Feeling ill at ease, she exchanged pleasantries with Gentle Deer, explaining she had meant to visit sooner but hadn't wanted to intrude. She saw Night Sun's heavy black brows rise accusingly at her lie.

Ignoring him, she made polite conversation with his grandmother, amazed at the aged Lakota woman's perfect command of the English language. As though she knew what Martay was thinking, Gentle Deer's sightless eyes crinkled at the corners and she said, "My grandson patiently taught me to speak the language of the white man." She looked fondly at him and added, "We had some good times playing school, did we not, Night Sun?"

"We did, Grandmother," he said, his drowsy eyes never leaving Martay.

Finding it hard to imagine Night Sun being patient with anyone, Martay said, puzzled, "But Night Sun just returned home. When . . . how did you learn English so rapidly?"

Gentle Deer's laughter filled the tipi. "I did not learn fast. Night Sun visit the white world each summer since he . . ."

"Grandmother," his slow, deep voice cut in, "explanations

are unnecessary." And he smoothly changed the subject, effortlessly catching, and holding, the interest of both women with an amusing tale of a prank his friend Lone Tree and the others had pulled on him up in the hills.

As she listened, Martay's eyes were drawn, of all places, to Night Sun's hard, lean buttocks as he continued to lie on his stomach. The fabric of his leggings stretched snugly across the taut flesh and she felt her throat go dry as he flexed his long legs and the muscles pulled and danced in his boyishly slim bottom.

It was the very first occasion when Martay imagined what it might be like to make love to Night Sun. Horrified that she could even consider something so scandalous, and at such an inappropriate time, she couldn't help herself. He was lying there flat on the floor, the firm muscles of his buttocks enticingly dancing and rippling under his buckskins, and Martay wondered how it would feel to be lying beneath him, to have his hard belly and slim hips pressing hers, his . . .

". . . and I assured him . . ." Night Sun stopped speaking. "Is something wrong, Martay?" he asked.

"What? No. No, nothing, I was just . . ." She swallowed, feeling the heat in her face, hoping to God he couldn't read her mind.

"You look a little warm," he said, and placing his palms flat on the floor, levered himself up. On his feet, he said, looking down at her, "Let's get some air." He put out his hand.

Still half lost in her guilty fantasy, she took it and, feeling the long, warm fingers close around hers, smiled dreamily at him, though she was speechless.

Outside he abruptly dropped her hand and said in a voice devoid of emotion, "I'll be gone today. You can either stay here with Grandmother or return to the tipi."

"No," she said, disappointed. "I don't want you to leave. Where are you going?"

"Never ask where I'm going," he said, his eyes chill. "If I

want you to know, I will tell you." He walked away. When he'd gone but a few steps, he paused, turned, and came back to stand before her. "Do you ride?"

"Horses?"

"What else?"

She brightened at once. "Why, yes, I do. I'm an expert horsewoman." She held her breath, waiting for an invitation to join him for a morning ride.

"Good for you," he said, and once more walked away from her.

Scar noisily sucked the last traces of meat from the bison rib, tossed it into the fire, and greedily grabbed another. When he'd finished a dozen of the succulent ribs, he wiped the juice from his scarred chin onto his calico shirtsleeve, belched loudly, and rubbed his greasy hands up and down on his muscular thighs, cleaning them on his soiled buckskins.

"Tell them they can come in now," he said to the Indian woman kneeling beside him.

Smiling, she invited the two waiting braves inside the army-issue tent that was pitched on a tree-sheltered bend of the Little Missouri River. Eagerly one brave pulled, from inside his shirt, a dog-eared envelope bearing a bright, shiny gold seal.

In his native tongue, he said, "You tell us if circle of gold have value?"

The Crow scout, full from a big meal, nodded with no enthusiasm. He had agreed to see the pair only because the woman now tidying his tent was the sister of one, and she had asked, just as she had crawled naked into his fur bed last night, if he would look at "a gold circle" her brother had found and tell him if it had worth.

Scar rubbed a coarse thumb over the shiny seal, then turned the envelope over. His beady eyes widened with interest when he saw the addressee: General William J. Kidd.

Pretending total nonchalance, the Crow scout unfolded the letter and read.

General Kidd:
   I have your daughter in a rock-concealed
   line shack exactly six miles northwest of
   Denver. Come alone within twenty-four
   hours and I'll trade her life for yours.
   Delay, and I will take her to the Dakota
   Territory.
   My bonafides? A scar down my chest
   from your saber. Remember Sand
   Creek, November 1864? I never
   forget.
   Night Sun
   Chieftain of the Lakota Sioux

Scar could hardly keep the excitement from his voice when he questioned the braves about how they had laid hands on the message. As they spoke, waving their arms, explaining how they'd killed the big prospector, the sturdy Crow scout was mentally counting his $10,000 reward.

"No value," he told the pair when he had learned all they knew about the letter. "None," he shook his head, and putting the letter back inside its envelope, unceremoniously tore it in two and tossed it into the fire, then motioned the disappointed pair away.

After they had gone, a broad smile slashed across his scarred face.

So the arrogant half-breed Sioux, Night Sun, had taken the general's daughter! Well, the general might get her back, but she wouldn't be the same, not after Night Sun had had her. No Indian ever hated the white man as much as that mixed-blood bastard.

Night Sun hated whites almost as much as he, Scar, hated Night Sun.

Scar's smile broadened.

As soon as he could learn where Night Sun had her, he would steal the golden-haired woman from his old enemy, collect the $10,000 reward, and be an honored hero.

The quick recollection of a fresh and pretty young girl standing in the morning sun at Fort Collins made the plotting Crow scout lick his lips in anticipation.

25

Martay glared at Night Sun's departing frame and wished she had not asked where he was going. She didn't care where he was going or when he would come back or if he ever came back!

But she watched until he was completely out of sight, and then, instead of returning to their lonely tipi, she started back inside Gentle Deer's lodge. With her hand lifted toward the flap, she hesitated, her attention caught by a maiden's happy laughter.

Martay froze.

The girl, small and beautiful, the very same one she had seen two mornings before smiling up at Night Sun, was rushing across the camp, hurrying in the same direction he had gone. She was going to meet him! The two of them were riding away from the village to . . . to . . .

"Peaceful Dove sounds far from peaceful this morning." It was Gentle Deer's firm, clear voice. Silently she had stepped up beside Martay. She was smiling, looking after the hurrying young maiden as if she could see her.

"Where is she going?" Martay wasted no time asking.

The old woman's face crinkled with pleasure. "She goes to say good-bye to her warrior; he will be gone all day. Then she will come to me and we will work on her wedding dress."

Martay felt her knees go weak and her heart sink. Dear God, Night Sun was marrying the girl! Speechless, she stood there watching as the laughing girl rushed after him. She felt a hand on her arm and Gentle Deer said, "Come inside. Keep me company today. Meet Peaceful Dove."

If there was anything she didn't want to do it was to spend the day with an old blind Indian woman and a young pretty one who was marrying the cold, heartless man who was holding her captive, but Martay nonetheless followed Gentle Deer back inside.

In minutes the beautiful young Lakota maiden, Peaceful Dove, joined them, and her eyes were so warm and friendly, it was impossible not to smile back at her when Gentle Deer introduced them. But Martay's jealousy flared as Peaceful Dove, undeniably one of the prettiest young woman she had ever seen, hugged Gentle Deer warmly, and chattering in the Lakota tongue, spoke Night Sun's name several times, her dark eyes flashing.

When the three women were seated, Gentle Deer reached behind her and brought forth a folded garment. Holding it up for Martay to see, she said proudly, "Peaceful Dove will wear this on the day she weds her brave, handsome warrior."

Her eyes clinging to the softest, whitest, prettiest leather dress she had ever seen, Martay could only nod and try to swallow and finally manage to say, "When is the wedding?"

Peaceful Dove understood the word wedding and happily answered, "The moon of drying grass."

Martay didn't understand a word she said. Gentle Deer repeated the words in English, then added, "September. Saturday, September twenty."

Only six weeks, Martay's busy brain shouted. In six weeks this beautiful smiling girl would be Night Sun's wife and he would bring her to their tipi and . . . and . . . What would happen to her then? And why had he brought her here?

Martay was confused and angry and jealous. But, for the first time in her life, she hid her true emotions. Forcing herself to smile back at the beaming Indian girl, she said, as calmly as possible, "I'm very happy for you and . . . and . . . Night Sun." Quickly Martay turned to Gentle Deer: "Please tell Peaceful Dove what I said."

The old woman chuckled. "Why are you happy for Night Sun?" she said. "Lone Tree is the one Peaceful Dove is to marry."

"Lone Tree?" Martay's eyes grew round. "You mean she's not . . . Night Sun isn't the . . ." Suddenly a weight lifted from her heart and Martay, looking straight at the pretty Indian girl, said, "Lone Tree?" The happy bride-to-be, hearing her beloved's name, nodded excitedly. "Oh, Peaceful Dove!" Martay said truthfully, "I am sooooo happy for you!" And she lunged over and hugged the other girl as though they were old, dear friends. Peaceful Dove, a placid, sweet young woman, hugged her back and said, *"Kola, kola."*

Gentle Deer gladly translated. "Friend. She is your friend."

"Yes," said Martay, "she is my friend!"

From that day forward, Martay spent her days with Gentle Deer. It was that or spend them alone, because Night Sun was rarely in camp. He never spent any time in their tipi. He rose early each morning, long before she awakened, and didn't return until late at night. More than one hot night she had lain awake listening anxiously for his footsteps only to fall asleep before he came. A couple of times she had half roused to see him across the tipi, his back to her, undressing in the shadows, and had lain there silent, trying to ignore the flash of bronzed muscular arms and long, lean legs before he stretched out in the darkness and promptly fell asleep.

That he was purposely avoiding her was all too evident,

and it baffled her. His coldness made her so angry that when their paths did cross, she went out of her way to be petulant and disagreeable. Once when Night Sun, in a hurry to be gone, complained that he couldn't find his canteen, Martay, poking fun at the customs of his people, tested his dark anger by saying "Why don't you just find it with your searching stones?" She was pleased to find she could still provoke him.

And provoke him she did.

His dark head snapped up. He spun around, whipped a fist out in the air and grabbed her by her belt. He jerked her up to him with such force, she heard the slap of leather on leather as their bodies collided. "I have," he said, his thinned lips only inches from her face, "had about as much of you as I can take."

Experiencing that familiar mixture of fear and excitement, Martay looked straight into his hard black eyes and, hoping to goad him into kissing her, said brazenly, "I don't think so. I think you'd like to take a lot more."

She trembled then, the heat of his closely pressing body enveloping her. Thrilling to the dangerous look in his eyes, she waited breathlessly, lips parted, anticipating his harsh, punishing kiss.

But Night Sun didn't kiss her.

His anger quickly changing to disgust, he said, "You're wrong. If I wanted more, I wouldn't have to take it." He set her back and released his grip on her belt. "You'd give it to me."

With his accusing words still ringing in her ears, Martay walked down the path toward Gentle Deer's, telling herself it was not true. She wouldn't give herself to him. Ever. She didn't want him; didn't even like him. Hated him.

And was no sooner inside the Indian woman's tipi than she was, as she did each day, asking questions about him. In only a few days she had learned more about the mysterious Night Sun from his grandmother than she had ever learned from him.

She had not learned, however, why she was with him.

Night Sun was, Gentle Deer told her, a "good boy" as well as a brave and handsome one. From the hour of his birth almost twenty-five autumns before, he had been the brightest spot in her universe. His father, a white trapper, had come to the Powder River Country one winter, and Pure Heart, Night Sun's mother, had fallen quickly in love with him. By the time the trapper left, promising to return, Pure Heart was carrying his child.

Martay had looked closely at the old woman's face as Gentle Deer calmly told of her unmarried daughter's becoming pregnant by the white trapper. Martay saw no censure, or shock, or displeasure on the weathered features. Only complete understanding and tolerance.

"A letter came for Pure Heart three months later," Gentle Deer went on. "James Savin wouldn't be returning to marry Pure Heart. He already had a wife, a white wife, who begged him to stay. He had told this wife about Pure Heart and his unborn child. He promised to help."

"Pure Heart must have been very sad," said Martay. "What did she do?"

"She grieved alone and never said anything against the man she loved. When she bore Night Sun, she gave all her love to him," said Gentle Deer. "And when the boy was old enough, she let him go to visit his father."

"Why? I would think she'd never . . ."

"She thought only of Night Sun. Not of herself. She wanted her son to know his white father."

Gentle Deer went on to tell an enrapt Martay that James Savin, Night Sun's father, had become a very rich man and that every summer from the time he was five years old, Night Sun was sent to spend some time with his father in Boston.

"My grandson knows the white man's numbers and letters," Gentle Deer said proudly. Martay only nodded, wanting her to continue. She did, saying that Night Sun had quickly learned English, was given music and art lessons, and was schooled in the customs and manners and dress of the white world. And when he became a man, she, Gentle Deer, persuaded Night Sun to take up his father's offer of a white man's education. So, at twenty, Night Sun, as bright as any young white man, went away to Harvard.

"By then," Gentle Deer explained, "James Savin's wife had died and he . . ."

Interrupting, Martay asked, "Why didn't Night Sun's father come back to Pure Heart after his wife died?"

Gentle Deer's sightless eyes lifted to Martay's face. "My daughter, Pure Heart, died long before James Savin's wife."

"Oh," Martay murmured, "I didn't know. How did it happen?"

"The bluecoats. They killed her at Sand Creek with the others."

Martay didn't dare breathe, much less ask where Sand Creek was and who the others were. Did the blind woman know that she was an American general's daughter?

Gentle Deer continued.

She told of the letters her grandson wrote while he was away, of his excellent marks at Harvard, of his hope to help his people by learning the law. She said that two winters ago Night Sun's father had died, leaving a large sum of money in trust for him, money he would receive when he turned twenty-five.

"He will be twenty-five in the moon of falling leaves," said Gentle Deer. "October."

She revealed many, many things about Night Sun, though never why he had captured Martay and brought her to his Dakota home. That remained a mystery and any time Martay asked about it, all she got was the wagging back and forth of Gentle Deer's gray head and Martay rightly guessed that the kind, aged woman didn't know.

Gentle Deer talked and talked, telling Martay something of her people's heritage, and while she did, she sewed beads on Peaceful Dove's wedding dress, her gnarled hands as deft and sure as if her vision were perfect.

Martay quickly grew fond of the wise old woman and little by little as the days went by, Martay, without even realizing it, began to adjust to life in a Lakota Sioux village. She still missed her home, her father and friends, but the luxuries she'd cut her teeth on seemed less important with each passing day.

It was no longer distasteful to eat the thin strips of meat that had hung in the sun to dry on racks. She was learning to like the bison jerky and often nibbled it while she listened to Gentle Deer speak of the old days. Gentle Deer taught her how to make pemmican. Seated under a shade tree, Martay enthusiastically pounded the jerked beef with a rock and then watched as Gentle Deer mixed the pounded meat with hot grease and dried berries. It was really quite tasty, and Martay was proud of her day's work.

With Peaceful Dove and Gentle Deer she went into the woods to pick wild grapes and chokeberries and raspberries, and upon commenting what a pretty day it was, heard Gentle Deer say, "In the autumn, when the Indian summer is upon us, there is no more beautiful place on earth than our beloved Powder River Country."

While Gentle Deer dozed on the banks, the two young women, kicking off their moccasins, jerked their dresses high and splashed out into a cold, clear stream, squealing and laughing like little girls.

And astride his gleaming black stallion, on a high point above on the river bluffs, a flint-faced Night Sun watched. Eyes only for the gilt-haired girl with the pale, perfect legs, he silently rebuked himself for coming here. He couldn't pretend he didn't know she would be here. He had visited his grandmother at sunup, long before Martay was awake, and Gentle Deer had told him she and the girls were going to Cave Creek to pick berries in the cool of the morning.

Night Sun shifted in the saddle.

Martay danced merrily about in the water for several minutes, going on and on about how glorious the cool water felt on her hot body. Feeling the heat in his own tensed body, Night Sun watched her climb out and, not bothering to lower her dress, spin dizzily about and collapse on the bank. She grabbed up a basket of the freshly picked berries, set it on her stomach, and choosing a huge, red raspberry, popped it into her mouth.

A sensual nymphet of the woods, Martay lay there in the grass, enjoying to the fullest the taste of the ripe, red berries and the heat of the hot Dakota sun on her face and bare legs.

Her long golden hair swirled about her head like a gleaming satin fan. Her luscious lips were stained red from the berries, and her pale, slender legs glistened with beads of water.

Night Sun, his dark gaze never leaving her, wasn't sure which he most longed to kiss.

The silky golden hair or the succulent red mouth or the bare creamy thighs.

26

"**Y**ou know why I summoned you here this morning?" Windwalker spoke in the Lakota tongue.

"Yes," said Night Sun, he, too, using their native language. "I have expected it."

Windwalker studied him with flat, dark eyes. "I have known you since the full-moon night of your birth. In all those summers, never have you behaved foolishly, as the other young braves." He let his words fall flat, the accusation in what was left unsaid.

Night Sun looked the aging tribal chieftain straight in the eye. "Now I have been unwise," he said. "I should not have brought the white girl here."

Windwalker slowly nodded. "This is true, my son. In so doing, you have put the entire Sioux nation in great peril." As he spoke, he lifted his arms and opened them in a wide encompassing gesture.

Night Sun suddenly felt a crushing sadness overwhelm him. Not because the Mystic Warrior was upbraiding him for his thoughtlessness, but because there was no longer "an entire Sioux nation" to be put into peril. Save for Windwalker's small band and one or two others hiding out in the hills, and Sitting Bull and Gall's people in Canada, all the mighty Sioux chiefs were dead or on the reservations, dancing to the white man's tune.

"Forgive me, Windwalker," Night Sun said, "I have acted as a white, not as a Sioux. I am sorry. What would you have me do to right this wrong?"

The older man's eyes softened with affection. "Do not look so sad, my son. The girl is unharmed; take her back to her people."

Night Sun swallowed hard. "I will do so. I can leave tomorrow at first light and . . ." A broad hand on his shoulder caused him to fall silent.

"No, Night Sun. Not tomorrow. Give her white father a couple of moons to worry. Then take her back." His dark eyes held understanding. "It is he who must suffer, not the girl. Do not harm her."

"No harm shall come to her." Night Sun paused, then added, "You know all, then?"

"That she is the child of the bluecoat who blinded Gentle Deer? I know. The gold hair, the green eyes. Is it not she?"

"It is."

The old chieftain opened his mouth as if to say more, decided against it, and abruptly brought the council to a close. "Go now and watch over the golden-haired one as if she were family. And when two moons have gone by, return her to her own family untouched."

"I will return her," said Night Sun, "just as she came to me."

"My heart is glad to hear you say so." Windwalker almost smiled then, and added, "The child-woman is handsome to look upon. As a young buck of only twenty-four summers, I am not sure I could have been trusted with her." He lifted his massive shoulders in a shrug.

Why do you think I stay away from her as much as possible? Night Sun silently replied. Aloud: "Again I offer my apology for putting our people in jeopardy. I will take the golden-haired one safely back and alone pay the price." He rose to his feet.

The old chieftain, looking up at him, said, "The price you pay may be a broken heart, my son." Night Sun looked at him questioningly, but he knew not to ask what the Mystic Warrior meant. "Go now," said Windwalker. The interview was closed.

It was late afternoon. A Saturday. The twenty-third of August. Martay Kidd's nineteenth birthday.

Alone in her silent tipi, she sat hugging her knees, trying very, very hard not to feel sorry for herself. It wasn't easy. Birthdays, from the time she was old enough to know what they were, had been very special to her. There had always been parties and presents and cakes and surprises.

There would be none this year.

No one even knew it was her birthday. She prided herself on the fact that she had told no one; counted it as a mark of maturity that she realized, without resentment, that these different people had no reason to celebrate her birthday. Here, unlike the world she came from, she was no more important than anyone else in the village.

Strangely, it didn't bother her too much. She was treated with kindness and respect, just as they treated each other, and she found herself treating others the same way. And there were times, at night when she was alone in her bed and thinking back to the old days, when she cringed recalling what a vain, foolish girl she had been.

Vanity had no place here, and that was odd, since these people—these proud Lakota Sioux—were universally conceded to be among the handsomest, most intelligent, and bravest of the Plains Indians. Physically and mentally superior, they were modest regarding their many attributes.

Martay found their attitudes unbelievable and refreshing,

and strove to be more like them, although she had far from mastered it yet. She was, after all, white and wealthy and used to admirers paying court.

Especially on her birthday.

So Martay was melancholy as she sat there alone in her tipi with no parties or presents or anyone to know or care that it was her nineteenth birthday.

Martay's head lifted from her bent arms when a shadow fell over the tipi opening. And her heart speeded when Night Sun's dark head appeared. Naked to the waist, he stood, for a long moment, looking down at her, an odd expression in his black eyes.

Then he said, "Come see what I've brought you."

Unable to believe her ears, Martay foolishly said, "You . . . you brought me something?" She remained seated there below him.

He smiled then and, bending from the waist, put his hands on her upper arms and effortlessly lifted her to her feet, which were bare. Looking down at the cute, naked toes, he said, "Where are your moccasins?"

Martay had no immediate answer. Used to servants, she had learned that keeping up with her own personal items was a hassle and more than once a hard-faced Night Sun had brought from his bed or from atop his chest or hanging on his lance an article of clothing she had carelessly tossed there.

Expecting him to be annoyed, she was relieved, and surprised, when he good-naturedly went in search of the missing moccasins. Finding one atop his fur bed, the other on the floor beneath his long-feathered war bonnet, he carried them to her and, ignoring the hand she reached out, crouched down before her.

"Give me your foot, Martay," he said, and his voice was level, pleasant.

She gladly obeyed. But when his long, warm fingers wrapped around her ankle and he lifted her foot, she grew so light-headed, she had to grab hold of his smooth bronzed shoulders to keep from falling. If he minded, or even noticed, he said nothing. He unhurriedly placed the moccasins on her feet, his dark head bent in concentration, his lean fingers brushing her sensitive skin, causing sweet sensations of pleasure.

Reflexively, her clasping hands tightened on him, sliding up closer to the curve of his neck and shoulder. Beneath her fingers the tendons tensed and corded and slowly Night Sun raised his head to look up at her. His hands circled her ankles, then slid slowly up her legs. In seconds his warm fingers were wrapped around the backs of her trembling knees.

"Night Sun," she managed weakly, her heart pounding furiously.

His black, tortured eyes slid closed and a strange sound came from deep inside his bare chest. He jerked her to him, and Martay cried out with shocked pleasure when he buried his dark face against her stomach and his questing hands moved up to cup the cheeks of her bottom.

He held her for only a second. One short never-to-be-forgotten second he clung to her as though he would never let her go, and Martay's assaulted senses recorded all the fleeting wonder of that moment.

Her hands went up into his silky black hair as she pressed his face more closely to her quivering belly, feeling the heat of his breath burning through the dress she wore, loving the way his big strong hands had moved intimately under her satin underwear to possessively clutch her bare, tingling buttocks.

As swiftly as it had happened, it was over.

He released her and rose, a faint residue of heat remaining in his beautiful black eyes.

"Sorry," he said, his voice as controlled as ever. "I'm sorry."

"But it's all right, I wanted . . ."

"No," he broke in, and vigorously shook his dark head, stepping away from her. "Come outdoors." He exited the tipi, not waiting for her.

Martay lingered for a brief time, puzzling over what had happened, and why he had stopped. Before she had time to come up with any answers, he was calling to her. She took a deep breath and hurried out.

Stone-faced, Night Sun stood between two horses. One was the magnificent black he rode, the other a shimmering sorrel. While the big black nipped playfully at his bare shoulder, Night Sun, holding the reins of the sorrel, said, "It's yours, Martay."

Martay stared at him. "You mean it? You're giving this beautiful horse to me? Why?"

His face softened at last. "Mare. It's a mare."

"I knew that," she said, coloring. "But why would you give me a mare?" She eagerly stepped forward to stroke the mare's velvet muzzle, smiling happily.

"Happy Birthday," he said softly.

Her eyes flew from the nickering mare up to Night Sun's dark face. Extremely pleased that he'd remembered and had surprised her with such a wonderful present, Martay impulsively threw her arms around his neck and thanked him.

"I love her! Oh, Night Sun, thank you, thank you!" Her cheek pressed to his, she couldn't see the mixed emotions reflected in his black eyes; was too excited to notice the minute trembling of his tall frame against her. Giving him one last eager squeeze, Martay kissed his smooth jaw and released him, saying, "May I ride her now? Where shall we go? Oh, I can't wait to . . ."

"I am busy, I can't . . ."

"Busy? But it's late afternoon." She gestured toward his bridled stallion. "If you didn't mean to ride with me, why did you bring the black?"

"I . . . ah . . . there's somewhere I must go." He didn't tell her that she had guessed correctly. He had meant to ride with her, but now he knew he couldn't trust himself. What had happened inside would happen again if he didn't stay away from her. And next time he had his arms around her . . .

"Let me go with you, Night Sun," she said. "I'll be no trouble, I promise." Her emerald eyes held a soft, pleading look.

"No," he said. "Beginning tomorrow you may ride each morning if you like. Speaks-Not-At-All will escort you."

Disappointed, she toyed with her new mare's bridle. "And will you ever ride with me?"

Night Sun didn't reply. He took the reins of both horses and led them away while Martay looked wistfully at him.

Sighing, she went back inside and flung herself down on her bed. And then it struck her. Night Sun knew it was her birthday. How? She had told no one. What else did he know about her? And where had he learned it? Who was this strange half-breed and what did he want from her?

She closed her eyes, opened them, and tried not to think about how she felt when he had knelt before her and crushed her anxiously to him. And could think of nothing else. Smiling dreamily, her senses stirred, Martay rightly surmised that if only she could find a way to be around Night Sun more often, something similar might happen again. Like the light of a new day dawning, it was suddenly clear to her that Night Sun stayed away from her on purpose. And she knew the reason why.

Martay's dreamy smile widened and she was far from unhappy on her nineteenth birthday.

Her happiness didn't last.

Night Sun returned the next morning, leading the new sorrel mare. Martay excitedly rushed out to meet him, hoping for a continuation of yesterday's pervasive magnetism between them. There was none.

He was distant and impatient. Accompanying him was the aged old brave Speaks-Not-At-All, leading a paint pony. Night Sun inclined his dark head to the old man. "Speaks-

Not-At-All is merely mute and deaf, not stupid. Don't treat him as though he were."

"I would never . . ."

"Yes, you would," he cut her off. "I hold him responsible for looking after you, so don't make it hard on him." Unceremoniously, he reached out, plucked Martay from the ground, and lifted her astride the saddled sorrel mare. "Give him trouble and you'll quickly answer to me."

"Why would I cause him any trouble?" she said, annoyed that he automatically assumed she would create problems for the old brave.

Night Sun shrugged, brought the reins over the sorrel's neck, and handed them to her. "If you have foolish notions of giving Speaks-Not-At-All the slip, let me warn you, there are dangerous renegade Crows hiding out in this valley."

"I'm not afraid," she said, and clicking her tongue to the mare, dug her moccasined heels into its flanks, anxious to be away from the dark, disagreeable man.

Night Sun's arm shot out and he grabbed the mare's bridle, halting its movement. He stepped up close to Martay, clutched the calf of her leg, and said, "Of course you aren't afraid. You're far too ignorant. But I'm warning you, if those Crows ever get their hands on you, you'll pray for death." He released her leg and nodded to Speaks-Not-At-All. The old warrior, standing stoically beside his paint pony, nodded back and climbed atop the paint's bare back. Night Sun's gaze swung back to Martay.

Wondering how she had ever imagined she could care for this sullen, insulting savage, Martay leaned close to his ear and said, "You know something, Night Sun. I don't like you!" And she jerked up on the long leather reins, wheeled her mare about, and thundered away. Speaks-Not-At-All followed right behind her.

Hands on his slim hips, Night Sun stood watching the pair gallop toward and soon disappear over the slope of the near horizon. Wondering how he could have, only yesterday, felt himself in danger of caring for such a belligerent, bothersome bitch, he said, "Good, goddamnit. I don't want you to like me."

27

Trembling with anticipation, she let her fingers flutter admiringly across his broad, bare chest and down his belly. He lay flat on his back, smiling with pleasure, his hand idly stroking the arch of her hip. Naked in the afternoon August heat, their bodies glistened with a fine sheen of perspiration.

Lazily he reached for her unbound hair and combed his fingers through its shimmering length. She lowered her mouth to his and licked at his full lips, teasing him, toying with him, until his fingers tightened in her flowing hair and he forced her mouth more fully to his, kissing her deeply, hungrily.

When finally their lips separated, she inhaled deeply, put her hands atop his wide shoulders and slid slowly, sensuously up and down his prone body until he anxiously grabbed her and rolled over, pushing her onto her back and moving atop her.

Inflamed, she murmured her gratitude when he swiftly took her once again, the third time he had enthusiastically made love to her since the noon hour. Anxiously, eagerly, they moved together, she admiring the contours of his passion-hardened face, he with his eyes tightly closed; and when their climax began, both were so lost in the lusty act and were making so much noise, they didn't hear the approaching horses.

But when, sated and breathless, they quieted and fell apart, she heard male voices and momentarily froze. Then, scurrying from the bed, she ran across the spacious room and, hiding behind the heavy drapery, cautiously peeked out.

Dropping the curtain as if it were afire, she flew back to the bed, repeating worriedly, "Oh, my God! Oh, my God!"

The big, tired man in the bed lazily opened his eyes and saw her stricken face. Alarm surging through him, he nervously swung his long legs over the bed's edge.

"What is it, Regina?"

"Larry, Larry, they're back! My husband and your father, they've come home!"

"No!" he said, not wanting to believe it, unease tightening his chest. "Dad's not due back from Denver for a couple of days and Colonel Darlington will be at Fort Collins with General Kidd until . . .

"They are both right downstairs! Quickly, put on your trousers and get out of my bedroom!"

"Regina, we're not in your room. We're in one of the guest bedrooms."

"Oh, dear God, where are my clothes?"

Martay found the wrinkled, mahogany-skinned old brave Speaks-Not-At-All to be the perfect riding companion. He could neither speak nor hear, so he smiled and nodded agreeably to anything she suggested. It made for some very satisfying one-sided conversations, allowing her to get a lot of things off her chest without the danger of her innermost thoughts being repeated.

That first morning she and Speaks-Not-At-All rode up onto, then along, the ridge paralleling the village, winding along the heavily timbered bluffs, looking at the busy camp below. After traveling less than a mile, Martay pulled up on her sorrel mare's reins, turned in the saddle to look at the old warrior, and hesitantly ventured, "I think your surly half-breed chieftain, Night Sun, is a real pain in the neck, don't you?" She favored him with one of her most appealing smiles.

Speaks-Not-At-All, anxious to be congenial, bobbed his head up and down and smiled back at her.

"I thought you'd agree. Has he always been such a moody bastard?" Again she smiled. Again he nodded, and she knew she'd found the sounding board for all her pent-up feelings.

Never one to keep things to herself, Martay told the trusted old warrior exactly how she felt about everything. Told him she was still in the dark and baffled by what had happened. That she didn't understand her capture; couldn't figure out why Night Sun hadn't ransomed her to her father.

And stroking the mare's sleek neck, she added as an after-thought that she couldn't fathom how Night Sun knew it was her birthday and why, when it was obvious he liked her no more than she liked him, he would give her something as valuable as the beautiful sorrel mare and hand-tooled Mexican saddle.

Two mornings later, while she and Speaks-Not-At-All stopped to water their horses, she wound the long reins around the saddlehorn and, lifting her hot hair up off her shoulders, said truthfully, "Speaks, I am so confused, I think sometimes I must be going crazy." He nodded and smiled at her. "You see, I know I should hate Night Sun, and I do, of course I do, but . . . but . . . there are times I . . . I feel as though"—she released her hair and shook her head, then continued— "Oh, Speaks, at times I think I love him. Can that be possible? Can I actually love a man I don't understand, a half-breed who has cruelly kidnapped me and brought me here against my will and treats me now as though I don't exist?"

Martay's smile had slipped as she spoke and her voice had

lowered, her tone grown wistful. She looked up to see the old brave studying her face, an expression of concern in his kind old eyes. Quickly she laughed and said, "You're right. It isn't love I feel for him. It's just that he's . . . well, let's face it, Speaks, he is the kind of man women find intriguing. He's brooding and somber and silent so much of the time, I can't help but wonder what he is thinking. Please tell me it's only natural for me to be helplessly attracted to him." She nodded her head, and taking her lead, he nodded and smiled eagerly, his watery black eyes twinkling.

"I'm glad you feel that way. I've been so worried, but that's foolish. Night Sun, for all his dark, masculine good looks, is cold and uncaring and I could never love a man like that. I feel better knowing we've got this cleared up. Thank you, Speaks. I appreciate your help. I'm glad you can see that he cares for no one but himself."

That same afternoon Martay, seated alone before Gentle Deer's tipi, looked up to see Night Sun, tall and commanding, striding unhurriedly through the camp, his hard, handsome face set, that all-too-familiar aura of impenetrability about him.

A near-naked little boy went running straight at Night Sun, and Martay was watching when the laughing, screaming child reached the unsmiling, silent man. In an instant Night Sun's face changed and he immediately crouched down, captured the tiny boy between his knees, and cupping the small, dark head in lean, gentle hands, gave his dirty, laughing face a kiss.

Martay blinked in disbelief.

And watched, entranced, as Night Sun teased and tickled the child, his own eyes crinkling at the corners, love and laughter shining from their black depths. Martay felt a lump form in her throat as tiny pudgy hands lifted to affectionately pat Night Sun's dark face and Night Sun made no move to avoid the poking, probing fingers, instead laughed heartily.

She caught herself smiling when Night Sun lifted the tiny

boy up and kissed his smooth chest, then playfully blew and bit on his bare tummy, snorting and growling loudly while the child squealed with delight and pulled Night Sun's raven hair, begging him to stop.

Only to beg him to do it "one more time" when Night Sun lifted his head.

As the long, lovely Indian summer days went by, Martay saw other signs of a gentle man beneath a foreboding exterior. She spent every waking hour, save for her morning rides with Speaks, at Gentle Deer's tipi and so was present, on more than one occasion, when Night Sun visited his grandmother. No man could have been kinder to the aging woman than he. He worried if he heard her cough, threatened if she didn't eat properly, listened intently, never showing any of his usual impatience, when she spoke fondly of the old days, recounting stories she'd told numerous times before. He was respectful, thoughtful, and affectionate, not embarrassed to kiss and hug his grandmother when he entered and left her lodge.

That he was idolized by the tribe was apparent. The braves looked to him as a leader, second only to Windwalker, none displaying any jealousy of his position, only complete loyalty and faith. The women looked on him as a benevolent god, the married ones felt honored if he took a meal with their families, the single maidens were awed by his physical beauty and air of command. The children worshiped him, sensing in him a kindred spirit, a boy at heart who loved to wrestle and shout and play just as they did.

The longer Martay observed him, the more in love she fell, and watching him with his people, the people he cared for and protected, Martay realized it was more than purely physical attraction she felt for him. Night Sun was a very lovable man. A remarkable man. A considerate, kind, thoughtful human being.

To everyone but her.

Determined she would change that, Martay went out of

her way to be more like the gentle, sweet-tempered people he loved so well. Taking her cue from them, she stopped complaining, stopped being argumentative, stopped being lazy. She was congenial, dependable, and industrious, and if Night Sun didn't notice, Gentle Deer did.

She praised Martay on tasks well done and asked if she would like a pretty new dress for Peaceful Dove's wedding. At once Martay said, "Oh, Gentle Deer, I do! I want a soft white dress as lovely as Peaceful Dove's."

"This cannot be, Martay. You are not the bride."

"No . . . I . . . I am sorry, I . . ."

"Do not apologize. I have a doeskin of palest beige; is soft as the velvet collar on the great coat my grandson once wore home from Boston. I have been saving it. We will make your dress from it."

Martay brightened. "Will you show me how to sew beads on it?"

The old woman reminded her, "When first you come to my lodge, you did not wish to learn."

"I know, but I've changed a lot since then, don't you think?"

Gentle Deer studied her thoughtfully with sightless eyes and said softly, "Don't change too much, child."

"Why not?"

Gentle Deer simply looked at her, a mysterious smile lifting the corners of her drooping mouth.

After her horseback ride each morning, Martay could hardly wait to get to Gentle Deer's. The new dress required a lot of time-consuming work and the wedding was less than two weeks away. She was looking forward to the big celebration along with the rest of the village and was still vain enough to want to be the prettiest woman there.

Well, the prettiest, after the bride.

Excitement rose as the day approached and she saw her

soft doeskin dress grow more beautiful with every colorful bead she painstakingly sewed to its yoke. As she sewed, she pricked her fingers more times than she could count, but refused to give in to the impulse to swear and complain and toss the garment aside.

It was to be a special occasion with all the Windwalker band in attendance. Including the elusive Night Sun. So Martay wanted, very much, to look so pretty, she couldn't keep from attracting his attention at the celebration and hoped the dress might help do the trick.

"Tell me again what the wedding festivities will be like, Gentle Deer," Martay said, and paused to suck at a pricked forefinger. She listened intently as Gentle Deer told of the feast and singing and dancing that would last until far into the night. So caught up was Martay, she didn't realize that Night Sun had come silently into the tipi and stood quietly behind her, listening too.

His grandmother knew he was there. Was even aware of the unguarded tenderness in his eyes as he looked down on the golden head below him. Felt the sweet aching in his heart as though it were in her own. Knew the instant Martay became aware of his presence.

And smiled when Martay, leaning her head way back, supported her weight on stiff elbows, looked smilingly up at him, and said, almost shyly, "Night Sun, will you dance with me at the wedding celebration?"

Gentle Deer was certain her grandson smiled warmly down at Martay when he answered, "Yes, my *Wicincala,*" then backed away and left.

Martay slowly lowered her head. *Wicincala.* He called her *Wicincala.* He had called her that once before, though she had forgotten about it until now. Now, as he said it, she remembered. It was when she was sick and he was bringing her to Windwalker. He'd had on that black tuxedo and they were atop his black stallion. She'd asked him not to let her die and he had said, "I won't, *Wicincala*. Never."

"Gentle Deer, what does my *Wicincala* mean?"

"Little girl," said the Indian woman, "my pretty little girl."

28

Saturday. September 20, 1879. A perfect Indian summer day on the east fork of the Dakota Territory's cold, clear Powder River.

Martay awoke with a start, turned her head quickly, and was relieved to see that Night Sun had already gone. She didn't want to see him today, not until they met at the wedding of Peaceful Dove and Lone Tree.

Full of energy and hope, she scrambled from her soft bed of furs, hurriedly washed her face and teeth, and drew one of her plain buckskin dresses over her head. Adhering to the new regimen she had set for herself, she fought the strong impulse to let the tipi chores go for the day, and instead went about tidying up, humming to herself as she picked up their clothes, swept the floors clean, and dusted the pine chest by Night Sun's bed.

She had been tempted, more than once, to look inside the chest where the man she loved kept his personal things, but she'd never given in. Hesitating now, she told herself she wasn't snooping, she wanted to give Peaceful Dove her fine pearls and earscrews for a wedding gift, and Night Sun had told her he would keep the jewels for her, in the top drawer of his chest. She could have them any time she pleased.

She pleased today.

So Martay didn't feel like an intruder when she opened the drawer and took from it the pearls. When she lifted the smooth leather envelope containing the jewels, her attention was drawn to a faded picture beneath. Eyes wide with curiosity, she lifted it from the drawer and studied the couple in the yellowing photograph.

A strapping, handsome man with dark hair stood with his arm around a tiny, beautiful Indian girl, a girl with the same eyes as Night Sun's. Black, beautiful eyes, looking up at the tall man with unveiled adoration.

Martay needed no one to tell her that the handsome pair were Night Sun's parents. Carefully lowering the crumbling photograph back to its place, she stopped and blinked when she saw another likeness smiling up at her.

A picture of herself.

Martay drew a shallow breath and nervously looked about, making certain she was still alone. Satisfied that she was, she eagerly lifted the newspaper article topped with the picture of her, only to see more pictures, more stories. Night Sun had apparently been tracking her movements from the moment she had reached Denver.

But why? Dear God, why?

Shaking her head in puzzlement, she skimmed some of the articles, then put them back where she'd found them, and saw a long, flat piece of black velvet, folded like a tall, narrow book. Intrigued, she let her fingers slide down its supple length, then curiously opened it.

Her face went hot, then cold, and hot again.

Lying on its specially cut bed of midnight-black velvet was a fragile ivory flower. A flower that had once been fragrant and seductive in the hot summer night. The long-stemmed white gardenia she had carried the night Night Sun took her from the Darlington party.

Martay's knees trembled and she felt for a moment she might cry.

The unpredictable Night Sun had saved her gardenia as though it were precious to him. He'd cut the black velvet collar from the great coat Gentle Dove had told her of, and had fashioned a luxurious resting place for the pressed flower.

"My Darling," Martay said aloud, and placed the flower, inside its black velvet covering, back exactly as she had found it.

Her heart sang as she hurried to Gentle Deer's lodge. And it continued to sing while she and the other young maidens readied the honeymoon tipi with sweet sage and *wacanga* to purify the newlyweds' first home. It continued to sing when, as a group, they went for Peaceful Dove, and together the six of them made their way to the river to bathe and wash their hair for the ceremony.

At last it was time for the wedding.

Martay did not wear her beautiful new doeskin dress. It hung, waiting, in Gentle Deer's lodge, where she would go at sunset to change for the big dance. For now she wore only a plain, serviceable dress, and her hair, parted in the middle, fell loose about her shoulders.

At straight-up noon, Windwalker seemed to appear out of nowhere. He wore no fancy garb, no shirt; his massive muscular shoulders and arms were bare. A hush immediately fell over the assembled crowd and everything took on a dreamlike quality.

Standing in a big open space under the clear blue sky, Martay watched as the strange, compelling ceremony unfolded. There was an altar. There was a peace pipe and lots of smoke. There was a bloodred blanket wrapped around the shoulders of Peaceful Dove and Lone Tree. Their wrists were bound together with a cloth and they clasped the sacred pipe, the aromatic smoke from the *kinnickinnick* swirling about their heads.

Windwalker, in his deep, bass voice, sang prayers over the happy couple, and although Martay could not understand his words, his powerful voice was beautiful and somehow very soothing.

While everyone's undivided attention was on the shaman and the wedding couple, Martay allowed her gaze to slowly sweep about, looking anxiously for that other mystifying man —the man who had kept and carefully pressed a gardenia because it had belonged to her.

He was easy to pick from the crowd. Taller by half a head than the braves surrounding him, Night Sun stood looking, not at Windwalker, not at the wedding couple, but directly at her. She'd caught him staring at her before, but always he'd hastily looked away. This time he didn't. He continued to stare at her with an unblinking intensity she could feel touch her as though his hands were on her.

His fierce scrutiny still scared her, maybe it always would, but it thrilled and pleased her as well. He cared for her, she knew he did, just as she knew that before another sun rose over his beloved Dakota Territory, she would be his in every way whether he was hers or not.

Trembling inside, she finally broke their locked gazes, forcing herself to look away, to return her attention, and her thoughts, to the wedding ceremony at hand.

"Walk hand in hand with the Great Spirit," Windwalker told the happy couple in Lakota and so brought to a close the somber rites.

If the impressive ceremony had been spiritual, with much mysticism and calling on the *Wakan Tanka,* the remainder of the festivities were of an earthly nature.

There was a huge, leisurely feast with juicy roasted elk and bison and vegetables and fresh berries. People were giving presents to the newlyweds, and when finally it was Martay's turn, she stepped forward and presented her pearls to them, the only thing she had to give, and a beaming Peaceful Dove kissed her cheek and called her sister, causing tears to spring to Martay's green eyes.

There was much laughter and joy and happiness. And before she knew it, it was time for everyone to go to their lodges and dress for the dance.

She searched anxiously for Gentle Deer, spotted her, and hurried to escort the blind woman back to her lodge. Once inside, Martay eased the tired Gentle Deer down to the floor, and went across the tipi to pull the flap securely closed. She then hurriedly stripped off the hot buckskin dress as well as her worn satin underwear. Wishing for a filled bathtub, or even for another bath in the cold river, she knelt naked before the pan of cool water Gentle Deer had provided, and washed her flushed face, her hot throat, her bare shoulders.

While she and Gentle Deer talked of the day's pleasures, Martay sponged her full, high breasts, coloring as they peaked into tight little buds when Gentle Deer mentioned Night Sun's name. Glad his grandmother could not see, she continued to bathe her heated flesh, wanting every inch of her body to be fresh and clean.

At last she rose, and stepping into the downy soft underwear Gentle Deer had made, she hesitated, unsure. The brief underpants were all; there was no chemise, nothing to cover her breasts. A soft chuckling made her turn her head.

Gentle Deer said, "Do not frown, child. The doeskin dress will cover you. Come, I will help with your hair. It is not necessary to wear the underwear unless you wish."

"I wish," answered Martay, and came to sit before the other woman.

As deftly as any sighted person, Gentle Deer drew Martay's long, heavy hair to the back of her head and began meticulously plaiting it into one plump, gleaming braid.

Naked save for the tiny doeskin underpants, Martay patiently sat there on her heels, feeling as though she might explode with excitement. Wishing Gentle Deer would hurry, not daring to say so, she imagined what it would be like when Night Sun saw her in the new dress.

At last the perfect braid was finished. Gentle Deer carefully wrapped the plait's end with strips of black velvet—velvet from the same source as that which cushioned a wilted gardenia—and placed her aged hands atop the bare shoulders of the girl before her.

She said, "I have fixed your hair like our people's because that is what you want." She gently squeezed Martay's shoulders and added, "But if he wants it loose and flowing, then let him have his way."

Martay turned her head as her speeding heart almost beat its way out of her bare bosom. She started to ask who, but didn't.

"I will," she said, and rose and went to get dressed.

The velvety doeskin dress felt soft and silky against her flesh. Looking into the mirror she had brought from Night Sun's lodge, she thought it was as beautiful as any fancy ball gown she had worn in the old days.

Tight across her breasts and hips, its yolk was decorated with narrow lines of colorful beadwork and dentalium shells. Around her narrow waist she tied a long belt with silver disks known as conchos. On her feet she wore fringed knee-high moccasins. Smiling at herself with pride and pleasure, she felt somehow new and good and different. A chill of expectation skipped up her spine and she softly laughed, thinking she was becoming like the Indians. She, too, could see things before they happened.

Could see that this night was to be a special one in all her life. Knew that she would indeed feel even more new and good and different by morning. She'd heard Night Sun say that white men saw so little, it was as if they used only one eye. Well, she was using both eyes now and she saw the two of them together. Night Sun and her. For the night or for a lifetime? That much she couldn't see.

Uncaring, she whirled about announcing, "I am ready, Gentle Deer."

"Are you?" said the blind woman, and Martay knew what she meant.

They joined the others just as the September sun was setting behind the distant Bighorn Mountains. Already the singing and chanting had begun and a handful of half-naked braves were dancing before a huge, newly built fire. Laughing maidens were clapping their hands and the old people were seated about on blankets, ready for an evening of fine entertainment. The beaming bride and bridegroom sat in a place of honor, watching the merrymakers.

Dropping Gentle Deer's hand at the edge of the crowd, Martay began to clap and pat her foot. In moments her hands, and her foot, stilled, her heartbeat quickened. She had become aware of Night Sun's presence, a presence so compelling, she could feel his nearness. As if guided by his silent command, she turned completely around, saw him at once, and felt her throat go dry.

He stood alone and apart, on a gentle rise fifty feet from her, a long, bare arm raised over his head, hand clasping the bough of a cottonwood. He, too, had changed his garb. Gone were the buckskin leggings and the fancy fringed shirt and the moccasins.

His tall, lean frame was covered with only a brief cream-colored breechclout and he looked more naked than clothed. Criss-crossing his bare chest were bandoliers decorated with buttons, elk teeth, and mother-of-pearl disks. His lengthening raven hair, glinting blue in the dying sunlight, was held back with a tight red headband, a few silky strands lifting in the gentle breeze from the river.

High on each leanly muscled arm was a wide band of polished copper, and anklets of shells adorned his bare feet. His skin was smooth and bronzed, and the sight of his bare, firm thighs and long, graceful legs, touched with the dying rays of the sun, made Martay long to run appreciative fingers from his naked hipbone all the way down to his bare, bronzed toes.

A savage lord. Arrogantly he stood there, feet apart, as still as a statue, the perfect male body outlined against a flaming apricot sky. In wonder Martay stared, and knew, at that moment, the reason she had never really cared for any other man; because the man she had always wanted, the man she had waited for, was standing there in all his splendid glory.

Primitive and proud and beautiful.

Someone grabbed Martay's arm as the sun slipped completely out of sight. Reluctantly tearing her eyes from Night Sun, she smiled warmly at the maiden, who was inclining her head toward the dancers. Nodding her understanding, Martay joined the revelers, watching and mimicking their footwork. Within minutes she had the intricate steps down and laughed nervously when someone handed her a gourd rattle.

The fire blazed high in the night sky. The drums pounded a provocative beat. Warriors passed bottles of wine around. Martay shook her gourd rattle, tossed her head about, but moved her body only slightly.

Night Sun came down to join the fun. He stood at the edge of the crowd, smiling easily, accepting drinks of wine and watching Martay dance. She looked stiff and embarrassed, out of her element. But beautiful. Breathtakingly beautiful. The soft doeskin dress clung to her high, lovely breasts and shapely bottom, and Night Sun was almost glad she was not completely at ease; if she relaxed and danced with the abandon of the People, she would be far too seductive.

Night Sun said yes to the offer of the whiskey being passed around and felt it burn down into his bare chest and arms. He was watching when one of the maidens handed a couple of *uncela* buttons to Martay. His first inclination was to step forward and warn her against the effects of the peyote. He stayed where he was. He would keep an eye on her. If she nibbled one or two of the buttons it would do her no harm. So long as she didn't accept more.

Having no idea what the girl had given her, Martay popped the tiny seed into her mouth and chewed, making a face at its bitterness. But the bitterness passed and she began to feel even better than before. She felt wonderful; alive and warm and happy. And relaxed; totally, completely relaxed, yet filled with a brand-new kind of excitement and joy.

Night Sun caught himself applauding when Martay began to dance more recklessly, her reserve quickly slipping away. Warmed by the whiskey and the fire and the sight of Martay sensuously swaying before him, he felt his own reserve slipping away, and his judgment with it.

He wanted the beautiful golden-haired white girl.

Had wanted her from the beginning. And he could have taken her any time he chose, but never had. How many nights had he lain there in agony, not touching her, though she slept not twenty feet from him. Why? What for? What difference did it make?

There was no longer any need for rape. He wouldn't be taking her with force, against her will. He could see in her expressive green eyes that she was his for the taking. So why not take her? After all, it wasn't as if he would be the first. He had told Windwalker he would return Martay to her people just the way she had come to him. He could do that and still have her. She was no virgin. Others had had her, he had no doubt. She was sister under the skin to the Regina Darlingtons of the world. Beautiful, spoiled, and wanton. Regina, and other rich white women, had given him some pleasant hours in bed and neither he nor they had ever regretted it. It would be the same with Martay Kidd. If they made love tonight, it would be, for them both, enjoyable, erotic, and easily forgotten.

Night Sun took another long pull of whiskey. He lifted the bandoliers up over his head and held them in one hand, idly slapping them against his naked thigh. His flat belly tightening, he dropped the decorative bandoliers to the ground and moved purposely forward, the shell anklets on his feet tinkling as he walked.

Martay, seeing him advancing, stopped dancing. She stood, the gourd rattle lifted over her head, and watched him come to her. Looking brazenly into his flashing black eyes, her whole being, every bone in her body, every hair on her head, was screaming for his touch.

Night Sun reached her.

For a long moment he stood there before her, unashamedly watching the lift and fall of her breasts as she began to slowly, seductively, roll her shoulders, enticing him, inviting him. The breath caught in Martay's throat when his warm hands spanned her narrow waist, then slid around to lock behind her. Wordlessly, he drew her to him.

"Night Sun," she said breathlessly, lifting her arms up around his bare, gleaming shoulders, the gourd rattle still clutched tightly in her right hand, "I feel so wonderful. Do you feel wonderful?"

Suddenly happy beyond belief, Night Sun laughed, bent his dark head, and said, "Yes, Martay, I feel wonderful."

She smiled dreamily. "Only thing is, I'm a little dizzy. Better hold me tightly or I'll fall."

His arms tightened around her and he pulled her closer to the heat and strength of his tall, lean body. "I've got you."

She sighed and laid her head on his shoulder. "Never let me go."

29

The night air had chilled, but the blazing fire burned high and fierce. The tom-toms, pounding out a savage beat, reverberated in rhythm with Martay's wildly drumming heart. She was dizzy and happy and hot, her legs weak from dancing.

For hours she and Night Sun had moved as one in a primitive, pagan dance of growing desire, their gazes locked, their lithe, graceful bodies sliding and swaying and rubbing in sensual, liberated freedom.

Martay leaned back in Night Sun's long arms and closed her eyes for a moment, finding it suddenly amusing that although her brain was quite foggy, her senses were keenly alert. Smiling dreamily, she thrilled to the myriad of sounds and scents that filled her with incredible pleasure and stirred her blood.

The pounding of the drums. The shouts and laughter of the happy dancers. The smell of wine on Night Sun's warm breath. The gentle tinkle of shells on Night Sun's anklets. The scent of Night Sun's heated, bronzed flesh.

Night Sun! Night Sun! Night Sun!

She opened her eyes, tightened her hold on his strong neck, and gave her gourd rattle a lazy shake. He let his hands slide down to her flaring hips, gripped her securely with long, spread fingers and urged her pelvis more closely to his. Erotically he rocked against her, making slow, lazy circles with his slim hips, undulating rhythmically. Through her soft doeskin dress and his brief breechclout, she could feel his heat and hardness, the physical proof of his desire. A desire for her and no other.

His hands, sliding lower, expertly guided her, lifting, lowering, moving her closer, urging her back, and she was helpless against such power and passion. He was, she realized, making love to her there in the blazing firelight while all the others danced around them, but she didn't care. She was hot and excited and oblivious to anyone save this dark god of love for whom she would do anything, anytime, anyplace.

Her clutching fingers slid on Night Sun's neck and she became aware, for the first time, that his chest and back and shoulders were slippery with perspiration. Bringing a hand down from his shoulder, she spread her fingers across his chest and blotted at the glistening beads of sweat covering him. Her hand was wet when she turned it over and stared at it.

"I'm hot too," she murmured, and directing his attention to the open throat of her dress, she put her wet hand inside, placed it atop the gleaming swell of her left breast, and lovingly rubbed his sweat on her heated skin. "I wish," she went on, "we could just pull our clothes off and dance naked."

Raising a dark hand, he placed long fingers on the pounding pulse point in her gleaming throat, then captured the tiny beads of moisture resting in its delicate hollow, and pointedly spread them on his lips. And licked them off.

"We will," he said, and the next thing Martay knew, he was leading her through the frenzied dancers. Caught up in their own wild enjoyment, the others never noticed. But silently observing from his solitary vantage point above, a stoic Windwalker's dark eyes narrowed as they followed the departing couple hurrying in the moonlight along the path toward Night Sun's lodge.

The Mystic Warrior shook his graying head.

Night Sun and Martay never knew. And had they known, they wouldn't have cared. The drums, the wine, the peyote, the weeks of fierce longing and painful self-denial had all converged to hurl them, at long last, on this special night of nights, into each other's arms.

They didn't speak on the way to Night Sun's tipi. Martay, hurrying to keep up with Night Sun's long, supple strides, clung tightly to his hand, as anxious as he to reach the privacy of their lodge.

When they ducked inside, Night Sun at last released Martay. It was dark inside; no fire was burning in the center; the only light was the wedge of moonlight coming through the open flap.

"I want to see you as well as feel you," he said, moving from her to readjust the smoke hole at the tipi's top, folding back the skins above until the tipi's interior was flooded with an abundance of bright, silvery moonlight. Then he crossed before her and, going down on one knee, pulled down the entrance flap and fastened it securely so that no one could enter.

He rose then and stood looking at her. Martay trembled when he moved, catlike, and came to stand before her. He was all Indian this night, from the top of his noble head to the soles of his bare feet. The burnished skin, the chiseled features, the awesomely black glittering eyes. Shadows played beneath his high, slanting cheekbones, and his mouth looked hard and determined and dangerous.

And Martay couldn't wait to feel that dangerous mouth on hers.

Night Sun lifted a hand to her hair. Cupping the back of her small, well-shaped head, he applied gentle pressure, urging her up onto her toes, even as he slowly bent his dark head to her. He leaned down and kissed her with a quick, feathery touch of his lips on hers, and Martay heard the brushing of seeds in her gourd rattle as it touched Night Sun's bare thigh.

He lifted his head, smiled at her, and took the rattle from her. Giving it one last playful shake, he tossed it across the tipi. His hands went immediately to the concho belt tied at Martay's narrow waist. Swiftly he untied it and stood for a second with it in his hands, folding it neatly, the sound of the silver disks clinking together loudly in the quietness.

Night Sun dropped the belt and put his hands on Martay's hips. While she looked up at him, unafraid, he pulled the soft doeskin dress up to her waist, paused, and said, "Lift your arms for me, sweetheart."

The endearment, coming from him, filled Martay with un-believable happiness. She would have done anything for him. Trembling slightly, she obeyed him, and feeling the soft dress come up over her head and off, she threw back her shoulders and lifted her chin.

And then it was Night Sun who trembled.

She stood there in the moonlight wearing only the soft doeskin underwear and the knee-high moccasins, and she was even more beautiful, more desirable, than he had hoped or imagined. The skimpy doeskin underpants rode low atop her hipbones and stopped high upon her pale thighs. Her breasts, completely bare, were full and high and stood out from her delicate ribs in proud, perfect mounds of creamy flesh topped with large pink-satin nipples that were, before his eyes, tight-ening into darkening buds of sweetness that tempted him to bend his head immediately and taste.

Instead he asked, very courteously, if he could unbraid her hair. Gentle Deer's words came rushing back: "If he wants to take down your hair, let him."

"Yes, if you like it better that way."

"I do," he said, and turning her away from him, unwound

the beaded black velvet adornment from the long braid, slipped it around the slender column of her neck, and tied it into a perfect bow at the side of her throat, then went about gently pulling the three large sections of hair apart. When at last it was undone, he combed his long fingers through the gleaming tresses and smoothed it down her delicate back. It fell almost to her waist, and the sight of it, shimmering there in the moonlight on her pale, bare skin, filled Night Sun with joy.

Impulsively he parted the long, silky hair down the middle of her head and swept it over her shoulders, then turned her to face him. The pale hair was very bewitching, spilling over her torso, but it partially hid her bare, beautiful breasts, so he impatiently swept it once more over her shoulders and released it, letting it fall down her back.

He said, "Dance with me, Martay?"

She said, "Yes. Oh, yes."

Night Sun put a long arm around her. His fingers moved slowly, enticingly, up her bare back, beneath the flowing hair that spilled over his arm. Gently he pulled her into his embrace and Martay trembled violently. Not with fear or apprehension or doubt. She trembled with the joy of being in his arms, of feeling the smooth hot flesh of his broad, hairless chest pressing against her sensitive nipples; his lean, hair-dusted thighs brushing abrasively against hers; his flat, sweat-dampened abdomen sliding sensuously on her own.

They danced there in the moonlight, the two of them. She in her doeskin underpants and knee-high moccasins, he in his brief breechclout, shell anklets, copper bracelets, and red headband. They could still hear the sounds of the tom-toms from the village, but they moved to a slower, more sensual tempo, finding their own pleasing, provocative rhythm.

Lost in wonder, Martay blinked when Night Sun's feet stopped moving. Questioningly, she looked up at him.

He put a hand on her bare shoulder and kissed her for the second time. For a breathless moment—so brief it seemed to her like a mere dreamlike flash—his lips moved ardently on hers, then released them.

"Martay, I want you naked. Take off your underwear," he said, his voice as warm and caressing as a summer breeze.

"No," she murmured, toying with the gleaming copper bracelets wrapped around his biceps, "you take off my underwear."

His heart hammering, his hands were at her waist by the time the last word left her mouth. He peeled the skimpy doeskin undergarment slowly down over her flared hips and released it. It whispered to the floor, pooling there around her moccasined feet. She kicked it aside.

Night Sun, stepping back, felt the blood rush to his already swollen groin as he admired the unclothed beauty standing before him. Her belly was so flat, it appeared concave; shadows played in the delicate hollows beside her rising hipbones. Her thighs were firm and gently curved, the legs long and slender. Her flesh was pale, its texture pearlized by the moonlight; and between her thighs, thick, shimmering golden curls, forming a perfect symmetrical triangle, gleamed silver in the night.

It was there that Night Sun's heated gaze lingered. A muscle jerking furiously in his jaw, he reached out and reverently swept long, dark fingers gently through those soft angel-curls, and he said, "It's this I want to feel against me when we dance."

Martay thought she would burst into flame as his hand possessively closed over her, the heel resting lightly atop her pelvis, the long, dark fingers caressingly cupping her, his black eyes lifting to hers.

She drew a shallow, much needed breath and said, "Night Sun, I want you naked. Take off your breechclout."

Recognizing his own words being recited back to him, he smiled and said, "No." Reluctantly moving his hand from her, he added, "You take off my breechclout."

He stood there then, unmoving, feet apart. Would she actually do it?

She did.

Unsure exactly how to go about it, Martay quickly found where the leather thong was tied atop his left hip, holding the strange garment in place. With shaking hands she untied the stubborn knot and pulled the breechclout away from his body. Fingers still clutching the soft rawhide covering, she stared with wide eyes at what she had undraped.

Rising there from swirls of thick blue-black hair was that pulsing, awesome maleness she had felt burning her through their clothing. Freed from its restraints, it sprang proudly up and out, a huge naked shaft of flesh like nothing she could have imagined. Never had she seen a man naked, and she was at once shocked and fascinated. His tall, bare body, to her, was beautiful, and this erect thrusting symbol of his masculinity was no exception.

Wide green eyes never leaving it, she said, "I want to touch you."

"Do it."

Martay shyly reached out, wrapped tentative fingers around him, and gasped when he jerked involuntarily within her grasp. Amazed by the heat and hardness and texture, she lifted her other hand to him and began, quite innocently, to eagerly run exploring fingers up and down the hard, impressive length of him. Night Sun was delighted. Martay was, without realizing it, proving to him she was exactly the kind of woman he thought. No inexperienced, innocent girl would be as bold as the blond beauty who was, at this moment, looking down at his straining erection as though it were something good to eat and driving him half crazy with her warm, practiced hands. Night Sun, looking forward to a long, hot night of lovemaking, abruptly jerked her hands away and pulled her back into his arms.

And again they danced there in the moonlight. The two of them; she in her knee-high moccasins and black velvet neckpiece. He in his copper arm bands and shell anklets and red headband. If dancing had been pleasurable before, now it was paradise. Unfettered by clothes, they swayed and pressed and undulated, their bare awakened bodies enjoying a degree of sensitivity unlike any either had ever before known.

While they danced there naked in the moonlight, Night Sun, his reserve totally swept away by the wine and whiskey and peyote and passion, honestly admitted to Martay that he wanted the night to be a very special one. That he wanted the two of them to stay naked in each other's arms until the breaking of dawn turned the silvery light now bathing them to the glaring sunshine of day.

He said he was going to make himself wait to take her completely for as long as he possibly could stand it, that he wanted them both to become so passionately uninhibited and highly aroused that by the time they fully surrendered to total possession and he entered her at last, they would be suffering a sweet, prolonged agony.

Martay, a total innocent in the ways of lovemaking, presumed she would grow no more excited than she was at this moment, dancing nude in his arms, feeling the throbbing, naked power against her belly; and since she was enjoying this gloriously erotic exercise in desire, she murmured her enthusiastic agreement to his plans.

They continued to dance, much, much slower now, barely lifting their feet, the shell anklets on Night Sun's feet hardly tinkling. He kissed her as they danced, short, brushing kisses at the beginning. Teasing little caresses, his mouth playing with hers, teeth raking across her full, soft lips.

But her prominent breasts were brushing tantalizingly against his chest and those soft silvered curls between her thighs and the warm satin flesh of her belly were cradling his tumescence so that he could hardly bear it. His hands slipped down from her waist to cup her bare buttocks and his open mouth came down aggressively on hers. Martay's opened to accept his kiss. Their teeth touched, his tongue caressed her lips.

Martay sighed as his kiss deepened and she felt the thrusting of his tongue deep inside her mouth. Clinging to him, she kissed him back with all the love and passion she felt for him. They kissed and kissed, each kiss growing longer, hotter, deeper. Their fevered breaths were loud in the quiet tipi, and their hands roamed anxiously and frantically gripped at slippery, naked flesh as they changed positions again and again, unable to get close enough.

Wildly, hotly, they kissed, their legs growing so weak with desire, they slowly slipped to the floor. Kneeling there in the moonlight, they continued to kiss as though they could never get enough of each other. Night Sun's hands were again cupping Martay's bare bottom, urging her to him as he kissed her greedily, hungrily, his tongue filling her mouth.

When finally their lips separated, Night Sun said raggedly, "Maybe it's time I take you to my bed."

"Yes," Martay agreed breathlessly, and trembled with pleasure when he sat back on his heels, bent to her, and pressed his lips to her left breast. "Night Sun," she gasped excitedly as his hot mouth enclosed the aching nipple in a gently sucking kiss. He allowed the wet little bud to pop out of his mouth, kissed the soft undercurve of her breast, then raised his head.

Lifting her easily up into his arms, Night Sun carried her to his soft bed of furs, gently placing her down. Martay leaned back, supporting her weight on stiff arms, and watched as Night Sun, on his knees beside the bed, pulled her long moccasins down her legs and off her feet, kissing each high instep as he bared them. He reached for the streamer of the black velvet tied around her neck, gave it a quick jerk, and slowly slid it from her throat.

He removed the copper bracelets from his arms, the shell anklets from his feet, leaving only the red band around his raven hair. He moved to her then, stretching out beside her in the moonlight, cupping a warm, full breast in his hand.

He said, "Now. Finally."

She asked, "We've waited as long as we can to make love?"

His rough thumb brushed her sensitive nipple. "No, sweetheart. I mean finally we are both completely naked. Isn't this better?"

"It is, but I . . ." Her eyes went to that heated rod of power jerking on his belly. "How long can you . . . I mean, will that . . . will you stay . . ."

His black eyes took on that fierce, intense expression. "Martay, never forget I am Indian. Indians are controlled and patient. Indians can wait forever." His expression softened then, and he added, "I didn't mean that I won't make love to you. I will." His hand slid up to cup the side of her neck, "I'll give you pleasure, sweetheart. What I said was, I'd like us to postpone reaching total fulfillment for a long time." He leaned to her and covered her parted lips with his own, easing her down onto her back as they kissed.

And then Martay found out what Night Sun meant when he said he would make love to her, would give her pleasure.

Like a master musician with a fine priceless instrument, he lovingly touched and stroked her body until she thought she would scream with the exquisite enjoyment. There was none of her flesh his warm, masterful hands did not claim, and she found herself anxiously arching toward the lean, brown fingers as they swept slowly, enticingly over her, his touch so light, it felt as if delicate rose petals were being scattered over her burning skin.

She lay there on his soft fur bed in the moonlight, her eyes opening and closing, while Night Sun stroked the gleaming hair of her head, her face, her throat. He touched her shoulders, skimmed his fingertips down the insides of her arms, and then back up. He circled both breasts, and ran the tip of his middle finger over each pointing, aching nipple.

And all the while he lay lazily on his side, looking at her with hot black eyes and murmuring encouragement and endearments in a seductive blend of English and Lakota, his deep voice as caressing as his hand.

His fingers swept down her flat stomach, her trembling belly, her long legs. He caressed her ankles, her bare feet, her toes. He pressed kisses to her open lips and told her that she was beautiful, so beautiful, he wanted to keep her like this, naked in his tipi forever, his sweetly willing prisoner of passion.

Completely in love and burning with desire, Martay assured him nothing would please her more. She said she wanted to be naked and beautiful for him always, to have his hands on her forever.

Night Sun eased her up and turned her on her side, so that she lay back against him, in the same position he was in, his body supporting hers. Martay sighed when he kissed the curve of her neck and shoulder. She lay comfortably back against his smooth, hard chest and instinctively squirmed her bottom closer to the heat and promise of that still-rigid shaft of extraordinary male power.

"Tell me, sweetheart," he said into her hair, "where you want my hand now."

Martay couldn't bring herself to answer. But she didn't have to. Night Sun's arm came around her and his warm palm flattened on her belly, then moved slowly down until it covered the golden curls between her thighs.

Martay put up no objection when he urged her left leg up and draped back it over his own legs, hooking it loosely, comfortably over his supportive calf.

His hand squeezed her knee, then moved slowly down to the inside of her thigh. Martay softly gasped when his fingers reached the thick triangle of curls, then slipped between to search out that tiny sensitive nub of female flesh. Her eyes closed with surprised ecstasy and her head dropped back on his shoulder as his fingers began their tender coaxing. Her healthy young body, stirred by his practiced, prolonged method of arousal, had produced a silky wetness that made his long, lean fingers glide easily over the fiery flesh and Martay experienced pleasure of a kind she had never known existed.

It was a form of splendid torture, and feeling as if she wanted it to last for eternity and at the same time praying for it to end at once, she writhed against him, shocked at what was happening to her, wondering fearfully what would happen if he should suddenly desert her, take his magical hand from her.

As though he had read her mind, Night Sun murmured against her ear, "We've all night. And all day. Let me love you, *Wicincala*. There's nothing I'd rather do than touch you this way."

It started then, triggered by his words. The sweet, frightening climax that caused Martay to cry out in dazed wonder. "Night Sun!" she sobbed as the fierce throbbing grew so strong, she was spiraling up into unbearable ecstasy.

"Yes, baby," he soothed, his fingers sliding faster, deeper, surer, giving her what she needed. Her arm flew back around his neck and her hand clutched frantically at the thick hair of his head.

"Night Sunnnnn!" she screamed as she exploded with heat and joy, feeling wave after wave of incredible tremors wash through her entire body.

"Good. Good, sweetheart," he praised, staying with her until her release was total. Then he hugged her tightly back against him, murmuring, "I've got you, sweetheart. Ah, that's good. Yes. Yes, baby."

When her slender body slumped tiredly against him, he gently turned her to face him. He kissed her tenderly, sweetly, cradling her head on his shoulder. Martay, exhausted, feeling all she wanted was to go to sleep, lay there limp in his arms while he kissed her repeatedly.

"Night Sun," she whispered against his moving lips, "I . . . I'm sorry. I don't think I can stay awake any . . ."

"I know, sweetheart," he said, continuing to take soft, plucking little kisses from her open lips. "It's all right. All right."

"Mmmmm," she murmured, and no one could have been more surprised than she when, a half hour later, with him continuing to cradle her in his arms and kiss her lips, her throat, her breasts, she was again stirring eagerly to his touch.

She was more than agreeable when he suggested she lie on her stomach. She gave his mouth a licking kiss and promptly stretched out on her bare belly, resting her weight on bent elbows.

Gently pushing her long, heavy hair to one side, Night Sun bent, kissed each rising shoulder blade, then climbed astride her. She didn't question him. She sighed and purred and laid her head on a bent arm while he leaned to her and kissed her back. Slowly, slowly he slid down her body, kissing her buttocks, her legs, her feet, his lips and hands setting her afire again.

Finally, he turned her over.

He sat back on his heels astride her, a beautiful naked savage. His black eyes gleamed and blue highlights played in his raven hair. His bronzed shoulders glistened with sweat and the white scar slashing down his smooth chest appeared to be of white satin.

That old familiar mix of fear and attraction was strong as Martay watched him poised there, waiting, staring unblinkingly.

Swallowing hard, she said, "I'm burning up again."

The fiercely beautiful savage leaned down, kissed her, and said into her mouth, "Me too, sweetheart."

Swiftly he moved inside her legs. "Never," he told her truthfully, "have I wanted a woman the way I want you right now."

Still he held back for a time, kissing her lips, her breasts, making sure she was ready. And when he finally thrust into her, he was so burning hot, he didn't, couldn't, care when he found that she was a virgin. The perplexing realization did jangle alarmingly in his brain for a split second, but then it was gone as the sweetness of her hot, tight body drove out all logical thought.

Martay was shocked by the white, hot pain she experienced and felt betrayed by her lover. But not for long. In moments, glorious pleasure made her forget there had been any discomfort. She opened her eyes to look at the dark, handsome face above hers as Night Sun moved his slim hips rhythmically, erotically, taking her with slow, insistent thrusts of his hard, aroused body. He clasped her hips and lifted her to him, tutoring her, guiding her. Martay learned quickly. When he drove into her, she eagerly tilted her pelvis, accepting him fully, wanting all he had to give.

They moved in slow, heated splendor, Night Sun repeatedly sliding almost all the way in, then retreating, holding back until he felt her release beginning, the spasming, the delicious clasping and gripping of her body around him. Only then did he change the tempo, speeding his movements, thrusting deeper, giving it all to her.

When it happened, she cried out, and cried out yet again when Night Sun, knowing she was there, finally let himself go. Martay felt the hot pumping liquid of love fill her, then overflow, and she gloried in the wonderful sensation. She wrapped her legs tightly around his back to draw him closer, hugging him to her while she kissed his dark jaw, murmuring, "Darling, my darling."

And through her mind flitted the giddy thought that she did indeed feel oh so new and good and different. Never again would she be as before. She belonged to Night Sun. She was owned, body and soul, by this handsome half-breed.

Would belong to him forever.

30

Regina Darlington, standing before the pier glass in her luxurious bedroom, felt a twinge of apprehension as she carefully examined herself. The doubt was not caused by the reflection she saw in the looking glass. She was, she knew, quite beautiful. The fashionable gown she had chosen for the evening, a shimmering bronze satin, had come straight from Paris. Her rich auburn hair was dressed elaborately atop her head with ropes of gold and pearls intertwined through the gleaming curls.

Regina drew a deep breath.

She was being foolish. Why should she feel threatened because Senator Berton had insisted that the two of them have dinner alone? She should be honored, not anxious. But she was anxious. She had not been alone with the senator since that hot afternoon she and Larry had very nearly been caught in a highly compromising situation.

Regina's knees went weak at the recollection.

Such a close call had left her almost ill for the rest of the day. It had been a nightmare. She and Larry Berton, stark naked, in one of the guest rooms, their clothes nowhere in sight. The two of them fleeing frantically through the carpeted corridor while the senator and her husband climbed the stairs. She had barely made it to her suite before Thomas opened the door and called to her, and she'd had a devil of a time explaining why she was so out of breath.

Regina shook her head as if to clear it.

Thomas hadn't suspected a thing, nor had the senator. She was just being foolish. The distinguished senator had quite simply invited her to join him for dinner this evening because he was leaving for Washington at week's end and he enjoyed her company. And besides, with Larry and the colonel away at Fort Collins, it was only natural that the two of them should dine together.

Regina began to smile.

The senator, with his thick silver hair and sophisticated charm, was an interesting, attractive man. The slight limp only added to his urbane appeal and she suspected it didn't hamper his performance in bed. There was, she happily surmised, a lusty, sexual animal beneath the veneer of the polished, aristocratic gentleman.

Her doubts pushed aside, an expectant, glowing Regina Darlington descended the giant staircase, eager for a pleasant, intimate evening with the powerful Virginia senator.

Any ridiculous unease she had suffered earlier dissipated completely as she sat across the candlelit table from her engaging dinner companion. Easily Senator Berton charmed her with his usual witty, informative conversation. That is, after he'd graciously kissed her hand, held it for a moment longer than necessary, and complimented her on her beauty.

Now as he sipped his wine and carved the rare roast beef, he smiled at her, his eyes twinkling, and Regina knew she'd been a ninny to have worried.

Taking a long drink of the vintage Lafite, she felt a familiar flutter of excitement begin in her stomach. Her husband, the colonel, would not be returning to the estate for another

four days. The senator's son, Major Berton, was not due back
for a week. They were, for all intents and purposes, alone here
at the foothills mansion. Finally the military guard surrounding the estate had been removed. All was quiet and peaceful
once more. The early autumn weather had chilled and a
warm, blazing fire was burning in the opulent drawing room.
Perhaps after a couple of brandies by firelight the silver-
haired senator would like to go upstairs and get more comfortable.

Regina looked at the senator's wide mouth. His lips were
gleaming wet from the wine. The fluttering of her stomach
grew more pronounced. Ah, yes, it promised to be a very
enjoyable night. That anticipated enjoyment drew closer
when, after finishing their rich dessert, she suggested brandy
in the drawing room.

"Splendid idea," said the senator, and came around to pull
out her chair. Once in the high-ceilinged drawing room, he
poured for them both, handed a glass to her, and touching his
glass to hers, said, "To the days ahead."

Smiling seductively, she added, "And to the nights."

She sipped her brandy while the senator downed his in one
swallow, then poured himself another. He drank down the
second glass, set the empty aside, and went directly to the
fireplace. Regina, watching him, noted the rise of his shoulders in his custom jacket as he drew a deep, long breath. He
turned to face her.

He said, "Mrs. Darlington, I'm certain you'd be delighted
if your husband were to receive a much deserved promotion.
Am I correct?"

"Why, I . . . Senator, nothing would make me happier."
Smiling at him, Regina felt she might laugh out loud. This
handsome Virginia senator so desired her, he was willing to
give her husband a promotion just to have her. My God, this
was even better than she'd hoped. A long, romantic night
with the senator and a long hoped-for promotion for dear,
sweet Thomas.

"I thought you'd feel that way, my dear," the senator said, "knowing what a devoted wife you are." Something about his smile, as he advanced on her, was all wrong.

Regina swallowed with difficulty. "I . . . I . . . try to be a good . . . ah . . ."

He had reached her. "Let us drop the pretense, Mrs. Darlington." He continued to smile.

Again inexplicably uneasy, Regina lifted a small hand to his crisp white shirtfront. Toying with a gold stud, she said, "Very well, Senator." She allowed her thick eyelashes to flutter down for a second, then looked him squarely in the eye. "Am I to assume you'd like to strike a bargain?"

"You are."

She laughed softly. "Shall we forestall any further discussion until we get upstairs?" She paused, inhaled, and added, "Say, to your room? Or would you prefer mine?"

"Right where we are is suitable, Mrs. Darlington."

"But, Senator," she said, starting to giggle nervously, glancing toward the open double doors and already weighing the merits of the expensive Persian rug in front of the fireplace as opposed to the long, soft sofa. "The servants, they . . ."

"You're quite right," said the senator. And he wasted no time crossing to pull the tall double doors shut. Turning, he said, "Now. About that bargain."

"Yes," she said, breathlessly, "name your terms." She placed a spread hand on her full, rapidly rising and falling bosom. "But first, may I make myself more comfortable?"

Crossing to her, he said, "By all means, my dear."

Senator Douglas Berton was amazed at the speed with which Regina Darlington divested herself of the shimmering bronze silk gown. In seconds she was standing in the firelight wearing nothing but a revealing bronze satin chemise, her silk stockings, and her dainty bronze satin slippers.

She was, he had to admit, stunningly desirable. So very desirable, he couldn't fault his healthy son for sampling her many charms.

He said, "Comfortable now, Mrs. Darlington?"

"Yes," she murmured, "but I'd like you to be comfortable too."

Thinking he'd be comfortable just as soon as he got out of that too-warm room, Senator Douglas Berton said, "You're a beautiful woman, Mrs. Darlington, and . . ."

"Thank you, Senator."

"So beautiful, I can't blame Larry for making love to you." He saw the alarm leap into her eyes.

"Why, I never in my . . ."

"You did, so let's not dillydally. My son is my whole life, Mrs. Darlington. That boy is all I have; my wife died years ago. Larry has a brilliant career ahead of him and . . ."

"I . . . I . . . know that, Senator. You've got it all wrong; I would never look twice at your son." She shook her head. "No, it's you I . . ."

He took a step closer and put his hands on her bare shoulders. "Mrs. Darlington, I've spent the last ten years keeping ladies like you away from my boy. I should have acted sooner this time, but I thought surely with your husband and the military around . . ." He shrugged. "You picked the wrong man, Mrs. Darlington. Chances are Larry will be at Fort Collins for another year or more, so I can't have you here in Denver."

"You can't have . . . this is our home, Senator. You can't just . . ."

"Yes, I can." He smiled then, and let his hands slide down her arms. "Don't look so glum. You'll benefit too. Colonel Darlington will be on the short promotion list and will get his star. You'll be transferred to the Presidio. Leading the life of a general's wife in the Bay City will be quite rewarding for a lady of your charm and beauty."

"Yes," she murmured, already seeing in her mind's eye a fine Telegraph Hill mansion with all the gay, cultured California set calling often to pay homage. "Senator, you've made yourself a deal."

"I thought so," he replied. "I'll see to the details as soon as I reach Washington."

"How can I thank you, Senator?" she said, aware of the strong hands still clasping her wrists.

The Senator's jaw hardened. "Stay away from my son!"

Scar slapped the Crow brave across the face. Bright-red blood spurted from the surprised man's split lip and ran down his chin. He didn't lift a hand to wipe it away, instead stood flat-footed looking at Scar.

Scar said, "I weary of these excuses you give, saying you learn nothing, you hear nothing." He stepped away from the bleeding man, dropped down onto the spread blanket, and motioned the woman forward to continue with his bath. Naked, he sprawled there on the blanket in the afternoon sunshine, leaning on an elbow while the dutiful Crow woman swiped at his scarred massive shoulders with a soapy cloth. "Sit," Scar commanded the bleeding brave. "And wipe your mouth."

The nervous brave did both, dropping to his knees as he blotted his ripped lip on a shirt sleeve. Averting his eyes from the angry naked man lolling immodestly before him, he said, "Scar, the fault is not ours. The girl may be with Night Sun. Windwalker's tribe never talks. And," he added, "if she is there, we can't just ride in and take her." His eyes were on the ground.

"Look at me, Kaytennae," said the fat, disgruntled Crow. While his woman lifted a heavy arm and soaped a furry underarm, Scar said, "Night Sun has the golden-haired woman. I want that golden-haired woman and I am going to have her. You find her or I'll"—he knocked the woman aside, reached out, grabbed his Colt .45, and cocked it— "I'll kill you and feed your bones to the dogs."

The brave nodded. "Let's head south tomorrow. Ride until the Little Missouri turns into the Belle Fourche. If we don't find them there, we can turn east to the Powder." He looked nervously at the big naked man with the cocked pistol.

Waving the Colt, Scar nodded. "Good. Tell the others we leave at daybreak. And tell them if they'll help me find her, they'll be rewarded. Now get away from here, I'm trying to get a bath." He laughed suddenly and laid the revolver aside. "I want to be nice and fresh for the general's pretty blond daughter."

General William Kidd stared broodingly out the window of his Fort Collins quarters. It was almost sunup on that cool September Sunday morning. His favorite time of the day. His favorite time of the year. But the morning, the season, brought him no joy.

His was a heart forever broken.

They weren't going to find her, he had finally faced it. His only child, his little girl, was gone, most likely had perished, and with her his joy in living. The sound of recall no longer stirred him. The sight of the blazing aspens beyond his open windows left him cold. Good food, good whiskey, good friends, no longer held any charm for him.

The general sighed and put his head in his hands.

Never did the darkness fall that he didn't hear her calling for him, the sounds of her sobs following him into fitful slumber. Never did the light of dawn touch his eyelids that he didn't tell himself this was the day he'd get her back.

But he knew better.

Martay was dead. He believed it. And, in a way, it was a comfort for him to believe it. Far better for her to be dead and in Heaven than held captive somewhere by some sadistic madman who . . .

Swallowing the bile that rose to his throat, the general raised his graying head. He rose and slipped long arms into his military blouse, buttoned the brass buttons up his still-trim frame, picked up his campaign hat and suede gauntlets, and headed for his office.

Within the hour he was seated across the desk from Colonel Thomas Darlington and the colonel was diplomatically questioning the general's decision to ride with a detachment being sent north toward the Canadian Border with hopes of a skirmish with hostile Sioux.

"With all due respect, General, you shouldn't make such a difficult journey."

General Kidd, hands laced atop his desk, thumbs idly twiddling, replied, "Colonel, if I don't do something, I shall go mad." His hands came undone and he pushed his chair back from the desk. "Since the search has terminated, I . . ." His shoulders lifted wearily in a shrug of defeat. "Besides, if our informers are right and Gall is planning to lead a band down into the Dakotas, I want to be there to face the red bastard!" His face flushed with color.

"Sir, I know you detest the Indians. We all do, but I've never understood . . . ah . . . that is . . ."

General Kidd bounded out of his chair. He strode to the window, looked out at the dusty parade ground, where a few troopers were exercising their mounts in the cool morning air. He turned about. "When I was a boy my family lived in Minnesota on a beautiful farm within sight of the Mississippi. My father's younger brother lived with us and I dearly loved my Uncle Dan. Dan was just a teenager himself, but I, being only six, thought he was a grown man and I wanted to be just like him when I grew up."

The General came back to his desk.

"One summer afternoon when my parents were in town and my uncle and I were down at the river swimming, a band of Sioux came riding up onto our property." General Kidd gritted his teeth. "They didn't harm me, but they killed my Uncle Dan." He closed his eyes, opened them. "Scalped him and left him to die. He bled to death in my arms." He rubbed a hand over his face. "Goddamn them all to eternal hell!"

"I can understand how you feel," said Colonel Darlington.

General Kidd nodded, calming immediately. "Strange, I hadn't thought about Dan in years. Sometimes I've almost forgotten why I hate Indians so much." He rose and went to study the calendar across the room.

He squinted. "September twenty-first," he said aloud. And Uncle Dan and the hostiles and Colonel Darlington were all forgotten. His eyes sad, he said wistfully to himself, "Fifty-seven days."

"I beg your pardon, General?" said Colonel Darlington.

"It's been fifty-seven days since I saw my child." He turned and looked at the seated man. "If Scar can't find her, then she can't be found." Tears sprang suddenly to his green eyes and his voice was rough when he said, "I won't see her again until we meet in Heaven."

31

The pale-skinned woman, her golden head resting on a sleek, coppery shoulder, was smiling in her sleep. The dark Sioux chieftain in whose arms she lay was not.

His black eyes troubled, Night Sun lay staring up at the ever brightening sunshine streaming down through the tipi's opened smoke hole. He'd not slept. Had not closed his eyes. He had, as promised, made love to Martay until "the dawn turned the silvery light bathing them to the glaring sunshine of day."

When dawn had broken, they had been making sweet, slow, lazy love, and by the time they reached total ecstasy, a rapidly rising September sun had washed their joined bodies with a soft pastel light. Afterward, Martay had fallen asleep in his arms.

Now, in peaceful slumber, her slender ivory body kissed by the soft pink sunlight, she seemed an ethereal, not-of-this-world creature. Surely no mere mortal could appear so angelic, so trusting, so heart-stoppingly beautiful.

Awed by the naked perfection in his arms, Night Sun, for

a long, silent time, had lain and looked at her, his eyes worshiping every gentle curve and plane of her bare body, every single silky eyelash, each long golden hair of her head.

He ran his fingers over her slender shoulder and down her arm. He touched an arched hip, a curved thigh, a dimpled knee. He carefully lifted a lock of her golden hair and stretched it across his bare chest, unconsciously pulling it along the white-satin path of his old scar.

He looked down at the streamer of gold lying in a valley of white on his dark skin. He shuddered and felt his chest constrict. And as though the soft golden hair were an evil, deadly thing, he brushed it away, anxious to have it off him, feeling his flesh suddenly crawl with distaste.

Night Sun ground his teeth.

Cold, harsh reality came flooding in with the encompassing sunshine. Regret and confusion plagued him. He was not proud of himself. He had taken Martay's virginity, and while he reasoned that she was only the rich, spoiled daughter of the soldier responsible for the scar down his chest and for Gentle Deer's blindness, it helped little.

The rising, gnawing guilt made him angry. Angry with Martay. He had naturally assumed, judging by her reputation and from observing her brazen behavior, that she was an experienced woman, that she'd had lovers.

Not at all happy knowing he was her first, Night Sun eased her arm from around his waist and moved away from her. Rising onto an elbow, he glared at the innocent-looking face. And his guilt and anger grew. Ashamed of what he had done, Night Sun, for the first time in his life, felt uncomfortable and remorseful lying naked with a beautiful woman to whom he had made love.

He shook his dark head.

Martay had led him to believe she was as worldly as Regina Darlington. He had presumed they could enjoy a night of lovemaking and there would be no regrets come morning. But he did regret it. He had promised Windwalker he would return his captive to her family exactly as she had come to him.

Night Sun felt a measure of unease mix with his displeasure. The Mystic Warrior was not easily fooled. Windwalker would know. And he would not approve of a trusted Lakota chieftain taking the innocence of a helpless white girl.

Night Sun rose. His face set in hard angles, he glared at the deceitful woman sleeping peacefully as though nothing had happened. Lying there below him, one knee turned out to the side, she was unselfconsciously displaying all her naked charms like the wanton he'd thought—hoped—her to be. And she was smiling in her slumber. While he became increasingly more tortured and repentant.

And angry.

Feeling the hot September sun slowly climb up her bare legs, Martay began to rouse. Eyes still closed, she stretched and sighed and erotically rubbed her bare belly against the soft fur bed, instantly recalling the night's lovely rapture. She reached a searching hand out toward Night Sun.

She patted lazily at the fur, swept her palm about, and finally opened her eyes. He was not there. Night Sun was not lying beside her. She had so wanted to open her eyes and see him sleeping soundly; longed to see those girlishly long black eyelashes making silky shadows atop the dark, slanting cheekbones.

"Night Sun?" she said, her voice heavy with sleep and affection. "Darling?" She yawned and rolled over onto her back.

And froze with fear.

The warm, passionate lover of the night had disappeared. In his place, a hard-faced, cold-eyed tribal chief in full regalia stood angrily staring down at her. His raven hair was formally bound with hand-embroidered felt. Ropes of rare turquoise beads hung from his bronzed neck. His fringed shirt and tight leggings pulled tautly on his tall, spare frame. His moccasined feet were wide apart. And in his long, lean fingers he held an elegant gold-and-wood hand-engraved walking stick with a solid gold head. He was rhythmically slapping the cane against his open palm.

"Night Sun?" she murmured, feeling uneasy and confused. "What . . . what is it?" She looked about for something to hide her nakedness. There was nothing. She sat up, curled her legs to one side, and crossed her arms over her bare breasts. "Why are you dressed like that?"

She flinched involuntarily when the cane's gold head struck the palm of his hand with a loud thud. And she flinched yet again when, deliberately slowly, Night Sun crouched down on his heels before her, his black eyes mean and accusing.

He pointed the cane at her. "Do you recognize this?"

Begging the tears that were stinging the backs of her eyes not to fall, Martay said, "I . . . it's a cane, I . . ."

"This, Miss Martay Kidd, is the walking stick Abraham Lincoln presented, long ago, to my grandfather, Walking Bear. Do you know why the great White Father gave this walking stick to my grandfather?"

Her bare body became covered with gooseflesh, Martay shook her head. "No. No, I don't, but I . . ."

"As a symbol of our tribe's sovereign authority." Night Sun's dark, scowling face darkened even more, and Martay gasped in surprised fear when he angrily snapped the walking stick across his bent knee and threw the shattered ends across the tipi. "Does it look like the Sioux has sovereign authority over this land?" He glared at her.

"I don't know, I . . . no, I guess . . ."

He rose to his full, imposing height, reached up behind his head, and in one swift movement jerked his fringed shirt off and dropped it beside her. He tapped his chest, making certain he had her full attention, then let his fingertips move slowly down the long white scar as she watched, openmouthed.

He said, "Know who did this to me?"

She shook her head. "No. I've asked and you would never tell . . ."

"The white man. A blue-coated trooper gave this to me. I was ten years old and unarmed."

"Who was he? Do you know?" she said, barely above a whisper, a hint of the awful truth dawning somewhere in her confused thoughts.

For a long, tension-filled moment Night Sun simply stared at her with those cruel black eyes. When finally he spoke, he said, "Last night should never have happened. You're white. I'm Lakota. Nothing can ever change that."

Hurt, and growing angry herself, Martay scrambled to her feet; stood there, naked, with her hands on her hips. "You're half white so . . ."

"No," he cut her off. "I am, and will forever be, a Lakota Sioux chieftain."

"Well, Chief, you sure liked making love to a white woman. How do you square that with your mighty Lakota conscience?"

He looked for a minute as though he might strike her. He said, "I can't." His frigid eyes traveled down her body. "Get clothed and stay clothed when I'm around."

"Not until you tell me what's wrong!" she shouted. "What happened between last night and now?"

"Nothing." He bent from the waist, picked up his discarded buckskin shirt, and thrust it at her. "Put this on."

"Why?" she taunted, and refused to take it from him. "I thought you liked me with no clothes. That's what you said. Said you wanted to keep me naked in your tipi forever."

Night Sun's eyes narrowed. "Stop shouting."

"I want to shout. I want all your fine, upright people to know what we've been doing. Remember what you were doing to me at dawn, Chief?" She saw the pain cross his face and was pleased.

"Don't . . ."—he shook his head— "do not call me Chief."

"Why not? Isn't that what you are? A proud Lakota chieftain who feels dirty this morning because he spent the night making love to the white enemy?"

His hand shot out and his long fingers captured her defiant chin. Holding it firmly between thumb and forefinger, he leaned to her and said, "What happened here last night had nothing to do with making love."

"It didn't?" she said, and suddenly she looked and sounded like a hurt, confused child. "What was it, then, if not love? I was making love to you. I thought you were making love to me." She lifted her hands to his trim waist. Frantically clutching at his bare ribs, she said, "But you weren't, were you? You were . . . you were just using me for a night of . . . it meant nothing to you. Dear God, you used me like . . . like a . . . didn't you?"

"I'm Indian, you're white" he said, as if that were an explanation.

"Answer me, damn you!" she shouted, tears beginning to pool in the corners of her eyes. "Were you just using me?"

"Yes. An Indian brave using his white captive," he said, meaning to hurt her, knowing that he had when the tears overflowed and streaked down her beautiful flushed face.

"I . . . I . . . you were my . . . there's never been anyone else," she said, beginning to sob openly, her heart broken. "D-did you . . . know . . . th-that?"

"I am sorry," he said, and feeling as though someone had plunged a knife deeply into his chest, Night Sun took her bare shoulders, set her back, turned on his heel and left her there.

Martay, trembling with emotion, slumped down to the soft fur bed, put her head on her bent arms, and cried uncontrollably. Her bare body jerked with her wracking sobs. She wept with despair and with shame and with fear. She had so completely surrendered her body and soul to a man who had used her callously. She was, he had coldly pointed out this morning, his white captive, to be used for his pleasure.

Used. What a horrid word. What a horrid reality. Night Sun had used her. Night Sun cared nothing for her. Night Sun hated her.

Instinctively, Martay turned into a fetal position, pressing her trembling knees firmly together, wishing the tenderness between her legs did not so vividly bring back all the pain and pleasure. Wishing she had never lain naked beneath a beautiful savage warrior. Wishing she had never felt his hands on her, his lips on hers, his body in hers.

"I hate you," she sobbed miserably, loving him, fearing him, knowing she must somehow get away.

Night Sun went at once for his horse. Ignoring the friendly braves' inquiries regarding his destination and the offers to ride along with him, he mounted the big black, wheeled him swiftly about, dug his moccasined heels into the beast's flanks, and shot away from camp. He thundered across the rolling plains while the hot autumn winds stung his face and burned his unblinking eyes.

His face set, his back rigid, he guided the mighty steed toward the distant *Paha Sapa,* his heart aching, his troubled spirit seeking solace. For three hours he rode without stopping, and then only to water his blowing, winded mount.

On the grassy, sloping banks of Belle Fourche River, Night Sun tossed the reins to the ground, threw a long leg over, and dropped to his feet. The thirsty horse moved forward, lowered his great head, blew in the water, lifted his wet muzzle, shook his head about. Then lowered it once more and began drinking greedily.

Night Sun lay down on his belly beside the huge horse. His hands on the bank, weight supported on bent elbows, he leaned far out and drank like a cat, his lips barely touching the water, his tongue lapping until his thirst was quenched.

He raised his dark head, wiped his mouth on a bare arm, and rose.

He waited until the black lifted his head and looked at him. Then he was up on its back again and they were splashing across the cold stream they had just drunk from. The sun was in the west when horse and rider reached the *Paha Sapa* —the sacred Black Hills.

At sunset Night Sun sat, tired and repentant, on a jutting precipice, very near the pit where he had sat as a boy for four days and four nights without food and water, seeking his vision.

Alone now in this sacred place, Night Sun sat, arms on knees, staring at the dying sun. He felt as frightened as he had all those years ago when he was sixteen. Then he was afraid of being alone and of the darkness and of dangerous animals. That did not frighten him now. He welcomed the solitude, looked forward to the covering blackness, appreciated the beauty of the bobcat. His was a far more formidable foe than loneliness or darkness or wild animals.

A slender golden-haired white girl.

32

In the days that followed, Martay kept her distance from her impervious captor. Hating him more than ever, she began seriously to entertain the idea of escape. It wouldn't be easy because Night Sun, as though he could see right into her thoughts, had withdrawn her riding privileges. Nevertheless, she began to make plans. Knowing that if she hoped to be successful, she must lull the cold half-breed and catch him off guard, she became, more than ever, the dutiful, model prisoner.

The two of them were never alone together; Night Sun saw to that. But when he visited his grandmother and found Martay there, she was quiet and courteous and effectively kept her fear and hatred of him from showing when their eyes infrequently met.

Determined she would arouse no suspicion, she kept her secret hurt submerged and treated Night Sun as if nothing had happened between them. He, too, behaved as if the long, intimate night in his tipi had never taken place and Martay supposed it was easy for him, since it had meant nothing. A few hours of amusement provided by his foolish white captive. A base hunger sated by using the closest available woman. A drunken interlude promptly forgotten with the return of sobriety.

There were hours when Martay was almost able to forget, herself. She purposely pushed from mind the way she felt when Night Sun had held and kissed and loved her. Shut her ears to the recollection of sweet love words he had murmured in the moonlight. Closed her eyes to the recurring sight of him naked and aroused and savagely beautiful.

Disciplining herself to conceal her thoughts on her upcoming escape, she was able, for the most part, to ignore his presence in the village. Night Sun helped. He stayed as far away from her as possible. Still, there were times when their being in the same place at the same time was unavoidable.

Like the day of the horse race.

For weeks there had been excited talk of the friendly rivalry between Night Sun and a strong, muscular brave known as Swift Eagle. Gentle Deer told Martay that when the two men were boys, they were the best horsemen in the village and that each year a horse race was staged to prove which rider's prowess was superior, which mount the faster.

What was the prize, Martay wanted to know? And felt a burning sensation in her throat when Gentle Deer answered.

"Then, the winner could choose any horse in the village." She fell silent, looked at Martay with those all-seeing sightless eyes, and added, "It is different now. Now they are no longer boys. They are men."

"The winner doesn't choose the horse he wants?"

Gentle Deer shook her gray head. "He chooses the woman he wants."

Martay felt she might be sick. Night Sun would win the race; she knew it. And then he would pick one of the pretty maidens and . . . and . . . do to the Indian girl all the things he'd done to her? Take one of the copper-skinned maidens to their tipi and make love to her for the rest of the day? Marry one of the pretty Lakota girls?

She didn't ask. She couldn't bear to hear the answer.

It would be like the old, happy times, Gentle Deer said. Night Sun on his black stallion and Swift Eagle on his chestnut gelding. Everyone would be there.

And everyone was. Including Martay.

Shading her eyes against the bright autumn sun, she stood with Gentle Deer and several chattering maidens, and watched as Night Sun and Swift Eagle, laughing and kidding each other, stood shaking hands prior to the race's start.

The two warriors wore only breechclouts. Their bare bodies had been oiled from throat to toes. Their thick black hair had been tied back with otter skins. Their feet were bare.

Martay had eyes only for the taller of the two. Night Sun, his bronzed chest and wide shoulders and long legs gleaming, looked as carefree and relaxed as if he were still a young boy racing for prized horseflesh. Her narrowed eyes slipped down to his groin, straining against the stingy covering apron of leather. He was no boy. He was all man and the race was for a woman.

In a daze she watched as the two warriors climbed on the bare backs of their mounts. The horses, as eager for the sport as their masters, shook their heads about and neighed and whinnied and acted as if they knew they were about to take part in a very important event.

Martay's gaze drifted from the leanly muscled thighs hugging shimmering black horseflesh up to the stallion's proud head. His eyes were big and excited, his ears pricked, and Martay knew he was receiving last-minute instructions from the man on his back. Silently, foolishly, Martay issued some instructions of her own.

"Please," she entreated inwardly, "let the chestnut win this one. I know you're the fastest, so does Night Sun, but must you prove it today? Can't you wait until next year's race? You see, I won't be here then. I won't have to watch Night Sun pick the girl he wants to . . . to . . .

Shouts rose from the crowd. The race was on. Holding her breath, Martay watched with the others as the black and the gelding galloped past in a cloud of dust, the warriors on their backs leaning low over their necks.

The distance was a mile. One complete circle around the village and back to the starting point. The horses' hooves striking hard dirt, the excited cries of the spectators, the pounding of her own heart, were the sounds Martay heard.

She could no longer see the riders; didn't know who was winning. It seemed an eternity before the speeding horses broke into view once more, heading for the finish line. Through the trees and scattered tipis she saw them and murmured soundlessly "No, no."

The big black was in the lead.

She couldn't bear to look. She couldn't bear not to. She saw the chestnut closing on the black. But only for a second. The black pulled away again, opening up the gap between them. The gelding did not give up. He found a new burst of energy and again pulled alongside the black. The two horses were shoulder to shoulder, galloping toward the finish line.

It was impossible to tell which one would win. The black's head would lunge ahead, then the chestnut would stick his nose past as, stride for stride, they flew for home. With only ten yards to go they were still running head to head when Martay saw it. A movement so slight no one would notice, and if they did, they wouldn't realize what had happened.

But she did.

She saw Night Sun's spread hand lightly slap the black's grinding, moving withers. The big stallion altered his stride minutely just as they drove for the finish line. The chestnut gelding won the race.

While all the others applauded and laughed and hurried to congratulate the winner, Martay remained where she was, knowing, as Night Sun knew, that he had thrown the race. He had handed Swift Eagle the race so that he wouldn't have to choose a maiden. Why that knowledge made her want to cry, she didn't know. But it did.

Late that evening when Night Sun returned to their lodge, she pretended sleep, just as always. But she couldn't sleep, and she knew that Night Sun couldn't sleep either. He tossed and turned and smoked in the darkness.

That he hated her was apparent, and while she lay there watching him lift and lower the orange-tipped cigar to his harsh mouth, its glow illuminating his face and chest, the awful truth, which she had been pushing to the back of her mind, became suddenly clear.

The trooper who had given Night Sun the mean, ugly scar down his chest was her father. That's what this was all about. Why Night Sun had brought her here. To get at her father. She was nothing more than a pawn in the game of old, enduring hatreds. Was it the reason he'd made love to her as well?

Feeling the hot tears spill down onto her folded arm, Martay continued to study his dark, handsome face through tear-blurred vision. It would be, she decided, the last night she would lie and look at him.

Tomorrow she would escape.

33

The next morning Martay waited until Night Sun was dressed. When his tall frame headed for the tipi opening, she rose up, clutching the fur covers to her, yawning, pretending she had just awakened.

"Night Sun." She spoke his name softly and saw the immediate tensing of muscles beneath the soft elkskin shirt that stretched across his wide shoulders.

"Yes?" he answered without turning.

"My mare so needs exercising. May I please ride her up on the eastern bluffs for a while this morning?"

She watched, not daring to breathe, while he stood there with his back to her, his hands flexing into fists at his sides. He was going to refuse. She knew it. He didn't trust her.

"I'll have Speaks-Not-At-All come for you in half an hour," he said, ducking his dark head under the flap, and was gone before she could offer thanks.

Martay's heart began to beat wildly. Throwing back the buffalo robes, she jumped up and hurried to dress. Knowing better than to do anything that might alert Night Sun, she didn't even consider taking anything but the clothes on her back. In a plain buckskin skirt and shirt and her knee-high moccasins, her hair pulled back and bound at the back of her head with a leather strip, she nervously paced, waiting for the old mute warrior.

And as she paced, her restless eyes touched the things that had grown familiar in the past few weeks—Night Sun's long fur bed, his eagle-feather war bonnet, his decorated lance. Feeling that unwanted lump rising to her throat, Martay paused, looked at his pine chest for a long moment, then moved slowly toward it. Quietly, carefully, opening the top drawer, she reached in and touched the supple black velvet enclosing her dried white gardenia.

Thinking that the wilted flower would be all that was left of her in Night Sun's life, she realized, sadly, she was taking nothing of him with her.

The near, distinctive sound of her sorrel mare whinnying a cheerful good-morning caused Martay to close the pine chest and rush toward the tipi opening. She stuck her head out, smiled warmly at Speaks-Not-At-All, and motioned to him that she would be right with him. Then, turning, she took one last, slow look around.

Martay swallowed, then swallowed again.

For the rest of her days she would remember exactly how this small, cozy lodge looked. Would recall the scent of sweet sage freshening the air, the feel of soft fur against her bare skin, the sight of Night Sun's dark head ducking through the flap.

She whirled about and rushed outside, took a long, deep breath of fresh air, and climbed atop her prancing sorrel. Slapping the long reins from side to side across the mare's sleek neck, she cantered the mount straight from the village, never looking back.

But a pair of intense black eyes were on her.

A shoulder braced against a tree, Night Sun stood, arms crossed over his chest, watching Martay and the old warrior ride out. The casual attitude of his long, lean body, the lack of expression on his face, belied the inexplicable unease he was feeling. Unemotionally observing her departure, he experienced an overwhelming urge to go after her.

Quietly grinding his even, white teeth, he pushed away from the tree and walked unhurriedly back toward the village.

Martay was uncharacteristically quiet as she and Speaks-Not-At-All rode across the countryside. Usually she kept up a steady stream of chatter as though Speaks understood every word. Not this morning. She knew the old warrior was puzzled by her silence; he kept looking at her with those sad, questioning eyes, and it made her feel worse than she already felt. But she hardened her heart, kicked her mare's flanks, and shot ahead, knowing what she had to do.

Speaks-Not-At-All, entrusted with her care, raced after Martay, just as she knew he would. She turned and smiled when he drew alongside her, and for a time the pair rode knee to knee across the great stretches of prairie grass and sagebrush. When they reached the beginning of the grotesquely carved buttes and rugged canyons, Speaks-Not-At-All motioned that it was time they turned back. He pointed up at the high white clouds building over the eastern hills.

Martay laughed gaily and indicated she wanted to ride just a bit further, just a bit faster. And all the while she was planning to elude him when they reached the rough, unbroken country that lay ahead. But when, half an hour later, they thundered into a shallow, curving sandstone canyon, Speaks-Not-At-All was still right at her side and she realized it was impossible to outride him.

Hating the thought of what she had to do, Martay slowed her horse so that the fall she must take wouldn't break her neck, then wasted no more time. Before Speaks could pull up on his mount, she tumbled from her mare's back and lay, unmoving, on the ground.

He was back to her in seconds, and Martay, lying in wait, her fingers clutching a large rock, waited until the sun was blocked from her view. Knowing then that Speaks-Not-At-All was between her and the sun, she opened her eyes just as the old warrior, on his knees, reached out to pat her cheek.

"Sorry, Speaks," she said, raised the rock, and struck him on the head. "Speaks!" she screamed when the old Indian crumpled to the ground beside her. Horrified, she shook him by the shoulder, immediately sorry for what she had done, begging him to open his eyes. But Speaks-Not-At-All was out cold.

For a long, miserable moment Martay sat there on her heels beside the unconscious warrior, debating what she should do. She could ride back to the village for help and . . . and . . . She envisioned a furious Night Sun, shook her head, and got to her feet. She hadn't hit Speaks that hard. Surely in few moments he would come to, find her gone, and go back to camp for help.

Still murmuring "I'm sorry, I'm sorry," Martay hurried to jerk up her mare's reins and remount. She galloped away, Speaks's horse running alongside her. For several miles she continued to ride fast, zigging around curves in a shallow canyon, plunging up and down up dry washes and dodging low-hanging tree limbs.

Nervously looking over her shoulder, half expecting to see Speaks running after her on foot, Martay finally slowed her mare to a canter. She had to get her bearings and decide where she would go. Frowning, she looked up at the changing sky. What had been a few high clouds an hour ago were now massive, white thunderheads boiling up, rapidly drifting west.

Martay pulled up on her mare. She had no idea in which direction she should ride. Where was the nearest town? The closest fort? She didn't know. She knew only that Denver was to the south and that Night Sun had taken her to a doctor in some small town on their way north to his camp. Maybe that town was close. Maybe she could get there in a few hours. So she turned south and hoped that she would reach civilization before nightfall.

* * *

Night Sun was restless.

He prowled the village impatiently, unable to fully focus his attention on anything. He kept looking at the sky, judging the length of time Martay and Speaks had been gone. When a couple of hours had passed, he went for his horse.

Alone, he rode out of the village, his Colt .45 stuck down inside the waistband of his tight buckskins. He wasn't sure what he expected to find, but an uncanny premonition of trouble had been nudging him all morning.

As soon as he left the village behind, Night Sun spoke commandingly to the black, and the big stallion went into an easy lope. Night Sun spoke again and the horse galloped rapidly toward the east. Soon horse and rider reached the place where Speaks-Not-At-All, having regained consciousness, sat on the ground, groggily rubbing his head.

Knowing immediately what had happened, Night Sun hurried to the old warrior and shook his dark head reassuringly when Speaks furiously signed that he had let Night Sun down, that the white captive girl had escaped. Wiping his eyes often as old men do, Speaks's hands trembled as he spoke with them, telling Night Sun all he knew.

"I will take you back to camp," said Night Sun, and refused to listen when the old warrior said he would walk back. Wanting to hurry, but far too respectful of the old man's dignity to lift him up onto the horse as though he were a child, Night Sun patiently waited while a still-dizzy Speaks mounted the black.

As soon as he was settled, Night Sun climbed up and was wheeling the horse about. At camp's edge, Night Sun pulled up, allowed Speaks-Not-At-All to climb down unaided, and said, his voice kind and level, "Do not worry. I will bring her back." He leaned down and affectionately patted the old Indian's shoulder. "I must go," he said "hurry home. It is going to rain."

* * *

Martay cautiously guided her mare through corridors of high, jutting ridges of rock and wrinkled draws. The sun intermittently went behind the heavy clouds and already the smell of rain was strong in the heavy air. She peered up at the towering bluffs and down at the deep ravines and wondered what this wild country might be like in a rainstorm.

She pulled up on the sorrel and stood in the stirrups, looking anxiously about for a path that would lead her to the top of the fluted ridges that rose threateningly around her. The rain-heavy clouds had again obliterated the sun. The air had cooled; a canyon wind had picked up and was blowing the ends of her blond hair into her face.

A distant rumble of thunder boomed, echoed, and died. And in the stillness following, Martay heard something else. Screwing up her face, she turned her head to listen, scolding her mare for neighing while she was trying to hear. The mare, dancing in place, was shaking her head, her ears pricked.

"What's the matter with you?" Martay asked the sorrel irritably, patting its neck, "be quiet, will you!" Then: "Oh, dear God," as she heard the distinct sound of horses' hooves striking hard ground and knew that her mare had caught their scent. She was in flight at once, her heart pounding, her busy brain asking how Night Sun could have caught up with her so quickly.

Her moccasined heels digging forcefully into the mare's flanks, Martay sensed rather than heard the other horses rapidly moving on her. The valiant mare gave it her all, but in moments the pursuers were closing the gap. The thought flicked through Martay's mind that she had been a fool to think she could ever escape him.

She cast a hurried glance over her shoulder, certain she'd see the dark, angry countenance of Night Sun. Her head whipped back around as the horrible truth dawned. It was not Night Sun pursuing her. The four Indians racing after her were not Sioux!

At that instant they overtook her and her worst fears were confirmed. A big broad hand reached out, grabbed her mare's reins, and jerked it to a plunging halt. Surrounded, Martay was too frightened to scream, too stunned to move. She was hauled down from her mare's back by a tall, powerful brave and shoved toward a big, ugly man with a badly scarred face.

The scarred Indian grinned, his hot beady eyes crawling over her. "We meet again," he said, and the recollection of a scarred Crow scout standing on the porch at Fort Collins brought with it a small glimmer of hope to Martay.

"Yes. Yes, you work for my father," she said, commanding her trembling knees to be still, her voice not to waver.

The squat Crow moved closer and said, "Scar works for no man." He reached out and touched a lock of her hair. "So . . . you are Night Sun's woman?"

"No. No . . . I . . . Will you help me get back to . . . to . . . Denver?" The other Crows, smiling and chattering in their native tongue, crowded around.

"Ten thousand dollars," stated Scar, staring at her.

"Ten thousand. . . . I don't . . . what . . ."

"You. You are worth ten thousand dollars."

"I am?" She was sure that was good news. "Yes! Yes, a reward. That's a lot of money." She attempted to pull her hair free of his blunt dirty fingers and tried to smile. "You'll be rich."

Scar said, pulling her closer by her hair, "Maybe I let the money go."

"Y-you would? Why?"

His grin broadened. "Maybe had rather have Night Sun's woman than all the white man's money."

Martay began to beg for her life, but it fell on deaf ears. Soon she was begging them to end her life.

Totally helpless against the four Crow hostiles, she was dragged, screaming, to a small grassy rise on the canyon floor. In moments she was lying spread-eagled, her arms jerked over her head, her legs pulled apart. Wrists and ankles were swiftly tied to stakes driven in the ground.

While the other braves went about gathering wood to build a fire, Scar pulled a long, sharp knife from the waistband of his dirty buckskins and crouched down beside Martay. The screams choked off in her throat when the huge, scarred Crow stuck the point of the gleaming knife directly into the laced opening of her shirt. With one deft downward slice, he severed the laces. The soft shirt was open midway down her torso and Martay waited, in agony, for Scar to jerk it apart.

He didn't.

He moved down and cut her knee-high moccasins off, and seeing the tiny bare feet, laughed with delight, a low guttural laugh. He touched fore and middle fingers to a bare sole and tickled her. She screamed and cried instead of laughing. He ordered her to be quiet and she did her best to obey, the tears continuing to stream down her cheeks as she hiccoughed with stifled sobs.

Scar, speaking in low, soft tones, told her exactly how he felt. As he began to cut her long, buckskin skirt, he told her he liked what he saw before him. A beautiful golden-haired white woman who belonged to the hated half-breed, Night Sun. He said he had wanted her that day he saw her at Fort Collins; was greatly tempted by her haughty beauty. Now he had her. Could do anything he pleased to her.

"Do you know what I'm going to do to you, Miss Kidd?" He pushed her torn skirt apart so that her long, slender legs were exposed. Martay didn't answer. Biting her lip to keep from screaming, she closed her tear-filled eyes.

She opened them when his big, broad hand abruptly grabbed her chin and he said, leaning close, "Ten thousand dollars is a lot of money to pay for a woman's body. I want my fill. When I'm through with you," he inclined his head, "my braves can have what's left." His hand slid down to her throat, his rough thumb rubbing familiarly, "When we're all done, that arrogant Sioux dog will no longer want you."

Choking, eyes wild, she stared fearfully at Scar as he slowly rose to his feet. Grinning down at her, the huge, repulsive Crow began undressing. He took off his shirt and leggings. He stood there, laughing, wearing nothing but a breechclout so brief, it rode low beneath his huge, shaking belly. He squatted down on his heels beside Martay, his fat knees apart, and commanded her to look at him.

The ugly naked Crow completely filled her vision. She could see only massive arms and scarred chest and powerful thighs and a bulging crotch barely covered by a strip of dirty leather. Ignoring the look of disgust and fear in her tear-bright green eyes, Scar reached out and slowly pushed at the left side of her opened shirt.

A great crack of lightning lit up the dark sky. The following thunder competed with Scar's lusty laughter as he exposed a trembling pale breast to his hot, eager eyes.

While the first sporadic raindrops began to pepper his broad back, the repulsive squat-bodied Scar taunted Martay, explaining that now he was going to cut all her clothing away.

"And when," he said, his beady black eyes glazing with desire, "you are lying pale and naked before me, I will . . ."

A shot rang out and Scar's words choked off in his throat as his eyes rolled back in his head. He dropped the knife and clutched at his chest.

Paralyzed with shock and fear, Martay heard more shots follow the first in quick succession, the sound of them mingling with loud, booming thunder, and in the blinking of an eye all the Crows lay dead or dying.

She screamed, looked up, and saw him.

Night Sun, standing tall and godlike in the rain, his raven hair blowing wildly about his hard, handsome face, the raised gun still smoking in his hand.

34

Her trembling lips formed his name in blessed relief, though no sound would come. Tears mixed with rain surged down her cheeks and she no longer struggled against the binding leather restraints. Her tensed body went limp with total release and her drumming pulse changed its rhythm.

Night Sun was here. She was safe.

Her grateful heart singing his name in a litany of thank yous, she watched him come to her, his wet, dark face rigid with wrath and hatred. When he stood just above, his narrowed black eyes fell on the fat Crow Scout beside her. He lifted a foot, set it squarely atop the dead man's thick neck, and ground his heel down with such fierce force, the scarred Crow's ugly face instantly became buried in the mud.

Night Sun picked up the discarded knife and swiftly cut the bindings from Martay's raw wrists and ankles. When he picked her up, the familiar feel of his lean strength caused her to sob out his name hysterically.

There was no reaction from him. While she clung to him,

crying and kissing his dark, wet face, he strode purposefully to the waiting black stallion, lifted her atop its back, and swung up behind her, then rode over to grab the reins of her sorrel mare.

A flash of lightning streaked across the black sky directly over the canyon, its dangerous, deadly charge striking a sturdy pine with such ferocity, the tree exploded. Thunder, so loud it vibrated through her cold, wet body, deafened Martay. Huge raindrops, driven by the rising winds, stung her face and bare arms and legs.

But she was not afraid.

There was no fear so long as she was enclosed in the strong, protective arms of this fearless Sioux chieftain. His power was mightier than the summer storm. His slow, steady heartbeat beneath her ear more fierce than the echoing thunder. The heat from his lean, coiled body could rival the electrical potency of the lightning.

So Martay relaxed completely in Night Sun's arms as the stallion, followed by the mare, thundered through the rain-drenched canyon. In moments Night Sun was guiding the big black under a low, wide ledge of sandstone. As soon as they were beneath the sheltering rock overhang, he shoved Martay from the horse and climbed down.

Chilled by the cold, driving rains, Martay stood shivering, arms crossed over her chest, her teeth chattering, the wet, torn buckskins clinging to her cold skin. Night Sun silently unstrapped a blanket from behind his saddle. She reached for it and was thoroughly puzzled when, instead of handing it to her, he tossed it to the ground scant inches from where the blowing, driven rain was peppering the stony apron of their dry refuge.

She looked questioningly up at him. His rain-wet face was still set in inflexible lines of menace. His eyes were as cold as the chill rains, his lips as hard as the granite enclosure where they stood.

Night Sun, relieved Martay was unharmed, angry with

himself that she could so frighten him, lifted a hand and wiped the rain from his rigid face. Seeing her standing there shivering, a mixture of heat and hatred jolted through him. His desire for her surged and awakened in him a sleeping brutality. He wanted her; he wanted to hurt her. Driven by an angered passion he did not fully understand, he reached out, took her arm, and roughly jerked her to him. His eyes holding hers, he raised his hands, curled long fingers into the torn opening of her buckskin shirt, ripped it apart, and shoved it from her shoulders.

His deadly black eyes on her rain-wet bared breasts, he spoke at last. "If a savage is to use you, I'll be that savage."

His mouth came forcefully down on hers. His sharp teeth nipped at her soft bottom lip, then released it. Immediately he deepened the kiss, his passion-hardened lips brutal in their invasion of her trembling mouth. He kissed her with fierce aggression, his hunger for her heightened by a raw need to punish her for scaring him.

Martay put up no fight. Grateful to be alive, relieved it was his arms she was in, his lean, hard body she was pressed intimately against, she willingly surrendered, kissing him back with a fervor that rivaled his. The long, demanding kiss was exactly what she needed and she sighed with pleasure as his tongue penetrated deeply. Eagerly she touched her tongue to his and felt him shudder against her.

Abruptly Night Sun raised his dark head. The expression in his eyes was a mixture of heat and cold, of lust and hate, of harshness and helplessness.

A muscle jumping furiously in his dark jaw, his hand came up to clasp and lift a soft, bare breast. His warm palm enclosed the nipple as his lips went to the side of Martay's throat. She felt his sharp teeth graze the sensitive spot just below her ear, and her pulse quickened as he hastily, hungrily, kissed a molten path to her breasts.

His hot, open mouth swiftly enclosed a peaking nipple and he slipped to his knees before her. He was not gentle. His arms went around her; his hands possessively gripped her bare back. Pulling her to him, he held her tightly, securely, while he sucked so vigorously at her breast, Martay winced from the pain-pleasure.

Her breath coming in short little flutters, she put her hands into his dark wet hair. Anxiously she gripped the silky locks, pulling frantically, urging him closer, even as she arched her back and leaned to him, enthralled by the exquisite enjoyment of his fiercely tugging lips and raking teeth. Making a strange little sound in the back of her throat, she watched his gleaming wet lips release her rapidly pinkening breast and move to the other.

No sooner was the small hard bud enclosed in the warmth of his mouth than he flutter-tongued her nipple, and Martay threw back her head, moaned with ecstasy, and murmured, "Oh, yes, Night Sun. Yes."

Surprised that such incredible joy could come from his lips enclosing her nipple, she gasped when his mouth opened wider to draw even more of her breast inside. That, too, brought added pleasure, and she watched, dazed with delight, as her wet, quivering breast seemed to disappear into his questing mouth as greedily he sucked, devouring her, thrilling her.

The first small hailstones hissed outside on the canyon floor as Night Sun knelt there under the rock overhang holding Martay against him, his mouth deserting her breast to slide hotly down over her narrow rib cage. When his lips touched the wet buckskin of her torn skirt, he lifted his head.

Feeling himself growing painfully hard beneath his tight buckskin pants, he was resolved to have her in any way and every way he chose. To teach her a lesson she would never forget. To ignore her pleas for gentleness and patience. So he ripped the soggy, tattered buckskin skirt from her just as a fierce gust of wind slammed into the scooped out enclosure, almost knocking Martay from her feet. With one steadying hand, he held her up. While the big black whickered loudly and nudged at Night Sun's shoulder, and fierce lightning skittered within feet of them, and the winds and the rains grew more angry and intense, Night Sun, as tumultuous and as violet as the worsening tempest, stripped Martay naked.

He sat back on his heels then, anticipating her fear, expecting the tears and the begging. But Martay defied him. Proudly she stood there, bare and wet and beautiful, her emerald eyes shining with unashamed desire, her hands outstretched to him, beckoning him to take what he'd unwrapped.

Watching her intently as though she were some strange, erotic apparition that would surely vanish in the mists, Night Sun shuddered, groaned, and reached for her, his hands roughly encircling her narrow waist. Martay, unafraid, looked steadily into his dark eyes, love and desire shining clearly in her own.

That open, inviting look, the brazen offering of her pale, beautiful body in sweet surrender, angered Night Sun. More determined than ever to shock her, he swiftly pulled her down, positioned her on her back atop the blanket, and stretched out beside her. A firm hand pressing her bare shoulder to the blanket, he brought a long leg over her knees to hold her down. His mouth lowered to hers then and he kissed her forcefully, deeply, his open lips twisting, slanting on hers. Martay felt the abrasive rub of his buckskins against her bare flesh as his chest pressed heavily on hers and his knee moved between her legs to nudge them apart. After just one deep, intrusive kiss, his lips left hers and immediately began moving aggressively down over her bare, tingling body.

Clutching at his shoulders, Martay murmured his name breathlessly and whispered, "Darling, take off your clothes. Your buckskins are scratching me."

He gave no answer. His eyes closed, his strong, possessive hands sweeping over her, he continued to kiss her naked flesh hungrily, feasting on her as though he would never get his fill. When his hot, open lips reached her bare belly, Martay shuddered, excited with pleasure. Night Sun turned his head from side to side, brushing his lips, his teeth, his tongue on her quivering flesh. His long silky hair, damp from the rains, fell around his dark, moving face to tickle and excite her.

Her hands clutching at the spread blanket, Martay lay there completely naked while Night Sun, fully clothed, pressed plucking kisses to her flat stomach as the high plains hailstorm raged around them. While his lips and tongue played passionately over her sensitive skin, Martay inhaled deeply of the rain-freshened air and smiled foolishly. Wonderingly, she turned her head and saw, as if in a dream, great balls of frozen ice fall from the stormy sky into the swirling waters surging through the canyon.

The violent winds continued to howl. The rains became torrential. The sky was as dark as midnight. The black stallion and the sorrel mare, standing not six feet away, whickered with nervous excitement, their eyes wild.

Unbothered by any of it, Martay felt absolutely no fear. She was not afraid of the late-summer storm. Nor was she afraid of the dark, handsome man furiously kissing her bare belly. She didn't understand him—she'd never been able to fully penetrate the mystery that was Night Sun—but she loved him with all her heart and soul. She was his. Would always be his. And he could love her in any way he wanted.

Night Sun's heated lips eagerly moved down, down until they touched the top edge of the damp golden curls between Martay's pale thighs. Immediately the blazing heat she'd felt since the first moment his lips had touched hers, became a hurting, painful need.

"Night Sun," she murmured.

Night Sun never lifted his head. On fire himself, hating her, loving her, wanting her with a dangerous, animalistic passion unlike any he'd ever known, he pressed his cheek to the soft gold curls even as his firm hands urged her legs to open for him. With sure, warm fingers he stroked the soft insides of her thighs until they parted to allow him total access. Then swiftly, deftly, as he did all things, he moved between her parted thighs without ever having taken his fingers from their silky insides, his lips from her trembling belly.

His hands went beneath her, his long, spread fingers clasped her rounded buttocks, and he gave her no opportunity to evade him. As though he truly were an uncivilized savage, she his white captive, meant only for his heathen pleasures, he said, his voice heavy with unchecked desire, "You are mine, Martay. You cannot escape me. No one will taste the delights of your body but me. It all belongs to me."

"Yes," she whispered, "it's yours. Take me, darling."

He looked up at her then, and try as she might, she could not read those Indian eyes. Holding her gaze, his dark face slowly, purposefully lowered into the golden curls, and when she felt his hot breath on her, Martay gasped. She gasped again when he kissed her. Kissed her just as though he was kissing her mouth, his lips and teeth touching her, caressing her. And when his beautiful eyes fluttered closed, the dark, girlish lashes shadowing his high cheekbones, he opened his mouth wider and she felt his tongue boldly stroke her, Martay winced and shuddered with shocked delight.

Hearing her sharp intake of air and feeling her quiver against him, Night Sun buried his face deeply in her. He loved her with all the fire and fury she inspired in him. His tongue quickly found and probed and stroked and circled the tiny nub of pleasure that was his intimate ally. Knowing he would set her afire, would shock and frighten her, he reveled in the knowledge. He would excite this naked temptress until she begged him for blessed deliverance. He would push her to the very limits of all-consuming human desire. He would show her that he held the very key to her ecstasy.

Martay was frightened.

Frightened by the height of her wild joy. Frightened by the depth of the love she felt for this dark man responsible for her rapture. Frightened that he would take his dazzling mouth from her and leave her burning with desire. It seemed there was nothing about her he did not know. It was as though every square inch of her body had been fashioned solely for him to explore, to awaken, to make his own.

She was his, all his. Nothing could ever change that.

The heat enveloping her escalated as he kissed and caressed her, his skillful loving pushing her toward a release so total, she fought against it. Her nervous fingers twining in his raven-black hair, she moaned softly and murmured, "No. Please, no."

Night Sun's hands tightened under her, his long fingers cutting into the tender flesh of her buttocks. His hot, open mouth sank deeper. His tongue stroked harder. He loved and licked and lashed her until soon it began; a mixture of agony and ecstasy so intense, Martay's slender shoulders rolled up from the blanket and she panted and pleaded and thought she could stand the fiery throbbing not one second longer. Wildly she clutched at Night Sun's dark, moving head, forcing his face more deeply into her even as her jerking pelvis surged up to meet his feasting mouth.

It seemed to last an eternity. That forceful, spiraling, scary hurting that only his hot, marvelous mouth could heal. Frantically she called out his name as her wrenching, frightening release buffeted her as though she were a leaf tossed about by the rain-driven winds.

Night Sun stayed with her, giving her all she needed, loving her so hotly, so intimately, he felt his own release dangerously close. When at last the involuntary jerking of her body had stopped and her grasping hands had released their hold on his hair, he brushed one last kiss to the inside of her trembling thigh and lifted his head.

She lay panting softly, her eyes closed, her tongue wetting her dry lips. There were no tears on her cheeks, no murmured scoldings for what he'd done, no attitude of shock.

Night Sun rose to his feet. Martay remained just as she was. She made no move to modestly close her legs. They were just as they had been when he lay between them. Parted, the slick, swollen sweetness between completely exposed to his hot gaze.

Martay's eyes opened to see Night Sun standing above, stripping himself of his clothes. She sighed with lazy happiness and watched appreciatively as his skin gleamed copper in a bright flash of lightning. Muscles played in his bare back as he peeled the wet buckskins down his long legs.

Naked, he stood there above, a bronzed god, fully aroused, his blatant masculinity a fascinating instrument of bold beauty to the woman who loved him. Awed by the proud, fierce sight of him, Martay trembled involuntarily.

Night Sun saw her tremble. He read quite a different meaning into her reaction to him. Now he had her as he wanted her. Afraid. Afraid he would fall to his knees and force himself on her while she was still shocked and shaken. And that was exactly what he would do.

Martay's breath quickened when his sleek animal body came down against her own. The smoothness of his chest, the crisp hair of his groin, the throbbing male power against her belly made her shiver with rising excitement. His mouth came down on hers. She tasted herself on his lips and, appalled, desperately tried to pull free. Night Sun refused to let her go. His tongue skimmed along her teeth, then penetrated deeply and he ground his open mouth to hers, holding her head immobile with the force of his kiss while she pushed futilely on his pressing chest.

His hand captured hers and drew it down to his aching arousal. He made her wrap trembling fingers around him, his own lean fingers guiding hers, showing her how. Their lips parted. He lifted his head and looked into her eyes, expecting to see distaste. He dropped his hand from hers, certain she'd jerk her hand away immediately.

Again she surprised him.

Her eyes filled with limpid desire, she gazed down on the rigid male flesh she continued to caress and she asked, quite seriously, "Does it feel best when I do it slowly, like this?"

She unhurriedly let her curling, caressing fingers slide the impressive length of him. "Or a bit faster, like this?" Her small, clinging hand moved up and down three times in quick succession before Night Sun, in agony, jerked it away, his expression one of confused anger.

Gripping her wrist, Night Sun pinned her arm to the blanket beside her shoulder and moved over her. Poised just above, he lowered his head and caressed her breast. His mouth quickly found a ripe nipple and his lips and tongue sucked it into a hard, darkened point of sensation while his hand swept down over her belly. Fingers slipping between her legs, he touched her, seeking entrance, and was amazed to find her already wet and ready for him.

His lips deserted her breast. He moved into position. Looking straight into her eyes, he gripped himself, placed the swollen head into her, and letting his hands move down under her hips to lift her to him, he slid deeply into her. She offered no resistance. No look of pain or discomfort crossed her face.

Their eyes locked. Both sighed with the pleasure of it and at once began to move together. In seconds their mating was as violent and as savage as the thunderstorms still raging beyond their bed of love. Panting and perspiring, Martay bucked against him, her pelvis tilting up to receive his driving, filling thrusts. Night Sun, his slim hips moving rhythmically fast, threw everything he had into her, each deep, quick stroke bringing them both closer to the edge.

When the total release came, both called out in their ecstasy, the sounds of their cries swept away on the galelike winds. Night Sun collapsed atop Martay, and when finally she began to squirm, he refused to let her go. Balancing his weight on his arms, he remained as he was, still buried in her, waiting. Waiting until her warmth could make him hard and ready again.

It didn't take that long.

Night Sun smiled when he saw, at last, a perplexed look come over her lovely face. Finally he had shocked her. That

aroused him totally. He grew very hard and heavy inside her.
At once he began the thrusting motions of lovemaking with
no preliminary kisses or caresses. That's the way he wanted it.
That's the way it would be. He would take his pleasure. She
would endure. He would show her, once and for all, that she
meant nothing to him.

Nothing.

But the warm, pliant body gripping his and the trusting
emerald eyes looking at him so lovingly and the soft, feminine
voice calling his name quickly changed all that. In seconds
Martay was moving perfectly with him and Night Sun was
murmuring her name and bending to press kisses to her
parted lips and painfully holding back so that he could take
her along with him on that magical journey to bliss.

35

The rains had stopped. Twilight was falling over the canyon. A peaceful quiet had replaced the thunderous roar of the afternoon's fierce rain and hailstorm. The lonely call of a distant whippoorwill was the only sound in the hushed evening silence. That and the occasional whicker of a restless black stallion.

Two tranquil lovers, their tumultuous passions quieted as the storm's, lay lazy and serene in their cozy high plains hideaway. Night Sun, flat on his back, was wide-awake. Martay, curled to him, her head pillowed by his supportive shoulder, knee on his stomach, dozed in contented exhaustion.

As he lay there with her soft, warm body pressed to his, Night Sun's thoughts grew increasingly troubled. Once again Martay had not behaved as he expected, as he intended, as he wished. Instead of a repentant, frightened, subdued female, he had had in his arms, through the glorious rain-drenched afternoon, a fire-blooded eager, adventurous lover whose wild, unchecked passion matched his own.

The vivid recollection of the long afternoon's loving, of all he had done to her, and all she had done to him, caused the confused Lakota chieftain to tremble suddenly. He trembled with fear. Night Sun was afraid. Afraid of the beautiful creature sleeping in his arms. Frightened deeply by the turbulent emotions the silky-skinned white girl so effortlessly stirred in him. Unused to fear, resenting its unsettling intrusion, Night Sun was angered by its unwelcome presence in his life.

His narrowed black eyes slid slowly down over the white, slender body intimately draped across the darkness of his. The forbidding sight filled his vision. It said it all. Pale white flesh against dark.

She was white. All white. Lily-white. He was Indian. More Indian than white. Two different worlds. She didn't belong in his. He refused to be a part of hers. She would not—he would not let her—mold and touch his heart the way she had his body.

They rode back to the Powder River camp in strained silence, Night Sun more distant than ever, Martay hurt and confused by the mystifying indifference after a day of such total intimacy. After repeated attempts to get him to tell her what was wrong, she gave up and, wearily resting her head on his shoulder, fought back the tears that stung her eyes.

Martay didn't question what the silent chief might do to her heart. He had already done it. He had taken it for his own. And now he didn't want it.

The pair reached the village shortly after midnight. Finally breaking the silence, Night Sun, lifting Martay from the horse, said, "Sleep. I'll tell the others we are back."

Not giving her a chance to reply, he turned and led the black away. Martay waited for his return, hoping, now that they were safely back in their lodge, she could get him to open up, to tell her why he refused to acknowledge what was between them.

But Night Sun didn't return after telling Windwalker they were back. He climbed the steep bluffs of the river and sat alone in the exact spot where once he had sat and watched Martay, her lips stained with berries, laughing on the banks below him, her dress pulled high up on her pale thighs.

Knowing he should send her away, wondering if it were already too late, Night Sun, tired from the long, lovely afternoon of lovemaking, strengthened his resolve to stay away from her. A couple of weeks and she would be gone. Back to where she belonged. Back to her world of foolish parties and adoring beaus.

Out of his hair. Out of his life. Out of his heart.

Martay, alone in their tipi, still wearing the shirt he had lent her, purposely brushed her nose against the rough sleeve and inhaled. The shirt smelled of Night Sun. His scent alone was enough to make her heart beat faster, her stomach flutter with remembered ecstasy.

Refusing to take the shirt off, she tiredly lay down on her fur bed, drew her knees up, and placed her pressed palms between them. Eyes on the empty bed across from her, she strengthened her resolve to not let this man stay away from her, as he had in the past. It wouldn't be easy, but she had to find a way—any way—to be around him so that he would finally see for himself that they were meant for each other.

That was the last thought in her mind when, still alone, she drifted off into exhausted slumber. She was not going to let Night Sun out of her sight.

As fate would have it, it was Gentle Deer's fragile, failing health that undermined Night Sun's firm resolve to stay away from Martay. And gave Martay the opportunity she was looking for to keep him close to her.

At sunup, after a sleepless night on the river bluffs, Night Sun stopped by his grandmother's lodge to say good-morning before returning to his own. His dark face immediately tightened when he saw the usually energetic old woman was still beneath her buffalo robes.

One look at the wrinkled face and he knew she was sick. Waving a dismissive hand at his worried questions, she said,

"It is just a head cold." She smiled then and, reaching out to touch a bare, bronzed shoulder, added, "If you choose to go about in the chill of morning half naked, you, too, will catch cold. Where is your shirt, Grandson?"

Night Sun, guiltily recalling where the shirt was, felt the heat rise to his face. Shaking his head, he placed her arthritic hand back under the warm fur robes and pulled the covers up to her chin. He sat down beside her.

He was still there when Martay came at midmorning.

Gentle Deer's cold worsened. Night Sun refused to leave her. So did Martay. And so it was that they were thrown together through the long, quiet hours of tending the sick old woman. When Gentle Deer was awake, Night Sun acted as though nothing were wrong between Martay and himself. When she slept, he rarely spoke, but his eyes met Martay's often and more than once, in their eagerness to fuss over Gentle Deer and make her more comfortable, their bodies accidentally brushed, their hands touched, and each time his breath caught in his throat.

For a full week Gentle Deer remained in her sick bed. Martay and Night Sun stayed with her. Day after day, night after night, they remained in Gentle Deer's lodge. The necessity of being together, the shared concern over someone they both loved; it was inevitable that Night Sun's coldness begin to slip away. How could he be angry with Martay when she was so tireless and sweet and uncomplaining in her care for his grandmother?

Late one chilly evening, while Night Sun sat smoking a cigar, his long legs crossed beneath him, he quietly watched Martay as she patiently spoon-fed his grandmother from a steaming bowl. Her golden hair was ablaze in the firelight, her perfect little mouth was turned up into the most disarming of smiles, her emerald eyes were filled with true affection for the old sick woman.

Night Sun's sharp teeth bit down on the cigar. Feeling far sicker than the woman being ministered to, he got up, came forward, and told the two women he would be back within the hour.

The cold air felt good against his hot face. He drew a deep, invigorating breath, ran a lean hand through his thick black hair, and started walking, considering a long night ride on the big black. After a week of being cooped, it would be relaxing to ride fast across the western plains in the moonlight. Ride until he was tired and sleepy and unworried.

Night Sun shook his head. He could not go for a ride. There was something he must do. Something he had put off too long. It was time he got it over with.

He went straight to Windwalker's isolated lodge.

Standing just outside, Night Sun foolishly rehearsed what he would say. It wasn't the first time. He'd gone over it dozens of times in his head. And it never sounded right. He ground his teeth. He had never lied to the Mystic Warrior. He'd not lie now.

As Night Sun stood there debating with himself, the flap of Windwalker's tipi opened and the graying chieftain stepped out into the night, a clay pipe in his hand.

Unsmiling, Windwalker said, "I have expected you."

Night Sun swallowed. "I have come."

The Mystic Warrior solemnly nodded. "I have had the *oinikaga tipi* prepared. We go there, cleanse our hearts and souls, smoke the pipe"—he paused, and staring at Night Sun, added— "talk."

Night Sun shook his head and fell into step beside Windwalker. Circling his tipi, they walked to the secluded sweat lodge in silence. Once there, both men stripped down to the skin, ducked inside the low, west-facing entrance into the small enclosure and sat cross-legged facing each other over the scooped-out circular hole at the tipi's center.

For a time, both were silent. Windwalker stared glassy-eyed at the "circle within the circle" and Night Sun knew what he was thinking. The small pit was a symbol, standing for life, which has no end. Plants, animals, men, are born and die.

But The People live.

Windwalker lit his pipe. Sweet-smelling smoke swirled about his head. He passed it to Night Sun, took up a decorated skin bag of cold, clear water, dipped a sprig of sage into it, and sprinkled water over the heated, glowing stones.

The ice-cold water hitting the red-hot stones produced a great surge of power, the unifying of the earth and the sky.

Night Sun inhaled deeply of the thick white steam. In moments, the heat had become so great, both men were sweating profusely, their bronzed bodies gleaming with moisture. They sat there quietly in the dark heat, smoking, relaxing, their lungs on fire. Night Sun closed his eyes and listened to the hiss of the ice water on the heated stones.

He felt the power, as he always did in the *oinikaga* tipi. He drew in long, cleansing breaths, and rubbed flattened palms over his chest. The power was penetrating him, filling him, healing him. Huddling there in the safe, hot darkness, Night Sun felt his body and mind become unburdened, and he tipped back his head and sighed dreamily.

"You will speak now." Windwalker's soft yet commanding voice disturbed Night Sun's sweet lassitude.

Night Sun's head slowly lowered. Lifting a hand, he wiped the perspiration from his eyes. He looked at Windwalker. The wise chieftain was staring, unblinkingly, at him. Waiting.

He had never lied to the Mystic Warrior. He wouldn't lie now. He was naked here in this comforting place, close to the earth and the spirit. He would offer no excuses. He would speak only the truth.

He said, "I am weak. Not fit to wear the name Lakota chieftain."

"Go on."

"I surrendered to the temptations of the flesh." He sucked in a deep, burning breath of hot steam. "I took the virginity of the golden-haired white captive."

"I know," spoke the Mystic Warrior, his flat dark eyes quietly accusing. "It was wrong, my son."

"Yes," replied Night Sun. "It was."

"You shame yourself. The Lakota does not take revenge on women and children."

Sadly, Night Sun shook his head. "I should not have brought her here. I am sorry I did. Sorry I harmed her."

"Despair walks with you," Windwalker said thoughtfully.

"Yes. I suffer."

Windwalker said, "If your heart loves this white maiden, you could . . ."

"No," answered Night Sun quickly, wanting desperately to believe it. "I desired her. That is all."

Windwalker solemnly nodded. "Then you must let her go."

Night Sun said decisively, "Yes. I will wait no longer to send her back. She'll go now. Tomorrow."

Windwalker's broad, solemn face softened a little, his eyebrows lifted, and he said, "She may not wish to leave us."

Night Sun's face remained stern. "She is the pampered rich daughter of an American general. Of course she wants to go. I'll send her back to her father."

"So be it," said Windwalker, and the light that had shown briefly in his flat dark eyes was gone.

Night Sun felt a little better.

The decision made, he returned to Gentle Deer's lodge. Later that night, after his grandmother was sleeping, he told Martay of his plan. He told her he was going to release her, set her free, send her back.

For a long, tension-filled moment she simply stared at him, her lips parted in disbelief. She was beaten. The attitude of his lean body, the determined line of his jaw. She had seen him thus so many times before.

Ungiving. Rigid. Unreachable.

She said, "Very well." And watching him intently, saw not so much as the flicker of a black eyelash in response. "I'll go home, but not until you tell me everything." She drew a much needed breath, squared her slender shoulders, and lifted her chin defiantly. "I demand it. You owe me that much."

Night Sun's inflexible posture gave way. His wide shoulders slumping slightly, he wearily sighed. He said, "Yes, I do. I know that."

"Then?"

He motioned her toward the lodge opening, indicating he did not wish to disturb his sleeping grandmother. But Martay put a hand on his arm when they reached it.

"We can't go outside," she told him. "We can't leave her."

He nodded and watched Martay sit down near the open flap. Like a little girl she wrapped her skirts around her legs and hugged her knees with her arms. He sat down to face her.

"This whole thing began one cold, snowy morning in 1864. I was ten years old and . . ."

Night Sun told her everything. He talked and talked, his voice low, level, his black eyes expressionless. He was, he said, as puzzled as she that her father had not come for her. He told of sending the message, of expecting the general to arrive at the Colorado line shack within hours after he had taken her from the Darlington party.

Martay, not moving a muscle, listened intently as the truth unfolded. And when finally it was all told and Night Sun fell silent, she studied the dear dark face before her as an inevitable truth dawned. If her beloved Night Sun and her father ever met, one of the two would die.

Martay rose.

"Thank you for . . . for . . ." She didn't finish the sentence. Her voice broke and she turned away. Over her shoulder she said, "I'll be in our . . . your lodge."

She hurried out into the night. Torn between her love for the half-breed chieftain and her general father, she went alone to the tipi she shared with the man whom, after tomorrow, she would never see again.

Night Sun, his heart squeezing painfully in his chest, remained where he was. Brooding. Lonely. Missing her already.

Across the lodge a wide-awake Gentle Deer, having heard every word that passed between the two of them, smiled to herself. And purposely waited, allowing her hardheaded grandson ample time to pine, Martay several long hours to wait.

At midnight the old Indian woman rose from her bed of furs and went to Night Sun.

She said, "A heart that cannot forgive will die."

He frowned at her. "Get back in bed."

"I am well. Go to your lodge."

He said, "I'll stay here until morning and . . ."

"You will go," said his grandmother. "You look haggard. Go home and sleep."

Too tired and troubled to quarrel, Night Sun rose, kissed her temple, and stepped out into the night. He considered climbing the bluffs, but his legs were tired, his back ached dully, and it was cold out. Automatically his steps took him to his own tipi. He paused just outside.

It was well past midnight. She would surely be asleep. He was exhausted, and tomorrow would be a long, trying day. So he ducked inside and quietly undressed in the darkness, taking care not to disturb Martay, asleep in her fur bed across from his.

Night Sun stretched out on his back, the heart inside his naked chest aching with unhappiness. He felt the burning tears spring to his eyes and tried to blink them away. He had not cried since he was ten years old. He blinked again and swallowed the choking lump lodged in his throat.

A cool hand touched his bare shoulder.

Night Sun slowly turned his head and saw a teary-eyed Martay beside him.

"I love you," she said, her tears overflowing when she saw the ones shining in his black eyes. "Don't send me back. I want to stay with you."

Her sweet, childlike admission was all it took. With a great groan of despair, resignation, and incredible happiness, Night Sun pulled the woman he loved into his arms and, unashamed of the hot tears spilling down his face, he murmured, choking with emotion, "From the first minute you looked up into my eyes on that moonlit veranda, I've known I would never let you go."

36

Her face buried in his warm, brown throat, Martay sobbed, "I thought you didn't want me and I . . ."

"Ah, *Wicincala,*" Night Sun managed hoarsely, eyes squeezed shut, arms pressing her tightly to his fiercely pounding heart. Loving her so much he had to control himself lest he crush the very life from her, he said, "I want you, Martay. I apologize for all I've done to you. I love you, *Wicincala,* I love you. Can you ever forgive me?" He pulled back a little to look at her.

"Y-yes . . . oh, yes," she cried. "Yes, Night Sun." Tears washed down her lovely face, but she was smiling and her eyes, those expressive emerald eyes that so intoxicated him, were shining with unveiled adoration and relief.

He smiled too, blinking back his tears and saying, "Don't cry, sweetheart. It's all going to be all right. Please don't cry."

"I . . . I'm . . . not . . . crying. . . . I . . ." Gulping for air, she laughed nervously, still continuing to cry.

"Hoksi cala," said Night Sun, his voice breaking, and cradling her head to his shoulder, he laughed too. For a time

they sat there, laughing and crying all at once, happiness and relief filling them with a new kind of joy neither was yet certain could last. They laughed and laughed, murmuring apologies, promising love, accepting forgiveness, and when finally their uneasy laughter subsided and Night Sun again pulled back to look at Martay, he shuddered and his hands trembled as he lifted them to frame her face.

All traces of laughter gone from his voice, he said, "I love you more than my life, Martay. I cannot live if you leave me."

"I'll never leave you," she murmured, her hands frantically gripping his trim, bare waist. "Never."

"Thank you, sweetheart," he whispered softly as he lowered his mouth to hers. He tasted the salty tears on her full, parted lips and moaned. Gently, lovingly, he kissed them away and silently vowed he would never again make her cry. "I love you," he said, pressing warm, sweet kisses to her wet, quivering lips, "I love you. If you love me, nothing else matters. Nothing."

"I do," she said happily, eagerly, "I do. I love you. And you really do love me, don't you?"

His black shining eyes held hers. "I worship you, Martay."

Their lips came back together in a gentle, lingering kiss. "I love you," she breathed into his mouth. "I love you. I love you."

Night Sun smiled and allowed her lips to play with his. She anxiously kissed him over and over again, pressing her fingers to his brown cheeks, turning her head first this way then that. Kissing at the corners of his mouth, licking and nipping a path along his full bottom lip, sucking at its wet inside, and all the while she was saying, as though the words were magical, as indeed they were, "You love me. You love me."

His breath growing short, Night Sun, letting his hands move down her arms to her narrow waist, felt his passion quickly rising and fought valiantly against it. He didn't want this beautiful woman in his arms to think that he only desired her; he didn't, he loved her with all his heart and wanted her to know it. But her honeyed lips were driving him half crazy and her bare breasts kept brushing tantalizingly against his chest.

Night Sun let out a small sigh of relief when at last Martay's lips left his. But his breath grew short when, placing a small warm hand atop his collarbone, Martay let her middle finger slowly glide down his long, white scar, murmuring, "Who hurt you? Was it . . . it was my father." She lifted knowing eyes to his.

Night Sun shook his dark head. "It doesn't matter. None of it matters."

"Oh, my love," she said, instinctively knowing it was her father's flashing saber that had left the scar, and before Night Sun could stop her, she leaned to him and pressed her lips to the scar's beginning point. "I'm sorry," she whispered, "sorry, sorry."

"Don't," he said, "it's all right," and touching her back, urged her to raise her head.

She didn't.

Against his warm, smooth skin, she said, "Let me kiss it. Let me heal it, Night Sun. Let me." His breath stopped completely as she opened her mouth and began kissing the scar's long bias path from left shoulder down across his rising, falling chest to his right hipbone.

His black eyes tortured, Night Sun looked down on the golden head bent to him and was helpless against what was happening to his body. Martay's soft, warm lips on him, her tongue wetly tracing the scar, brought on an immediate, achingly complete arousal, and he was as powerless against her as if he were an unarmed warrior pitted against his fiercest well-armed foe.

For the first time such a thought brought a small smile of pleasure to his lips. He no longer had to fight her. The battle was over. Both had won. This beautiful golden-haired girl,

bent to him, lovingly kissing his belly, was no longer his enemy. She was his love. His love. His woman. Soon, his wife.
And she loved him just as he loved her.

Martay's mouth had reached the scar's end. With her
tongue she circled Night Sun's rising hipbone, her unbound
golden hair falling around her face, pleasantly tickling his
chest, his belly, his thigh.

Martay lifted her head a little.

She turned her face toward that throbbing, thrusting masculinity rising on his bare belly, and Night Sun, his face
flushed and hot, said in a low, strangled voice. "Forgive me."

"For what?" she asked, her curious, caressing eyes never
leaving that impressive symbol of male power and potency.
"It's beautiful," she said, "all of you is beautiful," and in a
quick, impulsive act that caused Night Sun to shudder violently, she lowered her head and swept the curtain of her long
golden hair directly over him.

"Martay," Night Sun groaned. Her thick covering hair
tickled and tormented; his pulsing erection jerked and surged
beneath the silky, covering tresses. "Ah, baby, baby . . ."

His voice was so strained, Martay became alarmed and
promptly swept the tumbled, teasing locks from him. Pushing
the offending hair over her shoulder and behind her ear, she
whispered, "Yes, darling," and bending to him, pressed warm,
loving lips to the jerking, engorged tip. When she touched her
tongue to him, Night Sun, his belly contracting painfully,
reached for her, jerked her up into his arms, and kissed her
hotly.

When their lips separated, he said against her cheek, "I
believe there are a few things I'll need to teach you about a
man's body, my love."

"Mmmmm," she sighed happily. "Will you teach me
about my body as well?"

"It will be my fondest pleasure, sweetheart."

"I'm glad," she said, "will you begin now?" Then, taking
one of his hands, she unselfconsciously drew it down between

her legs. Night Sun touched her and found her already hot
and wet. "There. You see," she said, "what does it mean?"

His lean fingers began gently caressing her as he smiled
and said, "It means, precious darling, that your husband is
going to be one lucky man."

Her face clouded a little. "Night Sun, you are going to be
my husband, aren't you?"

He continued to stroke her, his fingers gliding smoothly
over satin, throbbing flesh. "Yes, *Wicincala*. Certainly." He
brushed a kiss to her forehead. "Do you suppose I'd ever let
another man touch you?" he said, his black eyes taking on
that intensity that had always thrilled and fascinated her. His
words were as arousing as his expertly stimulating fingers
when he added, his voice deep and assured, "No other's hand
will know you like this, no mouth but mine will taste the
sweetness of your kisses." He shifted, agilely moving so that
she lay upon her back, he over her. His hand finally forsaking
her, he moved between her widely parted thighs. Poised just
above, the tip of his hard, heavy masculinity pressing her
moist, burning flesh, he said, "Mine will be the only body to
give and take pleasure from yours."

On fire, in love, Martay said breathlessly, "Give pleasure
to me now, Night Sun."

Night Sun leaned down and enclosed a hard, darkened
nipple in his mouth and sucked gently for an instant. Rising
once more, looming over her, his weight supported on stiff
arms, he said, "I love you, Martay. I belong to you." He
smiled then, a slow, sexual smile that burned right through
her, and added, "If you want me, take me."

"Yes, I will," she breathed, and without hesitation reached
for him. Wrapping her fingers eagerly around the hard, hot
thickness, she guided him easily into her waiting warmth, and
all the while their heated gazes were locked; loving emerald
eyes snared by intense black ones.

It was a never-to-be-forgotten moment between them, and
the knowledge, shared for the first time, that they were in love

with each other, that nothing else mattered, that the world around them could not intrude, added a sharp, glorious, abandoned edge to the mating.

No sooner had Martay's loving hand released him to her receptive body than she began to feel the onset of total ecstasy. Her eyes still trapped by his, she said truthfully, without a trace of shame or embarrassment, "You are right, my love, I've much to learn about our bodies. Already it is starting for me and I don't think I can stop it."

Feeling as though he himself would explode at any second, Night Sun immediately began the rolling, rapid movements of his slim hips, driving into her with a force she craved. "Don't try to stop it, sweetheart. Let it come. I'll take care of you. Just keep looking straight into my eyes." He thrust hard, almost withdrew, then thrust deeply again. "Look at me while you climax, Martay."

"Oh, God," she moaned, feeling herself slipping close to the edge, her fingers grasping at his flexing biceps, fingernails digging into the smooth bronzed skin. "My God . . ." She surged up against him, moving with him, riding toward that rapturous crest and, still looking into his eyes, she sighed, "You are a god to me, Night Sun. A beautiful god." Her building climax was lifting her, driving her, loosening her tongue. "Come with me. Come in me. I want to feel you come in me. My darling. My god."

"Don't speak like that," Night Sun said. "I'm no god. I'm very human and . . . and . . . ahhhhh," he groaned, unable to hold back his release any longer. Hotly he poured into Martay while she murmured breathlessly, "Oh yes, yes, I feel it . . . yes," and looked unwaveringly into his jet-black eyes.

When it was over and both had regained their breath and their racing heartbeats had slowed, Night Sun dropped a kiss to her shoulder and said, "I don't think gods behave like that."

Inhaling deeply of his clean, masculine scent, Martay said,

"Pity the poor gods then." She kissed his ear. "And thank heaven we are only mere mortals."

Night Sun laughed.

Rolling over, bringing her with him, he laughed. The laughter rumbled through his chest and filled the woman who loved him with peace and happiness. Rarely had she heard him laugh; never had he laughed with her. The sound of his deep, merry laughter brought almost as much bliss as his expert lovemaking.

For the next couple of happy, carefree hours, the naked pair laughed and teased each other. They kissed and caressed and spoke nothing but lovers' foolish nonsense, exploring and enjoying their brand-new relationship. Not thinking past the moment, basking in the warm, encompassing sunshine of new and enduring love, they touched and sighed and yawned and stretched.

And laughed.

Finally, lying cozily, safely, in each other's arms after another impulsive, white-hot surge of passion had caused them to mate wildly, anxiously, then left them spent, the star-crossed pair, reluctant to release their fragile hold on elusive happiness, knew it was time to discuss their uncertain future.

"I won't," said Night Sun softly, stroking Martay's tumbled golden hair, "send you back. I'll go in myself. Tell them I have you and . . ."

"No!" Martay, protesting immediately, raised her head from his chest to look at him. "No, Night Sun. The Army will kill you." She paused, closed her eyes miserably, then opened them. "He'll kill you. I know my father." She pressed her cheek to his chest, again closing her eyes. "Let's not go back. Let's stay here and . . ."

"And spend the rest of my days looking over my shoulder? No, *Wicincala*. I'm going in and settle this."

Hot tears immediately sprang to Martay's eyes. Hugging him tightly, she said, "You can't go. I won't let you."

"I must go, Martay."

Her head shot up and she looked pleadingly into his dark eyes. "We've only just found each other. Is one night all we're to know of happiness?"

He smiled at her. "No, baby. We'll have lots of nights. And days and years."

"I'm scared," she said. "Don't leave me, please don't."

"I am going," he said, and Martay knew that nothing she could do or say would change the mind of this proud, stubborn Lakota she so loved. Still, she felt compelled to try.

She said, "Night Sun, there are two things in life my father cares about. One is the Army. The other is me."

"I'm sure that's . . ."

"Let me finish. When he learns it's you who captured me, do you really suppose he will let you live, much less marry me?"

Night Sun's eyes clouded slightly. "I hope so. If I can allow him to live after what he did . . . it won't be easy. For him or for me. But I love you and he loves you, so . . ." He shrugged bare shoulders.

Martay shook her head. "He'll never accept it, never. I love you so much, I am willing to go for the rest of my life without seeing my own father. Doesn't that mean anything to you?"

"It means everything."

"Then why must you go back?"

"Martay, although it would be hard to make you believe it, I've always prided myself on being a man of some honor." She opened her mouth to interrupt, but he silenced her with a forefinger to her lips. "I've been less than honorable in what I've done to you, and I'm not proud of it. I would like to make it right."

She brushed his hand from her face. "Haven't you heard one word I've been saying? There is no making it right. My father will kill you! He will, I know it."

"It's a chance I must take. For your sake as well as mine."

"For my . . . ? If you're doing it for me, then don't. I just want . . ."

"Martay, you said yourself your father loves you very much. I know you love him as well and I know that the day would come when you'd resent me because I took you from him."

"No, that's not true. You're all . . ."

"It is true. Maybe not right now or even next year, but it would happen. You would miss him and want to see him. And you would begin to resent me because I'm the one responsible for your being separated from him."

Martay stared at him. She knew it was true. She loved Night Sun with all her heart, but she still loved her father. She always would. "What are we going to do?" she said sadly.

Night Sun put a hand behind her head and urged her lips down to his. He kissed her softly and said, "We are going to face this together. I will go back and do whatever it takes to make things right. And when I've convinced your father that I love you and will take good care of you, I'll come back for you. We'll be married and . . . and . . ."

She slowly lifted her head. "And what? Will we . . . will we stay here or . . ."

"I'm not sure, *Wicincala*. I'm like you, you see. I love my grandmother the way you love your father. I've always promised her that as long as I'm alive, she can continue to live in freedom on these plains she loves."

Understanding fully, Martay nodded. "When will you leave?"

Her beautiful emerald eyes were so sad, Night Sun said, "How would you like to spend a few days alone with me before I go?"

Instant joy flooded her face. "Yes! Oh, yes. We'll stay here in your lodge and not let . . ."

"No, I've an even better idea. I'll show you some of this rugged, beautiful country. Would you like that?"

"Like it? I'd love it! When can we leave?" She began kissing his dark face eagerly, saying, "When? When?"

Laughing, he said, "We could go right now, but . . ."

"Yes!" she quickly agreed, and starting to get up, said, "I'll put on my . . ."

"You'll put on nothing," he said, interrupting, "until I've made love to you."

Martay cut her eyes to his groin. She laughed happily. "Night Sun! Again?"

Grinning, he pulled her down to him. "Again."

37

Windwalker was smiling.

Gentle Deer was too.

The Mystic Warrior and the blind woman were pleased. Their hearts were a little lighter than usual on this chilly autumn morning as they nodded and smiled and assured one another that they had known all along the young, strong chieftain, Night Sun, was a decent man who would not disappoint them.

The aging pair prided themselves on having correctly divined the future; of having seen a golden-haired child-woman coming into their lives, and, with her beauty and spirit and goodness, changing hatred to love, despair to hope, the end to the beginning.

Long before Night Sun had brought the *wicincala* to their high plains village, The Mystic Warrior had seen her in a vision.

Unclothed and unashamed, she stood in the late afternoon sunlight atop a rugged pink palisade high in the sacred Black Hills. Her pale, slender arms outstretched, her golden hair falling about bare shoulders, she beckoned to an unseen lover far below her in the lush green valley.

A mighty Lakota chieftain, the muscles of his back and legs straining and pulling under sweat-slick skin, agilely climbed the steep, forbidding rocks to claim the child-woman for his own.

The fierce warrior reached the pale-skinned woman and enfolded her in his arms. The beautiful naked pair mated there on the rocks in that most holy place as the *Wakan Tanka* looked down on them and blessed their union.

Gentle Deer, with her sightless eyes, had seen even more than Windwalker.

In a recurring vision, she had seen her grandson and the child-woman together. And she had seen the new life that their love had produced. A strapping son with golden skin and coal-black hair and bright green eyes.

So now the two old seers, Windwalker and Gentle Deer, speaking in their native tongue, sat together in the quiet of early morning, talking of the young, healthy pair who had ridden out of camp at sunrise.

Night Sun had come to Windwalker's lodge well before the first hint of light had appeared in the eastern sky. He had told the Mystic Warrior he loved the golden-haired woman and that he was going to make her his wife. He would, he said, ride back to the Colorado Territory and try to make peace with her soldier father.

Then Night Sun had asked for Windwalker's understanding and his blessing. He wanted, he said, to take the *wicincala* up into their sacred Black Hills, to show her the places dearest to his Sioux heart, to spend a few precious days alone with his woman before facing the future.

Windwalker had told him to go at once. To guard the woman with his life, and to cherish her as if she were his own flesh.

And as soon as Night Sun and Martay had departed, the Mystic Warrior had hastened to Gentle Deer's tipi, knowing she would be as joyous as he that Night Sun had finally cast off the cloak of foolishness and admitted his love for the white captive.

And now Windwalker and Gentle Deer beamed and planned and felt as though a small part of them and their band might live on. They spoke wistfully of the distant days gone by, hopefully of the uncertain days yet to come. They smiled and shook their heads and felt almost young again.

And neither dared speak of the fear that remained, even now, in their hearts. The fear that was always with them. The fear that threatened their dreams.

The fear that the very same blue-coated soldier who had blinded Gentle Deer and left Night Sun scarred, would kill the proud young chieftain they loved more than life itself.

Night Sun was smiling.

Martay was too.

Knee to knee they rode across the rolling plains in the bright morning sunshine. Both were filled with untapped energy, although neither had slept. The night had been spent making love and making plans, and before there was a morning sun they had packed up their gear and were anxious to leave.

Martay, astride her sorrel mare, her heavy blond hair tied back off her face, had borrowed from Night Sun a pair of soft elkskin trousers and a bright-red calico shirt. The pants were very snug over her rounded bottom; the pullover shirt was large and loose, and the opening kept parting to reveal to Night Sun glimpses of bare, firm breasts.

She was young and cute and devastatingly desirable to him. There was about her a wide-eyed provocativeness that only a very young girl could carry off; that purposeful flaunting of her recently discovered sexuality and freedom.

Just looking at her brought about a feverish sensation of lust that almost overpowered him. Gritting his teeth, he was tempted to reach out and grab the sorrel's bridle, pull Martay from its back, drag her to the ground, and strip those tight, tight pants from her.

He forced his eyes toward the distant horizon, and pointing, said, "We'll reach the Belle Fourche River by noon. We'll stop and eat there and take a bath if you'd like." She was nodding furiously. He smiled and continued. "After a short rest we'll ride on, and by nightfall we'll reach the Hills. We'll skirt around Fort Meade," at the words Fort Meade, Martay saw a minute tightening of his lean jaw, "and reach our most holy place, *Mato Paha,* well before sundown."

She flashed him a playful smile. "All that sounds fine, except . . ." She paused and wet her lips with her tongue.

"Except what?"

"Let's not spend the night at *Mato Paha.*"

"Why not? Bear Butte—the white man's name for it—is a beautiful place. It means sleeping bear."

"I'm sure it is beautiful. But it's holy, and you can't make love to me there. Can you?" Her smile had gone; she was serious.

Charmed, he said, "Ah, *Wicincala,* do not worry. I will place you atop the Altar of Stone and worship you." He winked at her and added, "And the *Wakan Tanka* and the spirits of all those who have gone before are welcome to watch."

Martay laughed merrily, the sound musical and happy on the fine morning air. She said, "I don't believe you, Night Sun."

His handsome face wearing a devilish grin, he reined his black alongside her sorrel, leaned toward her, reached out and laid a hand on her ivory throat. While the horses continued to walk at a slow, even pace, he let his fingers travel down to her breasts, which were revealed in the half-open red shirt.

His palm covering a rapidly blossoming nipple, he said, "Ah, Miss Kidd, you will be sorry you doubted me."

And with a swiftness that left her breathless, Night Sun plucked her from her mount and drew her atop the big black.

While Martay laughed and hit at him and screamed for him to let her go, he handled her as though she were no heavier than an infant, positioning her so that she sat astride, facing him, her long, slender legs drawn over his hard thighs.

Tying the reins of Martay's mare around her slender ankle, he draped the black's reins over its sleek neck, ignoring Martay's protests and threats and declarations that he was crazy. The black, well trained, pranced proudly on, commanding, in charge, his steady gait unchanged. The mare, a trifle confused, docilely followed alongside, the movement of the bit in her mouth controlled by Martay's ankle.

"Now," said Night Sun, his hand back inside Martay's red shirt, "kiss me, Captive."

Laughing, Martay happily threw her arms around his neck and kissed him. They rode on that way, kissing there atop his moving horse, each kiss growing longer, hotter, their hands growing restless, roaming, touching, their passions flaring. In minutes Night Sun had taken off Martay's red shirt and she hadn't tried to stop him. But she did demand that he take off his as well.

On they rode, both naked to the waist, Martay's breasts pressing insistently against Night Sun's smooth chest, their mouths combined in ever lengthening, hungry kisses. When finally his heated lips left hers, and Martay, faint and trembling, leaned her head against his shoulder, she heard him say into her hair, his voice heavy with desire, "I want you."

"And I want you," she replied, her pulse racing. "Where can we go?"

"I want you here," said Night Sun. "Atop my horse."

Martay, weak from his kisses, said, "You mean it? Up here?"

"Yes. Now. Here."

"Anywhere you say, darling," she murmured.

"I love you," he said, and untying her mare's bridle from her ankle and tying it around his own thigh, he moved Martay about so that she was draped across the saddle before him. Balancing her there, he undressed her, and when she was naked he put her back as she had been, facing him, legs draped over his.

Then he said, "Unlace my trousers."

Nodding, she anxiously loosened the leather laces over his groin, pulled the opened fly apart, and gave a strangled little sigh of excitement when he burst free, huge and hard and ready to give her pleasure. Fascinated, she reluctantly lifted her eyes to his for further instruction.

"Lick all four of your fingers, *Wicincala,*" said Night Sun, a vein throbbing on his forehead, his dark face flushed. Martay lifted her hand, turned it over, put out her tongue, and licked at her fingertips while Night Sun watched. "Yes," he praised, "like that. Lick them good. Make them wet." Martay turned her hand about to show him her gleaming fingers. He nodded his approval and said, his thick black lashes lowering over smoldering black eyes, "Now make me wet."

Martay willingly did as he asked. She lowered her hand to him and lovingly rubbed her fingers over the pulsing, velvet tumescence until he was shiny wet. Her breath coming fast, her swelling breasts tingling, she again lifted her eyes to his. His hands went to her rounded buttocks as he said, "Climb on to me, *Wicincala.*"

As though it were the most natural thing in the world, Martay did just that. She carefully, slowly impaled herself upon that glistening rod of male strength and felt that she was the powerful one when Night Sun, his long fingers kneading the flesh of her bottom, said huskily, his breath hot upon her face, "Make love to me. Do it until you bring me. Drive me mad with your body. Do it, *Wicincala,* I know you can. Love me, *Wicincala,* love me."

His words were a bluntly sensual invitation for her to satisfy him and Martay, ever the adventuress and longing to prove her untried prowess, was thrilled and challenged by it.

"I will," she said with conviction, and putting her hands into Night Sun's thick raven hair at the sides of his head, she kissed him, thrusting her tongue deeply, boldly into his mouth, and while she was kissing him she began to move her hips in an erotic, grinding motion.

Had an unsuspecting traveler happened across those dusty plains that fine September morning, he would have seen a sight so uncommon, he would not have believed his shocked eyes.

Atop a moving big black stallion, a beautiful blond woman, as naked as Eve in the Garden, was draped astride a copper-skinned Indian in tight buckskins. The blond woman was loving the bronzed savage with a total, uninhibited abandon that would have made the Gods of Love blush.

But there was no one within miles of the shameless lovers, and it was a good thing, because Martay, determined she would give her handsome Sioux the loving of his life, wantonly ground her pelvis down on him, gripping him, squeezing him with her burning body until she drew a deep, shuddering climax from him.

Proud that she had managed to hold back long enough to bring him the pleasure she had so wanted to give him, Martay let herself go. She called out his name and clung to his bare shoulders as her hips did a frantic dance and she felt the glorious sensations that never failed to astound her.

When at last all the tiny tremors had subsided and she lay draped upon Night Sun's chest, she heard him say, with the faintest trace of a chuckle in his low baritone voice, "Any more doubts about when and where we will make love, Captive?"

Martay lifted her head as reality returned.

"Dear Lord above, what have we done?" she said, looking about in disbelief, blinking in surprise at the neighing sorrel tickling her bare foot with its velvet muzzle. "Mounted atop a horse . . . and I'm . . . Night Sun, this is terrible! I am terrible!"

Night Sun laughed and hugged her. "Terrible? Hardly, *Wicincala*. I for one don't know when I've enjoyed a horseback ride more."

38

There they were. In the distance, directly ahead. Rising abruptly in the middle of the Great Plains. The Black Hills of Dakota. From where Night Sun and Martay rode, still several miles west of the Hills, the towering dark-green ponderosa pines looked a deep blue. When they had been even further away, the towering hills had appeared black.

Night Sun pulled up on his big stallion; Martay followed his lead, turning her mare about, riding back to him. They sat there mounted, looking to the east, as the sun behind them slipped lower in the clear September sky. Night Sun's black eyes, locked on the rising wonder before him, was silent.

When he spoke, he said, more to himself than to Martay, "For as long as the sun shall shine and the rivers flow."

Martay, attuned to his somber mood, waited a respectful pause, then said softly, "Tell me about it, Night Sun. I know that the Black Hills . . . they belong to the central government now, don't they?" She looked directly at him.

His eyes were still fixedly staring straight ahead. She saw him swallow. He said, "These hills have always been used by my people for hunting and spiritual purposes. In 1868 the President signed a treaty deeding to the Sioux seven million acres of land. The Black Hills are at the very center of that land." He stopped speaking; a muscle was flexing in his jaw.

"Go on. Please."

"This was to be ours 'for as long as the sun shall shine and the rivers flow.'" His gaze swung to her at last. "The white man thought this land worthless, so he didn't mind if we heathens had it. But then in 1874 a yellow-haired soldier rode up into The Hills to look for gold."

"General Custer?"

Night Sun nodded. "The boy general told anyone who would listen that there was gold here. Overnight, miners began pouring into our Sacred Hills. A couple of years later General Custer came after Sitting Bull and Crazy Horse and Gall, and the battle of Greasy Grass—what you call the Little Big Horn—was fought. It was called, by the whites, a 'bloody massacre.'" Night Sun shook his head. "The foolish general bragged and let it be known he was coming, and then was shocked when our people were waiting to protect their land, their women and children, from him."

Martay was watching Night Sun's dark, rigid face. "Were you here? Did you . . ."

"I was in Boston reading law." He looked her straight in the eye. "Martay, if I had been here, I would have proudly ridden with Crazy Horse. I would have protected what was ours."

"I understand," she said.

He went on. "After Custer's fall, anti-Indian feelings were at a fever pitch, so in seventy-seven, just nine short years after the 1868 treaty, the government cheated us out of this land and forced our people onto reservations." He took a long, slow breath. "Last year the Army built Fort Meade right in the shadow of *Mato Paha,* our most holy place, to protect the mining digs in The Hills from the hated Sioux."

Martay wasn't sure what she should say. She had heard,

from her father and his officers, an entirely different version of what had happened at Little Big Horn. It had been a merciless slaughter, they had said—a bloodthirsty massacre perpetrated against brave, unsuspecting United States soldiers riding peacefully across the high plains.

Who was she to believe?

Night Sun caught her troubled look. He softened his expression, smiled, reached out, and patted her knee. "I am sorry. Don't fret, *Wicincala*. You had nothing to do with any of it, and I should not have burdened you." He leaned close, kissed her cheek, and said, "I'll race you to the Hills."

Cares were forgotten as Martay immediately dug her heels into the mare's belly and shot away, shouting over her shoulder, "Catch me if you can, Indian!"

"Here I come, pale face!" Night Sun thundered after her, raising his flattened palm to his lips to give loud Indian war whoops that made Martay shriek loudly with feigned fear.

Like carefree children, they played for the rest of the afternoon. Racing, pursuing, overtaking. Shouting, laughing, kissing. Martay squealing and screaming and threatening. Night Sun growling and roaring and subduing.

They reached the entrance to The Hills, riding into *Mato Paha* an hour before sunset. Awed by the beauty surrounding them, Martay followed Night Sun's pointing finger to a rising table of rock.

"The Altar of Stone," he said, and she nodded, staring up at the impressive granite palisade, shaped exactly like an enormous pulpit altar, it's smooth, flat top bathed a bright blood-red by the last rays of a dying sun.

While Night Sun tended the horses and unloaded their gear, Martay, promising she would not go far, set about exploring the rugged wonderland. Night Sun made her promise she would call to him every five minutes so he wouldn't worry. She agreed.

When he had rubbed down the horses and tethered them, and gathered firewood, and set up their night's camp, he

looked about for Martay. As promised, she called to him. He
followed the sound of her voice, lifting his eyes up to the
Altar of Stone. He saw her and blinked in disbelief as his
heart began to beat in his ears.

Unclothed and unashamed, she stood in the late afternoon
sunlight atop that rugged pink palisade high in the sacred
Black Hills. Her slender arms outstretched, her golden hair
falling about bare shoulders, she beckoned to him.

His dazzled eyes never leaving her, Night Sun hurriedly
stripped down to the skin. Then, lithe and quick like the
mighty Lakota warrior he was, he climbed up to her. The
muscles of his back and legs straining and pulling under
sweat-slick skin, he agilely ascended the steep, forbidding
rocks to claim her.

Wordlessly he encircled her narrow waist with his hands
and lifted her high up over his head. Wrapping a strong, supportive arm beneath her bare bottom, he held her there, her
pelvis pressed against his chest, her breasts just above his upturned dark face. Martay, gripping his bare shoulders, looked
down at him and whispered, "I love you, Night Sun."

He kissed the pale, sun-pinkened belly before him. "And I
worship you, *Wicincala.*"

And as the last faint rays of the sun washed their bare
bodies with a heavenly pastel light, Night Sun gently placed
the woman he worshiped down upon that smooth stone altar
and kissed every inch of her flesh, reverently adoring her with
his lips, idolizing her with tender caresses, exalting her with
his masterful hands, until Martay was sighing and squirming
and anxiously reaching for him.

When the sun finally slipped below the distant horizon,
leaving only a lingering pale purple afterglow, Night Sun lay
down upon his back and drew Martay down astride him.
While the fireflies came out in the darkened canyon below and
a night bird called to its mate, the beautiful naked pair made
fiercely passionate love there atop the high, smooth Altar of
Stone.

* * *

The hours were priceless, exquisite, golden. Alone in the Hills, away from his people, and from hers, the man and the woman came to know each other better.

Martay learned that her handsome lover was all she had thought, and more. Not only was he a strong, intelligent, loyal Lakota chieftain who revered his people and feared no man and loved as fiercely as he hated, he was also kind and sensitive and had a wonderful droll sense of humor.

Night Sun found that the woman he adored was more than he had dreamed of in a mate. She was not just extraordinarily beautiful and bright and delightfully passionate, she was also surprisingly sweet and thoughtful and charmingly witty.

Unlike the Indian maidens he had grown up with, she was not shy and withdrawn; she was a talkative, opinionated woman who was curious about everything and anything and not the least bit shy about asking if she wanted to know something. Nor was she reticent in answering any question he might have.

It was long after the sunset lovemaking on the stone altar. With night, a deep chill had settled over the Hills, and the lovers, though still quite naked, lay snuggled in their soft furs under the cold stars near their flickering campfire.

Martay, lying warmly atop Night Sun, her toes curling on his shins, her arms folded on his chest, face atop them, was looking into his jet eyes, questioning him about the women in his life.

Enchanted, he stroked her back and teased, "Need you ask? You've seen the way the maidens at the village look at me."

Martay, pretending anger, reached up, grabbed a handful of raven hair, and gave it a none too gentle tug. "You are conceited!"

"Mmmm," he said. "And what about you? I watched you back in Denver." His laughing eyes turned serious. "How many, *Wicincala?* How many men have there been in your life? Ten? Twenty? Fifty?"

Martay could have named a half-dozen young men who had feverishly courted her in the past two years, but meant it when she said, to the dark man lying beneath her, "What difference does it make? They weren't you." And she gave his stern mouth a kiss.

"I am a jealous man, Martay."

"Be jealous," said she. "If you are not certain you were the first and only man to make love to me, then I don't care to be wasting my time on such a thickheaded dunce anyway." She again kissed his mouth.

Night Sun laughed and squeezed her tightly. Lowering his voice to a deep, threatening boom, he said, "White woman foolish, make fun of dangerous savage."

"Mmmm," she responded, yawning lazily, and sliding off him. "Savage not dangerous enough to suit white woman." She draped an accusing hand across the soft flesh of his groin and shook her head.

"Why you . . ." He grabbed her, rolled her over, growling and biting her neck while she laughed. Then the growls and laughter died and the kisses that followed turned into white-hot passion that quickly heated the cold, starlit night.

They slept late the next morning, broke camp at noon, and rode south through the Hills while crested blue-jays chattered in the pines and beavers worked industriously in the cold, clear streams. Through canyons and gulches they traveled at a lazy, leisurely pace, while over their heads, the heat of a broiling Dakota sun was filtered by the lush, green branches of towering ponderosa pines.

It was a breathtaking fairyland, and Martay felt as though she could stay forever, just winding her way through its wonders atop her sorrel with Night Sun at her side on his black.

At midafternoon they stopped to rest. They swam in a stream so cold, their teeth chattered and Martay's pale flesh turned blue. Then they lay in the dappled sunlight and let the late-autumn heat warm their bare wet bodies.

When Martay saw Thunderbird mountain, she begged to climb it. Doubtful about allowing a soft, city-bred young lady to attempt such a perilous feat, Night Sun shook his dark head.

"No, *Wicincala*. It's not as easy as it appears."

"Can you climb it?"

He laughed and said, "I'm an Indian."

She looked up at him. "That's your answer too often, 'I'm an Indian.' You think Indians are the only surefooted people in the world?"

Still grinning, he replied, "We are pretty hard to beat, my love."

Wrapping her arms around his trim waist, Martay hugged him and said, "If I promise not to complain, will you let me climb it with you?"

He sighed and kissed her nose. "When you look at me like that, I'd agree to just about anything."

Warning her he would change his mind if she refused the rope he was tying around her waist, Martay stood dutifully still and allowed him to rope them loosely together. Minutes after they had begun climbing, she was glad he had insisted. Her right foot lost its hold and she slipped, only to be immediately yanked back up by the rope.

"You all right?" he asked, his eyes troubled.

"Just fine," she said, dusting her hands on the seat of her buckskin breeches. "What are we waiting for?"

His face relaxed and he turned and began climbing the sharp, jutting rocks with swift, deft skill, pulling Martay up over crevices and drops she could not traverse. More than once he bent down and she would step up on his back or he would make steps for her of his hands and feet and she would ascend them.

It was great fun for her. And for him as well. He laughed when he caught her crawling on her hands and knees, and for a time he stood watching, arms folded over his chest, before he took pity on her, bent down, grabbed her wrists, and hauled her up to him. Lifting her into his arms, he climbed the rest of the way carrying her.

And when they stood victorious at the summit, Martay put her arms around his neck, kissed him and, out of breath, said apologetically, "Would you be terribly disappointed in me if I told you I'm too tired to go back down."

Night Sun framed her face with his hands, and while the winds howled around them on that high precipice he kissed her with such devastating tenderness, Martay felt for a moment she might cry.

"You could only disappoint me if you stopped loving me," he said, his thumbs skimming over her bottom lip.

Martay trembled. "Darling, I'll always love you, always."

He smiled down at her. "In that case, I will carry you back down the mountain." He picked her up. "Trust me?"

"With all my heart."

39

The following afternoon they reached Wind Cave. Wide-eyed and curious, Martay clung to Night Sun's hand as together they explored the quiet, vast underground cavern. Colorful limestone formations rose imposingly from the floor or hung perilously suspended from the ceiling. Suffused sunshine, invading the depths through narrow overhead crevices, lighted their way and gave the cool stone palace an ethereal appearance. Martay had never seen anything like its stark, silent grandeur.

"When I was a boy," said Night Sun, his resonant voice echoing through the wide rock corridors, "I thought the people of our tribe who had gone on to the land of afterdeath could hear me when I came into Wind Cave to speak with them."

He stopped walking, released Martay's hand, turned, and lifted her up to sit atop a flat piece of stone, directly below a slanted shaft of hazy sunlight. He stood facing her, his hands resting on her knees, and continued. "I talked with my mother and my grandfather often in this peaceful place." His face was in shadow; Martay could not read his expression, but his voice was low, soft as he said, "I told them of the things that were happening to our people; I asked Grandfather for advice." Night Sun fell silent, his hands moving restlessly up Martay's trousered thighs.

"And did he give it?" she asked softly.

Night Sun's bronzed face abruptly came out of the shadow. "Yes," he said, his black eyes somber. "Walking Bear told me I should always listen to Gentle Deer. He said that I must go to my white father, study at the white man's school, and learn his numbers and letters. . . ." His wide shoulders slumped almost imperceptibly and his throat contracted. "Because the sundown of Lakota Coyote—the Sioux Nation—was quickly reddening the western sky."

Martay touched his dark cheek. "Tell me about your white father, darling. Is he . . ."

"James Savin died a couple of years ago," said Night Sun with no emotion. "He was a wealthy man; now I'm a wealthy man. Or will be next month when I turn twenty-five." He climbed up on the rock to sit beside Martay. "Savin was a trapper when he met my mother. He came into our village, saw her, wanted her, and took her, failing to mention that he had a wife back east." Night Sun smiled suddenly and casually pushed the hair back from his forehead. "My father was a great charmer, Martay. The People, including Walking Bear and Windwalker, fully approved of James Savin."

Martay reached for Night Sun's hand; held it in both of hers atop her lap. "And your mother, she fell madly in love with James Savin?"

"So they tell me. It must have been love, because after only one short winter with Savin—a few weeks—she never gave any of the braves a chance. She remained faithful to James Savin until the day of her death."

"How sad," said Martay, imagining the hurt and loneliness the Indian woman had endured. "Did you see your father often?"

"From the time I was six years old I was sent east to spend time with him each summer."

Night Sun, warmed by the love and understanding flowing from Martay, told her things he had never told another living soul. With no trace of self-pity, he admitted that he had been miserably out of place in his father's fine eastern mansion. Said there were so many strange new things to learn in the white man's world that he was far more frightened there than he had ever been riding his pony alone on the plains.

He told of the understandable resentment of his father's wife toward him; said Mrs. James Savin was unable to hide her dislike for the half-breed son, a product of her husband's infidelity with the "dirty squaw woman."

"She said those words to you?" Martay was horrified.

"Only on those occasions when she lost her temper because I had clumsily knocked over a priceless vase or had come upon her so quietly, I scared her." Night Sun laughed then, and added, "Or for any of a dozen other equally annoying transgressions."

Night Sun continued to smile easily, but Martay's heart hurt for a frightened little boy alone in a strange world he did not understand, subjected to the coldness of a bitter wife who saw, every time she looked at his dark face, the eyes of the other woman. The pretty Indian woman who had shared her husband's bed.

"I don't like Mrs. James Savin," said Martay heatedly, angry with the faceless woman for taking out her pain and frustrations on an innocent child.

"Constance Savin is dead, *Wicincala*. She contracted influenza five years ago and lingered three weeks." He glanced at Martay. "She wasn't really a mean woman; put yourself in her place." He shrugged.

Martay did. She imagined being married to Night Sun and having him go away while they were still newlyweds. Of his making love to another woman. Of fathering a child that was not hers.

"I would have been very hurt and very jealous."

"Exactly. And Constance Rood Savin was embarrassed as well. She was refined and genteel; came from an old monied family. It must have been a nightmare for all her upper-crust friends to find out about me."

Martay was shaking her head. "I'm surprised your father . . . that is . . ."

"Me too. Most men would never have acknowledged my existence." Night Sun leaned against the wall of rock behind them and pulled Martay back against him. "I want to know more about you. Tell me about your mother. Was she as pretty as you?"

Martay smiled and snuggled to him. "My father said she was the most beautiful woman in all California. That's where they met and married." She looked up at Night Sun. "You're not the only one who is wealthy. I own producing gold mines throughout Northern California and the Sierra Nevada. My mother left them to me."

Martay, always a talker, enthusiastically told Night Sun of her childhood in the Chicago mansion, of missing the mother who died when she was four, of being spoiled and catered to because the staff felt sorry for a motherless little girl whose military father was always away.

She admitted that as she grew up she did pretty much as she pleased and had decided, early on, against marriage and motherhood in favor of a life of travel and adventure.

"And do you still feel that way?" asked Night Sun in that voice that could woo seductively and caressingly; or command in such a way as to compel obedience.

Martay turned in his arms. "No! I want to be your wife and have your children."

He smiled and put a hand to the slender column of her throat. "Ah, can I ever really capture a spirited woman in whose veins a rover's blood flows?" His fingers stroked downward.

Her emerald eyes flashing, Martay said forcefully, "I'm not a rover! I just want to be your wife."

He gently tipped her head back, bent, and kissed the hollow of her throat. Against the sensitive flesh he murmured, "I hope a bit of the rover remains, my sweet. A wife of mine may find it necessary to do a bit of roaming." His tongue wet a small patch of ivory skin, then he blew gently on the dampened flesh.

Her breath growing short, Martay said, "I've no objection to roaming, so long as you roam with me."

Night Sun pushed her loose red shirt off a fragile shoulder and kissed the side of her throat, his lips moving to the curve of her neck and shoulder. He whispered, "Have you any objection to my mouth roaming over you?"

She laughed, breathlessly. "We don't have . . . the bedding's outside."

"Mmmm," he murmured, continuing to caress the tempting pale flesh he was baring. "I'll bet we can manage without it."

Martay soon found out they could manage quite well without their buffalo furs. In minutes Night Sun had undressed her and himself. He draped his shirt over the rock where they had sat, allowing it to fall over the edge, like an embroidered scarf adorning a side table. He then turned Martay about so that her back rested against the shirted rock.

He said, "I've been wanting to do this," pulling her up on tiptoe, "since the night we danced at Lone Tree and Peaceful Dove's wedding."

"Do what?" she sighed, her heart racing, her breasts flattening against his warm chest.

Night Sun hunched down and entered her while she gasped and threw back her head. "This," he said. "I've wanted to make love to you while we're both standing."

"W-why . . . ?" she whispered, not really caring, already glorying in the strange and wonderful sensations evoked by this strange and wonderful new position.

Rising once more to full height, Night Sun said, "When we danced, you fitted against me so perfectly." He slipped a hand around her right thigh, gently lifted her leg up and hooked it over his supportive arm. "I wondered then if you'd fit on me as perfectly as you fitted against me."

Martay was beginning to take panting little breaths as Night Sun filled and stretched her and pleasure spread rapidly, astonishingly, from that heated place where their bodies were joined to encompass her entire being.

"And . . . do . . . I?" she managed, short of breath.

"My Martay," was all he said, but she knew the answer was yes. And looking directly into her eyes, Night Sun made love to her standing there in a filtered shaft of honeyed golden sunlight that embraced their bare, linked bodies.

"Night Sun, this is . . . this is . . . wonderful," sighed Martay, her arms looped around his neck, diamonds of perspiration dotting her face, throat, and breasts."

"Isn't it," he said, and bending, gave her an openmouthed kiss as his taut, lean buttocks rocked rhythmically to her.

Highly excited, feeling as though she were literally being speared by Night Sun's hard, piercing lance, she loved every thrilling second of the unorthodox mating. Their damp bodies slipped and slid and did indeed fit perfectly. And Martay, femalelike, fleetingly worried, in the middle of her growing ecstasy, that she was not as fresh as she should be, that the perspiration of sexual excitement might be unpleasing to her lover.

Night Sun, the veins in his neck and arms standing out in bold relief, his chest drenched with sweat, read the foolish doubt in Martay's emerald eyes.

Thrusting deeply, he murmured, "You look and feel and smell like heaven."

They spent the night in the cave, choosing a spot for sleeping where slices of silvery moonlight made the thick darkness around them less forbidding. Still, Martay clung tightly to

Night Sun and slept with one eye open, wondering about bats and other night creatures that shared their quarters.

Sunrise seeping down to them was a welcome sight to her, and Night Sun didn't have to ask twice if she would like to ride on for an hour or so before eating breakfast.

They continued to drop steadily south, in no particular hurry, until at midmorning Night Sun pulled up on the big black, stood in the stirrups, and grinned.

"We're there," he announced.

"We're where?" said Martay.

"The *Minnekahta*. The Place of Warm Waters."

Martay squinted and saw in the distance a white vaporous cloud rising from the rocks. "Night Sun! May I bathe in the warm waters?"

"That's what they're for, *Wicincala*. Come." He kicked his horse into a trot and Martay anxiously followed.

She oohed and aahed with pleasure when she sat carefully down in the moccasin-shaped bathtub scooped out of the rock. And she squealed with childish delight when Night Sun splashed in with her. Seating himself behind her, he pulled her back between his bent knees and Martay lay comfortably relaxed in the hot, steamy water with her back resting on his chest.

"This is luxury," she said. "Like a real honest-to-god bath in a real roomy tub."

His dark head resting against the rock tub's edge, Night Sun, his black eyes closed, arms wrapped around Martay's waist, teased, "Is that what you prefer?"

She said, "Don't tell me you don't wish for it now and then, because I won't believe you."

He grinned, eyes remaining closed. "I did live in your world long enough to be seduced by some things."

"Ah-ha," she said, hugging his strong, slippery arms. "What else did you get used to?"

"Let's see," he mused lazily, opening his eyes and bending

to sprinkle kisses over Martay's wet shoulders. "Aged brandy. Fine cigars. Silk sheets. Good music."

Martay clucked her tongue accusingly and raised a hand up to caress the damp hair by his ear. "I thought so. You're a fraud, my handsome half-breed friend."

"I've thought the same of myself many times," he said, lifting his head.

Martay quickly turned about in his arms. "Night Sun," she said anxiously, afraid she had gone too far; had hurt him, "I was teasing you, darling. I know that you are . . ."

"Caught between two worlds, Martay," he interrupted, his black eyes intense. "I know that. I don't fully belong in either."

"That's not true! I've seen you in the village, you are one of them. You're a respected Lakota chieftain and you . . ."

"Am I? I'm not so sure. There have been times when I am not certain I would have returned to the Dakotas if not for my grandmother." He toyed idly with Martay's damp golden hair, twisting gleaming strands around his long fingers. "You guessed correctly. I grew soft in the East, and while some whites made it clear that I was not welcome in their presence, my fellow student and good friend, Drew Kelly, never minded that I was half Indian. "Nor," Night Sun added teasingly, "did the ladies."

Martay made a face. "I'll just bet they didn't!" She smiled then and told him, "Night Sun, you aren't soft, you're human. There are good things in both worlds; they are just different, that's all."

"Well, *Wicincala,* one thing is certainly the same, whether here in The Hills or in Chicago, Illinois."

"Really? What is it?"

He wrapped her wet hair around his hand, urged her head back against his shoulder, and kissed her. "Making love."

She smiled. "That's true, I suppose, but I'd like, someday, to make love to you in a Chicago bed just to prove the point."

"I'll see to it," said he. "In the meantime, how do you feel about making love here in the *Minnekahta?*"

Martay stared at him, "Is that possible?"

"And pleasurable," he smilingly assured.

She laughed happily and gave his wet, sensual mouth a kiss. "Who needs silk sheets?"

It was their final morning in the Black Hills.

When they rose, they would leave behind this lush, private world of splendor. And in twenty-four hours Night Sun would head south for Denver to face General William Kidd.

It was not quite sunup, but Night Sun was wide-awake. Martay was sleeping peacefully beside him, turned facing away, backed up against him, her warm back and bottom pressing his side. He eased up onto an elbow and looked at her.

A bare white shoulder peeked from under the warm furs; her golden hair was a silky mass of tumbled curls around her sleeping face. She looked as innocent as a child, and as helpless; and he wondered, for the thousandth time, if he hadn't been grossly unfair to her.

Snatching her from a world of ease had been abhorrent enough, but then to make love to her when she was alone in his camp and vulnerable. That was unforgivable.

Night Sun tenderly pulled the covers up over her shoulder.

She thought she would be happy in Dakota with him, but would she? Could a beautiful young woman who had been raised in a mansion with servants really be content in a crude tipi on the plains? Would the love she now felt for him quickly turn to resentment and hate?

Troubled, Night Sun rose as the first light of dawn tinged the eastern sky a gunmetal-gray. Shivering in the chill morning air, he stood for a moment, naked, yawning and stretching, his legs apart, hands clasped behind his head. Eyes locked on the changing sky, he flexed the muscles of his upper body. His tight stomach caved in under his ribs, his chest expanded.

Night Sun abruptly drew a startled breath and looked down. Martay, as naked as he, was kissing the arch of his bare right foot.

"*Wicincala,*" he said, "what are you doing?"

She gave no answer. She continued to kiss him, her lips moving from the smooth flesh of his foot up his hair-dusted leg as she crouched there before him, hands spread out on the soft grassy ground. Speechless, hardly daring to breathe, Night Sun remained motionless as her lips, open and warm, continued traveling slowly upward to his tensed thigh as she rose to her knees before him.

Night Sun's black eyes rolled back in his head as flames of heat licked at him and his body responded to the burning fire rapidly engulfing him. Already his erection was fully formed and aching for her touch.

Martay's lips were brushing kisses to the inside of his thigh, and Night Sun, groaning, put a hand to the crown of her head, his long fingers flexing involuntarily in the silky locks.

His dark face hardened with passion, he said, "You don't have to do that."

She inhaled deeply of his clean male scent. "I want to," she whispered. And nuzzling sweetly, her lips and nose pressing ever closer to that stiff, surging proof of desire, she continued to tease and toy with him, brushing kisses up over his taut belly, licking a path along the line of thick raven hair leading downward from his navel, murmuring softly, "I love you, Night Sun. I'll always love you."

Kneeling there before him, Martay put her hands to his lean hips, clasped him possessively, threw back her head, looked up, and gently commanded, "Look at me, darling."

His legs apart, his hands restlessly touching her shoulders, every muscle in his tall bare body tautened with sweet agony,

Night Sun looked down at her, his eyes shining with a hot light.

"Don't," she whispered, "think that I'll ever be sorry you took me." She hesitated, then finally touched her lips to the straining, throbbing masculinity rising directly before her face. He shuddered violently and could not quell the moan that tore from his chest. "I won't be," she told him, and licked a wet, hot line up the rigid length of him. "And you won't be either."

Night Sun rocked back on his heels and let out a loud groan of ecstasy when her warm, wet mouth enclosed him. Both his hands anxiously came back to clasp her head, and any doubts he had entertained were swept away; quickly forgotten in the face of physical pleasure. He stood there in the rising sun with his beautiful naked woman kneeling between his legs, loving him so sweetly, so intimately, he felt as though he could stand there forever, looking down on the golden head bent to him, feeling the tug of soft, warm lips on his blood-filled flesh, marveling at the exquisite touch of her tongue licking and lifting him dangerously close to exploding fulfillment.

Drawing a strangled breath, Night Sun reluctantly urged her head away, forcing her mouth to leave him. He fell to his knees to face her, his black eyes tortured, his chest heaving, perspiration dotting his hairline despite the chill of the morning.

Martay knew the man she loved was more aroused than he'd ever been before. Armed with the knowledge, she wrapped her arms around his neck and whispered pleadingly, "I know my father. I'm afraid you'll be killed. Don't go back." She pressed her burning cheek to his. "If you love me, say you won't go back."

40

But Night Sun would not agree.

As much as he loved Martay, he refused to give in to her wishes that he remain safely with her; that he not return to Colorado. And as they rode back to the village that warm afternoon, Martay, casting loving glances at his handsome copper face, smiled wistfully at the irony of his refusal.

This proud, stubborn man she so loved, the one person on earth she could not live without, was the only male she had ever known whom she could not bend to her will. And that was why she so adored him. From their first minute together, he had been unmovable.

He still was.

There on her knees at sunrise she had handed him her very soul, had offered her body for any kind of pleasure he desired, had willed him to lose himself so completely in her he would agree to anything. Wildly, ravenously, he had made love to her, loving her more fiercely than ever before, taking her again and again to frightening heights of ecstasy, and all the while she had pleaded with him to say he wouldn't go to

Colorado. That he would honor her wishes. He would stay with her.

He never did.

Throughout the prolonged lovemaking he remained mute, his black eyes speaking for him, telling her he loved her, but that he would not budge from his decision. And even when, near hysterics from the continuing carnal pleasure that was spiraling her yet again toward that awesome pinnacle, she began to cry, Night Sun took her skillfully over the top, but promised nothing save the fact that he would love her for as long as he lived.

They reached the village at four that afternoon. Standing silent sentinel outside their lodge, was Speaks-Not-At-All. It was the first time Martay had seen the old warrior since the morning she had effected her escape.

A sudden rush of affection, mixed with guilt, came over her, and dismounting, she hurried to him, put a hand on his stooped frame, and said over her shoulder to Night Sun, "Tell Speaks-Not-At-All that I am sorry. I ask his forgiveness for hitting him; I would like to be his friend."

Night Sun, winking at Speaks over Martay's head, said, "Tell him yourself, *Wicincala*."

Turning, she questioned, "How can I? He is mute."

Night's wide, sensual lips turned up into a satanic grin and he told her, "Speaks reads lips. And"—he crossed his arms over his chest to deliver the final blow— "he understands English."

Horrified, Martay looked from Night Sun to Speaks-Not-At-All. Smiling sheepishly, the old Indian bobbed his gray head. Her gaze flew back to Night Sun. He was laughing aloud.

"You are the devil incarnate!" she accused angrily, her face aflame, and through her mind ran the times she had talked openly to the old warrior about Night Sun.

Untouched by her insult, Night Sun pulled her, struggling

and incensed, back against him, locking his arms around her slim waist. Both faced the still-smiling Speaks-Not-At-All. From above Martay's ear, Night Sun teased, "That's your own guilty conscience bothering you, my love." Then to the old warrior, "Speaks, have you ever repeated anything a person told you in confidence."

Violently the old man shook his head, his watery eyes looking straight at Martay. She softened at once. Putting out her hand, she smiled, and speaking very slowly, very distinctly, said, "Will you be my friend? I've a feeling there will be many occasions when I wish to say things about this exasperating man that I don't want repeated."

A bony old hand gripped hers with surprising strength, and Speaks, without uttering one sound, assured Martay that all her secrets were safe with him.

"How is Grandmother?" Night Sun abruptly changed the subject.

At once the old warrior's face took on a worried expression. Night Sun, releasing Martay, said, "She's ill again?"

Speaks nodded.

"Will you see to the horses, old friend," said Night Sun, and taking Martay's hand, led her directly to Gentle Deer's lodge, his face reflecting his worry.

Inside, Windwalker looked up, nodded to them, rose, and silently vanished. Gentle Deer's weathered face broke into a wide grin when she heard the handsome pair, and immediately she struggled to rise.

Dropping to one knee beside her, Night Sun stayed her with a firm hand to her shoulder. "Lie back, Grandmother," said he, "Martay and I will sit here close and tell you of our wonderful adventures in the Hills."

The concerned pair stayed with Gentle Deer for the rest of the afternoon. As dusk came on, Martay rose, kissed Gentle Deer's cheek, and thoughtfully giving the old woman a few moments alone with her grandson, went outdoors, where the Mystic Warrior waited in the shadow.

When she had gone, Night Sun, holding Gentle Deer's hand, said, "I could wait to leave for Colorado until you feel better."

She smiled, her dark eyes disappearing into the wrinkled folds of tissue-paper-thin skin. "You might have a long wait, *Hanhepi Wi.*"

Gentle Deer had not called him by his Lakota name in years. It was as though she knew she would not be calling his name after today. When several minutes of talking quietly together had passed, Night Sun lifted her thin hand up to his chest, covering it with his own, and said, "I will leave at daybreak tomorrow. You and I will say good-bye now."

"Yes," she croaked, "we say good-bye now, *Hanhepi Wi.*"

Night Sun squeezed her hand, then gently placed it under the covers. He kissed her cheek, rose, and crossed the tipi. Gentle Deer stopped him, softly speaking his Lakota name again.

Night Sun paused, pivoted, and looked at her.

She said, squinting, her blind eyes watering, "Stand there for a moment and let me look at you."

A tremor of unease shooting up his spine, Night Sun asked, "Which one, Grandmother. You or me?"

She understood the question. He, like her, had the strong premonition that they would not see each other again in this life. He was asking which one of them was to die.

Through sightless eyes she studied his dear, dark face for long, silent moments. And saw a squalling, healthy baby that had brought such joy into all their lives. She saw a brave ten-year-old boy at Sand Creek with blood running down his thin chest. She saw the a slender twenty-year-old sullenly going away to learn the white man's numbers. Lastly, she saw a strong, handsome warrior returning to his tribe with a beautiful golden-haired child who would become his woman. A woman who would give him every reason to live.

But she had never lied to her grandson. She would not lie now.

"I do not know," she said tiredly. "I hope it will be me."

It was past midnight.

Night Sun and Martay lay quietly in the cozy firelight of their tipi. They had remained at Gentle Deer's lodge while she had slept, never knowing they were there, until Windwalker returned at eleven o'clock and gently commanded Night Sun to leave the sleeping sick woman in his care for the night. To go and rest for the long ride that was ahead of him come morning.

In silence they had returned to their lodge and Night Sun, going directly to his pine chest, had removed some paper and a pen. Face harsh in concentration, he had written out his will. Then, folding it neatly, he had tied a leather strip around it and put the packet back inside the chest.

Martay knew she didn't have to question him. He would tell her if it was something that concerned her, so she went about preparing the things he would need for his trip. When she placed the bundle beside his Winchester, she looked up and saw him watching her.

He held out his arms. She went into them.

"I made out my will, *Wicincala,*" he said.

"No," she began, "please . . ."

"You will find it in the top drawer of the chest," he continued, as though she had not spoken. "I left a half of everything to you"—he pulled back to look at her— "and I hope you'll not mind; I left the other half to a new school they are starting back east this year to educate Indians. The Carlisle school in Pennsylvania is meeting in an old army barracks and I want . . ."

"Giving money to them is a wonderful idea," she said quietly.

He smiled. "You're a very understanding woman. I love you."

"If you do, will you . . ."

"No, *Wicincala,* I won't." He dropped his arms away and stepped back.

"Wait," she said, advancing on him. "You've not heard me out. I was going to ask if you'd allow me to cut your hair before you leave."

Night Sun grinned and lifted a lean hand to the flowing raven locks. "I thought you liked my hair. What about those times when . . ."

"I do, but . . . you'll be safer if you look more like . . . like . . ."

"A white man?"

"Yes. More conventional." She gripped his upper arms. "You'll be riding into Denver and I'm so afraid someone will . . ." the words trailed off.

Her emerald eyes looked so worried, Night Sun said, "There's a small pair of scissors in my chest." He touched her upturned chin. "I brought them back from Boston for Grandmother and she refused them."

"Get undressed," ordered Martay, and went for the scissors. While Night Sun made faces, Martay, on her knees behind him, snipped away the long midnight locks. When she had finished, the Lakota warrior, Night Sun, once more looked like the learned law graduate, Jim Savin. Admiring her work, Martay said, "When you get to the outskirts of the city, promise you'll change clothes. I packed the things that—"

"You are getting mighty bossy," he said, running his hands through his newly cut hair. "And, I, sweet, have an order for you."

"Yes?"

He reached out and curled a long finger down into the opening of her shirt. "Take off your clothes."

"Anything you say."

So now the naked lovers lay in pensive silence, each carefully memorizing the sight, smell, and feel of the other. Night

Sun's warm hands moved slowly, searchingly over the soft curves and tempting hollows of Martay's slender frame, as a blind man might study an intriguing surface with his fingertips.

It was the same with her.

She stroked his chest, his sculptured shoulders, his rib cage, wondering, with choking terror: Would this be the last time she would be allowed to feel the pleasing texture of his smooth, bronzed skin; to run her fingers through the thick, shorn black hair; to marvel at his strong, steady heartbeat beneath her fingers?

Neither meant it to happen, but soon bodies stirred to the touch of adoring hands, and passion flared. Temptation passed through them like a gentle sigh and they came together there in the firelight, mating silently, the unspoken love shining from their locked eyes.

If the coupling at sunrise had been wild and frenzied, this joining here in their lodge was the opposite. Slowly, leisurely, they made love, Martay exercising her newly discovered ability to hold back her release; Night Sun, skillful in the art of prolonging pleasure, doing so with controlled expertise.

It was the most beautiful and fulfilling act of lovemaking ever to occur between them. For more than two hours they languidly, wordlessly tempted and taunted and teased and touched and took each other to paradise.

And when it was finished, as if some lovely, spiritual ceremony had touched and soothed their souls, leaving them blissfully exhausted and at peace, they fell asleep in each other's arms.

The next morning Martay tried very hard to be brave when the time came for Night Sun to leave. Forcing herself to wear a smile that would have illuminated the gloomiest night, she stood with a hand possessively riding Night Sun's back while, holding the whickering black's reins, he talked quietly with the Mystic Warrior.

At last Windwalker put a broad hand to Night Sun's shoulder, gripped him for an instant, released him, and walked away.

Night Sun turned to Martay.

Her brilliant smile slipped and she fought back the hot tears that were stinging her eyes. Knowing that they had said earlier, in the privacy of their tipi, all there was to say, and knowing if he said anything now, those tears would surge down her cheeks, Night Sun climbed atop the big black, intending to kick the mount into a hurried gallop and depart.

But mounted there above, he looked down into the sad, beautiful eyes of the only woman he had ever loved and felt his heart kick painfully against his ribs.

"Wicincala," he said softly, soothingly, the deep timbre of his voice a gentle caress. He leaned down from his pony to kiss her lightly on the mouth. Then he righted himself and rode off at a trot.

41

Martay stood watching until the last fine dust kicked up by Night Sun's horse had dissipated in the still morning air. Only then did she turn and walk slowly back toward Gentle Deer's lodge.

Just outside she paused, drew a deep, slow breath and squared her shoulders. Forcing herself to smile, she ducked inside, determined to be brave and cheerful, to hide her choking fear from the sick old woman.

Gentle Deer's sightless eyes were closed; she was sleeping peacefully. Relieved, Martay gently sighed, closed the tipi flap, and silently took a seat beside it. Her throat hurt from needing to cry. All morning she had forced herself to be strong, to be as courageous and stoic as a Lakota woman would be. She hadn't wanted Night Sun to ride away from a weeping, clinging woman.

But now he was gone and Gentle Deer was sound asleep, and Martay felt her firm resolve slipping away. The tears she had held back for so long sprang to her eyes and overflowed.

Folding her arms atop her bent knees, she leaned her head on them and quietly cried, her heart breaking.

"Do not weep." Gentle Deer's calm voice caused Martay's head to snap up.

Dashing at the tears with the backs of her hands, Martay sniffed and said foolishly, "No . . . I'm not . . . I . . . how are you feeling this morning, Gentle Deer?"

"Better than you," replied the wise woman. "Come here, child."

Martay quickly moved across the tipi, falling to her knees beside Gentle Deer. Gratefully clasping the offered hand, she squeezed the gnarled fingers and admitted, "He's gone, Gentle Deer, and I'm worried."

"I know."

"I love him so much and I fear he will never come back to me." Martay shook her head, the tears continuing to fall. "I couldn't stand it, I couldn't." Her fingers tightened on Gentle Deer's. "Night Sun will be gone forever and I'll have nothing of him, nothing."

"I cannot know if my grandson will return safely to you," said Gentle Deer. "But even if he does not, you will always have a part of him." She smiled knowingly.

"No, I won't, I . . . He'll be . . . I don't understand. If Night Sun doesn't . . . I . . ." She fell silent and her mouth rounded into an O of surprise and comprehension as Gentle Deer's meaning began to dawn. She stared openmouthed at Gentle Deer.

Gentle Deer nodded. "You carry my grandson's child, do you not?"

"I don't know, I . . ." Martay's teary eyes were wide, her high brow knitted. She had not considered such a possibility, and yet since the night of Peaceful Dove's wedding—the first time Night Sun had made love to her—she had not . . . there had been no . . . "Oh, Gentle Deer, could it be?" She dropped the old woman's hand and quickly placed both of hers atop her flat stomach, spreading her fingers, touching inquiringly, hopefully.

"Yes," said Gentle Deer quietly. "The bloods of two great families merging." She smiled again. "The blood of my beloved husband flowing in your child's veins."

Nodding, Martay said excitedly, "And the blood of my mother and father as well."

The old woman again reached for Martay's hand. Holding it tightly, she said, "Your unborn child is very precious to us all. The others live on in him." Her wrinkled face held a peaceful, happy look.

Martay, feeling suddenly lighthearted, smiled and said, "Him? You're so certain it will be a boy?"

"I am," said the old woman. "The last Lakota chieftain."

"The last?" Martay's smile fled.

"Yes. The days of my people are over. If he lives, you must persuade Night Sun to go to your world; to raise his son in the white world."

"That is your wish?"

Sightless eyes crinkled. "No, child. That is how it must be."

Night Sun rode like the wind.

Anxious to reach his destination, he pushed the valiant black to the limits of its amazing stamina, and pushed himself as well. Horse and rider thundered across the vast rolling plains, the stallion willing to lay down his life for the man on his back. The man on his back willing to lay down his life for the beloved golden-haired woman he had left behind in the Powder River village.

His starkly chiseled face set in fierce concentration, Night Sun was oblivious to the winds that stung his sunburned cheeks and caused his black, unblinking eyes to water. With single-minded determination he rode swiftly toward the rendezvous that could mean his death.

That realization caused a sharp pain to shoot through his

chest even as it brought a rueful smile to his lips. How many times he had faced death over the years and never known fear. His life had never seemed that important; if it continued or ended, did it make a difference? Whether he killed or was killed by his enemy was simply a decision made by fate, accepted by him.

Now it was no longer so.

He wanted to live! Wanted to live as never before. Now there was enhanced meaning to his life; it was richer, fuller, happier. How he longed to live; to love and protect that golden goddess he worshiped, to lie with her in his arms each night, to be at her side when she bore his sons and daughters, to grow old with her in peace and comfort.

The smile left Night Sun's face.

Chances of a future together were almost nonexistent and he knew it. There was little doubt that the man he was riding to face, Martay's father, would kill him. There would be no time for explanations or calls for understanding. The blue-coated trooper who had left scars on both body and mind so long ago was not the benevolent kind.

Night Sun's shoulders slumped.

So be it. He would not raise a hand in defense against the general. He loved the general's daughter too much. He could not kill her father and live to see the censure and sadness in her beautiful green eyes. He, Night Sun, might not live to see Martay again, but General William J. Kidd would.

Those thoughts were walking through his mind when, six days after leaving Windwalker's Powder River camp, Night Sun saw the gas lights of Denver twinkling below in the distance.

Almost as exhausted as the prized beast he was astride, Night Sun blinked his burning eyes and rolled his aching shoulders in a circular motion. Patting the black's lathered neck, he said soothingly, "Old friend, just carry me down to the center of town and I'll allow you to rest until morning. A rubdown and a bucket of oats for you; a bath and a bed for me." He lifted a bronzed hand and pushed back his shorn hair. "Then tomorrow we face General Kidd."

The winded horse neighed and shook his tired head and needed no further coaxing than Night Sun's deep, gentle voice saying, "Let's go, boy."

It was nearing midnight when Night Sun dismounted before the large, lighted Broadway street home of his old Harvard classmate, Drew Kelley. Fortunately, Drew himself answered the door, saving one of the sheltered house servants the shock of seeing an unkempt, buckskin-clad Indian standing on the shadowed veranda.

And a trail-weary Night Sun from having to explain.

"Jim!" said Drew Kelley, grinning broadly, embracing his friend. "Come in, come in! It's good to see you. Hell, you just disappeared. I went to the Centennial one afternoon and you . . ."

"Drew, can I stay the night?"

"As long as you wish," Drew said enthusiastically, drawing Night Sun into the foyer. "I'll have your horse tended right away. What brings you back to Colorado?"

"I've come to see an Army general," was Night Sun's straightforward reply.

Puzzled, Drew Kelley said, "Oh? Any particular one?" He propelled the taller man into the library.

"General William J. Kidd."

Drew Kelley stopped and stared at Night Sun. "Jim, I guess you haven't heard the news."

"What news?"

Drew gave no immediate reply. He crossed the spacious room to the mahogany desk. From its gleaming top he picked up the latest edition of the *Rocky Mountain News.* "Read this, my friend."

Night Sun took the newspaper, quickly read the headlines, and said aloud, "No. God, No."

* * *

The midday fog was beginning to clear over the Presidio. Sergeant Major Bert Hallahan, his light eyes reflecting the shock of what he had just read, donned his garrison cap and left the post telegrapher's office. Deaf to the familiar screechings of the low-flying gulls, Hallahan made his way directly to the post commandant's office of the newly arrived General Thomas Darlington.

Polished black bootheels clicking together as he came to attention, Sergeant Hallahan saluted the tall, slim general.

"Telegraphic dispatches from Washington City, sir," said Hallahan, holding out the report.

"At ease, Sergeant," said General Darlington, "how goes the battle with that renegade Indian, Gall?"

Sergeant Hallahan swallowed. "None too well, I'm afraid." He nodded at the folded yellow missive Darlington held in his hand. "General William Kidd was mortally wounded leading a charge against Gall at sundown yesterday afternoon."

Disbelieving, General Darlington looked at the young soldier as though he had spoken in a foreign language.

"Jesus God!" he exclaimed, feeling his knees suddenly gone weak. "That can't be! General Kidd was . . . the Army wouldn't risk an experienced military strategist like him."

General Darlington dropped into his chair and began to read, shaking his head all the while. "Merciful God, I can't believe it." His stricken face reflecting his outrage, he read and reread the message and lifted angry eyes to the young officer across the desk. "The hostile, Gall? Was he . . ."

"Gall was routed and forced to surrender, sir."

"I hope the red bastard hangs. My old commanding officer, General Kidd, was one of the finest officers this country has ever had."

"Yes, sir."

General Darlington suddenly sighed. "I can but hope the general's at peace now."

"Sir?"

"General Kidd's daughter was kidnapped from a party at my Colorado home last summer. The general was never the same after that." Darlington slammed a fist down on his desk in frustration. "I feel responsible for both their deaths."

"Nonsense, General."

"Is it, Sergeant? If Mrs. Darlington had never hosted that damned party . . ."

"Which reminds me, General. Mrs. Darlington has asked for my help with the gala you two are having this Saturday evening. I told her I would check to see if you can spare me one day this week."

"What was it she wanted you to do, Sergeant?"

The handsome young noncommissioned officer lifted wide shoulders in a shrug. "Not certain, General. Mrs. Darlington just said I should plan on being at the Telegraph Hill mansion for the better part of the afternoon."

General Darlington, his thoughts still on the loss of Bill Kidd, said distractedly, "It's quiet around the post now. Go this afternoon if you like."

"Yes, sir."

A weary, worried Night Sun rode back into the Powder River village one quiet, cloudy afternoon. Dreading having to tell Martay that her father was dead at the hands of a Lakota Chief; dreading even more what the shocking news might do to their relationship, Night Sun headed straight toward his lodge.

Immediately spotting that golden head among all the dark ones, Night Sun dismounted, tossed the reins to a beaming boy, and started to her.

As though she could feel his presence, Martay looked up, saw him, and formed his name on her lips, though no sound came. Her heart beating wildly, she started running. He stopped and waited for her to reach him.

Calling his name, she fell into his arms and, burying her

face in his throat, said, "Oh, my darling, you're back. You're back."

"*Wicincala,*" he said, drawing her into his close embrace.

"Night Sun, my love, I have sad news," said Martay, then pulled back to look up at him. "Darling, Gentle Deer. She's . . ." He nodded, silencing her, knowing what she had to say.

Night Sun hugged her tightly, then silently guided her to their lodge as the first drops of a cold autumn rain began to fall. Inside he set her back, his hands lightly gripping her arms, and said, "*Wicincala,* I, too, have sad news. Sweetheart, your father is dead. He was killed in battle by the Lakota war chief Gall in a skirmish in northern Dakota." He waited, hardly daring to breathe, while the force of his words penetrated.

"My daddy is . . . Daddy . . . no. Dear God, no!" And she threw her arms around Night Sun's neck and sobbed uncontrollably.

"I love you, *Wicincala,*" he said, tears wetting his bronzed cheeks. "I am sorry. Sorry your father is gone. Sorry my grandmother is gone." His arms tightened around her.

"Yes, yes," she sobbed. "Oh, my darling, I'm so glad that I have you. Promise you'll love me always, no matter what. Swear that I'll never lose you."

The sobbing young woman had no idea how relieved the worried Lakota was to hear her say those words to him. "Never," he promised, kissed her tear-reddened eyes, and drew her gently down onto his fur bed. Holding her on his lap, Night Sun rocked Martay as though she were a child. She cried out her grief on his shoulder while a cold rain pummeled the tipi over their heads.

When all the tears had been shed, the pair stretched out and talked quietly, exchanging favorite memories of the loved ones they had lost. It was Martay who, finally growing weary enough to be sleepy, said, "It's so final, isn't it, darling; Gentle

Deer was your only family and Daddy was mine. Now both are gone and we have no . . ."

"We have each other, *Wicincala,*" he said, kissing the top of her golden head. "Together we will have a family, our family."

Martay looked up at his handsome face, recalling Gentle Deer's prediction that already she was carrying his child. She started to tell him. But she was not sure she was pregnant, so instead she said, "Yes, darling, we will. Make love to me, Night Sun."

At dawn Martay stirred and wakened. Night Sun, exhausted from his long journey, slept on. Kissing her forefinger, Martay placed it an inch from his sensual lips, then withdrew it. Taking great care not to disturb him, she inched out from under the warm furs and, naked, shivered in the chill morning air.

Her buckskin dress lay beside the bed where she had hastily discarded it. Sitting on the furs, she pulled the dress over her head and rose to her feet. Pushing her tumbled hair behind her ears, she slipped her bare feet into a pair of moccasins and, casting one last look at the sleeping man, stepped out into the gray dawn.

The village was quiet, all the Lakota still sleeping warmly in their tipis. Martay was glad. She wanted, needed, solitude. A few moments to herself for a last good-bye to the father she had loved so dearly.

Agilely she climbed the bluffs overlooking the placid river, chose a soft grassy spot directly below a high shelf of rock, and slowly sank to her knees. Sitting back on her heels, Martay looked up at the gray dismal Dakota sky and felt the loss, the sadness, press down on her chest.

Before her lifted eyes was the well-remembered vision of a large, spectacularly-garbed silver-haired man of great strength and power, whose very existence had made her feel safe and cherished.

Martay, feeling lost and lonely, said aloud, "Oh, Daddy, how I shall miss you."

Again her tears started. She let the tears slide down her cheeks unchecked as she wistfully recalled how protected she had felt with her father's comforting arms around her. She bowed her head. Quietly she cried; a lost child.

A movement caught her eye.

Martay warily lifted her head. The sun was rising to dispel the last wisps of mist over the rocks. And from out of that mist stepped Windwalker, the slanting golden light of the new-risen sun lighting his broad, chiseled face. He was in full regalia. The fringed buckskin shirt pulling across his massive chest was decorated with narrow lines of beadwork and gleaming silver conchos. His graying braids were fur-wrapped and in his hand was an eagle-bone whistle.

There before her eyes was the welcome vision of a large, spectacularly-garbed silver-haired man of great strength and power.

The Mystic Warrior came silently down to her, put out his hand.

Looking straight into her eyes, he said solemnly, "In the far-distant past I had a beautiful daughter. She contracted the fatal disfiguring disease the white man calls the pox. She was taken from me to join the *Wakan Tanka*." His broad, firm hand gripped Martay's small one and his voice was low and soft when he said, "You will be my daughter now."

His heartfelt words and his powerful presence brought a loud, choking sob from Martay's tight throat. Gratefully she fell against his massive chest and felt herself quickly enclosed in a pair of strong, comforting arms.

A father's safe arms.

It had been more than a week since Night Sun's return. It had rained every day—a slow, drizzling autumn rain falling from a low, heavy sky.

Night Sun and Martay stayed secluded in their lodge, listening to the rain beat down on the taut skins of the tipi and discussing their future. Windwalker, like Gentle Deer, had urged Martay to convince Night Sun he should take her back to live in the white man's world. She wanted to please the Mystic Warrior as well as the dear departed Gentle Deer, but most of all she wanted the man she loved to be happy, so she told him one rainy night, after they'd made love, that they needn't go back.

Drawing lazy, teasing circles on Night Sun's bare chest, she said, "There is actually no reason for me to return to the Gold Coast. I have no family there."

Night Sun captured her roaming hand. "And there is no reason for me to remain here. Gentle Deer is gone."

"But the Lakota way of life . . ."

"Is gone as well, *Wicincala.*" His black eyes held a wistful expression. "Our long, hard fight with the white man is ending. Most of the People are already on reservations. Windwalker told me yesterday he is weary of the struggle, of seeing the young ones without enough to eat. He's taking his band in before the harsh winter begins." He closed his eyes, opened them. "I can best help my people by living in your world, but promise me that every summer you'll come with me back here to this place I love so much."

Martay nodded. "I promise." She bent and kissed Night Sun's chest. Her lips against his warm, smooth flesh, she said, "But, darling, what of your safety? If we go back, they will arrest you and . . ."

"No, sweetheart," he said, smiling boyishly at her. "Under the white man's law, a wife is not required to testify against her husband. And you are the only person who knows that I kidnapped you."

Martay began to smile too. "When do we get married?"

"As soon as we get back to your world."

Martay's smile turned to a frown. "You know, I suppose it's foolish but . . . I . . ."

"What, *Wicincala?*"

"I would like to be married here in the Powder River camp by Windwalker." She looked closely at him to catch his reaction.

"A fine idea, but it won't be legal in your world."

"I know. We'll get married again, but it would mean a lot to me." She smiled at him, knowing he was pleased.

"Thank you, *Wicincala,*" said Night Sun. "It would mean a lot to us as well."

"So? When do we marry?"

Night Sun pulled her down atop his chest. Kissing the shiny crown of her head, he said, "We should wait until the rain stops, don't you think?"

"Mmmmm, yes."

"Tell you what, we'll keep an eye on the *mastekola.*" Martay lifted her head, her eyes questioning. "The lark," he explained. "The lark is a weather forecaster, sweetheart. There will be good weather whenever it flies straight up."

"Are you teasing me, half-breed?"

"Would I do that?" he said, his black eyes flashing as he pulled her back down and kissed her.

They lay quietly then, talking, planning, looking to the future ahead in Chicago, he assuring her they would often visit Windwalker and the band; that their going back would be best for his people. With his education he could help protect them from the one-sided treaties of the past. It was late when finally they fell asleep, the gentle rain still beating down over their heads.

When Martay awoke the next morning, she no longer heard the drumming of the raindrops. She quickly wakened Night Sun.

"Do you hear it?" she asked.

Yawning, he said sleepily, "Hear what? I hear nothing."

"I know," she said, jumping up. "Hurry, let's go out and look for the *mastekola.*"

Looking at the adorable naked woman whose emerald eyes were as wide and excited as those of a child, Night Sun grinned and obediently rose. In moments the pair, holding hands, stepped out of their lodge.

It was Martay who saw it first. A lark was sitting in the low bough of a conifer tree not ten yards from the tipi.

"See!" she said, pointing. "Now what?"

Smiling, Night Sun nodded and slipped his arms around Martay's waist. Softly he said, "We wait."

Martay, holding her breath, stared at the lark. The tiny bird gave a few jerky movements of its head as though it knew the humans were watching him. Then he flapped his wings and flew from the leafy conifer.

Straight up toward the clouds.